TELL THAT TO MY HEART

(BOOK 1 IN THE HEARTSHAPED SERIES

ELIZA J SCOTT

This book has been edited in British English (BrE) and therefore uses British spellings.

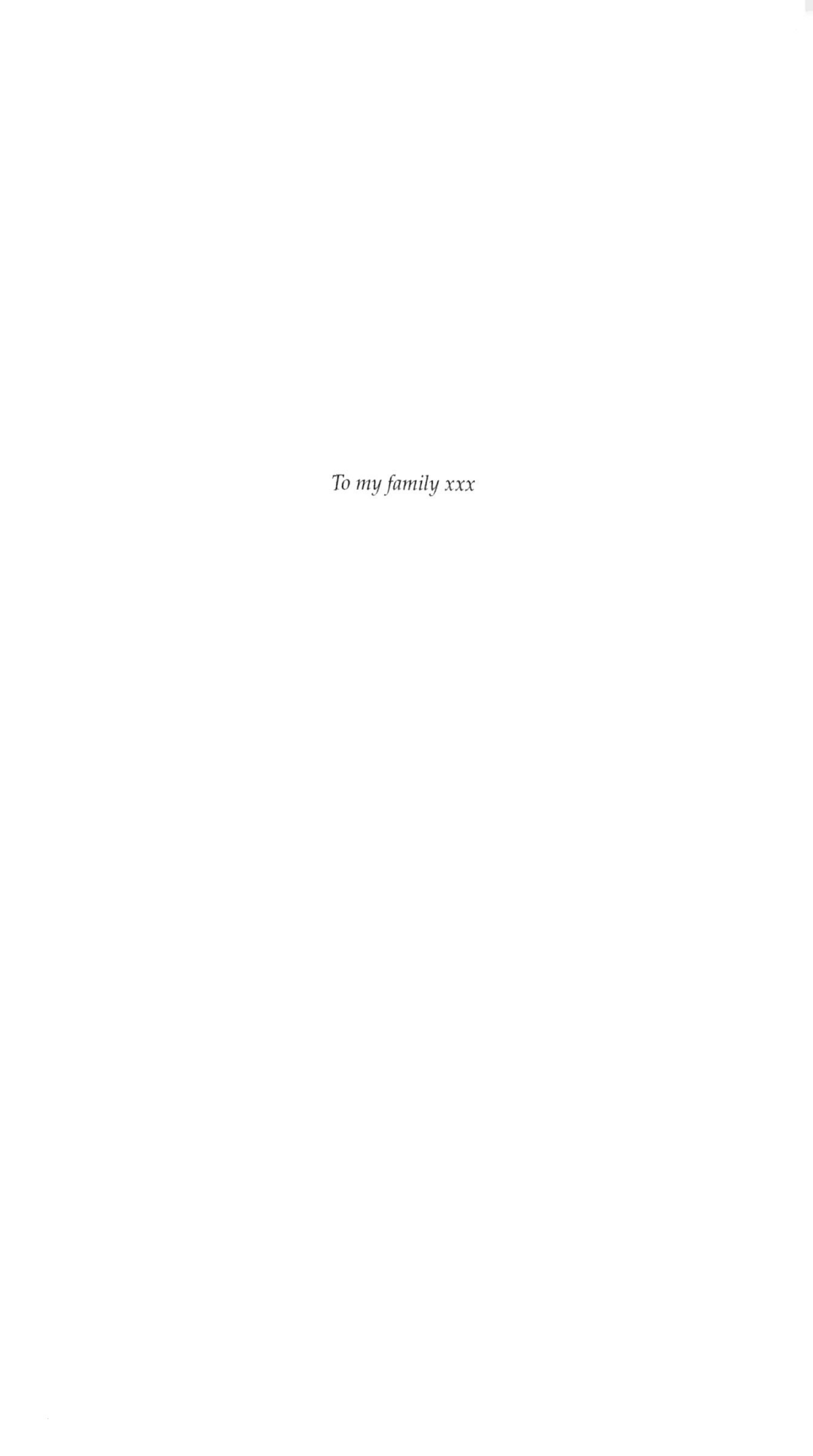

To my family xxx

1

'THANKS.' Mim flashed the driver a quick smile before leaping down from the bus that had ground to a halt halfway along Gillygate in the centre of York.

'No worries, love, mind how you go.' He winced as she narrowly avoided colliding with a cyclist who'd been weaving his way in and out of the static line of rush-hour traffic.

'Yikes!'

'Watch where you're bloody-well going!' The cyclist turned, his eyes full of anger. 'Stupid bloody woman.'

'Alright, keep your hair on.'

Thanks to the seemingly never-ending roadworks that had sprung up everywhere around the city, the bus had been stuck in bumper-to-bumper traffic for the last twenty-five minutes, creeping along at an agonisingly slow pace, fumes from the many exhausts swirling around in the damp October air. Mim's stress levels were soaring; she was going to be late for work. Again.

'S'cuse me.' She squeezed through a couple of early morning shoppers who were ambling along, blocking the pavement and too deep in conversation to notice her impatience bubbling up behind them. They stood aside, one of them shooting her a filthy look as she hurried by.

With her long blonde hair flying out behind her, Mim managed a short burst of running before she hit another wall of people. 'Flaming hell,' she muttered, doing her best to edge around them. Her long legs took a few strides before she reached the next obstruction. 'Sorry, can I just get through, please?'

She raced along, taking a quick leap to the right to avoid the snapping jaws of a snarling Yorkshire Terrier. 'Yeah, yeah, when you're big enough, squirt.' She landed in a muddy puddle that splashed up her leg. 'Drat!'

Taking advantage of a clear stretch ahead of her, Mim ran with long, thundering strides, one hand gripping onto the backpack that was slung over her shoulder, the other holding her phone – she'd already texted her best friend and co-worker Anna-Lisa, warning her of her lateness and asking for her to cover for her. Her mind was so focused on getting to work and trying to ignore the tight feeling in her chest, she didn't see the tall, dark-haired man stepping out of the coffee shop until it was too late. She lunged sideways to avoid him, clipping his arm with her backpack and skidding in a small pile of soggy leaves in the process.

'What the …?' He shook hot coffee from his hand, sending Mim an angry look.

'Arghh!' She thrust out her arms. *Don't hit your head! Don't hit your head! Don't hit your head!* Everything seemed to grind down into agonisingly slow motion; a cyclist swerved around her, she heard gasps from a group of women huddled nearby, and snorts of laughter from a gaggle of teenagers who were obviously bunking off school. There was a resounding thud followed by a clatter as she landed in an ungainly heap on the ground, her phone skittering across the cobbles, coming to a halt perilously close to the wide-toothed mouth of a drain. She lay there frozen, all but for her chest that was heaving as she struggled to catch her breath. She took a moment to gather her thoughts. The message that her knee was throbbing finally reached her brain – it would be a miracle if she hadn't put a hole in her tights. A stinging sensation in her hands joined the chorus and tears of embarrassment started swimming in her eyes. She sniffed, quickly blinking them back. *Don't cry! Don't make a show of yourself, you're a grown woman, not a child! But, ouch! Bloody ouch!*

'Are you alright down there?'

She glanced up to see the man she'd just bumped into looking down at her, his dark eyes twinkling. Though her throat felt tight, she did her best to swallow her tears as she made a clumsy attempt to stand up, humiliation colouring her cheeks. 'Yes, I'm fine, thanks.'

'Here, let me help you.'

Strong arms pulled her to her feet. She watched, her face burning more furiously, as he bent to pick up her backpack then reached for her phone. 'There you are. I'm afraid the screen on your phone's cracked.' He handed them to her, brushing away the wayward strands of hair that had fallen over her face, the sudden intimacy sending a spike of electricity through her. In spite of her embarrassment, it hadn't escaped Mim's attention that he was seriously good-looking. Tall, dark and handsome; he was just her type. Her already scarlet face flushed even brighter.

'Thank you.'

'And I think you might need a new pair of tights.' His dark eyes glittered.

She glanced down to see a large hole glaring at her, a ladder already hurrying its way down her shin. 'Oh, bugger. They were new, I just bought them at the weekend. They were expensive; they're special thermal ones.' *And exactly why do you think this stranger needs such details?*

'Ah.' Amusement tugged at the corners of his mouth.

'And I think you might need a new shirt – sorry, by the way.'

His eyes followed hers to the coffee stain splashed down his front. 'Hmm, unfortunate timing.'

Mim suddenly remembered the cause of her haste. 'Look, I'm honestly really sorry for bumping into you and for making a mess of your shirt, but I'm late for work again and I've got a horrible feeling my old dragon of a boss is looking for any excuse to sack me, so I've got to dash. Bye and thank you. And sorry, again.'

'Hey, no worries. Good luck with your horrible boss.'

'Thanks, I'll need it.'

She pushed on, ignoring the thrumming ache in her knee and cursing the smashed screen of her phone. *Not far now*! She was nearing the snickelway that gave a short cut to Smiddersgate, the street of mediaeval timber-framed buildings where she worked; she was hoping to slip down it but her heart sank when she saw road-works blocking the way and a sign proclaiming: "No Access". 'Bugger!' She stopped, resting her hands on her thighs while she considered what to do. Her lungs were squeezing ever tighter, creating a pain in her chest, making her breathing ragged. There was no alternative, she'd have to go the long way round. Why, oh why, had she moved out of her house on the edge of the city? She never had this problem when she lived there; a quick bike ride and she was at work in under twenty minutes.

She continued her race along the York-stone pavements, her heart pounding almost as loud as her boot-clad feet. 'Jeez.' She gasped, pressing her hand against the stitch that had started stabbing into her side, while her lungs protested as she tried to force a gulp of air into them. *Nearly there, Mim, keep going.* She jumped down off the kerb and onto the road to dodge a young mum with a pushchair who was negotiating the path with a businessman and his pull-along-case.

As she ran, Mim did her best to block the rising feeling of nausea that had started swirling around her stomach which exercise always seemed to induce. *Lord, I must be North Yorkshire's most unfit twenty-six-year-old!* She hated running; she was rubbish at it. Always had been. Always would be.

Her body continued to object as she ran down Smiddersgate.

'Phew!' The main door to the wonky, wattle and daub building that housed Yorkshire Portions Magazine where she worked as a marketing assistant was a welcome sight. Mim paused for a moment, hoping to steady herself and calm her breathing. She pulled her hair away from her clammy neck and slipped her phone in her pocket. 'Right, here goes.' Once inside, she headed to the back stairs and tiptoed her way up, hoping to weave her way around the rabbit warren of rooms and corridors before slipping surreptitiously into her office.

'Morning, Jemima.' No such flaming luck.

Mim's galloping heart plummeted to her feet as a line of sweat trickled down her back. She looked up to find her boss, Susan Pallister-Biggs, owner editor of Yorkshire Portions Magazine and stuck-up, snooty bag, at the top of the stairs, hands on sturdy hips, pinning her with her infamous steely glare. As usual, Susan's hair looked like it hadn't seen a hairbrush in weeks, the short, salt and pepper curls sticking out as if she'd had a fright. The look was topped off by a smear of what looked like dried egg yolk running down the front of her blouse. She was the only one at work who used Mim's full name. Being addressed as Jemima always made her feel like she was in trouble, which she invariably was with Susan and her equally pompous sub-editor business partner Kenneth.

'Morning, Susan. I'm really sorry I'm late, roadworks again; there's even more of them today, they're everywhere, I think they're breeding, it's causing mayhem.' She was still gasping for breath, her pulse thrumming in her ears.

'Well, whatever the reason, you can make up the time you've lost by working through your lunch break. We've got heaps to do today, as you're very well aware. And look at the state of you with your hair all over the place and that hole in your tights; please don't tell me it's the latest fashion trend.' Susan's imperious voice was really beginning to grate.

'Of course, I was going to do that anyway.' *What bloody lunch break?* Mim couldn't remember the last time she hadn't worked through at least part of hers, even when she hadn't been late.

The magazine's rapid rise to success had taken all at Yorkshire Portions by surprise, resulting in Susan becoming increasingly competitive with their peer publications, pushing to feature more appealing, fresher articles in theirs. She made no secret of wanting their magazine to be the best. The increased workload this had generated meant that the magazine had become horrendously understaffed. But, instead of employing new "team members", as she liked to call them, Susan had merely allocated those who were already there with extra job titles, and naturally, extra responsibility – not that this was reflected in an increase in salary. If anyone was brave enough to draw the situation to her attention, she would simply dismiss them with a wave of her diamond beringed hand and say that she was dealing with it. This had resulted in everyone being stretched to the limits, and the general feeling that something or someone would break before too long pervaded the air. The situation was laughable, since rumour had it that she was loaded, and it didn't sit well with her staff that they were working for a mean penny-pincher who put frugality before staff worth or morale.

Mim reached the top of the stairs, but instead of stepping to one side to let Mim pass, Susan remained rooted to the spot, appraising her with a critical eye. It made Mim feel even more uncomfortable. 'S'cuse me, I just need to…' As she went to squeeze past her boss, her nostrils were assaulted by the woman's familiar fusty odour, generated by her apparent reluctance to wash her clothes. Mim couldn't help but scrunch up her nose and hold her breath. It put her in mind of a jumble sale and the smell generated by piles of unwanted, long-forgotten clothes that had been lurking at the back of so many wardrobes for years.

'Honestly, Jemima, close up you look even worse, anyone would think you'd been sleeping rough.'

'Sorry, I had a bit of an accident on the way here.' *You've got a bloody nerve commenting on my appearance; at least I'm not wearing my breakfast. And when was the last time your hair saw a brush or shampoo for that matter, eh? And don't speak about homeless people in that disparaging way, you snotty old boot!*

'Hmphh. I think you did. But never mind that, now you're here you can get me a coffee, then I want a word with you in your office.'

'Oh, okay.' If Mim's heart could have sunk any lower it would have; Susan's words spelt doom.

'Well, what are you waiting for? Don't just stand there gawping at me. Go on. Chop, chop. Go, go, go. I've got to contend with the new art director starting today on top of everything else, and I need a coffee before I can face any of it.' She made a shooing motion with her hands, the stones of her enormous diamond ring glittering in the artificial light.

'Sorry, yes, coffee.' *That'll be in my role as "Office Dogsbody" no doubt.*

Mim worried at her bottom lip as her mind began scrambling over her boss's words. *Ughh!* What did Susan need to speak to her about so urgently? If it was something bad, surely she wouldn't want to do it in the office Mim shared with Anna-Lisa and Aidey; that would be way too awkward on so many levels. Even so, she wouldn't put it past her boss; Susan was infamous for her shocking lack of sensitivity when it came to people's feelings.

With a variety of scenarios whirling around her mind – all involving her being handed her P45 – Mim made her way along the oak-panelled landing to the pokey little kitchen, its familiar smell of damp making her nostrils twitch. She checked the kettle for water and flicked the switch; she could murder a coffee herself. An image of the response *that* would elicit from Susan pushed the craving right out of her mind. Instead, she slugged back a quick glass of water, wiping the drips from her chin with the back of her hand. That would have to do for now. She washed her hands, wincing as the water made the grazes sting. As she dried them, her eyes were drawn to a wide scrape down the sleeve of her prized leather jacket; it must have happened when she fell. 'Oh, no!' Her heart sank. It was her pride and joy, and it had taken ages for her to save enough cash to buy it; she hadn't even had the flaming thing for six months.

Wiping it with a dampened corner of the tea towel didn't help; she'd google how to fix it, or email the store and ask their advice. There was no way she was going to stop wearing it.

The sense she was being watched took her unawares, making her shiver. 'Ughh! Stop it!' she remonstrated with herself. But paranoia was becoming an increasingly common feeling as an uneasy air of change had begun to permeate the office at Yorkshire Portions, slipping under doorways and lurking in dark corners, making everyone feel they had to watch their backs. Such an atmosphere had the potential to be divisive and Mim was thankful that the friendship she shared with Anna-Lisa and Aidey was strong enough to ward off any potential discord between them, quashing any negativity before it had chance to take root.

While she waited for the kettle to boil, Aidey eased into her mind; what exactly was going on there? Four weeks ago, one chilly Monday morning, Susan had marched into their office and announced that she was changing his role from art director to designer and picture editor which she said was a job he was much better suited to, the new art director apparently being somebody they'd headhunted and who was "made for the role". Mim's heart had gone out to Aidey, who had listened, his kind face disguising the anger he felt, as Susan blatantly bulldozed over his feelings. She'd even had the audacity to suggest that he should be grateful he wasn't taking a pay cut. Up to that point, Mim had thought Susan's lack of sensitivity couldn't surprise her. Now, nothing would; which made this morning's imminent conversation all the more worrying.

As Mim headed along the corridor to her office, a vaguely familiar voice floated down towards her. She frowned as it triggered a warning in her gut and set her hackles up. Her mind leapt at the hazy wisps of memory that hovered around the edges of her mind, trying to link the voice to the person, but she still hadn't managed to put a face to it by the time she'd reached the door. Warily, she pushed it open to find that the usual friendly atmosphere of the room had been whipped away and replaced by one of heavy discomfort. She glanced between Anna-Lisa and Aidey who gave her matching concerned smiles. She turned to her desk to see the owner of the voice sitting there, a challenging glint in her eye as she held Mim's gaze.

2

A GASP ESCAPED Mim's lips, betraying her shock before she had chance to stop it. It was as if the lid was lifted on a box of emotions she'd kept packed away, buried in a deep, dark place. Suddenly, they came rushing at her, crowding her mind, creeping up her spine, their force taking her by surprise. 'You!' Her voice was barely above a whisper. The girl responded with a flick of her eyebrows.

Mim swallowed and took a deep breath, hoping she gave an outward appearance of calm. It had been several months since she'd last set eyes on this individual, and it had taken a second or two for it to register just who she was. The girl's previously light brown locks had been replaced with a curtain of glossy black hair and a heavy, blunt fringe, the style finished with a vibrant turquoise dip-dye. It had thrown Mim for a moment, until the arrogant, self-assured expression triggered a painful memory. One Mim would rather forget.

'Where the hell have you been, Jemima? I only asked you to make me a coffee, not go to Brazil for the beans.' Susan's words brought her back to the moment, the accompanying disingenuous smile could easily have been mistaken for a sneer, and Mim didn't have the will to respond.

'Hi there, Jemima, you look surprised to see me,' said the girl, taking a sip of tea from Mim's mug.

'Oh, erm, yes, I am.' *Major understatement!*

'You two know each other?' asked Susan.

'Er, kind of,' said Mim.

'You could say.' The girl smirked as she swivelled on Mim's seat. It took every ounce of Mim's strength not to reach over and yank her out of it.

'I assume you're not going to hang on to that until it gets cold?' Susan took the cup from Mim.

'Oh, no, course not.'

'Right, well, you won't need me to introduce you to Honey, but you will need me to tell you that she's the new marketing forward-slash PR assistant and you need to show her the ropes; take her under your wing and look after her.'

New marketing assistant? Since when? Take her under my wing? Look after her? Like bugger I will! She's the last one who needs looking after; she should come with a warning: "Watch out! I'm trouble". Sensing everyone's eyes upon her, Mim pushed her thoughts out of the way. 'Oh, right, okay.'

'Right, now we've got that sorted, I'll leave you to get on. Aidan, Anna-Lisa, that includes you, too. The people in this room seem to have forgotten we have a deadline looming. And you're not the only one who's late today, Jemima; I need to find out where that bloody new art director's got to.' She flicked her beringed hand at them and left.

Susan had barely had chance to leave the room before Honey spoke. 'Jemima, before we go any further, can I just say that I hope you're not going to hold it against me about what happened with Rick. After all, it was hardly my fault; he didn't tell me he already had a girlfriend.'

With her mind reeling, Mim slipped off her leather jacket and hung it on the hook on the back of the door, then picked up her floral backpack. *Who are you trying to kid? You knew full well he had a girlfriend.* 'I'm not going to hold anything against you; it's in the past.'

'That's good. It's just at the time, you seemed a little … what's the word? Gutted.'

'It is, good, I mean; you did me a favour.' Mim let a beat pass, ignoring Honey's last barb, aware of Anna-Lisa and Aidey's silent observation. 'Right, we'd better get started.' She looked across at the new girl, expecting her to get up out of the seat but all she got was a self-assured smile.

'Honey, you need to go and get yourself a chair, you're in Mim's at the moment and she needs to sit in it herself to be able to start work,' said Aidey. 'You can use the spare computer on the desk beside you, you just need to grab something to sit on.'

'Yes, there's a couple of spare office chairs in the room next door; you can go and chose one from there.' Anna-Lisa made no attempt to disguise the cool tone to her broad North Yorkshire accent.

Honey pulled herself up and pushed past Mim. 'Right, I'll do that then, shall I?'

'Good idea,' said Mim.

She watched Honey leave the room before she spoke again. 'Okay, so this is officially the morning from hell. Any idea what's going on? And thanks for that by the way, I don't think she'd have budged if it hadn't been for what you said.'

Anna-Lisa, the magazine's petite editorial assistant, mimed tearing out her soft-pink bob. 'Arghh! Morning from hell is an understatement! Susan's managed to get a bee in her knickers over the weekend and is on the bloody warpath more than usual. And as for her latest recruit, she totally knew what she was doing, sitting in your seat like she owned it; it's so obvious it's someone else's desk, what with all the stickers on the computer, manky dead flowers in the vase and stuff on the desk.' She cast her eyes over the said "stuff", which could justifiably be referred to as "mess". 'She's just being a cow. What the hell have we done to deserve having Honey Blossom pigging Blenkinsopp working here? Please tell me it's all just a horrible nightmare and I'll wake up from it soon.'

'More to the point, what's poor Mim done to deserve this? There's obviously some unpleasant history between the two of you,' said Aidey.

'Ughh! You could say.' Mim flopped into her seat, rubbing her forehead with her fingers. Adrenalin was coursing round her bloodstream, pushing her stress levels to new heights. 'How come you two know her, though?'

'She did some work experience at White Sprite Media when my sister was working there a few years ago. Felt more like a lifetime apparently; let's just say she left a bit of an impression: lying, chasing after the blokes, just generally causing mayhem, and a lot of clearing up after her when she'd gone. Since then, I've heard her name mentioned in relation to a few other companies – never anything complimentary or positive,' said Anna-Lisa. 'And it looks like she's still continuing with the ridiculous sassy teenager act she had at White Sprite Media, even though she must be in her twenties now.'

'Yeah, she must be, and I can remember the horror stories you told me,' said Aidey. 'And I still find it hard to see how her name matches what I've heard of her personality; surely a name like Honey Blossom conjures up images of someone sweet and nice. Are you sure it's her real name?'

'From what I can gather it is; it hardly suits her, does it?' said Anna-Lisa.

'Not from what I've seen so far. Let's hope our first impressions are wrong, otherwise things are going to get even worse round here,' said Aidey.

'Oh, please don't say that.' Mim reached into her backpack and pulled out a packet of penny sweets, setting it down on the desk.

'She's not the one who Rick cheat … I mean, she's not the tart who threw herself at Rick, is she?' asked Anna-Lisa.

Mim nodded. 'She's the one, though, surprisingly, I never knew her name.' She removed last week's bunch of faded pink gerberas from the squat glass vase on her desk and threw them in the bin; she wouldn't have time to replace them today.

'Typical. My sister said she threw herself at every man in her path, preferably if they were attached. Seems to like the challenge, or the need to have what somebody else has.'

Mim cast her mind back to the night she'd seen Rick kissing the girl at the back of the Highway Man pub. She flinched, the memory still raw. The girl in question had appeared on the scene a few weeks beforehand, albeit lurking in the background, her voice and laugh just that little bit too loud. She always seemed to be around when Mim was with Rick; she'd even noticed the girl watching them intently on several occasions. And whenever Mim had caught her eye, the girl would smirk, which triggered a feeling of unease that had felt almost sinister. She couldn't explain it at the time, but it hadn't taken her long to find out why.

MIM WAS SITTING at the bar of the Highway Man, waiting for Rick when a text message pinged on her phone. She snatched it up and read it, a frown drawing her thick, dark eyebrows together.

'If you're wondering where your boyfriend is, you'll find him round the back of the pub.'

'What?' She read it again before glancing around the room,

wondering if it was someone there who'd sent it. But the place was full of regulars, and there was nothing revealing in their behaviour. Her heart started thudding, and her stomach twisted into a tight knot as that old familiar feeling started to creep its way up inside her. She checked the number; it was no one from her contacts list. 'Not this again.' She slid off her stool, slinging her bag over her shoulder.

'You okay, love?' the landlord asked.

'I'm not sure, Mick.' Mim made her way to the back door, apprehension pulsing around her body with every step. She'd only just set foot in the beer garden when she spotted a couple getting intimate by the stone outbuilding, the man's hands roaming enthusiastically under the girl's top.

Though he had his back to her, Mim recognised the floppy black hair, the long, muscular legs and the battered leather jacket: Rick. As if on cue, the girl opened her eyes and smirked over his shoulder, waving her mobile phone at Mim. Rick turned, his face dropping as it registered he'd been caught red-handed, the girl's lipstick smeared across his mouth along with his guilt.

Mim fled back through the pub and out into the street, tears pouring down her cheeks, her heart shattering into tiny pieces as she left the scene of his betrayal. It was bad enough that she'd seen him cheating on her, but what hurt her the most was he didn't even try to apologise or make excuses.

'Why her, why here?' said Mim.

'God only knows, but it sounds like it's not going to be easy for you working with her,' said Aidey.

'And you look knackered, hon, I thought you said you were having a quiet weekend but you look like you've been partying hard.' Anna-Lisa peered closer at Mim, scrutinising the dark circles under her eyes.

Mim lowered her voice. 'I wish; I spent the weekend at home working on that little freelance marketing job for the organic cosmetic company; you remember, the one who got in touch a couple of weeks ago. I went to bed early every night, but as soon as my head hit the pillow, that was it, my mind just took off and I couldn't get to sleep until well into the early hours.'

'Oh, Mim, you're going to have to do something about that before it gets out of hand, insomnia can make you ill, you know,' said Anna-Lisa.

'Yeah, and that's the last thing you'll need now you've got "you-know-who" working beside you,' said Aidey.

'Hmm, no doubt about it, she's got an air of trouble about her ' said Anna-Lisa. 'We'd better watch out; from what my sister says, she's a bitch!'

'Who's a bitch?' Honey pushed the door open with the chair.

'Oh, just someone you don't know,' said Anna-Lisa.

'S'alright, I can manage, I don't need any help, this chair isn't heavy or anything. My godmother won't mind that a big strapping bloke let her favourite goddaughter struggle while he just sat there watching and not lifting a finger to help.'

'Godmother?' said Mim.

Honey set the chair down. 'Yep, didn't you know? Auntie Susan's my godmother.' She paused for effect. 'Will here do?'

Alarm bells started clanging loudly in Mim's ears; if she didn't need the job and the money, she would have made a bolt for the door right there and then. Instead she pushed down the feeling of despair. 'Yep, there's fine.'

3

MIM LOGGED in on her computer before checking the list of jobs she hadn't managed to cross off her "to-do" list the previous Friday, which had turned out to be more manic than usual, thanks to being sent off at the last minute to pick up the invitations for the Yorkshire Portions Christmas party from the printers at the other side of the city. Being scatty, lists were essential to her daily routine – both at home and at work – and the only way she could keep some semblance of order in her life. They still didn't stop her from the occasional bout of forgetfulness though, like the time she'd forgotten to organise a wedding anniversary bouquet of flowers from Kenneth to his wife. She hadn't actually forgotten, she'd crossed it off her list instead of the item below it. The ensuing bollocking from Kenneth meant it was something she hadn't done since.

'What the bloody hell are you playing at, you stupid girl? Are you deliberately trying to wreck my marriage?' he'd yelled at her. She'd looked at him with morbid fascination as his porcine eyes had bulged, while his face had puffed up like an over-inflated bull-frog and turned a vibrant shade of red that crept up over his bald head and gleamed through his comb-over. He'd looked so ridiculous, she'd felt a giggle rising inside her, and it had taken every ounce of self-restraint she'd possessed not to let it escape in a noisy snort. Only when he'd threatened her with the sack had it leached away, her amusement hastily replaced with panic. She'd really had to grovel to keep her job that day.

How the hell is it my job to order his wife's flowers for their anniversary? My job title is "Marketing Assistant", not "General Sodding Dog's Body"! she'd fumed silently.

Luckily, Mim had a friend who worked at Bloomz – York's most exclusive florists – and a quick phone call had resulted in a hastily put together bunch of flowers that saved the day, and Mim's neck. Yep, that would go down as an all-time low at Yorkshire Portions Magazine. But not as low as the arrival of Honey Blossom Blenkinsopp.

MIM WAS busy designing a Facebook advert, chewing on a mouthful of sweets, when the phone on the desk she shared with Honey rang with an internal call. She waited a moment, hoping Honey would answer it. But the ringing continued while Honey's attention remained fixed on her mobile phone.

Mim glanced over at Aidey and Anna-Lisa who were looking daggers at the new marketing assistant. She pushed the half-chewed sweets into the side of her mouth so she could speak. 'Can you get that, Honey?'

'I'm busy.'

Yeah, busy scrolling through your Instagram feed!

Anna-Lisa's top lip curled into a snarl, while Aidey rolled his eyes. Mim hastily swallowed the sweets and snatched up the receiver, trying to keep the impatience out of her voice. 'Hello.' Her heart sank as Susan's officious voice barked in her ear.

Seconds later, she replaced the handset and got to her feet, shaking her head as she left the room, aware of three pairs of eyes on her. It wasn't even ten o'clock, yet today was already going from bad to worse. Susan's latest demand had been for her to make coffee for the new art director who'd just arrived, and boy did it stick in her throat.

Where the bloody hell in my job description does it say that I'm the office sodding junior? Begrudgingly, Mim threw the coffee granules into the mug, not caring how it would taste. Well, that wasn't strictly true, at this very moment, she'd be quite happy if it tasted vile; it would serve the new art director right, he should be making his own coffee. And he needn't get any ideas, thinking he could just click his fingers and she'd jump to make a coffee whenever he wanted one. Not a chance. The bottle of cheap washing-up liquid caught her eye and, for a fleeting moment, she considered adding a quick squirt of it to the mug; that would ensure the art director wouldn't ask her to make him a drink ever again. *Yep, start as you mean to go on, Mim! Genius!* The thought briefly lifted her spirits and a small smile hovered over her mouth. *It would probably make him fart bubbles!* She stifled a giggle at that.

Her annoyance resurfaced as she chuntered her way to Susan's office. Biting down on her emotions, Mim knocked on the door and walked in. 'Here's the coff—' She stopped dead in her tracks, shock whipping her words right out of her mouth as a bolt of attraction simultaneously shot through her. There, standing right in front of her, was the man she'd bumped into, the resultant coffee stain glaring at her accusingly from his pale blue shirt. 'Oh,' was all she could think to say as the distinctly masculine aroma of his cologne infiltrated her senses.

'Hello, is that for me?' The man held out his hand for the mug, his disarming smile revealing Hollywood-white teeth with a barely discernible snaggle to his right canine that was indescribably appealing.

'Oh, er, yes, it is.' He was tall, much taller than Mim's five-feet-ten, with high cheekbones so razor-sharp you could slice cheese with them, and a hint of dark stubble that grazed his strong jaw. *Mmm-hmm, delicious!* Her state of shock after her fall at their earlier meeting must have numbed her senses at the time; he was even more good-looking than she remembered, intimidatingly so, in fact. And he knew it. He was exactly the sort of man that would have you tongue-tied and feeling awkward without uttering a word or lifting a finger. But Mim couldn't take her eyes off him, drinking in his floppy hair that was as black and glossy as a raven's wing, set off by a pair of almond-shaped eyes so dark they were like beads of Whitby jet, glittering with a hint of amusement and a splash of wickedness. There was no denying it, he was dangerously good-looking, with an irresistible air that screamed bad-boy. And Mim had a weak spot for bad boys.

'Jemima!' Susan's voice crashed into her thoughts. 'Let go of the mug; give the man his coffee!'

'Oh, yes, of course.'

'Thank you.' His mouth twitched as he took the cup.

A wayward ripple of desire travelled through her body.

'Jemima, this is Caspar De Verre; he's our new art director. Caspar, this is Jemima Dewberry, our marketing assistant.'

'How do you do, Jemima Dewberry, though I do believe we've already met,' he said.

Oh, that smoky voice, how I'd love to hear it whispering sweet nothings in my ear!

'You have?' Susan looked from Caspar to Mim. 'There seems to be a pattern forming this morning.'

'Yes, I, er, well, it was when I was rushing to work this morning…'

Caspar tapped the coffee stain on his shirt and Susan's face darkened. 'Don't tell me you're responsible for that, Jemima?'

Mim was snapped back into the moment. 'Well, yes, but it was an accident. I was running, and my backpack…'

'Oh, for goodness' sake, girl, I don't know what's got into you recently. I do apologise, Caspar. Jemima is like a walking disaster area at the moment.' She scowled at Mim.

Caspar held his hand up. 'Hey, it's really not a problem, and it was actually my fault, I wasn't looking where I was going and stepped out in front of Jemima; she didn't have time to dodge out of the way, and if she had she would've run into the path of a car.'

'Hmphh. Right, well, thank you, Jemima, you can get back to your desk. Have you finished that ad yet?'

'Almost, I just need—'

'No need for explanations, go on, back to work.' Susan waved her hand, making sure Caspar got a good glimpse of the diamonds adorning it.

'Okay.' *Keep your knickers on, and if you didn't treat me like the office flaming doormat, then I'd have had it finished last Friday.*

'Thank you for the coffee, Jemima.' Caspar flashed her a heart-melting smile which, despite the negative feelings that were simmering away inside her, made her heart squeeze.

'You're welcome.' She gave a small smile back before heading through the door and stomping down the hall, humiliation making her cheeks flame.

Once back in her office she felt all eyes on her.

'So what's he like?' asked Anna-Lisa.

'Please don't tell me he's as old as Kenneth and the other old crocks that work here; this place needs some young, fit guys to liven things up a bit. No offence.' Honey looked across at Aidey.

'None taken,' he said.

'Aidey's not an old crock, is he, Mim?' asked Anna-Lisa.

'No way, he's only twenty-eight and he's attractive.' Mim was too busy shooting Honey a look to notice Aidey's face flush to the roots of his dark blond hair. 'Anyway, the new bloke's called Caspar De Verre, or something like that, I'd say he's mid-thirties, and he seems okay.'

'Did I hear my name being mentioned?' Caspar walked in with Susan who was taking him round the office and introducing him to the rest of the staff.

Mim felt a rush of excitement. 'Oh, er—'

'Caspar, this is Aidan Lister, he's the picture editor, forward slash, designer I was telling you about, and the girl with the hair like candyfloss is Anna-Lisa Swift, she's our editorial assistant, forward slash, copy editor and proof reader. Over here is Honey Blenkinsopp, Yorkshire Portions' new marketing assistant forward slash PR assistant, and you've already met Mim.'

Mim groaned inwardly; if she noticed the change in tone of Susan's voice when she moved on to her name, then the chances were everyone did.

'And what's Mim's role?' asked Caspar.

Oh, that'd be doormat, forward-bloody-slash dogsbody!

'Oh, she does the same as Honey. Though she also writes the occasional article for the magazine,' said Susan.

'Yep, we're the same rank,' said Honey, surprising her new work colleagues by adopting an affected little-girl voice.

'Ah.' Caspar looked from Honey to Mim then to Anna-Lisa whose non-verbals spoke volumes.

'You didn't tell us he was absolutely drop-dead gorgeous, Jemima!' Honey hardly waited for the door to close before she rounded on Mim, her voice back to its usual tone. 'What's the matter with you? That would've been the first thing I'd have mentioned.'

'Just goes to show not everyone's like you, doesn't it?' said Anna-Lisa.

'I wonder if he's new to the area? I wonder if he's got a girlfriend? He might like someone to show him round, take him to the best bars, the best places to eat, that sort of thing. I'll go to his office and ask him when Auntie Susan's stopped dragging him round the building. And don't forget, *I* saw him first.'

'He's not my type,' said Anna-Lisa.

'Yes, but he's Jemima's type, isn't he, Jemima?'

'Trust me, I don't have a type at the moment; you're welcome to him.' Mim bit down on the urge to come back with something cutting, ignoring Honey's smile and the mocking look in her eyes.

4

WITH NO FURTHER demands from Susan, the morning went surprisingly quickly, and, despite the occasional surge of stress flooding her chest whenever recent events pushed their way into her thoughts, Mim had managed to make a satisfying dent in her to-do list.

She loved her job, well, she enjoyed the marketing and social media aspect of it, and was getting more and more satisfaction out of writing articles, but she was beginning to resent the extra "dogsbody" bits that were starting to take over. They were adding to her unhappiness at Yorkshire Portions, and making her regret giving up her job as a marketing executive at Minster Digital, an ambitious up-and-coming digital company that were gaining themselves a decent reputation. Mim had been happy there, but it had always been her dream to work for a magazine, so when her sister, Josie, had dropped into the conversation that a friend of hers had mentioned there was a marketing job going at Yorkshire Portions Magazine, Mim hadn't wasted a second, and applied straightaway. She'd watched its rise from a small on-line local lifestyle magazine run by Clarissa Pallister-Biggs, daughter of Susan, to the almost overnight success it had become today. Susan had taken over as editor and brought in her nephew Simon as publication manager, re-launching it as a glossy magazine that now rubbed shoulders with the best lifestyle publications that graced the shelves of the supermarkets. But, as Mim soon found out, all that glitters is not gold.

Though the interview had gone well, as soon as she'd met Susan and Kenneth, the bubble of excitement she'd bounced in on was immediately burst. The pair had an unpleasant, superior manner and she was hard-pushed to say who was the more arrogant. It had come as a surprise when she was offered the role, having resigned herself to her application being unsuccessful on the grounds that she simply wasn't posh enough and didn't meet their exacting standards. And, though a feeling in her gut was sending out warning signals, Mim did her usual, and let her heart rule her head, pushing her doubts, and her initial dislike of the couple, out of her mind, accepting the job without a moment's consideration. She'd taken it, knowing it was for less money, but with the promise of a generous increase in salary once the magazine had properly found its feet. However, despite the magazine thriving and having an increasing readership, no such pay rise had been forthcoming, and Mim didn't have the courage to ask for one.

The one good thing to come out of working for Yorkshire Portions was her friendship with twenty-seven-year-old Anna-Lisa, whose forthright manner, dry sense of humour and dirty laugh Mim adored; she was the stereotypical Yorkshire woman, called a spade a spade and, despite her diminutive height of five-feet two, was utterly fearless and wouldn't think twice about telling you if she didn't like something. You definitely knew where you stood with Anna-Lisa, and Mim respected that. She also had a penchant for piercings and sported a silver nose ring, and tragus piercings in both ears, while the outer edge of her ears were decorated with an array of silver studs. And her view of love was the polar opposite to Mim's. Where Mim wore her heart on her sleeve, Anna-Lisa kept hers very much locked away. Growing up in care and a variety of foster homes had seen to that. Anna-Lisa lived with Caleb, her boyfriend of the last two years, and her affection for him was as close to being in love as she would ever care to admit, though his fondness for computer games was beginning to grate.

There was Aidey, too; he'd become a good friend. Mim had known him before she'd started at the magazine; he'd been in the same year at school as her older sister Josie and had hung around on the periphery of Josie's friendship group. He was quiet, thoughtful and easy to be around; there was no hidden agenda with him. He was easy on the eye, too, with his moss-green eyes, smattering of freckles, spiky dark blond hair and tall, broad-shouldered physique. At six-foot-three he was a good five inches taller than Mim. She would class him as one of her best mates now, but when she was a teenager, she'd harboured a crush on him; one that she'd shared with no one, not even Josie.

She didn't like the way he was being treated by their bosses. She knew he was seething about having his role changed, but it hadn't stopped him from giving his job his all. *They should bloody well be grateful to have him!* She peered over her monitor, observing his kind face, looking for traces of unhappiness and hoping what had happened wouldn't make him start looking for a different job, though she wouldn't blame him if he did.

The mushrooming feeling of unease in the office didn't help and nor did the increasing references to her being inadequate. It had begun to chip away at her confidence, but not as much as the appointment of Honey, who'd sat beside her all morning, resisting the tasks she was asked to undertake, doing nothing more taxing than watching vlogs on her phone or taking selfies and posting them on Instagram. A perfect example of nepotism if ever there was one. Well, there were quite a few at Yorkshire Portions Magazine, actually; Mim was beginning to wonder how many more Pallister-Biggs friends and relations would end up working for them.

'So, how's it going? Has Jemima been showing you what to do, Honey, dear?' Susan bowled into the room and Honey sat to attention.

'I've been really busy, done loads, Auntie Susan, haven't I, Jemima?' There was that irritating little-girl voice again.

Mim felt herself bristle. *Busy, my arse! You've done naff all except stuff your face with my sweets!* 'Yes, very. Been rushed off your feet,' Mim said through clenched teeth.

'Good, good, I was a bit worried there might not be enough work for two of you.'

Susan's words sent a shiver down Mim's spine. *Why employ Honey if you thought that?*

'Right, I'm off on my lunch break,' said Honey as soon as Susan had left. 'Anybody want to join me?'

'I've got some catching up to do,' said Mim. *After what you did, hell would freeze over before I'd go anywhere with you.*

'No thanks, I want to finish this restaurant write-up,' said Anna-Lisa.

'Aidey, fancy going for a coffee so you can fill me in on all the office gossip?'

'No thanks, I want to finish editing these pictures before I go out.'

'Hmph. Your loss. I might as well go and see if I can tempt Caspar to do something with me.' She arched her eyebrows suggestively as she pulled on her jacket.

As soon as Honey left, it was as if the room breathed a sigh of relief, the tension dissipating as the door clicked shut behind her.

'Jeez! This is going to be hell, she's so full-on,' said Anna-Lisa. 'And that daft little-girl voice she does sometimes, what's that all about?'

'Mmm. It is a bit odd, and I must admit from what we've seen so far, she hasn't got a great attitude,' said Aidey.

'Please tell me this isn't happening.' Mim put her head in her hands. 'Please tell me I'm in a horrible nightmare and I'm going to wake up and find out none of it's true.'

'Trust me, I wish I could; the only thing I've heard about Honey Blossom Blenkisopp, is that she spells nothing but trouble. In fact, I'm surprised Susan and Kenneth haven't heard about it, or realised what she's like,' said Anna-Lisa.

'Yeah, she hasn't been here five minutes but she's already changed the atmosphere of the place,' said Aidey.

It wasn't like him to comment, which made Mim think things must really be as bad as they seemed.

'As if it isn't crap enough having the Pallister-Biggs breathing down our necks. Did I tell you what Simon said to me last Friday just before we finished?'

'I dread to think,' said Mim. She popped a sweet into her mouth before offering the bag around. 'I'm afraid there's not much choice since Honey's decided she can help herself to them.'

'No thanks,' said Aidey.

'No thanks. Anyway, there was just me and him in the office, and he asked me if I had any plans for the weekend and if I fancied doing any "over-time" with him.' Anna-Lisa made finger quotes around the words. 'You should've seen him leering as he said it. Even put his arm round me and managed to "accidentally" touch my boob. Urghh! Gives me the creeps just thinking about it! Honestly, I was so tempted to yank his ridiculous man-bun right off his head and stuff it up his nose.'

'I can just imagine you doing that, as well,' said Mim.

'Me, too.' Aidey chuckled.

'Well, could you blame me? It looks like some sort of rank birds' nest. Granted, on some blokes it would look stylish, but on him, it just looks like a fusty old granny bun.'

Mim and Aidey looked at each other and burst out laughing.

'Not so sure many blokes could carry one off, actually; I certainly couldn't.' Aidey ruffled his short, blond hair.

'That's because you're more rugged; Simon's a runty little dick,' said Anna-Lisa.

'There's a compliment in there somewhere, Aidey.' Mim giggled, her eyes roving over the undulations of the muscles visible beneath his navy-blue long-sleeved t-shirt. A warm, unfamiliar feeling washed over her.

'Yeah, well, honestly, he made my skin crawl. And if he lays a creepy bloody finger on me one more time, he's going to get a knee in the nads for his trouble,' said Anna-Lisa.

Aidey winced. 'Ouch! That'd fettle him.'

'It's nothing more than he deserves. He's a bit too hands-on for his own good. I saw him with his arm around the new intern, what's her name? Sara? Poor kid looked really uncomfortable; her face was like a beetroot. Come to think of it, where is she? I haven't seen her today, and it would be her that Susan would usually send to make coffee, not me,' said Mim.

'She left,' said Aidey.

'What do you mean, she left?' asked Mim.

'She texted me this morning to say that she hated it here and she wasn't coming back anymore,' said Anna-Lisa, fiddling with a tragus piercing.

A frown gathered between Mim's eyebrows. 'You mean after Susan bawled at her last week?'

'Mmm-hmm.' Anna-Lisa nodded.

'Can't say I blame the lass. I saw her leaving the old trout's office on Friday afternoon, she had tears pouring down her cheeks. I think she left just after that,' said Aidey.

'That bloody woman's got a nerve! Those poor interns are treated like dirt, and Susan walks around like she's doing them a massive favour; like it's some kind of honour to be working here for nothing while they have them running around after them.' Anna-Lisa looked livid. 'And you should see the emails she sends them; they're so arrogant and full of uppercase letters to make sure the poor kids are in no doubt that she's yelling even then. I saw one the other day, it was just awful, there was no "hello", no "thank you for working your butt off for free for us". Just bare-faced bad-manners and bullying.'

'Yeah, coming here straight from university must be a horrible introduction to your working life,' said Aidey.

'Everything alright, folks?' Clarissa Pallister-Biggs, the magazine's editorial assistant popped her head round the door, her dark, glossy hair shining.

'Fine thanks, Clarissa,' said Anna-Lisa, while Mim and Aidey just smiled.

'I'm popping to the Nutmeg Tree and just wondered if you fancied anything bringing back? Coffee? Hot chocolate? Slice of cake?' Her smile lit up her pretty face.

'No, thanks,' said Mim.

'Thanks for the offer, but I'm going to head out just as soon as I've done this,' said Aidey.

'Yep, me, too, but thanks anyway,' said Anna-Lisa.

'Okay, see you later.'

Mim turned to her friends. 'Do you think she heard us?'

'I hope not.' Aidey frowned.

'I don't think she did, we were talking quietly, and the floorboards are so creaky on the landing, they make it difficult to hear anything else when you're walking along them,' said Anna-Lisa.

'Hmm. But I heard Honey's voice when I was walking along the landing; before I realised it was hers,' said Mim.

'Well, that's because she's got a massive gob and a voice like a foghorn.' Anna-Lisa laughed. 'I don't think we need to worry about Clarissa hearing us.'

'I hope not; I wouldn't want to hurt her feelings,' said Mim.

Twenty-three-year-old Clarissa was the only likeable member of the Pallister-Biggs family, the "stuck-up-arrogant-prat-gene" having by-passed her. Unlike her mother and her older cousin, Simon, she was amiable, hard-working and kind-hearted. But, much as they were fond of her, it still didn't stop them from treating her with more than a little caution. After all, as they regularly reminded one another, blood is thicker than water.

~

'ALL ALONE?'

Mim's bubble of concentration was punctured. She looked up to see Caspar standing in the doorway, wearing a lopsided smile, his dark eyes twinkling at her. Her stomach looped-the-loop sending a wave of excitement through her.

'Er, yes, I'm working through my lunch … thanks to all the roadworks, my bus got me in late this morning so I need to catch up.' *Earth to Mim, he's well aware you were late this morning! Don't forget, he's wearing the consequences down his shirt.* She felt her cheeks begin to blaze, partly down to her earlier actions and partly down to what the glint in his eyes was doing to her insides. *Oh, my days!*

'That's very noble of you.'

'Not really, there's just lots to do.'

'And what about the new girl, Honey, is she busy, too?'

'Mmm. We're all busy.' *Tread carefully, Mim, don't expose yourself by criticising other staff; you don't know his motives for asking. You're in the crap already, you don't want to get any deeper.*

'Ah, okay. And do you live far out of the city?'

'I live in Skeltwick; it's usually a fifty minute bus ride away – it takes in a lot of the other villages – but that seems to have at least doubled with all the roadworks.'

'Ouch, that must mean you get home quite late then?'

'Mmm-hmm.' Mim nodded, wondering where the conversation was going.

'Tell you what, why don't I give you a lift home tonight? Sounds like I'm heading in your direction and I'll avoid the bus route which should shave a chunk off your journey time.'

'Oh, you don't have to, Aidey's already offered—'

'And is Aidey going in that direction anyway?'

'Well, I'm not sure…'

'That's settled it then; it makes sense that you come with me and save Aidey from having to go out of his way.'

'Oh, okay, if you're sure?'

'I'm positive.' Caspar winked at her and headed back to his office.

What was that all about? Mim gazed after him, her libido raging into life; the effect Caspar De Verre was having on her, anyone would think he bathed in concentrated pheromones. She swallowed and took a deep breath, hoping to marshal her wayward senses that had spent the morning being bombarded by myriad emotions. Mim's thoughts were interrupted by the shrill ring of the phone on her desk.

'THERE YOU GO. One chai tea latte and one salted caramel muffin.' Aidey set the brown paper bag down on Mim's desk. 'You can't go all day without having anything to eat, you'll keel over.'

'Thanks, Aidey, you're a babe; you got my favourite, how thoughtful. What do I owe you?'

'Nothing at all. Just get it down you while the tea's still warm.'

'Are you sure?'

'Positive, enjoy. I think Anna-Lisa's bringing you some more sweets seeing as though Honey devoured most of yours this morning. And I got these as well. I spotted them as I was heading past Bloomz and thought I'd snap them up for you seeing as though you had to chuck the last ones.' He handed her a small bunch of her favourite pink gerberas.

'Oh, Aidey, that's so lovely, thank you.'

'No worries, I just thought you needed cheering up a bit.'

'Ahh, how sweet.' Honey came into the room, the familiar sneer-like smile on her face. 'Got the hots for Mim, have you, Aidey?'

'Don't be ridiculous, Honey. Aidey's one of my best friends.'

'That right, Aidey?' asked Honey.

'It's spot on, we've known each other since school; I was in the same year as her older sister Josie; we used to hang around in the same group.'

'Hmm. I'll believe you; thousands wouldn't.' Honey sniggered.

Mim felt anger rear up inside her at the girl making fun of Aidey. She gave her a pointed look, noting that Aidey had busied himself at his desk, his cheeks burning so brightly his freckles had all but disappeared.

'Do you ever have anything nice to say, Honey?' Anna-Lisa arrived in the room and glared at her.

'Yes. And I wasn't being horrible; I was just pointing out the obvious.' She glared back.

'No you weren't, you were being bitchy and not stopping to think about other people's feelings, as usual.'

'What do you mean as usual?'

'What I mean is you're always passing snidey little comments about people – particularly Mim and Aidey – without thinking for a moment how it might make them feel.'

Honey gave a derisory snort.

'Just leave it, Anna; it's okay,' said Aidey.

'See, he's not bothered. And anyway, what's with your name? Couldn't your parents spell or something?'

Mim glanced across at Anna-Lisa, her heart going out to her friend; after spending so many years in care, any mention of her parents was a touchy subject for Anna.

'What do you mean? Not that I think you're anyone to talk about names, Honey Blossom.' Anger simmered just beneath the surface of Anna-Lisa's words.

'Well, they obviously can't spell, can they. I mean, "Anna-Lisa", what's that all about? The name's "Analise"; it's German or something, and it's not two names stuck together with a hyphen: "Anna-Lisa". I should know, one of my cousins is called Analise.'

'There are loads of names out there that have a variety of spellings actually, Honey. And it doesn't matter how Anna's name's spelt, it's how her parents wanted to spell it,' said Aidey.

'Exactly,' said Mim. 'Look at the name "Caspar", you can spell it "ar" at the end, or "er"; it's up to whoever's choosing the name.' As soon as she'd used Caspar as an example she wished she hadn't. Why couldn't she have chosen a name like Graham or Stephen, instead of drawing attention to herself?

'Oh, trust you to have to bring Caspar into it,' said Honey, wearing her trademark smirk.

'Oh, why don't you just bugger off?' Anna-Lisa muttered under her breath.

'What was that?' asked Honey.

'Everything alright in here?' Susan peered around the door, making everyone jump.

'Everything's fine, Auntie Susan, isn't it, folks?' Honey beamed a fake smile around the room which resulted in a less than enthusiastic response from her colleagues. 'Although, I think Anna-Lisa was just saying something, weren't you, Anna-Lisa?'

The atmosphere in the room became even more intense. Mim held her breath, anxious for where this was going to go. She caught Aidey's eye; he looked as uncomfortable as she felt.

Anna-Lisa shook her head. 'Nope, don't know what gave you that impression.'

Susan glanced between Honey and Anna-Lisa. 'Good, good. Now, back to work everyone, there's lots to do today. And I hope you're getting caught up with your tasks after this morning's fiasco, Jemima?'

'Yes, I worked through my lunch and—'

'I'm not concerned about details, all I care about is that you get the work done.' Susan waved her hand dismissively, the stones of her ring flashing in the light, as she left the room.

Mim was fed up of Susan trying to humiliate her in front of other people, most of all Honey. *Rude bloody bully! Why does she think it's okay to talk to me like that?* She looked across at Anna-Lisa who pulled a face and crossed her eyes. Mim felt a small smile tug at the corners of her mouth.

5

'YOU READY, JEMIMA?' Caspar stepped into the room, his smile making her stomach perform somersaults.

She checked the clock on the wall; it told her it was almost five o'clock. She'd been so busy, the last hour and a half had flown by and she hadn't noticed it getting dark outside nor the Victorian style street lights flickering to life. 'Oh, not quite; I'd lost track of time.'

'No worries, I'll be in my office when you're ready.'

'Oh, okay.' Mim could sense three pairs of eyes on her, one particular pair boring into her like laser beams.

'What does he mean? Why does he want to know if you're ready?' asked Honey.

'Erm, he's heading my way, so he's offered to drop me off at home.' She'd been so engrossed in her work, she'd forgotten to mention anything to Aidey, and judging by the look on his face, he was thinking she was pretty rude. *Oh, bugger! I seem to have mastered the act of annoying people today.*

'I thought Aidey was dropping you off?' Anna-Lisa didn't sound very happy either.

'I know, but Caspar popped into the office when you were all out at lunchtime and said he was going my way anyway – and I know you'd be going out of your way to take me home, Aidey, which didn't seem fair once Caspar had offered. I'm sorry I forgot to say anything sooner, it slipped my mind.'

'It's okay, I totally understand.' Despite his reassurances, Mim couldn't help but think that Aidey looked hurt and it tugged at her conscience.

She looked up at Anna-Lisa whose expression she couldn't read, but somehow managed to make her feel uncomfortable.

'Caspar to the rescue, eh?' There was no mistaking Honey's sarcastic tone.

Oh, bugger off! 'You're making it sound like it's something more than it actually is,' said Mim. 'As I've already said, he's heading my way, Aidey would be going out of his way to drop me off, which, again, as I've already said, didn't seem fair or make sense. It's as simple as that.' She shut her computer down, straightened her stack of notebooks and stood up. 'Right, I'm off, see you tomorrow; and thanks again for the offer of the lift, Aidey.'

'No worries, see you tomorrow.'

'See ya,' said Anna-Lisa. She was still wearing that odd expression; Mim could almost say it bordered on disapproval. She'd text her later tonight and explain the situation, hopefully that should sort things out.

Ughh! There were so many unspoken messages swirling around the Yorkshire Portions office today, she'd be glad to get through the door and get out of the building.

~

'So where are you parked?' asked Mim.

'Just along here, then take a left,' said Caspar.

'Ah.'

In a moment, he'd stopped beside a grey metallic sports car. 'Your carriage awaits, madam.' He opened the door and took a low bow, waiting for her to get in.

'Oh, wow! This is your car?'

'It is.'

'It's amazing.'

'Thank you, I'm glad you like it.'

'I love it.' Mim slipped into the deep leather seat, her eyes taking in the luxurious, state-of-the-art interior, wondering how he could afford a car like this on magazine wages.

Once behind the wheel, Caspar nosed his way out of the carpark and eased into the growing swell of rush-hour traffic. 'Sod this,' he said. In a flash, he'd taken a sharp left which led to what Mim had always assumed was a dead-end. At the end of the road, he took a right and followed a rabbit warren of roads that appeared to by-pass the bulk of the nine-to-five heave of traffic. Before she knew it, they were on the dark country lanes to Skeltwick.

As they drove along, and despite Mim being thrilled to be taken home by Caspar, she felt a faint underlying prickle of unease. She hugged her backpack to her chest like some sort of security blanket, wondering where the feeling had come from.

She was relieved to find that conversation flowed, and was that a hint of flirtation she detected? Her heart fluttered with excitement while an annoying, nagging doubt prodded her, reminding her of her recent resolution of being done with men, especially the ones that came with a bad boy vibe. Aidey sprang into her mind – the very antithesis of a bad boy – and the indiscernible look on his face when she'd told him she wouldn't need a lift; something told her it had hurt him a little. She felt a pang of guilt; the last thing she wanted to do was hurt him, he was one of her best mates. She'd speak to him tomorrow, make sure they were okay.

'Which way's your house?' asked Caspar when they reached Skeltwick.

'Just head straight on, then take the right directly after the White Swan pub on the corner, take the second left, head up the little hill and it's the first cottage on the right.'

'A village pub, eh? How quaint; it looks charming. You'll have to take me for a drink there some time.' He turned and flashed her a smile, his dark eyes twinkling in the lights of the dashboard.

'Definitely.' Mim's heart flipped. Her heartache of a couple of months ago was shoved unceremoniously out of her mind, and the niggling feeling in her gut quashed. 'There, that's my house, you can just stop on the road in front of it.'

As Caspar slowed down and pulled up outside the neat, double-fronted sandstone cottage, Mim's mind was in turmoil. *What happens now? Do I invite him in for a drink or will that make me look like a desperate saddo? Or, worse, will he take it as an invitation for something else, because judging by the vibes that I've been getting from him, it wouldn't surprise me if that was on his mind?* She rummaged in her rucksack for her keys, her mind searching for what to say. 'Right, thanks for dropping me off.'

'Pleasure. Don't know about you, but I could murder a coffee.'

'Oh, right, yeah, would you like to come in for one; a coffee, that is?'

He laughed. 'Yes, what else would I come in for?'

'Oh, er, a cup of tea?' *What? Tea? Why would I say something like that?* Mim climbed out of the car and scurried up the short path to her front door, thankful that the street lights cast a soft glow, conveniently disguising her blushes.

All fingers and thumbs, she went to push the key into the lock but dropped them in her haste. As she bent to pick them up, Caspar asked, 'Do you know the relevance of the initials and date above the door here?' She was relieved that he appeared oblivious to her clumsiness, instead his attention was on the heavy stone lintel above the doorway. He ran his fingers over the age-smoothed "JC & AC" that were neatly carved there, with the date "1745" sitting directly below them.

'Um, I think it's the date of a wedding, or something like that. My sister knows more about it; said something about seeing names fitting those initials in some ancient deeds for the property or a copy of some old will or old legal document, something like that anyway. Her husband Russ researched the history of the house and found out all sorts; he's really into things like that.'

'Wow, fascinating stuff.'

Once inside the small hallway, she flicked the light on and, taking advantage of Caspar's interest in the door, quickly snatched the bath towel she'd left drying on the sturdy column radiator, shoving it out of sight in the understairs cupboard.

'This is very sweet,' said Caspar. 'I love rural Georgian architecture; the fact that it's got all of the formal symmetry you associate with the style, while maintaining a distinctly countryside influence.'

'The cottage actually belongs to my sister and brother-in-law; I'm house-sitting for them while they're in Qatar. There's no way I could afford to rent somewhere like this myself, never mind buy.'

'Qatar? That's a far cry from North Yorkshire. What are they doing over there?' He followed Mim into the kitchen. 'Oh, and this is just lovely. He glanced around at the duck-egg blue shaker kitchen, the low beamed ceiling and the quaint Yorkshire horizontal-sliding sash windows.

'Er, excuse the mess; I meant to tidy up at the weekend but never quite got round to it. I'll have to do it soon, though, before Josie –

that's my sister – Skypes me; she likes to check on the house and make sure I'm looking after it properly.'

Caspar's eyes swept over the detritus that littered the granite worktops, the dirty dishes piled high in the sink. His eyes alighted on a couple of dog bowls on the floor. 'You have a dog?'

'Ah, yes, well, no, well, yes; actually, he's Josie's but she didn't want to take him with her – thought it wasn't fair – so I'm looking after him, but he goes to the pet-sitter during the day when I'm at work. As a matter of fact, you can make the coffee while I go and get him; it's just a few doors up. I'll be two ticks.' Mim thrust the jar of coffee into his hand and dashed out of the door before he had time to argue.

The moments away from Caspar gave her time to regroup. Her insides were a melting-pot of emotions swirling and sloshing around; the one with the loudest voice yelling that he was hot to trot and just her type, others flagging up danger signals, warning her to keep her distance. She was sorely tempted to turn a deaf ear to the latter ones.

Arriving at Wisteria Cottage, Mim grasped the gleaming brass door-knocker and gave the front door a resounding thud. It set off a round of barking from the depths of the house, the familiar deep tones of her sister's Labrador, Herbert, making her smile.

'It's alright, calm down you two, it'll just be your mum, Herbs. Maisie, will you stop your yapping, please?' In a moment, light flooded the doorstep and a solid black Labrador lunged at her, closely pursued by an excitable black cocker spaniel. 'Woah, hello, Herbs, hiya, Maisie. Hi, Carly.'

Carly brushed a straggle of hair off her face. 'Sorry, Mim, I couldn't grab hold of them in time, little buggers. They've been extra excitable today for some reason, egging each other on and getting up to mischief in the garden.' Carly's elfin face, petite frame and blonde ponytail belied her thirty-six years. She was wearing her "dog walking" clothes of faded skinny jeans and an over-sized checked shirt that looked as though it belonged to her husband Owen.

Mim looked up from stroking Herbert's big, square head. 'Oh, no, nothing too drastic, I hope.'

'No, all harmless, quite funny actually, mostly involving running up and down the kids' slide and digging a hole in the new flower bed.'

'Digging a hole? No! Herbert, what have you been up to?'

Herbert wagged his tail, looking pleased with himself.

'Don't worry, I spotted them just in time before any real damage could be done, but let's just say there was mud flying everywhere for a short while. Anyway, petal, don't just stand there on the doorstep, come on in for a coffee; the kids are round at my mum's and Owen's not going to be back for at least another hour, so we've got plenty of time for a chinwag.'

'Actually, if you don't mind, I won't. It's just, well, I've had a lift home – the traffic and roadworks are horrendous in York and I was late to work this morning, so … anyway, the person who gave me a lift is currently making coffee in my kitchen, and I'd better head back there before he wonders where I've got to.' Mim did her best to sound casual, trying not to betray the fact she fancied the pants of the mystery driver.

'Oh, it's a "he" is it?' The look in Carly's eyes told her she'd been rumbled.

'Yes, he's the new art director at work – Caspar – he was heading this way, so he thought—'

'And does he, by any chance, happen to be drop-dead gorgeous and make you want to rip his clothes off?'

'Erm, well—'

'I'll take that as a yes.'

Mim felt her face flush. 'Listen, thanks, Carly, I'd best get off, you're letting all the warm air out of the house standing here chatting to me. Thanks for having this naughty boy. Come on, young man, let's get you home before you cause any more mischief.'

'Never mind Herbert causing mischief, you'd better make sure your "lift" leaves before the resident curtain-twitchers get themselves in a tizz about him and set the local rumour mill in action. You'll be in danger of your sister finding out about what you've been up to before you do!' Carly giggled, grabbing hold of Maisie's collar. 'Come here, madam, don't go getting any ideas about following Herbert home.'

'Ugh! Don't remind me about the dreaded curtain-twitchers. They need to find something more exciting to do with their lives than poke their noses into other people's business. Anyway, thanks again, Carly; I'll see you in the morning.'

'See ya, don't do anything I wouldn't do.'

'Not sure there is anything you wouldn't do.'

'Cheek! Actually, that reminds me, are you still okay for my kinky underwear party next Friday?' Carly had raised her voice for the benefit of resident busy-body Pat Motson who lived a few doors up at Cuckoo's Nest Cottage. She gave Mim an exaggerated wink, pointing in the direction of their nosy neighbour's house.

Mim nodded, stifling a giggle; her friend had a mischievous streak, and so did Mim. 'So, is there any truth in the rumour the new vicar's wife's coming too?'

'Absolutely; apparently she's very keen. Deb invited her, not thinking for a minute she'd accept, but didn't want her to feel left out.'

'Really?' She noticed a movement in the curtains of Cuckoo's Nest Cottage, a narrow chink letting a sliver of light sneak out. No doubt Mrs Motson's outrage would be going stratospheric anytime soon.

'Really.' Carly clamped her hand to her mouth as she struggled to keep her laughter under control.

'In that case, you'd better make sure she knows exactly what a kinky underwear party involves; we don't want her thinking it's something like kitchenware.'

'Good point, that would be a shocker for her wouldn't it? Imagine her taking something phallic home and using it to stir the vicar's soup!' The dirty laugh Carly was struggling to hold onto escaped, making Mim giggle too.

'Oh, don't! You've no idea what mental image has just forced its way into my mind. I'm off before you say anything else.'

'Hah! See you in the morning, chick. Have fun.'

Mim hooked her fingers under Herbert's collar and made her way down the path. She couldn't help but chuckle; Carly wasn't really having a kinky underwear party, it was her turn to host the monthly get-together of their group of friends from the village. And it was the first time Gemma, the vicar's wife, had been invited.

Mim had barely got the door open when Herbert hurled himself down the hallway, barking at Caspar who was sipping coffee in the kitchen.

'Herbert! Sit!' She ran towards the Labrador, grabbing hold of his collar and pulling him back. 'What's got into you? Behave!' The Labrador sat, a low growl emanating from deep within his solid body.

'Does he always greet strangers this way?' asked Caspar.

Herbert's growling got louder.

'Shush, Herbert! No, I don't know what's got into him, he's normally really friendly, too much so.'

Caspar eyed the Labrador warily before turning to Mim. 'I made you a coffee, didn't know if you took milk or sugar, so I just left it black.'

'Thanks, I just take a splash of milk.' She could feel Herbert pulling on his collar as Caspar added milk to her mug.

'There you go.' He slid it across the granite top of the large island towards her. Herbert took exception, barking and growling again, his hackles raised.

'Herbert, will you please stop it!' Mim looked across at Caspar who'd lost his confident air and was now looking quite frightened.

'What's the matter with him?'

'I don't know; I've never seen him like this before.'

'Can't you shut him up?' Caspar asked.

'Erm, right, yes, I'll try. If you stay where you are, I'll pop him in the utility room and shut the door.'

'I like the sound of that.'

Though it niggled her, Mim turned a blind eye to the cold tone of his voice. She loved Herbert and wasn't completely comfortable with putting him in a room on his own when he hadn't seen her all day, especially when this was his home; after all, he was only looking out for her.

'Sorry about Herbert, he must be feeling protective.' Mim led Caspar to the living room, the Labrador's objections now muffled in the background thanks to the solid doors and thick walls of the cottage. She sat down on the large, squishy sofa, expecting Caspar to take one of the chairs, and was surprised when he sat beside her.

'No worries.' He smiled, and Mim noticed the look of unease in his eyes had been replaced by the self-assuredness of earlier. 'This is a fantastic room, by the way; your sister and brother-in-law have good taste.' He sat back, his eyes roving over the beamed ceiling, the large, carved fireplace in butter-coloured sandstone and the tasteful soft-furnishings. It was the one room Mim had consciously kept tidy, in readiness for the Skyping sessions with her sister.

'Mmm. I like it,' she said. 'It's cosy, especially with the fake wood-burner on.'

'It's fake?'

'It's oil; Josie couldn't stand the mess of a real one, too much dust apparently.'

'Can't say I blame her.' He stretched his arm along the back of the sofa. Mim could feel the warmth of his skin radiating onto the back of her neck; it sent a wicked shiver of excitement through her. 'So are you going to enlighten me as to why you think your boss is a "dragon" – as you put it – or why you think she's looking for an excuse to sack you?'

'Ah, I shouldn't have said those things.' *Bugger! He didn't waste much time in bringing that up, did he?*

Caspar laughed. 'It's okay. I won't repeat it, I was just wondering what made you think that; from what I saw today, you seem to be a hard worker.'

Mim scrambled through her mind for a reason that would sound plausible; she didn't know yet whether Caspar could be trusted. 'Well, it's just that I seem to annoy her quite a bit at the moment.'

'Ah, care to elaborate?'

Was it just her imagination, or had he started playing with her hair? Her stomach looped-the-loop and she swallowed. 'Well, things like me being late, though I do set off in what should be plenty of time but with all the roadworks, I just seem to get later and later every morning. That and my scattiness don't seem to go down very well.'

'Some people find scattiness appealing.'

'Well, I've never met anyone who does.'

'Yes, you have.'

'I have?'

He nodded.

'Who?'

'Me.'

'Oh, right.' Mim's breath caught in her throat and butterflies took flight in her stomach. *Oh, my days! What is he doing? Is he flirting? Of course he's flirting, you silly woman! What should I do? Should I flirt back? Oh, flippin' heck, I swore off men after my last pathetic excuse of a relationship, and the fact that I work with him is a recipe for disaster. Yes, but he's gorgeous! Those eyes…* And yet… There was something, a little niggle in a dark recess of her mind, prodding her, warning her to be careful, which was, at this very moment in time, something she'd really rather ignore.

'You do know you're a very attractive woman, don't you, Jemima?'

Me? I'm like a flaming ungainly elephant! 'Erm, am I? And it's Mim, by the way, not Jemima; I'm only Jemima when I'm in trouble.' *Actually, from what my gut's telling me, I'm in serious trouble right now.*

'Okay, Mim, in answer to your question, yes, you are very attractive; you've got the most incredible blue eyes.'

'I have?'

'Mmm-hmm.'

Mim wasn't an obvious beauty, but she was striking. She had large ice-blue eyes, set ever-so-slightly too far apart, framed with thick, dark lashes. Her nose was long and aquiline and her mouth, with its full lips, could be described as being a little too wide. Her thick, naturally mouse-brown hair that she'd disguised with a mixture of blonde highlights, could be justifiably considered straggly and unkempt at times. As for her figure, she'd claim to be slightly over-weight, and couldn't remember a time when she hadn't been conscious of her height and gangly limbs that always seemed to be getting in the way or knocking things over, herself included.

'Oh.' She was conscious of him staring at her with those black eyes that were glittering with a delicious hint of danger.

'Yes, you're what I'd call a classic pre-Raphaelite beauty.'

'Are you taking the mickey?'

'No, not at all, I'm being perfectly serious.'

'I think you are; I hate my nose, it's way too big, my eyes are googly, and as for my mouth, it's massive; makes me look like I've got trout lips.'

'You're much too self-critical; I'd say your looks are most definitely more than the sum of their parts, and that's how you should think of them.'

'Er, what does that mean?' *He's making me sound like some sort of mathematical problem; and I bloody hate maths!*

'It means that, added together, your features make you incredibly beautiful.'

'They do?' Mim swallowed. Their eyes locked and her heart flipped as she wondered where this was going, after all, they'd only just met. But, before she had chance to ponder the matter further, the ring-tone of her mobile phone started to spill from the pocket of the leather jacket she was still wearing. Their moment of whatever it was had disappeared before it really got started. *Bugger!*

'Right, I think that's my cue to leave.' Caspar drained his mug and set it down on the table in front of the sofa.

'You don't have to, I'll call whoever it is back later on.'

'It's fine, I need to be getting back.'

'Oh, okay.'

'I could pick you up in the morning, if you like?'

'Isn't it out of your way?' Mim followed him to the front door, the sound of Herbert barking in the background.

'Not really, maybe five minutes at most. It'll mean you'll get to work on time and won't get into any more trouble with your "dragon" of a boss – and please don't quote me on that last bit.'

The lopsided grin he gave turned Mim's insides to mush. 'Well, if you're sure.'

'I'm sure; I'll pick you up just before eight.' He leaned forward and kissed her cheek, his five o'clock shadow brushing her skin and sending delicious ripples of anticipation through her.

She closed the door, leaning against it as she processed what had just happened. Her heart was racing in that familiar way it did when she was on the cusp of becoming involved with someone that she knew, deep down, she shouldn't. The buzz it gave her was more exciting than any sugar rush.

The sound of Herbert whining pulled her out of her musings. 'Alright, Herbs, bide your passion.' She made her way to the utility room and opened the door. The Labrador shot out, nearly knocking Mim off her feet as he raced towards the living room. 'Hey, go steady, Herbert!' She followed him, watching as he gave the room a thorough sniffing, his hackles raised and his tail swaying in an agitated way, before trotting to the front door. Only when he was satisfied that Caspar had left did his usual happy demeanour return. He pressed his head against Mim's thigh and nudged her hand for a ruffle of his ears.

'What's got into you, lad? It was only Caspar, and he's nice.' She tried to ignore the niggle that prodded her from the back of her mind, telling her that dogs had a strong intuition about people. And from what she could gather, Herbert thought Caspar was not what he appeared to be; in canine language, he wasn't to be trusted.

6

Mim plumped up her pillow for the umpteenth time, and pulled the duvet closer to her chin. She'd been lying awake for the last hour and a half. After the day she'd had, her body was tired and she was feeling emotionally drained, but sleep was cruelly eluding her. As if on cue, as soon as she'd closed her eyes, her mind had started racing; it had thoughts that needed addressing and apparently wouldn't settle until they had been – over and over again.

Mim had felt emotionally drained for as long as she could remember and she knew it had a lot to do with her dubious choice of boyfriends. Well, it actually had everything to do with her dubious choice of boyfriends. Just when she thought she'd found "the one", and she was in a relationship that might actually be going somewhere, she'd discover that the said boyfriend had other ideas and, more often than not, other girlfriends.

'Phfft!' Mim moved onto her side, pulling the duvet over her head, blocking out the bright harvest moon whose iridescent glow was reaching in through the chinks in the curtains.

Thoughts of work crept in, making her heart thud in a disagreeable way, a hint of panic worming its way around her body. What was going on at Yorkshire Portions? She was sure Susan's irritation with her wasn't simply to do with her being late on the odd morning, after all, Mim always made the time up. Yes, she couldn't argue that she was scatty but, even if she did say so herself, Mim was good at her job, and tackled everything that was thrown at her with enthusiasm – even if it didn't remotely resemble anything in her job description. She'd been told many times by her co-workers that her bosses took advantage of her good nature, but the people-pleaser in her hadn't minded that much. Until today, and the arrival of Honey Blenkinsopp. Then, she really bloody minded.

On paper, her role at the magazine was her dream job, but recently it had become something she increasingly disliked. Her weekends had always been precious, but were even more so now, with the thought of returning to work on a Monday morning throwing a damp, heavy cloud over her Sunday afternoons, making her mood slump as low as the autumn mists that hung over the village at this time of year. She took a deep breath and rubbed her eyes, but as much as she was beginning to hate her job, she didn't want to lose it.

The conversation she'd had with Anna-Lisa rolled into her mind. Mim had rung her back after Caspar had left, anticipating what her friend was going to say.

'Be careful, Mim, there's something about him that makes me feel uneasy,' she'd said. 'He's just a bit too smooth for his own good.'

'There's nothing to be careful about; Caspar just gave me a lift back home, I made him a coffee, then he left. That's all.' Mim had pulled a face, knowing if it was anybody else but Caspar, she'd be sharing the finer details with her friend, hoping to get her slant on things, but something had made her hold back. And, if she was completely honest with herself, she felt the same unease about him as Anna-Lisa, only Mim, as usual, chose to ignore it.

'Hmm, well, if you're sure. But there's definitely something about him I don't trust; he's just too sure of himself and I get the feeling he's used to women jumping as soon as he clicks his fingers.'

Is that what it looks like I've done? No, of course not; there was nothing to jump at, he was doing *me* a favour – and Aidey, too – giving me a lift home so it meant Aidey wouldn't have to go out of his way. Anna-Lisa's got him all wrong; her best-friend protective side has gone into over-drive. I know she means well, after what happened with Paul and Matty, and Connor, and Rick. Uhh! Rick, what a weasel! Mim punched her pillow and switched sides, closing her eyes tight shut. The less she thought about that worm of a boyfriend the better.

She'd be the first to admit that there was an indisputable pattern in her choice of boyfriends. But what she'd chosen to ignore was the pattern of disquiet in her gut, the warnings that she'd only get hurt, that no good would come of it. With each and every man she'd dated, it had been there, but the thrill of temptation had been stronger, the addiction to that particular element irresistible; it had won out every time. And Mim showed no signs she was learning from it.

An hour later, she was still wide-awake, listening to the shrieks of the barn owls calling to one another from the fields at the back of the house. Her heart was thrumming with anxiety as her worries and doubts got the better of her, pushing sleep even further from reach. 'What am I doing wrong?' she asked herself, not for the first time. And, hard as she tried to fight them, she felt tears prickle at the back of her eyes, as thoughts of Rick pushed their way through. Usually, in the cold light of day, she could keep a lid on her feelings and the memories of what had happened, but in the small, dark hours of night, it was a different matter; there was no escape.

'This is no good!' She flicked on the bedside light and threw back the duvet. Sitting on the edge of the bed she rubbed her hands up and down her face. The insomnia had been dragging on for weeks and the more Mim tried to get to sleep, the more impossible it seemed. She'd worked out she'd been surviving on a measly three hours' sleep a night, and it was having a knock-on effect on her well-being; her psoriasis had re-appeared with a vengeance, its objection at the stress she was putting her body through manifesting in rough, scaly patches on her abdomen as well as the base of her spine and the tops of her arms. Ever since she'd been a small child, she'd always had a splodge of it somewhere on her body, but as soon as anxiety took hold, the rash would flare up almost overnight.

With a sigh, Mim pushed her feet into her slippers, pulled her dressing-gown on and headed downstairs. There was no point fighting a losing battle; she'd make herself a mug of hot milk and cinnamon, just like her beloved Grandma Joyce used to do for her whenever she stayed over at Primrose Cottage. She couldn't face another night of lying in bed, the dark shroud of insecurity creeping over her, squeezing and twisting in her chest, making it difficult for her to breathe. Getting out of bed was the only way she'd be able to shake it off.

Herbert, apparently used to this new routine, heaved himself out of his bed, his tail wagging sleepily as he wandered over to her when she appeared in the kitchen. 'Hi there, Herbs, sorry for waking you. How do you fancy some nice, warm milk, eh?'

Mim set a pan of milk on the gas hob, her mind crowding with the events of the day, each one jostling for prominence. She wandered over to the table and flopped onto a chair. Herbert followed, rested his large square head in her lap and gazed up at her with kind eyes. Mim smiled and smoothed his ears. 'I wish my life was as simple as yours, lad.' Herbert wagged his tail. 'Actually, forget I said that, Herbs; it can't have been much fun for you when your family of four years upped sticks and left the country, leaving you with your scatty Auntie Mim. That must've felt pretty crappy and confusing; trust me, I wouldn't want to be left with me.'

Herbert whimpered and nudged her hand, keen for the ear smoothing to continue. Mim obliged until the sound of the milk frothing and bubbling furiously on the hob interrupted. 'Bugger!' She jumped up and raced to the stove, turning the heat off just in time before the milk spewed out of the pan. 'Blimey, that was close.'

She filled a mug with the milk and poured the rest into Herbert's bowl, adding a dash of cold so he wouldn't have to wait to drink it.

While the Labrador was noisily lapping the milk from his bowl, Mim headed back to her seat, cradling her mug in her hands and inhaling the comforting cinnamon aroma. The first thought that entered her mind was Caspar and that deliciously dangerous smile of his. It was fair to say, he ticked all of her boxes – apparently ticking some she didn't even know she had. But she couldn't help but wonder why he was paying her such particular attention. What did he mean by driving her home, paying her compliments that she knew she'd accepted clumsily – if she'd even accepted them at all? Part of her didn't know whether he meant what he said, or if he was secretly laughing at her. Whatever it was, she knew she'd find it very easy to fall for his lines; after all, she had a track record for it.

Honey's face pushed thoughts of Caspar out of the way. Why did she, of all people, have to get a job at Yorkshire Portions? Mim closed her eyes and scrunched up her face. 'Ughh! What have I done to deserve that?'

Herbert, who'd done a thorough job of checking that every last drop of milk had been removed from his bowl and was now busy licking the floor around it, looked up at her. As if reminded of her turmoil, he trotted across to her and sat at her feet. Mim looked down at his handsome face and couldn't help but laugh at the line of milk that edged his lower lip, tiny beads of liquid hanging from the bristly hairs. Just then, his tongue shot out and swept, lizard-like, from one side of his nose to the other before he leaned forward and released a loud belch.

'Charming,' said Mim. 'Don't think you're ready for fine dining just yet, are you, Herbert?' He wagged his tail, before slumping to the ground, making himself comfortable on her slippers.

After a good twenty minutes of wrestling with the things that had thus far deprived her of sleep, the power of Mim's worries suddenly seemed less daunting. As far as Caspar was concerned, she decided she'd take his smooth words with a pinch of salt, but if he was up for a bit of no-strings fun, then where was the harm in that? It might even do her a bit of good. After Rick, there was no way she was going to get attached to a man for quite some time. But if a gorgeous bloke was going to pay her some much-needed attention, then a bit of a laugh and a cheeky little dalliance wouldn't hurt anyone; she'd play it cool and play him at his own game. There was absolutely no way she was going to fall for his charm the way she had with the others; they could keep it light and casual. It wasn't Mim's usual style, but since her usual style had caused her nothing but heartache, then she figured it was time to change tack and try something new. And she chose to defy the little warning voice that said her heart was in danger of getting hurt again. *Not this time. This time, I'll have the upper hand.*

She looked down at Herbert who was sleeping contentedly at her feet, his gently rhythmic snoring joining the nocturnal creaks and groans of the house that Mim had become so used to she barely noticed them. She took a mouthful of milk, licking the froth from her top lip.

Honey was a trickier one to manage. From Mim's experience – and from what Anna-Lisa and Aidey had said earlier in the day – Honey was manipulative, spiteful and most definitely not to be trusted; they'd all have to watch their backs with her around.

Thoughts of Honey had segued into insecurity about her job, and a new ripple of concern swept through her. What was going on there? Wouldn't it have made sense for Mim to be the senior marketing assistant and for Honey to be her junior? It would certainly have helped make the dynamics easier, particularly working alongside a forceful personality like Honey's. Mim couldn't shake the nagging doubt that Susan wanted rid of her; certainly the way the woman had been treating her recently gave her good reason to feel that way. Maybe it was time to start looking for a job elsewhere; after all, the one she'd got hadn't lived up to expectations and she hadn't been happy there for a while.

Mim yawned and glanced at the clock; it was a good forty-five minutes since she'd first come downstairs. The talking to she'd given herself combined with the soothing effect of the warm cinnamon-infused milk had worked wonders and she was relieved to find that sleep was finally seeking her out.

She eased her feet from beneath Herbert's solid body, making him groan. 'Right, young man, time for bed.' He looked at her with bleary eyes before heaving himself up and wandering over to his bed.

Upstairs, she climbed into bed, plumped up her pillow and allowed sleep to claim her before her thoughts got chance to bloom out of control and logic escape her.

7

THE WEEK CONTINUED in much the same way as it had started, though thanks to Caspar, Mim hadn't been late for work once. Bizarrely, that seemed to disappoint Susan, and Mim still couldn't shake the feeling that her boss was looking for reasons to find fault with her. It hadn't gone down well with Honey either and she'd had more than a little of the green-eyed monster about her, quizzing Mim relentlessly about Caspar, wondering as to the topic of conversation on the drive to and from work, whether he just dropped her off at home, if he'd ever been into the house, or, more importantly, if he'd ever mentioned a girlfriend. The questions were fired at Mim like bullets from a machine gun, and repeated more assertively if her answer was less than satisfactory.

'So, you're telling me you haven't actually asked if he's got a girlfriend?'

'No.'

'Why not?'

'Well, he's never brought it up, so I didn't think it was my place to; it's none of my business,' said Mim.

'Well, surely if he had a girlfriend, he would've mentioned her. Has he asked you if you've got a boyfriend?'

'Not really.'

'What do you mean, not really?'

'Jeez, give it a bloody rest, Honey,' Anna-Lisa had snapped.

'I'm only asking a simple question; I don't know why Jemima's finding it so hard to answer it.'

'Maybe it's because she's sick to death of being interrogated. And here's an idea, why don't you go and ask him yourself if you're so interested?'

Honey had responded by pulling a face at Anna-Lisa before adopting her usual petulant pout, while Aidey had given Mim a sympathetic smile.

Each night, after driving her home, Mim had invited Caspar in for coffee. She was disappointed that Herbert hadn't thought him any better for knowing. In fact, the Labrador's reaction to him was getting more alarming with every encounter; at the last one, Herbert had lunged at Caspar, his teeth clashing menacingly. She'd never seen this side to Herbert before, and it had been a struggle to hold onto his collar. Much as she didn't like to admit it, the reasons for his behaviour were giving her cause for concern. But each night, Caspar banished her doubts as he lavished her with compliments, delivering lingering kisses to her cheek before he left, his exotic cologne swirling around her nostrils and tapping into the part of her brain that triggered an attraction alert. And despite her resolve, he was beginning to worm his way into her affections.

'Lord, Mim, I swear I could lose myself in those stunning eyes of yours,' he'd said on Thursday evening as they were sitting side-by-side on the sofa. Mim had held her breath, her heart racing as he'd leaned in, convinced that he was about to kiss her. Instead, he'd held her gaze and given her a lopsided, snaggle-toothed smile that had reached right inside her and played havoc with her surging libido.

'Coffee?' asked Mim. It was Friday evening and Caspar had just pulled up outside her cottage.

'Actually, how about a glass of this instead?' He reached behind him and produced a bottle of red wine. His eyes twinkled dangerously, triggering a flurry of butterflies in her stomach. 'It's been quite a week, I think we've both earned it.'

'You won't catch me arguing with that.' Mim grinned, ignoring the alarm bells that were clanging in her mind. She blocked them out, instead focusing on the swell of happiness that filled her heart as she made her way across the path to her front door. 'I'll just open up;

you make yourself at home while I go and get Herbert. Wine glasses are kept in the cupboard on the wall next to the back door.'

'Okay. And, Mim…'

'Yes?'

'Don't be long.'

'I won't.' A smile lit up her face as she headed along to Carly's, almost giddy with excitement, wondering if tonight was going to head where she hoped it would. She ignored the twitching net curtain as she passed Cuckoo's Nest Cottage; what a thrill she'd be giving nosy-parker Cath Motson.

'Now then, hon, come in.' Carly stepped back, opening the door of Wisteria Cottage wider as Herbert and Maisie shot out, propelled on a jet of enthusiasm and mischief.

'Woah, you two, bide your passion!' Mim laughed.

Herbert ran around her, hotly pursued by Maisie, his whole body wiggling with happiness, his tail swooshing in the smaller dog's face. Maisie snapped at it excitedly, eliciting a yelp from the Labrador. He stopped in his tracks and shot his canine friend a look of disbelief, making Mim and Carly giggle.

'Honestly, you two,' said Carly. 'You're like a pair of excitable toddlers who've been fed a vat load of e-numbers.'

'Have they been like this all day?' asked Mim.

'No, it's only when you get here that they start the comedy double-act.'

Mim couldn't help but laugh at her friend's description.

'Have you got time for a cuppa or are you rushing back for a coffee with Mr Tall, Dark and Dangerous?' asked Carly.

Dangerous? The word sent a spike of uncertainty up Mim. 'Oh, er, yes, we're having wine tonight, seeing as though it's Friday and we've had a bit of a full-on week. And, out of interest, what makes you think he's dangerous?'

'I just mean he has a classic sort of bad-boy look, albeit a posher version, all wrapped up in designer clothes – just from what I've seen when he's been leaving your place – kind of like Dracula in that handsome, irresistible sort of way; you know he's bad but the temptation's too great to resist, kind of thing.'

Mim laughed, she knew what Carly meant; it was exactly what made him so appealing to her.

'And wine, eh? Looks like he won't be driving home tonight, then. Can you imagine all that fodder you're giving nosy Cath

Motson? She'll be in her element having something new to spy on; her curtain twitching'll be cranked up into overdrive by the end of the night!'

'Ughh! Don't!' Much as she hated the thought of being the subject of tittle-tattle, Mim couldn't help but giggle.

'Yep, news of what you've been up to will be round the village before *you* even know about it. But just look at it this way, petal, while she's gossiping about you, at least she's leaving someone else alone.'

'That's very true and when you put it like that, I suppose I can tolerate the thought of it. Anyway, I'd best get back but we can have a catch up over the weekend if you're around?'

'Sounds like a plan. Owen's out with the lads tomorrow night, why don't you pop round then – bring Herbert – and you can fill me in on the Dark Count.'

'The Dark Cou ...?' The penny dropped and Mim giggled. 'Ah, you mean Caspar.'

'Mmm-hmm. I'm looking forward to hearing all about him. Anyway, get yourself home; it's Friday night and you've got a hot man and a cheeky glass of wine waiting for you.'

'I do indeed.' Mim smiled, feeling a flutter in her stomach. She turned to the Labrador and clicked her tongue. 'Come on, Herbs, let's get home. See you, Carly and thanks for having this boy.'

'No probs. Have fun. See ya.'

As soon as Mim opened the door to the cottage Herbert's hackles rose and he started growling and barking alarmingly. Mim, keeping a tight hold of his collar, led him straight along the hall, through the kitchen and into the utility room. 'Sorry, Herbert, but if you behaved yourself and were nice to Caspar you'd be able to join us.' She closed the door quickly, ignoring the niggle that Herbert's reaction to Caspar's presence created, dumped her backpack on the nearest dining chair and headed to the living room where she found Caspar sitting on the sofa, glass of wine in hand.

'Ah, here you are at last.' He picked up a large glass of wine from the coffee table and handed it to her. Mim took it, smiling as she sat beside him.

'Ooh, thanks, I need this.'

'Cheers to Friday night and the start of the weekend.' He clinked his glass against hers.

'I'll drink to that. Cheers.' She took a sip of wine, the rich berry flavours dancing on her tongue, spreading a wave of warmth down her throat as she swallowed. 'Mmm, that's good.'

'I'm glad you like it, it's a goodie. It's from my parents' wine cellar, I brought it specially for tonight.' He turned to her and started twirling a strand of her hair around his finger, his eyes fixed on her intently.

'You did?' Mim's heart started racing as excitement buzzed through her.

'Mmm-hmm.' He nodded, releasing her hair before running his finger down the side of her face. 'What are you doing to me, Mim Dewberry? You've got me totally captivated.'

'I have?' *Woah! I've never captivated anyone before! Things are looking up!*

'Surely you can see that? Why else do you think I've been picking you up of a morning and dropping you off at night?'

Mim swallowed and shook her head, doing her best to ignore the butterflies that were fluttering like crazy around her insides. 'I, erm, I don't know.'

'It's so I get the chance to spend more time with you, get to know you better, of course. Did you really think I was just doing it because I was passing?'

'Yes, I did; that's what you said.'

'Well, that was true for the first night, but after that I've had to make a special detour; I live on the other side of York.' He set his wine glass down on the coffee table and turned back to her.

'What? You come all this way just because … because you—'

'Yes.' He gave her a heart-stopping smile before cupping her face in his hands and pressing his lips against hers, kissing her softly.

Mim let out a groan as she felt herself melting into him, her resolve of not taking things seriously leaching away as his tongue parted her lips and found hers. Before she knew it, he was undoing the buttons of her fitted black shirt, tugging it out of her skinny jeans. 'Wait! Not here.' Reality kicked in and she leapt to her feet.

'What? What do mean?' He pushed his fringe back with his hand, frustration in his eyes.

'It's my sister.'

'Your sister?'

'She's fussy; a little bit house-proud, and she'd have a fit if she thought I'd done anything I shouldn't be doing on this sofa. It cost her a fortune; she had to have it specially made.'

'But how would she know?'

'Well, she wouldn't, not really, but I would. I'd know, and I'd never be able to look her in the eye, then she'd probably get suspicious which would make her know that I was hiding something.'

'Okay.' He looked confused and not a little put out.

'I just wouldn't be able to relax; she'd be at the back of my mind the whole time. The last thing you want when you're having … when you're getting … oh, bugger, I'm making a mess of this. What I'm trying to say, but making a right arse of it, is that I don't fancy having Josie on my mind when we're … you know… doing it. Do you see where I'm coming from?'

'I think so, but it's a bloody shame, that's all I can say.'

'Oh!' Mim's eyes grew large and she started to giggle. 'I didn't mean we couldn't, you know … do it anywhere else in the house, well, maybe not Josie and Russ's bedroom, but my bedroom is absolutely fine. Or the bathroom, and maybe even the kitchen table.'

'The kitchen table? Sounds interesting, but wouldn't your sister be fussy about that, too?'

'Hmm. Now you come to mention it, she probably would be a bit iffy about it, actually make that very iffy; we'd best keep the kitchen table off limits … and now I come to think of it, the bathroom, too, actually; she has this weird extra sense and seems to know about things like that, at least she did when we were teenagers. It was actually a bit spooky – not to mention annoying – and I've kind of got the feeling things haven't changed.'

'Right. She's quite something, this sister of yours.'

'Oh, she is, you wouldn't believe.'

'I think I'm beginning to.'

Mim's thoughts slowed down a gear, as she became acutely aware she'd been gabbling. She looked up at Caspar, trying to assess his feelings. He stood before her, hands on hips, gnawing at his bottom lip. Had she put the dampers on things tonight? Her heart suddenly slumped; she hoped not.

Aware of her watching him, a lopsided smile spread across his face. He stepped towards her and repeated the tantalising kiss of earlier. Mim's heart surged and her knees went weak. She gasped as he pulled away. 'The bedroom it is then,' he said, his eyes dark with lust. 'Lead the way.'

~

'WOW! THAT WAS AMAZING.' Mim flopped back onto the pillow, her raggle-taggle hair splayed out around her.

Caspar lay beside her, sweat glistening in the thick, dark hairs of his chest. 'You're one hot lady, Mim Dewberry.'

'I am?'

'You are. And you've got the most amazing body on you; it's deliciously voluptuous.'

'Is that a fancy way of saying I'm fat? And I'm sorry for not warning you about my psoriasis, but it's not exactly sexy talk, is it? And it's having a bit of a flare-up at the moment which is annoying.'

'Hey, no need to apologise at all, I hadn't even noticed it; I was too distracted by all of the delights you had on offer. And you need to stop putting yourself down; you're gorgeous and womanly and have a great personality too. It's a heady old combination, Mim. You need to start appreciating what you've got.'

'I'm not sure about that; you're just being kind.'

'You're totally wrong there. Haven't you seen the way Aidey can't take his eyes off you? He has the hots for you, big time.'

'Aidey? Don't be daft, we're just mates; he doesn't think of me in that way and vice versa. Besides, we've known each other for donkey's years; if anything was going to happen between us I dare say it would've done so by now – not that it ever would.' Mim quickly batted thoughts of Aidey out of her mind; she didn't want to loiter on how hurt he'd looked when she'd turned down his offer of a lift home in favour of Caspar. Instead, she wanted to focus on Caspar's wonderful words.

'Hmm, I'm not so sure – about how he feels at least. But, as I was saying, you really are completely and utterly desirable. And your cleavage in the blue and white striped top you were wearing to work earlier this week was enough to turn a strong man's knees to jelly.'

Mim giggled. 'Really?'

Caspar turned to face her. 'Really; I don't know how I managed to concentrate on my work that day thanks to you.'

Mim's heart soared with happiness. The nagging doubt she'd harboured about him all week slipped away as she basked in the glow of his words. Gone, too, was the resolve that this would simply be a bit of fun, a meaningless dalliance. If Caspar wanted something serious, he could have it.

He reached across and pulled her close to him, pressing kisses to the top of her head. 'Listen, I've been thinking and, much as I'd like nothing better than to have you on my arm and let the world know about us, I think it's probably a good idea if we keep things to ourselves for now, don't you? So, it might be for the best if we don't mention any of this at work, you know how nosy people are. And I quite like the idea of just the two of us knowing; it adds to the excitement, don't you agree?'

'Oh, okay, I suppose so.' She pushed a feeling of disappointment out of the way.

'Mmm, and something else to keep to yourself, I've got a sneaking suspicion that Clarissa is quite keen on me, if you know what I mean? She's a lovely girl, very attractive, but I just don't think of her in that way. She could only ever be a work colleague to me, but we don't want her old dragon of a mother pushing her nose in, do we, nor that little madam Honey? Imagine the trouble that could cause.'

'True.' Mim could imagine her boss wouldn't be pleased to find out she was having a relationship with her new golden boy. Honey less so. Still, she couldn't help but feel disappointed and not a little confused.

'Yes, I just think it's better off all round if we keep things to ourselves. It can be our little illicit secret. Just think of all those delicious stolen moments in secluded dark corners, your lips on mine, all that passion building during the day, bubbling over; it'll make it all the more exciting for when we get back here in the evening.' He dropped a kiss on the tip of her nose.

'Mmm, when you put it like that...' And, much as she liked the sound of it, there was that little niggle making itself known again. Mim wished it would bugger off.

8

Mim woke early for a Saturday; she wasn't used to sharing her bed with someone else and Caspar seemed to take up an awful lot of room – not that she was complaining by any stretch. She'd hoped to wake up in his arms but instead he was sprawled across the bed, leaving her a tiny sliver on the edge and next to no duvet. Still, she didn't mind; last night had been amazing, way beyond her wildest dreams. She'd lost count of how many times they'd made love, only getting out of bed to get something to eat or to let Herbert out for a toilet trip in the garden. Mim felt a sudden pang of guilt for the Labrador, he'd had a pretty crappy night. He was used to spending his evenings stretched out in front of the stove in the living room, snoring blissfully, not cooped up in some poky utility room in case he savaged the guest. She'd make it up to him; he deserved a little treat or two.

She squinted at the alarm on the bedside table, but not having her contact lenses in meant its face was just a blurry haze. Judging by the level of light in the bedroom she guessed it was around eight-thirty. Herbs would need letting out. She peered at Caspar, his face squished into the pillow, his breathing soft. Her heart gave a little squeeze as she remembered the words he'd used last night: deliciously voluptuous, gorgeous, amazing body. She wriggled her toes in delight before throwing back the duvet. She looked down at herself, smoothing her hand over the soft round of her stomach. *Hmm, that's not exactly how I'd describe myself.*

Caspar stirred and Mim hurriedly tiptoed across the room and swiped her dressing gown from the hook on the back of the door. She didn't want him to see her stark naked this morning; in the cold light of day, he might be forced to eat his words.

Downstairs, Herbert was in raptures at seeing her, spinning around and wagging his tail so hard his whole body shook. 'Morning, handsome, how are you today?' She bent down and held her arms out to him. The Labrador shot over to her, resting his head on her shoulder, his broad tail swishing back and forth over the floor. She smoothed her hand down his solid, silky back. 'Ahh, that's a mighty fine greeting, lovely boy. I'm really sorry about last night. I'll make it up to you, I promise. How does a nice juicy bone from the butchers' sound?'

On hearing the word "bone" Herbert sat to attention, his ears pricked. He let out a little whimper, making Mim chuckle. 'I'll take that as a yes, then, shall I?' She didn't like the fact that she'd have to pop him back into the utility room before Caspar came downstairs but she didn't want a repeat of last time. Herbert's reaction to Caspar did set alarm bells ringing again but, this morning, she didn't want to pay too much attention to them.

She was sipping tea, gazing out of the window and admiring the view down the length of the garden and onto the fields beyond when Caspar first appeared. Sensing him behind her she turned to see him bare-chested, wearing nothing but his boxer-shorts, his floppy hair looking sexily ruffled. A bolt of lust spiked through her alongside a feeling of uncertainty; after last night, she could argue they'd got to know one another pretty well in a physical sense, but emotionally, well, that was a different story.

'Morning.' She hoped she sounded casual. 'Cup of tea?'

He yawned and ruffled his hair, rolling his eyes towards the utility room where Herbert had struck up his barking and growling. 'I'd prefer a coffee, thanks.'

'Coffee it is.'

As she went to flick the kettle on, she was surprised to feel Caspar's arms slipping around her waist, his face nuzzling her neck. The heady, warm scent of their bed, still lingering on his skin, was delicious.

'Actually, put that coffee on hold and come back to bed with me.'

Oh, that voice!

He turned her round and kissed her deeply. How could she refuse?

'SO WHAT ARE your plans for today?' Mim tried to keep her voice neutral. She was struggling to contain the hope that he'd suggest they do something together, and desperately didn't want to sound needy or clingy, especially at this early stage of their "relationship".

Caspar propped himself up on his elbow and slowly traced his finger from her chin all the way down to her stomach then back again, running it back and forth over her plump bottom lip. 'I'm afraid I've just got time for a quick coffee, then I've got to head off. How about you?'

Disappointment made her heart sink though she tried not to show it. 'I'm going to take Herbert for a good long walk then maybe meet up with Anna-Lisa. And I'm going to Carly's for a drink tonight; I think I'll see if Anna wants to join us; we can have a good girly catch-up over some Prosecco.' She flashed him a wide smile, hoping she'd made herself sound busy and popular, and not like some friendless saddo who would be waiting at home, doing nothing, seeing no one, until he clicked his fingers. *Been there, done that, not doing it again. Ever! No matter how hot you are, Caspar De Verre.* It still didn't stop her from wondering what he was doing with the rest of his day.

'Well, your day sounds a whole lot better than mine. I've got to help my parents; they've got a business and I work for them from time to time. And, unfortunately, today is one of those days.'

'Oh, what sort of business is it? Is it in publishing?'

'No, it's nothing remotely like publishing; let's just say they've got their fingers in lots of pies, but it pays pretty well, so I can't complain too much. Anyway, about that coffee...' With that, he pushed the duvet back and climbed out of bed.

UNLIKE MIM, Herbert seemed thrilled that Caspar had left. He shot out of the utility room and raced around the house, sniffing everywhere, deep growls emanating from him.

'It's okay, Herbs, he's gone, though I don't know why you don't like him; he's really nice when you get to know him.' Herbert didn't look convinced as he made his way over to his bed. 'Trust me, he is.' Again, Mim pushed the unwelcome niggles to the back of her mind.

Herbert looked up at her and wagged his tail, making her smile. She ruffled his velvety ears. 'Right, I'll have a quick shower, then I'll take you for a nice long W.A.L.K.'

9

HERBERT WAS DANCING from paw to paw as Mim clipped the lead to his collar. 'Excited are we?' He replied with a whimper before having a quick nibble of her thick plait that had snaked over her shoulder. 'Thank you, young man, that's enough of that.'

As soon as she opened the door, he was off, dragging her out onto the step, jumping about in sheer delight. 'Bide your passion, lad, there's no rush, we've got all day.' Mim couldn't help but laugh.

With Herbert eagerly pulling on the lead, they made their way along the old York flagstone footpath, taking a right at the end of the row of cottages on Smeathorn Lane and heading towards to the well-worn track of the public bridleway that ran parallel to the broad, sweeping fields of Low Woodside Farm, a small wood nestling beside it. 'Herbs, sit.' The Labrador obeyed, allowing Mim to unhook the lead from his collar before he shot off into a nearby hedgerow that was apparently brimming with tantalising smells.

Mim threw the lead over her shoulder and sauntered along the lane, her hands thrust deep into the pockets of Josie's padded waxed jacket. With the unsettling events of the week pushed to the back of her mind, Mim relished the new feeling of lightness her evening with Caspar had bestowed upon her. It had silenced the background anxiety that had been her constant companion for months, always chattering away like incessant white noise.

Overhead, the sky was a broad splash of cerulean blue, punctuated only by the occasional wisp of white cloud floating by. Birds were chattering away ten-to-the-dozen in the trees, their exuberance making Mim smile. The air was filled with the earthy smell of autumn, tinged with a whiff of burning leaves from a bonfire at one of the allotments that sat side-by-side on the edge of the village; a higgledy-piggledy cluster of sheds and vegetable patches, divided up by makeshift fences of corrugated iron and random pieces of wood cobbled together. She inhaled deeply and sighed; it was the perfect day for a walk in the countryside. Indeed, the weather seemed to be making up for delivering days of patchy rain throughout the previous week. And today was awash with glorious mellow golden sunshine that danced over the fields and peered through the branches of the trees. Those that were still in leaf were now sporting the rich shades of autumn, their burnished golds, reds and bronze shining in the sunshine. The River Skelt that wended its way through the villages on its way to York could be seen glittering through the hawthorn hedgerows. The air was crisp, the warmth of the sun just taking the edge off the slight nip in the breeze. Mim loved feel-good days like these; what a pity, she thought, that Caspar couldn't join her.

Caspar. The thought of him sent a wave of happiness through her. Not in her wildest dreams had she ever thought she'd attract the attention of a man like him. Yes, he fitted the bill of her usual type, ticked all her boxes, but he had something extra too; he was more polished than her previous boyfriends, more sophisticated, more mature. And that combination scared her slightly. She ignored the little voice that said, "more dangerous". Why on earth was he interested in a girl like her? Surely he was better suited to Clarissa who was groomed and elegant. No doubt about it, they'd make a very attractive couple. Not wanting to dwell on that thought, Mim quickly pushed her doubts out of the way, remembering the wonderful things he'd said to her the previous evening, his voice seductive and velvety. The memory made her shiver with delight; he'd made her feel special and desirable. None of her previous boyfriends had ever done that.

'Oh, Lord.' She could feel herself falling for him. Hard. And, as much as the little warning voice was jumping about in her mind, trying to get her to listen, the pull of Caspar was just too strong. *He's not like the others, he's different. He won't treat me badly. I just know it.*

Mim and Herbert headed further along the track which had become quite muddy in parts, and she was glad she'd decided to wear her wellies. She edged around the deep, dirty puddles while Herbert bounded straight through them with little regard for the consequences. 'Ughh! Herbert! You're going to need a shower after this.'

Aware of the thudding of horse's hooves gaining on her, Mim turned to see the vicar's wife Gemma on her chestnut mare. 'Morning, Mim, how are you? Woah, Starlight.' She gave Mim a warm smile as she pulled on the reins.

'Morning, Gemma, I'm fine, thanks. Just making the most of the lovely weather. How about you?'

'Good, thanks, same here. The children are out and about on their bikes and David's tackling some pruning in the garden, so I thought I'd grab the opportunity to go for a ride.'

Gemma's glossy, dark hair and rosy-apple cheeks lent her an air of wholesomeness.

'I don't blame you, it's glorious. By the way, are you going to Carly's next Friday?'

'Wild horses couldn't keep me away, I'm really looking forward to letting my hair down.' Gemma winked at Mim and urged her mare on. 'Come on, Starlight. See you later, Mim, enjoy your walk.'

'Bye, Gemma.'

As she continued on her way an enormous buck hare shot past her, racing from the razed stubble of the corn field and into the hedgerow, apparently escaping the clutches of the buzzard that had followed him and was now circling above, calling out in consternation. Herbert stopped in his tracks, front paw poised in a classic gundog pose, his gaze following the gap in the hedge where the hare had disappeared.

'Don't even think about chasing it, Herbert.'

The Labrador turned his head to her, wagged his tail and continued trotting along the lane, his nose fixed to the ground as he went. Mim watched him, smiling; he was such a lovable character.

They continued along the track, Herbert tirelessly running backwards and forwards, beating Mim's step-count several times over. As they approached the small packhorse bridge, a cluster of bullfinches flitted across her path like a squadron of tiny Spitfires, landing on their target of cow parsley skeletons with skilled precision. They gripped onto the swaying stalks, pecking at the seed-heads, punctuating their snacking with bursts of chatter. A moment later they flew off, a flash of vivid orange against the blue of the sky.

The birds triggered a memory of walking along this very path with her grandparents and Josie when she was only about eight or nine. They'd seen bullfinches that day, and had marvelled at their vibrant plumage and formation flying. Mim recalled how Grandad John had told them that the name for a collection of bullfinches was a "charm". Mim had been thrilled to hear that wonderful description. Lovely Grandad John and his easy-going temperament, he was a mine of information, never seeming to tire of her and Josie's endless questions. "What's this, Grandad? What's that, Grandad?" Mim had asked him once how many steps it would take to get to the moon. He'd laughed, ruffling her hair affectionately, and told her he loved her imagination, and that she must never stop thinking that way.

Thoughts of her grandparents naturally turned to her mother, wondering what she was doing now. Mim felt her mood dip; her relationship with her mum Jeanette had always been tricky. It had been a while since she'd heard from her – getting on for eighteen months – her texts and phone calls going unanswered, emails, too. The last time they'd been in the same company, they'd parted on bad terms and Mim guessed that Jeanette was still licking her wounds. It was fair to say that Mim was still smarting too. But, she figured, there are only so many times you can forgive your mother for stealing from you and lying to you.

Mim's father had walked out on them when she was just five years old, leaving in a hail of bitter words. He'd returned sporadically over the years, his winning words and easy smile charming his way into her mum's good books again. Each time, he and her mother enjoyed a cringingly passionate reconciliation, taking to their bedroom for several days and leaving Josie and Mim to fend for themselves, until the day, when Mim, aged eleven, had come home from school to find her mother heartbroken; her father had gone again. He hadn't said goodbye, and Mim hadn't seen him since.

What followed was a pattern of her mother taking up with a succession of inappropriate men who were always destined to treat her badly; they'd move in, take up residence on the sofa along with control of the TV remote and, when they'd fleeced Jeanette of every penny she had – even the paltry savings in Mim and Josie's piggy-banks – they'd dump her unceremoniously, leaving her sobbing and fit for nothing for weeks. It was hardly the best example to set two impressionable young girls. Thankfully for Josie, being older, she'd found it easier to see things from a different perspective. Early on, she'd made up her mind that she wasn't going to follow their mother's pattern. *Her* life, she'd told Mim, was going to be different. She was going to marry someone decent and kind, and even then, not until she was absolutely certain they both loved each other equally. She was going to steer well clear of the sponging layabouts their mother had favoured. Unfortunately for Mim, she, it seemed, had been too young to make such observations, and had grown to view their mother's relationship history as the "norm"; the template for all relationships. And so far, she'd followed her mother's example to the letter.

To make matters worse, in the process, their mother appeared to have subtly reversed their roles; she'd become the child, the one who needed protecting, nurturing and the offering up of financial support. Mim and Josie had unwittingly taken on the role of parent, until the day their mother had pushed them too far.

The events of eighteen months ago were something of a turning point. Jeanette had landed on the doorstep of the house Mim shared with a couple of other girls on the outskirts of York, her eyes swollen with tears, her hair dishevelled, her hands clutching two bulging suitcases, begging for a bed for the night. 'Oh, Mim, love, can I come in? Me and Terry have split up and I've got nowhere else to go. Can I stay with you? It'll just be for one night, that's all. I'll find myself somewhere else tomorrow, I promise I will.' She'd broken down and sobbed, and though Mim had felt a variety of conflicting emotions – as well as a hefty dose of déjà vu – how could she refuse?

Mim had given up her bed for her mother, herself sleeping on an ancient blow-up air bed that had all but deflated by the following morning. And, just as she had expected it would, one night became a week, and a week became a month – until the day Jeanette had been asked to leave.

Mim had found herself in an uncomfortable position on several occasions when her housemates had grumbled that her mother had been helping herself to their food, taking all the hot water and, worse, smoking in the house when they'd asked her not to, making everywhere reek of stale cigarettes. They'd been reluctant to mention anything until things had got too bad which had made Mim feel terribly guilty. On top of that, all Jeanette appeared to do was lie in bed for most of the day, not lifting a finger to tidy up after herself or make the effort to look for a job. She'd more than outstayed her welcome.

Up until that point her mum had spent many tedious hours explaining how her relationship with her latest boyfriend Terry had fallen apart – the usual story – and Mim had listened, her anger gradually building at her mother's self-pity. Why, at her age, had she not begun to realise that attaching yourself to men like him was doomed to end in heartbreak? 'We did try to warn you, Mum,' she'd said. 'We could see he was no good for you.'

'Yeah, well, I thought he'd be different, he seemed so charming, not like the others. And, anyway, I thought you were just jealous.'

'Jealous? Of you going out with *him*?'

Jeanette had nodded. 'Yeah, he told me you fancied him, had been flirting with him something shocking. Which, if I'm honest, I was a bit put out about; it's hardly appropriate, is it?'

'And you believed him?'

'Well, yeah, why wouldn't I? You didn't have a boyfriend of your own, you'd just been dumped by that loser you were going out with, and Terry's a bit of a dish. He said it was embarrassing how you were coming on to him, but I didn't say anything to you because I didn't want to cause any trouble.' Jeanette had pursed her lips together and sniffed.

'He said *I* was coming on to *him*?' Mim's anger had boiled over. 'The lying scumbag! Let me tell you this, Mum, I wouldn't have touched that slimy creep with a bloody barge pole. And it was *him* coming on to *me,* not the other way round. I don't want to go into any details but put it this way, there was no doubt about his intentions. What he said was so gross, it makes my skin crawl just thinking about it.'

'That's a lie, I don't believe you! Terry would never do anything like that; he didn't fancy you! You just wanted what I had. He was really into me – until the money ran out.' Jeanette's voice had tailed off.

'Yeah, well, that says it all, really, doesn't it?'

'What do you mean?'

'Let's not pretend it hasn't happened before, Mum. How about Lee, or Nozza, or Stevo…' Mim had counted them off on her fingers.

'That's not fair! You don't know what it's like being me. My situation is all your father's fault. If he hadn't left, I wouldn't even be in this mess, with no home, no security, no one to care about me, having to do everything on my own. It's alright for you.'

'Mum, you can't keep blaming Dad for the bad choices you've

made; don't you think it's time you took some responsibility for yourself? There's loads you could do to turn your life around. You're attractive, you could get yourself a job, you could—'

'You really don't understand, do you? Thanks for absolutely nothing. When you were growing up, I spent all my time trying to find a man to be the perfect father figure to you and our Josie. I was desperate to replace that loser who had the bloody nerve to call himself your father; about as much use as a chocolate fireguard he was. Had to put up with loads of crap from even more useless bloody men, all for you two. Fat lot of good it's done me.'

Mim had shaken her head, exasperated at her mother's response. 'You can't blame Josie and me either. And besides, we had Grandad, he more than made up for us not having a dad around; he was the perfect father figure for us, you know that. And Grandma Joyce, she was the perfect mo— Well, she was perfect, too.'

Her words had hit a nerve, or rather, the words she'd almost said. Jeanette had shot her a look, pouting like a petulant child. It had only served to infuriate Mim.

But it was true, and they both knew it.

Whenever she thought of her grandparents, Mim felt a huge rush of love for them, followed by a feeling of guilt that she didn't hold the same affection for her own mother. She often wondered if that made her a bad person. But regardless of that, not a day went by when Mim wasn't thankful for the happy times she'd had staying at her grandparent's cosy little home full of love, warmth and the lingering aroma of Grandma Joyce's delicious baking. The handful of happy memories Mim had of growing up had all been created there, or on the long walks on sunny days when they'd taken a picnic to have in the sprawling parkland of Eskelby Hall. There was always a bottle of Grandad's homemade ginger beer, fizzy and feisty – and just a little bit too hot for Mim, but she'd loved it all the same because it had been made especially for her and Josie. *Especially* for them; that simple gesture had made Mim feel incredibly loved and special. She recalled how their excitement had built as he'd got ready to pop the cork, the bottle held away from them, their eyes scrunched in anticipation. 'Ready, girls? Let's count, one, two, three…' Pop! 'Woah!' He'd laugh out loud, his eyes sparkling as he splashed the liquid into their red plastic beakers. How Josie and Mim had loved those days.

She could clearly remember the feeling of excitement when the red and green checked rug had been shaken out and thrown down onto the uneven ground under the branches of a sprawling chestnut tree. She and Josie had pounced, eager to help Grandma Joyce set the picnic things out, a cacophony of birdsong and the hum of plump bumblebees playing in the background. Mim was easily distracted, running off after butterflies who flitted around, dancing in the sunshine, believing them to be fairies in disguise. Or if it was a little breezy, she'd jump up and help Grandad John look for stones to weigh the corners of the picnic blanket down, walking off together, her tiny hand in his huge, work-roughened paw. Afterwards, armed with their brightly-coloured fishing nets, he'd take them to the little stream that burbled through the grounds of Eskelby Hall. Mim had always hoped to catch a huge trout to take home for tea, but all they'd ever caught were tiny little minnows which they slipped back into the stream with a resounding plop, laughing as the fish wriggled off, continuing with their day as if nothing had happened. They were the happiest of times, and Mim was grateful for every single one of them.

The crunch came with her mother when Mim's housemates had asked her to meet them at the local coffee shop; they needed to speak to her, they'd said. Mim had a horrible feeling she knew what they were going to say: it was time for her mum to leave. And she'd been right. Her friends had worded their grievances as kindly as they were able, but it was still glaringly obvious that Jeanette had taken horrendous liberties with their good nature. But it still didn't make it any easier for Mim to tackle.

Jeanette had responded with a spiteful rant; didn't she know how selfish she was, how she didn't deserve to have a mother.

"Well, not one like you.' The words had flown out of Mim's mouth before she'd had time to stop them.

'You ungrateful little bitch!' Jeanette had followed up with a stinging slap to Mim's cheek before storming out of the room.

That had been the last exchange between the pair.

By the time Mim had returned from work the following day, her mother had gone. As had the small stash of money she'd kept hidden in her knicker drawer. Worse, cash, perfume and expensive makeup products had all disappeared from the bedrooms of her housemates. Mim shuddered at the memory.

As she continued on her walk, her eyes fixed to the ground, thinking about the conversations she'd had with her mother about her poor choice in partners, it gradually dawned on her that she'd had similar conversations with Anna-Lisa and Aidey about her own disastrous relationships. Granted, they weren't exactly the same, but there was a familiarity in the pattern which couldn't be denied. It made Mim feel inexplicably angry with her mum and even angrier with herself. Why couldn't she be more like Josie? She sighed and kicked a stone, watching it bounce along the track. But this new relationship with Caspar felt different.

Once again, she ignored the annoying little niggles at the back of her mind; she was going to prove them wrong.

Conscious that thoughts of her mother had dampened her mood, she picked up a stick, whistled for Herbert and threw it. 'There, you go, Herbs, fetch!' She smiled as he bounded after it, large velvety ears flapping behind him; "fetch" was his favourite game, one he was happy to do till the cows came home.

In a moment he was in front of her, the stick between his teeth, a victorious look on his face. 'Good lad,' she said. He dropped the stick at her feet and looked up at her expectantly. 'You want another go?' He wagged his tail and gave an excited whimper. 'Go on then, fetch that.' She put all her strength into throwing the stick so it soared through the air, laughing as Herbert tore after it, picking it up and giving it a thorough shaking. You couldn't be anything other than happy around that boy, she thought.

In the distance she noticed a woman jogging towards them and, judging by the long, blonde ponytail and purple and black running gear, it was her friend Amy.

'Hiya,' said Amy as she approached Mim. Herbert trotted over to her. 'Hiya, Herbs.'

Amy jogged on the spot when she reached Mim, her ponytail swinging from side-to-side. Her cheeks were flushed and her breath was coming out in puffs of condensation in the cool air.

'Hi, Amy, gorgeous day,' said Mim.

'It is, especially after all that rain we've had.'

'Tell me about it. Are you going to be at Carly's next week?'

'Sure am, I'm looking forward to it. Will you be there?'

'Yep, though I should probably warn you that Carly's been joking that it's actually a kinky underwear party; purely for the benefit of Pat Motson and her cronies.'

Amy threw her head back and laughed. 'I love it. When did she do that?'

'The other night when I was collecting Herbs.'

'Fabulous! The way that woman's gob works – Pat's I mean – it'll be all round the village now, and half way round Ellerthorpe as well.'

'Well, let's hope the vicar doesn't hear about it since Gemma's going to be there. I'm not sure he'll want his parishioners thinking his wife's been buying a load of kinky stuff to liven up their bedroom antics!'

'Hah! That would be hilarious. Though I wouldn't want it to put Gemma off joining us; she seems lovely and a bit of a laugh,' said Amy.

'I agree, but I do like the thought of winding Pat Motson up, especially after she tried to contact our Josie to tell her I was making a mess of her house and had never had the hoover out, or swept the garden path.'

'Miserable old bag, she's got too much time on her hands.' Amy flicked a look over her shoulder. 'Anyway, I'd better get off. See you later, hon.'

'Yep, see you,' said Mim.

Mim decided to turn back once she'd reached the style in the drystone wall. It was caked in mud and looked even more rickety than when she'd last climbed over it. The temperature had dropped, making her nose feel chilly and her fingers and toes numb. And, judging by the way he was panting, she figured Herbert had enjoyed a good enough run around for the last hour and a half so wouldn't be too reluctant to go home. She'd nip into the butchers en route so she could pick up the bone she'd promised him. She turned and whistled for him as she pulled her gloves out of her pockets. 'Come on, Herbs, let's head home.' The Labrador came bounding over, his tongue lolling, his tail swishing happily.

They were three quarters of the way back when Mim's mobile phone pinged. She furtled about in her pocket and retrieved it to see a text message from Anna-Lisa.

Are you free this afternoon? Do you fancy meeting up? We could take Herbs for a walk. Ax

Mim tapped out a quick reply.

Am free, would love to meet up. Just on a walk with H, too knackered for another one! How about a drink at the pub? Been invited to Carly's for a drink tonight. You're welcome to come too. You can stay over at my house if you like. xxx

Anna-Lisa's reply landed almost immediately.

Fab! Sounds great! How about lunch at the pub instead of a walk? Ax

The thought made Mim's stomach rumble; she hadn't eaten much the previous evening and had only had a couple of slices of toast for breakfast. She typed her reply before the notoriously capricious local mobile phone signal had chance to slope off.

Ooh, yummy! If they're still serving. Is 2ish okay? xxx

Again, she didn't have to wait long for Anna-Lisa's reply.

Perfect! See you then! Ax

Once back in the village, Mim headed towards the main street where the little cluster of shops were located on the edge of the well-tended village green. She passed old Billy Stainthorpe, wrapped up tight in his dark grey overcoat, a thick woollen scarf tied snuggly around his neck, his flat cap pulled down low on his head. He walked badly, as did his equally ancient wire-haired terrier Rinty, whose whiskers were as grey as his owner's. The pair looked at Mim with equally rheumy eyes. 'Now then, Mim.' Billy raised his wooden walking stick at her in a friendly gesture.

Herbert ventured across to Rinty, pleased to see a familiar friend. 'Morning, Billy, morning, Rinty. How are you keeping?'

'Fair to middlin', lass, can't grumble.'

'That's good. And it's a lovely day.'

'Aye, it is that. It's a right good 'un. Best enjoy it; it'll be winter before we know it, and I can feel it in my bones that we're going to be in for a bad 'un.'

'Oh, no. That's not good news. Anyway, I hope you and Rinty enjoy your walk. I'll see you later.'

'Aye, cheery-bye, hon.'

Mim stopped outside the neat Georgian building that was Finkel's butchers, a mouth-watering display of homemade pies, sausage rolls and plump joints of meat set out in the window. She bent to fasten Herbert's lead to one of the hooks on the wall. 'Here we are, Herbs, your favourite shop in the whole wide world. You wait here, while I nip in.' The Labrador's eyes were fixed firmly to the line of juicy game birds that hung from meat hooks above the window.

'Mim, save yourself the trouble, love. We were expecting you to call in so we got me laddo's bone ready.' Keith Finkel, owner of the shop, came out waving a white plastic bag at her, his butcher's hat pushed back on his head.

Herbert whimpered, shivering with excitement as drool started to form at the corners of his mouth.

'Oh, thanks, Keith, that's really good of you. As you can see, he knows exactly what's in there.'

Keith gave a throaty laugh. 'Aye, nowt as greedy as a Labrador, is there? Governed by their bellies, they are.'

'You're not wrong. I'm sure Herbert would eat until he burst.'

Next stop was the village shop where Mim stocked up on essentials as well as her favourite penny sweets and a bottle of Prosecco to take with her to Carly's that night.

'Looks like a weekend survival kit in there.' Lou handed her the bag of shopping, making Mim laugh.

'You're not wrong. Actually, I've been meaning to ask, are you going to Carly's next week?'

'Aye, are you?'

'Yeah, I'm looking forward to it, seems ages since our last get-together.'

'It does. Though, I must tell, you, Carly was in here earlier and told me what she'd said about the kinky underwear thing. You can imagine the fun I had with nosy Pat Motson when she came in for her bread and newspaper. And I might have mentioned a male stripper would be joining us, too.'

Mim burst out laughing. 'You did what?'

'I couldn't help myself. I overheard the spiteful old witch having a bitching session with Cath Jones at the back of the shop. Pulling everyone apart they were. I've no time for the pair of them. Pass themselves off as holier than thou, but haven't got a nice word to say about anyone.'

'You're right there. But how on earth did you find a way to tell Pat Motson about a stripper going to Carly's?'

'Well, I just sort of dropped it into the conversation.'

'As you do.'

'Exactly! I just asked Pat if she'd be joining us, and wondered if she'd got one of the kinky underwear catalogues to order from in advance. Then I just sort of mentioned how a much-in-demand male stripper by the name of Hosé Horny was going to be there. And I might've told her that she'd need to be quick if she wanted to tuck a tenner in the waistband of his underpants 'cos they wouldn't be on for long.'

'You didn't?'

'I did.'

'You're wicked! Does Carly know?' Mim could barely speak, tears of mirth pouring down her cheeks.

'Yep; she thinks it's fabulous.'

'Yes, I can imagine she would. Well, I'd best head back home, Herbert's desperate to get stuck into the bone Keith from the butchers gave him. And he's also in desperate need of a bath; judging by the smell of him, he's been rolling in fox poo again, little sod.' Mim gathered up the bag from the counter. 'I'll see you later.'

'See you, chick.'

10

IT WAS JUST after one forty-five when Mim heard the sound of Anna-Lisa's car pull up in front of the cottage. She ran to the door, happy to see her friend. Though they worked together, they hadn't had a proper chance to mull over the events of the previous week, nor have a proper chinwag about anything else, and Mim was looking forward to spending time with her friend. Herbert was hot on her heels, his tail wagging enthusiastically. 'Hiya, Anna, need a hand bringing anything in?'

Anna-Lisa slung her burgundy backpack over her shoulder and closed the door before heading round to the boot of the car, the buckles of her favourite chunky biker boots jangling as she walked. She was wearing a pair of black skinny jeans with slashes to the knees, and an oversized black and white dogs-tooth coat over a pink slogan t-shirt. Her candyfloss-coloured hair had been scraped up into a messy bun, fine tendrils falling softly over her pretty face. 'You can grab this for me if you like.' She pulled out a bulging carrier bag. 'Supplies for tonight.'

'Ooh, fab!' Mim flicked her plait over her shoulder and headed down the path. She went to open the gate but the solid body of Herbert was in the way. 'S'cuse me, Herbs, you're going to have to get your nose out of the way if you want me to open it.'

Herbert took a step back, shooting out as soon as he was able, charging over to greet Anna-Lisa. 'Hiya, gorgeous boy, how are you?'

She bent to stroke his head. 'I swear you get more handsome every time I see you, you really do.'

'That's probably because he's just had a shower after spending most of his walk charging through muddy puddles then rolling in a load of fox poo. I can't tell you how glad I am that Josie and Russ saw fit to install a shower for him in the outbuilding. I dread to think how hard it would be to get him in the bath, or the mess it'd make. Not to mention how much Josie would hate *that* idea. Anyway, at least he's clean now, but he got bored of me drying him so he smells a bit of wet cabbage, I'm afraid, which I can promise you is infinitely better than the way he smelt before.'

Anna-Lisa crumpled her nose. 'I'll take your word for it. Anyway there's a T.R.E.A.T. for him in the bag, along with wine and nibbles for tonight – they're for us.'

Herbert's ears pricked up and his tail swished happily.

'Good to know.' Mim took the bag. 'And you do know he can spell, don't you?'

'Ah, I'd clean forgotten.' She glanced at Herbert who had a hopeful look in his eyes.

'And you wouldn't believe how many T.R.E.A.T.s he's had today; he's been very spoilt.'

'Nice jeans by the way, are they new?'

'Thanks, yep, I picked them up in the sale. I've been after a pair of these for ages and snapped them up as soon as I saw them reduced. They're perfect for getting my wobbly bum and fat podge under control; they give it a bit of much-needed scaffolding.' Mim patted her stomach.

Anna-Lisa tutted. 'You haven't got a wobbly or fat anything, never mind bum or podge for that matter. Stop putting yourself down, Mim.'

'You only say that because you haven't seen me naked.'

'True, and can I just say, much as I love you dearly, I'd like it to stay that way.' Anna-Lisa giggled. She followed Mim down the hall, Herbert trotting close behind, her face a picture when she took in the state of the kitchen. 'Jeez, Mim, what have you been doing? It's a tip in here; anyone would think the place had been ransacked.'

Mim set the carrier bag down on the table, reaching inside for the wine. She had the good grace to look sheepish. 'I know, I didn't mean for it to get this messy but with everything that's happened this week, I just couldn't face cleaning. I'm going to tackle it tomorrow in case Josie Skypes. Anyway, let's forget about the mess for now; I'll pop this in the fridge, but don't let me forget to take it out before we go to Carly's.'

'I won't. And can I just say, there was some frantic curtain twitching going on along at Cuckoo's Nest Cottage when I arrived. I've never known it so bad. I wonder what could be the cause?' There was a hint of sarcasm in her voice.

'You won't believe it when I tell you.'

'I bet I would.'

'What do you mean?'

'Could it be something to do with the appearance of a certain dark-haired gentleman dropping you off and picking you up this week?'

'Oh, no, it's not that.'

'Really? Don't tell me she hasn't noticed the Dark Count and his fancy car.'

That's what Carly calls him, too. 'Ah, well, I suppose she has but that's not what I meant.' Mim felt her cheeks flush. 'It's to do with some of Carly's mischief. Come on, let's head to the pub while they're still serving food, and I'll fill you in on all the details when we get there.'

THE TWO WOMEN found a sunny table in the cosy bar of the pub. The mouth-watering aroma of roast dinners – something the pub had gained quite a reputation for – filled the air, making Mim's stomach rumble. She sat on the banquette, glad to feel the soothing rays of the sun warming the back of her neck. Herbert flopped down on the floor beside her while Anna-Lisa went to order their food at the bar.

'Here you go, get that down you.' Anna-Lisa set a large glass of cider down on the table in front of Mim. She pulled out a stool opposite and sat down before taking a slow sip of her pint of beer. 'Mmm. That's so good.'

'Cheers,' said Mim, raising her glass.

'Oops, sorry, I was so keen to get that down me I forgot! Cheers to the bloody weekend at last.' Anna-Lisa clinked her glass against Mim's.

'My thoughts exactly.'

'And what a week; if feels like about a dozen of them have been crammed into one. And I've hated pretty much every minute so I dread to think how it's been for you.'

Mim sat back and sighed. 'It's been pretty shitty at work, I have to say, what with Honey and all the weirdness with Susan, but other stuff hasn't been too bad. Except how could I forget I've gone and wrecked my prized leather jacket, look. I've tried to fix it, but nothing seems to work. I'm gutted.'

Anna-Lisa gave the scuffed sleeve of Mim's leather jacket a cursory glance before fixing her friend with a steely gaze. 'Hmm. Shame, looks like you've taken the top layer of dye off. And what do you mean about other stuff not being too bad?'

Mim felt a surge of excitement as Caspar crept into her mind, replaying their illicit night of passion, the feel of his hands on her body… Her stomach leapt and she felt her cheeks flush. His words telling her to keep their relationship a secret flashed before her. But she and Anna-Lisa shared everything…

'Come on, spill, I can tell you're keeping something from me. Is it to do with the Dark Count?'

Oh, if only I could tell you!

'Stop calling him that.' Mim laughed. Her mind was whirling, she so desperately wanted to share her news with her best friend, tell her how she was feeling, explain how this with Caspar was different. But at the same time, she didn't want to break his trust, didn't want to hear Anna-Lisa's warnings.

In the end, it didn't take her friend long to wear her down. 'I thought we were best mates, Mim; looked out for each other, shared everything. What's changed? It's like you suddenly don't trust me or something.'

'I do trust you, honest I do, Anna, it's just—'

'What? Did he tell you not to say anything? Please tell me you're not going to let a bloke come between us; we're best mates.'

'I would never do that, Anna, you know how much I value our friendship, but Caspar told me it was probably best to keep us a secret.'

'You're an "us" already? That didn't take long, and why doesn't he want you to tell anyone. You're a babe and lovely with it; he should be wanting to shout it from the rooftops.'

Mim could sense her friend was trying to hide the fact that she was a little put out by the revelation, and was keen to smooth things over. 'It wasn't so much you, but he doesn't want the bosses to find out in case they get funny about it, you know what they're like. And Susan in particular seems to have got it in for me at the moment, you know that.'

'Hmm. It still doesn't mean you couldn't tell me; we've always told each other everything. It just makes me feel a bit worried that he's said that, that's all. It seems a bit off. But, cross my heart, I won't breathe a word to anyone.'

'Thanks, Anna, and I know you're suspicious of him, but he's really lovely when you get to know him, and he makes me feel special. Really special. The things he was saying to me last night … he told me that I'm beautiful and "deliciously voluptuous" – which I know I'm not but he made me feel that way last night – and no one else has ever said anything like that to me before.'

'Oh, Mim, chick, you are special but you've dated so many losers they've made you lose sight of that fact. I love you to bits and just don't want to see you hurt, that's all. I want you to be happy and be with someone who really deserves you. Aidey's been worried too.'

An image of Aidey's kind face flashed across Mim's mind, his green eyes smiling, his hair standing on end as it always did thanks to his habit of pushing his fingers through it, the sprinkling of freckles across his nose. It triggered a feeling of warmth inside her. He was a good sort, Aidey, someone who made her feel safe, like the world was a better place when she was with him. Yep, he was definitely one of the best mates a girl could have.

Mim sighed. 'I really appreciate your concern, and Aidey's too, but I don't need you to worry about me, I'm fine. I'm actually worried about Aidey; he hasn't been himself at all this week, which is understandable with everything that's happened.' Time to turn attention away from herself.

'Too true, he's had a totally crap week, what with how Susan's treated him. He's worth more than that, and he's so good at his job, or should I say, *was* good at his job, now that the Dark Count has stepped into his shoes and taken it. Not that he won't be good at what he's doing now, but his heart's not in it. I actually wouldn't be surprised if he leaves, nor could I blame him.'

'Yeah, that had crossed my mind. It'll be a shame if he does, but in all honesty, I can't really see myself being there for that much longer, whether it's because Susan finds some reason to sack me, or because I find another job before she gets the chance.'

'Seriously, you're thinking about leaving?'

Mim took a sip of her cider and nodded. 'The thought had crossed my mind after Honey's arrival.'

'Jeez, it'll be totally shite if both you and Aidey leave. I don't think I could stand it on my own without you. Clarissa's okay, but she's not you two, and she'll always be a Pallister-Biggs no matter how much she wants to fit in with us.'

'Yeah, she's a nice lass. I feel sorry for her being part of that family.'

'Me, too, especially when she's the talent behind the magazine while Susan and Kenneth brazenly take all the credit.'

'True. Anyway, how are things with you and Caleb? Is he still driving you bonkers with his computer games?'

'Uhh, please don't mention those bloody games! He spends more time playing them and communicating with his friends than he does talking to me. I swear if he spends much longer in that spare room – or "computer room" as he now calls it – I'll forget what he actually looks like.'

'Has it got that bad?'

'Well, maybe that's a slight exaggeration, but he does spend the bulk of the time he's at home in there. Feels like he only ventures out to eat, bathe and sleep.'

'Oh, dear.' Mim's heart went out to her friend. Though Anna's exterior gave the impression she was as hard as nails, Mim knew beneath it was a centre as soft as marshmallow. Her friend's tough childhood had left its mark; she rarely talked about her feelings and was as tight as a clam as far as matters of the heart were concerned. But it was obvious to Mim that, despite Anna's declaration that she didn't believe in love, deep down, she was pretty keen on Caleb.

'Yes, "oh dear". He doesn't even meet up with his friends physically anymore, they seem happier to chat via that daft dragon game. It's all very odd. Anyway, that's enough about him, I intend to enjoy myself tonight while he's the sadster at home in a poky little room with nothing but a computer for company.'

'I'm sorry to hear it's like that for you; don't forget, I'm here if you ever need to talk, chick.' Mim knew not to push her friend; she'd open up when she was ready.

Their conversation was interrupted by the arrival of Julie the landlady holding two plates of steaming food in her hands. 'Hello there, ladies, two roast dinners for you.'

'Mmm, smells delicious, thanks, Julie,' said Mim.

'And mind the plates; they're red-hot.'

'Will do, thanks for the warning.'

Herbert sat to attention, his eyes flicking greedily from plate to plate.

'This isn't for you, Herbs. Lie down, please,' said Mim.

Herbert looked at her with pleading eyes.

'And the woeful, please-feed-me-I'm-starving look won't work either, you've had loads to eat today, any more and I think you'll pop. Lie down, please.'

With a noisy harrumph, Herbert obeyed.

'Good lad,' said Mim.

Julie threw the tea-towel she'd been using to hold the plates over her shoulder. 'So, what's this I hear about Carly having a kinky underwear party, and is there any truth in the rumour that there's going to be a rather hot male stripper? Oh, and is the vicar's wife's going? And, more importantly, if it is all true, how do I get myself an invite?'

'What's this?' Anna-Lisa looked at Mim, her eyes like saucers. 'You've never mentioned any of this before, I thought it was just the usual wine and catch-up night.'

Mim giggled and gestured for them to move closer. Lowering her voice to a whisper she said, 'It's not true. Carly just started the rumour about having a kinky undies party to wind Pat Motson up, and it was Lou who added the bit about Hosé Horny the male stripper.'

'Oh, that's hilarious,' said Julie, giggling.

Anna-Lisa burst out laughing. 'Hosé Horny, I love it!'

'Shhh,' said Mim. 'We mustn't let folk find out it's a joke, we really want the curtain twitchers to think it's true. Carly wants to see how long it'll take to get round the village.'

'Uhh, it won't take that miserable old bugger long to spread the word,' said Julie. 'She's a right gossip.'

'That's an understatement,' said Anna-Lisa.

'Carly just wants to have a bit of fun with this, then we can all thoroughly enjoy the sight of the woman getting egg all over her face when she finds out she's had the mickey taken out of her,' said Mim.

'Brilliant! Be sure to keep me posted, but in the meantime my lips are sealed. And now I'd best get back to the bar, there's a queue forming and Bill's looking a bit flustered. Enjoy your food, lasses.'

'Fancy a coffee?' asked Mim. She was in the kitchen of Pear Tree Cottage with Anna-Lisa. Herbert had flaked out in his bed and was snoring softly.

'Sounds good. That's the worst thing about having a drink in the afternoon; it makes me feel so sleepy. I need a nice strong hit of caffeine to wake me up or I'll end up snoring my head off like Herbs.'

'Same here, and looking at him, anyone would think he'd had a couple of pints, too.'

Since Mim had shared her news about Caspar, a subtle air of awkwardness had hovered between the two friends. Mim felt torn; the attraction to Caspar was powerful, drawing her in, already she was totally in his thrall. But she valued her friendship with Anna-Lisa. She and Aidey were the best friends Mim had ever had; they had each other's backs and were loyal to the core. Certainly, they'd helped her recover from a broken heart more times than she cared to remember, taking her out when all she felt like doing was hiding under the duvet, making sure she ate well when all she wanted to do was stuff her face with crisps and sweets. The pair had developed quite a repertoire in an effort to cheer her up, particularly after her painful split from Rick, with Anna-Lisa doing silly dances and pulling funny faces, and Aidey telling his seemingly never-ending supply of eye-wateringly bad jokes that were so corny you couldn't help but laugh. Or wrapping his arms around her, holding her tight when she broke down, making her feel the world wasn't such a bad place. Mim was all too aware how lucky she was to have such loyal and caring friends, and she'd do all she could to hang on to them; they – along with Josie – had become the constants in her life since her grandparents had died, and she valued them enormously.

'I love this house.' Anna-Lisa broke the silence. 'It's always sunny and bright. It must've been hard for Josie to leave it, especially after they spent so much time and money doing it up.'

'I think it was, but the job offer was just too good for Russ not to take up; he'd been head-hunted so it was a bit of an honour really. And the fact that they didn't have to sell it helped; I think it would've been a different story if they had. Josie likes the idea of coming back here in a few years' time.'

'Ah, another one, I seem to be hearing more and more about that.'

'What do you mean?'

'Head-hunting; don't forget, according to the Pallister-Biggs, they headhunted the Dark Count,' said Anna-Lisa.

'Oh, right, yeah, I suppose.' Ordinarily Mim would be desperate to use mention of her latest romance to wax lyrical about it, relishing the feeling as her heart filled with happiness. But since Anna-Lisa wasn't exactly giving off positive vibes about Caspar, she resisted the urge and bit the words back, even though, at times, her enthusiasm almost got the better of her and they got precariously close to slipping out. Mim decided a change of tack was needed. 'Actually, I need to get the place tidied up a bit before Josie Skypes. She'd have a fit if she saw the state of this room.'

Anna-Lisa giggled, looking around her at the piles of dirty crockery littering the surfaces, the bin spilling over and the dirty paw marks covering the tiled floor. 'It is a bit of a pigsty, but at least you keep the living room tidy-ish, I suppose. Tell you what, why don't I give you a hand to tidy up now? It'll save me from falling asleep in my coffee which I'm at serious risk of doing, then I'll struggle to wake up in time to go to Carly's.'

'Really? You want to tidy? Well, personally, I can think of better ways to spend my Saturday afternoon.' Mim felt a wave of tiredness wash over her; she sat back in her chair, stretched her legs out and yawned. *Hmm, maybe Anna-Lisa has a point.*

'Clearly.' Anna-Lisa arched an eyebrow at her friend, making her laugh. 'Well, what else can we do, other than fall asleep? We've got a good few hours before we go to Carly's; we could get this place looking spick and span in that time.'

'Great,' said Mim, putting little enthusiasm into the word; she was as messy as her friend was tidy.

'Brilliant! Let's get cracking.' Anna-Lisa jumped up and clapped her hands. Mim watched as she made her way to the iPod dock, selected a playlist of motivational dance music and turned the volume up. 'Come on, you scruff, lead me to the dusters.'

Mim got to her feet with a groan.

A COUPLE OF HOURS LATER, the friends were standing in the newly-gleaming kitchen, admiring their handiwork. 'Wow! This place has never looked so good since Josie left,' said Mim. 'I'll be able to bring my laptop in here without worrying about what she thinks if she Skypes tomorrow.'

'Told you you'd be happy you listened to me.' Anna-Lisa stood, hands on hips. 'And, I know you've had a lot on your mind this week, so I'll make allowances for you not being in the mood to tidy up, but *please* try not to let it get into such a state again. That mug was absolutely gross! I reckon I'll be having nightmares about it. I've no idea what was in there, but I swear you could have a conversation with it. And the gunk in the bin was literally fermenting; I'm surprised you aren't sharing the house will all sorts of vermin. You've got to promise me you won't let it get as bad as that again.'

Mim giggled. 'I'll do my best. Promise.'

'Good. Right, we've got ten minutes to get ready. Let's get cracking – and don't forget that wine from the super-sparkly, newly-gleaming fridge.'

'I won't, and by the way, thanks, Anna.'

'You're welcome, chick.'

11

'COME IN, LASSES.' Carly stood back, holding the door wide open to let Mim and Anna-Lisa into the hallway of Wisteria Cottage. Maisie shot out, dancing around Herbert's legs like it had been years since they'd last met, before running back inside with him hot on her heels and heading straight for the kitchen. 'What are those two like?'

'Love's young dream?' Mim laughed.

'Something like that,' said Carly. 'It's been a lovely day, but it isn't half nippy now, get yourselves in out of the cold.'

'You're not wrong, even though we've only walked about two strides from Mim's I'm absolutely nithered.' Anna-Lisa's words hung in a plume of condensation.

'I know, I can't believe how chilly it's got since lunch time,' said Mim, shivering. 'Where are the kids?'

'Tucked up in bed, fast asleep. They've had a busy day, what with swimming lessons and a birthday party. It was a case of a quick bath and bed when we got home; the pair of them were asleep as soon as their heads hit the pillow.'

'No wonder after all that,' said Mim. 'Actually, I could've gone to sleep myself this afternoon but Anna-Lisa had us cleaning.'

Carly closed the door behind them, shutting out the cold night air. 'Really? Cleaning what? Ooh, thank you, girls.' She took the bottles handed to her by Mim and Anna-Lisa, freeing them to hang their coats up and kick their boots off.

'Mim's place, or should I say, Scruffpot's place. It was like a right pig-sty; I'm still traumatised.'

'Cheek, it wasn't that bad,' Mim said with a giggle.

Anna flashed her a look that said "really?".

'Well, maybe it was just a little bit.'

'It so bloody-well was, and now I'm desperate for a drink to help me recover from the whole shocking experience.'

'Right, let's go and crack open one of these little beauties then.' Carly headed down the hallway that led to the large contemporary kitchen.

'Ooh, it's so lovely and toasty in here,' said Anna-Lisa.

'Mmm, it is. And it's good to see Herbert doesn't waste any time in making himself at home.' Mim smiled at the sight of him curled up with Maisie on the brightly coloured mat in front of the Aga.

'Right, ladies, park your bums wherever you fancy,' said Carly.

'I like the look of your new stools at the breakfast bar, how about we sit there?' Anna-Lisa made her way over to them.

'Sounds good to me,' said Mim.

'Ah, yes, they arrived the other day; I'm chuffed to bits with them.'

Anna-Lisa pulled out one of the metal and oak bar stools and sat down at the huge island unit. 'This is my dream kitchen, Carly. I have serious kitchen-envy whenever I come here.'

'Thanks, chick, it's been a real labour of love sourcing everything, but we got there eventually.' Carly turned to reach for glasses in one of the wall cupboards. 'What do you think we should have first, fizz or wine?'

'Oh, I'm easy, I'll drink anything,' said Mim.

'Er, tell us something we don't know, Mimbo,' said Anna-Lisa with a chuckle.

Mim stuck her tongue out at her friend.

'Exactly what I was going to say.' Carly giggled. 'How about you, Anna? Are you fizzing or wining?'

'Ooh, I think, as it's Saturday, we've got to start with a bit of fizz, don't you?'

'I like the sound of that,' said Mim, rubbing her hands together.

'Couldn't agree more; Saturday night should always start with fizz.' Carly grabbed three flutes and placed them next to the bottles on the island. She picked up the Prosecco, eyeing it warily. 'Have either of you got any better at opening these things since we last tackled a bottle? I seem to recall most of it ended up on the floor; I was sorely tempted to get down there with Maisie and Herbert and lick it up.'

Mim giggled at the memory. ''Fraid not – er, and I'm sorry about that, but unless you want a load of froth around your kitchen and dripping off your walls, I'd best not touch it.'

'I really don't fancy that, especially since I've just painted them,' said Carly.

'Pass it here; I'll have a go, though I'm not promising anything.' Anna-Lisa took the bottle from Carly and began peeling the foil back before tentatively tackling the cork. All three women winced as she began carefully easing it out, their expressions changing to surprise when it suddenly shot out with a resounding "pop". It ricocheted off the ceiling and hit Herbert square on the backside. The Labrador barked and jumped up, looking around for the perpetrator while Maisie looked on in bewilderment.

The three friends fell about laughing. 'Oh, I'm so sorry, Herbs, I didn't mean to do that, I was trying to avoid the bi-fold doors and the newly painted walls,' said Anna-Lisa.

'You're lethal with those things, Anna!' said Mim. 'If I remember rightly, the last time you opened a bottle, it hit a load of glasses and shattered them to pieces.'

'Yep, I think we should leave it to Carly next time.'

'Oh, bugger, I really can't see me doing any better than you two,' said Carly as she filled the glasses. 'Any road, bottoms up, lasses. Here's to Saturday night and a good old girly chin-wag.'

THE EVENING PASSED QUICKLY, the three friends relaxing into their usual easy-going banter, sharing the events of the week. By the time they'd finished the Prosecco and moved on to Chardonnay, Mim was beginning to feel a little tipsy. It didn't help that her contact lenses had decided to float about on the surface of her eyeballs, making it even more difficult to focus.

'So come on then, Missy, are you going to spill the beans about what's going on with you and the Dark Count?' Carly raised an enquiring eyebrow.

'That's what I call him, too!' said Anna-Lisa.

Oh, bugger! Mim had been hoping the subject of Caspar

wouldn't crop up. Though, if she was completely honest with herself, she had thought it a bit too good to be true that they'd got to almost nine o'clock and there'd been no mention of him. Up to that point they'd been laughing about the growing mischief of the kinky underwear night and the fun they were having winding up Pat Motson and her cronies. But now, it seemed, it was time to discuss Caspar, and Mim was feeling torn. If it had just been Carly and her, she would've been able to go into raptures about him. With Carly not having met him, she hadn't had the chance to form a negative opinion of him like Anna-Lisa seemed to have, so she wouldn't be in a position to throw a wet blanket over her enthusiasm. But having Anna-Lisa there, and knowing how she felt about Caspar, meant she'd have to considerably restrain herself. And that wasn't going to be easy, especially after she'd been drinking Prosecco.

'There's no point looking all innocent, like there's nothing to tell, we both so know there is, don't we, Anna? There's no way on this earth that someone as hot as him can stay the night with a hot-blooded, sexy little minx with legs that go on forever like you and nothing happens. If I was in your shoes, lady, I wouldn't be able to keep my hands off him. Oh, and if you do actually say nothing happened, we won't believe you for a teeny-tiny minute.'

'Actually, I'm not sure I want to know,' said Anna-Lisa.

Mim felt a mix of relief and hurt at Anna's response. 'Anna-Lisa doesn't approve, do you, Anna?'

Anna-Lisa swirled her wine around her glass. 'It's not that I don't approve, it's just that I worry about you, after what you've been through, that's all, and you were so devastated after Rick; I don't want to see you as upset as that again.'

'Well, like I've already told you, there's no need to worry. Caspar's different to the others; he's not going to treat me badly like they did. Honestly, I know it; he's a decent bloke.'

'Ooh, so something is going on between you, then.' Carly's eyes widened.

Alcohol had pushed Mim's inhibitions away along with her regard for Anna's concerns. She felt a rush of happiness surge through her. 'You've got to promise me you'll keep it to yourself.'

'I promise, cross my heart,' said Carly.

'Well, it's early days and I can't really say too much, except last night, was, well, O.M.G., I seriously went to heaven and back.'

'Woah, you little vixen, Mim Dewberry. Does Josie know of the soaring temperatures at Pear Tree Cottage?'

'No! And she's not going to find out!' Mim felt a sudden pang of worry; something told her Josie wouldn't approve of Caspar either. She glanced across to Anna-Lisa, whose expression had turned serious. 'Can't you just be happy for me, Anna?'

Anna-Lisa reached across and took Mim's hand. 'Oh, hon, I want nothing more than to be happy for you, honestly. It's just you haven't known him five minutes and already you've fallen hook, line and sinker. After what you've been through, and the number of times you've been hurt, I just don't want you to have to go through that again; you were wrecked after Rick, and it took you a long time to get back to your normal happy self again. You'd be exactly the same if the situations were reversed, you know you would.'

'Anna's got a point, chick, and it's the sign of a good friend who's prepared to say things you might not necessarily want to hear.' Carly turned to Anna-Lisa. 'So why does Mim think you don't approve of the Dark Count?'

'Because she doesn't make it a secret!' Mim gave a small laugh.

'Well, for one, because I've seen this pattern so many times before and, well, it's not that I don't approve of him – that's not my place – it's just that, well, you know when you get a feeling about someone and it makes you uneasy? Well, it's kind of like that. I suppose you could say my gut's sending me warning signals about him and it's making me wary. Sorry, Mim.'

The room suddenly took on an awkward mood. Carly pressed her lips together, looking at Mim intently. 'Right, and how many times have we had conversations where we've said you should always trust your gut?'

'Too many times,' said Anna. 'Just promise me, Mim, if you get an uneasy feeling about anything or anyone – I don't just mean Caspar – you'll listen to it and not ignore it like you usually do.'

Mim could feel her heart pounding, partly because she felt a prickle of annoyance with her friends, and partly because she knew they were right; hadn't she pushed that same little niggle about Caspar – and so many other boyfriends – to the back of her mind, refusing to listen to it? And what about Herbert's reaction to him? That was totally out of character. But what the hell? You could be wrong about people, couldn't you? Wasn't it unfair to judge on first appearances? She liked him, he liked her, and that was all that mattered. She took a deep breath. 'Listen, I really appreciate you both looking out for me, but in this instance I think Anna's wrong, I really do. But, anyway, when I first kind of got an inkling he liked me, I made the decision to allow myself a little bit of fun; surely you don't think there's anything wrong with that? He's seriously hot, and ticks a load of my boxes, so I'm prepared to enjoy it while it lasts, and take the risk of it being short-lived.' She shrugged. 'When did a bit of no strings fun hurt anyone?'

'As long as it is no strings and you don't end up getting your heart broken again.' Anna looked at her. 'And it's not just my gut-feeling, he's really cocky, too, the way he struts about the office like he owns the place; I can see that slime-ball Simon and him locking horns before too long.'

'Hmm.' Mim had to agree with Anna about Caspar and Simon locking horns; there was definitely a hint of rivalry between them.

'And what does Aidey think of him?' Carly shot Anna-Lisa a loaded look which didn't go unnoticed by Mim.

'He feels the same as me; he doesn't want Mim to get hurt.'

'Well, he hasn't said anything to me, but I should imagine he's got other things on his mind, it can't exactly be easy for him having to work alongside someone who he's had to essentially give his job to.'

'Yeah, that was a shameful thing your bosses did.' Carly shook her head. 'I know I've only met him a few times when he's called in at the pub with you guys, but I got the impression that he's a really lovely lad. Has he got himself a girlfriend yet?'

'Nope, he's still single, though from some things he's said, I kind of think there's someone he really likes but I'm not so sure she knows it,' said Mim.

Carly gave Anna-Lisa another knowing look.

Mim took a sip of wine; her friends' comments about Caspar had niggled her a little and she was trying to resist the urge to say something defensive. But the words were hovering precariously on the tip of her tongue and popped out before she had chance to stop them. 'Anyway, Anna, you're not exactly overjoyed about how your relationship with Caleb's going, so it just goes to show no one's perfect.' As soon as the words had left her mouth, she wished she could snatch them back. She sensed Carly looking from her to Anna as the air of awkwardness intensified. *Why did I have to go and say that?*

Anna-Lisa met her gaze, a hint of hurt in her eyes making Mim feel terribly guilty.

'Tell me about it,' Anna-Lisa said. 'I'm not fooling myself about how things are with Caleb and me, and if I'm being brutally honest, I'd say we're on borrowed time. But – and I know I'm going to sound like a right hardened cow – I'm not going to be gutted about it, and my heart won't be broken, that's still safe and sound in here.' She patted her chest. 'Not that I'm saying that's a good thing; it's because I intend to keep myself safe so I won't let anyone in. I'm not as lovely and warm as you are, Mimbo.' She reached across and rubbed her friend's arm.

Mim smiled and gave Anna-Lisa's hand a squeeze. 'You're not a hardened cow, Anna; you're the most kind-hearted person I know. You've had it tough, so it's only natural you're wary. I only wish I could be more like you. You're the best friend anyone could ever have.'

'Right back atcha, chick.'

'What a pair we are, eh?'

'Yep, just as well we've got Carly to keep us right.'

Carly got to her feet. 'Well, I think you're both totally fabulous, and I don't know about you, but I've got the munchies. I think it's time I put the pizza and garlic bread in the oven.'

'Good plan,' said Mim.

12

As a rule, Mim usually despised Monday mornings with a passion, the dread for them starting as an annoying little niggle from early Sunday afternoon, building gradually through the day until it had begun to dominate her every thought, eventually manifesting itself into a troubled night's sleep. But this Monday morning was different. This was a Monday morning she'd been looking forward to for the whole weekend for one simple reason: Caspar.

'Morning.' Her heart fluttered as she slipped into the heated leather seat which felt divine on her cold legs. The spicy scent of his cologne hit her nostrils and mingled with the aroma of new car, instantly catapulting her back to Friday night. She felt a frisson of excitement and looked across at him, unable to control the huge smile that was currently splitting her face in two. He looked unbelievably handsome in his crisp blue shirt, open at the neck, that set off his pale complexion and dark hair.

'Morning.' He leaned across, cupping her cheek with his hand and kissing her deeply, sending a host of butterflies running riot around her stomach. It took every ounce of her strength not to pounce on him and drag him back into the house for a hot and steamy replay of Friday night. 'Mmm. That takes the sting out of a dreary Monday morning.'

Oh, that voice! Oh, that kiss! Oh. My. Days! She pressed her lips together, running her tongue along them, savouring the taste of him. It sent a shiver of delight vibrating through her.

'I missed you.' He kissed her again, making her groan.

He missed me? Caspar De Verre actually missed me? Her heart soared. 'I missed you, too. Actually, you don't fancy popping into the house for a few minutes, do you? I'm sure we've got time.' She arched a suggestive eyebrow at him, making him smile.

'Much as I love the sound of getting up close and personal with your hot little body again, I think I'd find it a considerable struggle to tear myself away from you. I don't think it would go down too well if we're late for work, do you? And it might make our bosses a tad suspicious, which is something we don't want.'

'Spoilsport!'

He threw his head back and laughed. 'It'll make it all the more worthwhile when we get back tonight.'

Mim hadn't thought of that. She looked at him and grinned, her toes wiggling with happiness. 'True.'

'Right, now we've got that sorted, we'd best head off; the sooner we get started, the sooner we get finished.' He winked at her.

'So, did you have a good weekend? How did helping your parents go?' she asked, buckling her seatbelt.

'Well, I seem to recall the weekend started off amazingly well, but I'm afraid to say, after the delights of Friday night and Saturday morning, much as I love my parents, working for them was a little bit of an anti-climax.' He cocked a knowing eyebrow at her before slipping the car into gear and pulling out onto the road. 'How about you? How was your weekend, Mim Dewberry – did I ever tell you how I love your name?'

She laughed. 'Thanks. Well, mine was pretty much the same as yours, really. Friday night was totally *amazing,* as was Saturday morning! Then the rest of the weekend was good, but no comparison. After you'd left on Saturday I went for a long walk with Herbert—'

Caspar gave a disapproving snort at the mention of the Labrador's name, stopping Mim in her tracks. A spike of annoyance shot through her, taking her by surprise; she didn't like him being dismissive about Herbert. She pushed the feeling away and continued. 'Anyway, it was such a lovely afternoon, really sunny and bright, we met loads of people we knew on the walk. Then, when we got back, Anna-Lisa came round and we had lunch at—'

Another disapproving snort from Caspar, cutting her off. Mim stole a quick look at him, but his face was impassive and his eyes were fixed on the road. Once more, she elbowed her annoyance away, pretending she hadn't noticed it. 'Then Anna went and suggested we tidy the house before my next Skyping session with Josie, so we did. Honestly, the place is gleaming; I've never seen it look so tidy since Josie left.'

'Well that's no bad thing.' He turned to her and chuckled.

'Hey, cheeky! Then later in the evening we went along to Carly's for a catch up over a drink and some pizza. It was fun, but not as much fun as Friday night; that will definitely take some beating.' She looked across at him, a beaming smile lighting up her face.

He reached over and squeezed her knee. 'I couldn't agree more.' He paused for a moment. 'You didn't mention anything about us to Anna-Lisa, did you? I know you're best friends and I know how you women love to share, but I really think it's the right thing to keep quiet about us at work for all the reasons I mentioned before – even from Anna-Lisa.'

He said "us"! We're an "us"! Mim was struggling not to tremble with excitement.

'You know how easily these things have a habit of coming out and Anna might let something slip to Aidey – no matter how innocently – then he might let something slip to someone else. Though, granted, it might not be so innocently with him, especially if he continues to see me as a threat to him. I wouldn't put it past him to do anything to stir up a bit of trouble behind my back.'

'Aidey? Aidey wouldn't do anything like that; he's not malicious; he's quiet, just gets on with his work. And he doesn't have bad bone in his body.' Though, she wasn't so sure that he didn't see Caspar as a threat after what had happened with his job. Still, she felt sure she could trust Aidey with her deepest, darkest secrets if ever the need arose.

'Well, that's what you think, but you didn't hear him having a go about me when Susan called him to her office on Thursday. I'd had to report some shoddy work he'd done as she was ready to heap the blame on my shoulders. Would you believe, he actually denied having done any of it? Said it was all down to me? I had to point out to Susan that it wasn't my style at all.'

'So what happened?'

'Well, she had to admit I was right and told Aidey it was the very reason I'd been brought in; said things needed to be slicker, cranked up several bloody notches now that the magazine was a serious contender and was playing with the big boys. He took it badly when she said it was time he pulled his socks up; but I have to say, she had a point.'

'Oh, poor Aidey.' Mim felt a wave of pity for her friend; his life at Yorkshire Portions had been turned upside down much more than hers had been. He hadn't even shared this bollocking from Susan that Caspar was speaking of; even so, it must have really upset him. No wonder he'd been quiet for the latter part of last week.

A frown furrowed her brow as she thought about Caspar's words; she couldn't help but think that something didn't seem right. Was he telling the truth? 'I don't get it. Aidey's always been known for being excellent at his job. Clarissa knew him from when she ran the magazine as a blog and used to get him to design graphics for her, then other people started to ask him too; he'd built up a good reputation, was really in demand. It was what made the bosses offer him the job in the first place, before anyone else jumped in and snapped him up.'

'Hmm. Well, something's happened to make him take his eye off the ball. Between you and me, he's lucky he's still got a job at all. If it was down to me he'd be out on his ear; he's lucky Susan's got a kind heart.'

Mim's eyes almost popped out of her head. *Kind heart, my arse! She's an evil old bag of the highest order!* She turned to stare out of the window, at a loss for words.

'Does he have a girlfriend?'

'Not at the moment, no. He was going out with a girl called Hannah for a while, but they split up a few months ago.'

'Hmm.'

Mim wondered what "hmm" meant, but for some reason, discussing Aidey's private life with Caspar made her feel inexplicably disloyal to her friend. She was relieved when Caspar was distracted by a call, and the conversation came to an end.

The pair continued their journey to York, with Caspar frustrated at not being able to put his foot down and let his sporty car eat up the miles thanks to the thick, patchy autumnal fog that lasted for most of the way. Conscious that he was going out of his way to pick her up, Mim had asked if he minded and was relieved when he reassured her he didn't; he said that he enjoyed spending the extra time with her. It made her heart sing in a way it wouldn't normally do at eight-thirty on a grey and misty Monday morning.

As soon as they arrived at the office Caspar slipped into work mode, though it didn't stop him from hastily drawing her into his office and kissing her passionately, making her body ache with desire. He pulled himself away, his dark eyes twinkling at her. 'There, that'll keep us going for a little while.'

'That's so not fair. How am I supposed to concentrate on my work after that?'

But Caspar didn't have time to reply since Simon bowled into the room without bothering to knock. He looked shocked to see Mim there, but it still didn't stop his eyes from travelling the full length of her long legs, a lecherous smile tugging at the corners of his mouth. It made Mim shudder. 'What are you doing in here, Mim? I hope you're not disturbing Caspar, he's a very busy man, you know.'

'No, I, er, I was just—'

'I asked Mim to stop off here so I could explain about an idea I'd had for an advertising campaign, but it's not urgent, I can do it later.' He turned to her. 'I'll give you a buzz later and you can pop back so we can discuss it further; should be fairly straightforward but I'd still appreciate your input.'

'Yep, that's fine. See you later.' She felt the heat of Simon's gaze on her as she left the room; it made her skin crawl.

Aidey was already at his desk when Mim arrived, and judging by the amount of work around him, he'd been there for quite a while. She regarded him for a moment; she was sure Caspar was wrong about his feelings for her, they were mates who went back a long way, that was all.

'Morning, Aidey. Good weekend?' Mim slipped of her chunky "new" leopard print faux fur coat and hung it on the back of the door. It was her latest charity shop purchase and she was rather thrilled with it, especially since it had been a steal.

'Morning, Mim.' His eyes brightened when he saw her. 'It was okay, spent most of it working. How about you?'

She felt a pang of guilt. Usually if Anna-Lisa was coming over to her house, she'd text Aidey and give him the option of joining them which he sometimes did. But for some reason, she hadn't done that this weekend, and now felt a little mean for it.

'I took Herbs for a couple of long walks, had a girly catch-up with Anna and Carly and even cleaned the house.'

He looked surprised. 'You cleaned the house?'

'Yes, and you don't have to look so shocked,' she said, laughing.

'I did it with Anna's help, well, actually she forced me into it. But I'm kind of glad she did.'

'What did I force you to do, Mimbo?' Anna-Lisa swung through the door, wrapped up well against the cold in her tweed overcoat, a grey beret set at a jaunty angle on top of her sugar-pink hair.

'I was just telling Aidey about our cleaning session.'

'Ughh, don't! I'm still recovering from it! Did she tell you about the mug we found, Aidey? I swear it had a new life-form growing in it; I'm totally convinced I saw a pair of beady eyes looking back at me from the deep, dark, depths.' She gave a theatrical shudder.

'Oh, ha-ha! Take no notice, it wasn't anywhere near as bad as Anna's making out.'

'It so was,' Anna-Lisa mouthed at him, making them all laugh.

'What's the joke?' Honey huffily pushed her way past Anna-Lisa.

'Oh, nothing,' said Anna. She pulled a face behind Honey's back.

The three of them watched as Honey stomped over to her desk, threw her bag down onto the floor and flopped heavily into her chair. She was in a bad mood and she wanted everyone to know about it.

They stole furtive glances at one another. Mim was generally regarded as a tolerant person, but she had no time for the girl; she viewed her as an obnoxious attention seeker which was clearly what this latest display of histrionics was all about.

'What's up with you? How come you've got a face like a slapped arse?' asked Anna-Lisa, bold as ever.

'I have not. I'm fine. I don't know what makes you think that. Don't go pushing the fact that it's Monday and you don't like it onto somebody else. That's a form of bullying, that is.'

Anna-Lisa splayed her palms at Honey. 'Woah! You can just stop right there. From the way you pushed past me and stormed over to your desk, it's pretty obvious to the rest of us that you've got a bad case of Monday-itis – which is absolutely fine as long as you don't try and push the blame of how you're feeling onto other people. None of us like Mondays, but we're grown up enough to just get on with it. But I'll tell you what, we'll leave you alone until you feel like being civil, okay?' She rolled her eyes at Mim and Aidey as she headed to her desk.

Mim looked at her friend with a feeling of admiration; she wished she had the balls to stand up to Honey's sort like Anna-Lisa did.

Sensing she was being watched, Mim turned to see Honey

looking daggers at her. It made her feel uneasy. Why was she getting the dirty look when it was Anna-Lisa who'd just put her in her place? She caught Aidey's eye; he'd clearly noticed it, too.

An hour later, the phone on Mim's desk buzzed with an internal call. Her heart sank; such calls usually meant Susan, something that was never a pleasant experience, least of all on a Monday morning. She picked the handset up with trepidation. 'Hello.'

'You do know you have an incredibly sexy voice, don't you?' It was Caspar, his voice smooth and chocolatey.

Mim giggled. 'Do I?' She sensed three pairs of eyes on her and tried her hardest to stop smiling.

'Oh, you most certainly do, you hot little minx.'

She caught sight of Honey's intense glare. 'Right, okay, yes, I'll do that,' she said, hoping she sounded work-like.

'I'm guessing the others are listening?'

'Yes, that's right.'

'So I'd probably better not tell you how much I'd like to lay you over my desk and peel down your—'

Gulp! That definitely wasn't work-talk and was making her feel all of a dither. She steadied herself. 'That sounds great. I've got some ideas you might like, too. I'll just grab my notebook and I'll pop down to your office straight away.'

Caspar gave a dirty laugh. 'Mmm. I like the way you're talking. I'll be waiting for you, don't be long.'

'I'll be there in a moment.'

'Who was that?' asked Honey.

'Caspar; he's got an idea for an advertising campaign he wants to discuss with me. We were going to do it first thing, but Simon needed to talk to him so we had to put it off, but Caspar's keen to get it moving.' Mim could feel the intensity coming from Anna-Lisa's side of the room, but knew better than to meet her friend's gaze; one glance and she'd be rumbled.

'Well, I should be there as well; it's not fair if he only wants your input, we're equals, my opinion's just as important as yours.' Honey pushed her mouth into its now familiar pout.

'He didn't ask for you, he just wants to discuss it with me. I can share the details with you afterwards and we can go over it together then.' Mim's words gave her a little fizz of pleasure.

Honey huffed and shook her head. But before she could say anything further, Mim pushed her chair back, snatched up her notebook and a pen, and disappeared through the door as quickly as possible.

'Sorry I took so long, Honey wanted to come, too, I had all on not to—' Before she knew it, Caspar was standing before her, his lips pressing against hers, his eager hands pushing their way up inside her top and underneath her bra, making her whole body pulse with lust.

'You're driving me crazy, Mim Dewberry.'

She groaned, returning his kisses with equal ardour. 'We'd best be quick.'

Seconds later the pair jumped apart when an assertive knock at the door took them by surprise. Mim gasped. 'Oh my God!' She hurriedly straightened her top and grabbed her notebook. Caspar scooped up a handful of papers from his desk.

'Come in,' he said.

The door opened and Honey appeared. Mim's heart fell. *What the hell? That bloody girl!*

'Honey, what's the problem?' asked Caspar, not hiding the impatience in his voice.

'I just thought that if you were discussing a new ad campaign, that I should be here, too. Save Mim having to repeat what you've said in case she gets it wrong or something. And I've got some really good ideas of my own I've been desperate to share but nobody seems to want to listen.' She spoke in the now familiar little-girl voice she used when speaking to Caspar and her bosses.

Ideas? What ideas? What a load of bollocks! And that bloody voice! Mim could feel her blood start to boil. What right did Honey have to try and undermine her in front of Caspar? Or anyone, for that matter.

'I can assure you, I have every faith in Mim's abilities to get an ad campaign right; her track record is proof of that. And, furthermore, if I'd wanted you to be present while Mim and I discuss it, I would've asked you to join us. But I didn't as I couldn't see the point in dragging both of you away from your desks. So you might as well go and get on with what you were doing while we finish off here.'

Honey stood there as if willing him to change his mind. 'But Mim hasn't given me anything to do.' She flashed puppy-dog eyes at him.

Jeez, the bloody bare-faced cheek of the girl! And since when exactly did I have to hold her hand? 'If you look at the to-do list on my desk, just do the next thing that hasn't been crossed off; I think it's some Twitter posts, they're fairly straightforward, if you just start drafting one of those.'

Honey mustered up her now familiar death-stare, directing it at Mim before flouncing out of the room.

Caspar pinched the bridge of his nose between his finger and thumb. 'How on earth can you be around that girl?'

'Trust me, it's not easy.'

'I can believe that; she behaves like a spoilt, moody teenager, especially when she uses that irritating bloody voice.'

'You're not the first person to have said that.'

'Hmm. Quite the passion killer, though, isn't she?'

Mim nodded, any last remnants of lust draining away. 'Just a bit.'

For appearance's sake, the pair ran over a few ideas for a new advertising campaign that could be linked in to a feature on the magazine's blog. If Mim was honest with herself, Caspar's suggestions weren't that ground-breaking, and Aidey's work was far superior and professional-looking. But she bit her tongue and scribbled his ideas down, using words of enthusiasm to massage his ego. She'd discreetly run them by Aidey and see if he'd help her. On second thoughts, would that be like rubbing his nose in it? Hmm, it probably would. She pushed that idea away; there was no way she was going to hurt Aidey's feelings or make him feel crap for the sake of Yorkshire Portions.

'You reek of Caspar's cologne.' Honey pinned Mim with a piercing glare when she returned to their office. 'And what were you doing before I came into his office? You both looked really shifty.'

'We weren't doing anything; we hadn't had time to do anything. Caspar had just started explaining his idea when you knocked at the door.'

'Yeah, well it was all quiet before I knocked; I couldn't hear anything being discussed.'

Oh, why don't you just bugger off, you evil little cowpat! 'That's because Caspar was gathering the papers together and thinking about things before he spoke, I was just waiting until he was ready.'

'Yeah, yeah, a likely story.'

Aidey shook his head. 'Will you let it drop, Honey? I'm trying to concentrate on this.'

'Yeah, can't you just give it a sodding rest instead of always having to make out there's something dodgy going on, or trying to stir up trouble. It's like being back in the playground! You'd be better off getting stuck into some work for a change, that'd keep your mind occupied and stop you from behaving like a spiteful child.' Anna-Lisa glared at her.

'What? I do not behave like a spiteful child! You've got no right to talk to me like that, I'm going to speak to my Auntie Susan, see what she has to say about how you lot have been treating me.' Honey stood up and flounced out of the room.

'I can honestly say I've never known anyone make my blood boil as much as she does!' Anna-Lisa sounded exasperated.

Mim rested her elbows on her desk and put her face in her hands. 'I know exactly how you feel but I don't have the energy nor the inclination to argue with her. No matter what you say, she always seems to have to turn it into an argument; she never backs down and it's draining. Isn't it amazing how just one person can totally change the atmosphere of a place?'

'Make that two people,' said Aidey.

'Too right. I know it's only Monday, but roll on the weekend,' said Anna-Lisa, eliciting half-hearted laughs from her friends. 'And, don't worry about Honey, she won't have chance to speak to Susan, she's in meetings all morning.'

13

Mim glanced up at the clock, and was relieved to find that it was almost lunch time; the morning had passed surprisingly quickly since her almost "moment" with Caspar. It had helped that Susan had left them alone for the bulk of the time except for when she'd blustered through the door demanding if anyone knew of the whereabouts of her diamond ring. Thankfully, Clarissa had found it on the windowsill in the kitchen, where her mother had left it when she'd taken it off to wash her hands. It was a scenario that happened on a regular basis – if it wasn't her ring that was missing it was her expensive pen, or her purse or her car keys – so no one was too alarmed; the woman was just too lazy to look for things herself, and making a hoo-ha about it meant that it would send her minions off, scuttling about looking for whatever it was she'd misplaced.

Honey hadn't returned to their room for a good hour after she'd flounced off in a huff, though Aidey said he'd seen her leaving Simon's room looking smug but slightly dishevelled, which explained why Simon had left them alone, too. The fact that they'd been joined by a new unsuspecting intern called Tamsin had meant Mim hadn't been called upon to make teas and coffees. And there'd been no sign of Kenneth since he wasn't expected to arrive until early afternoon owing to a dental appointment. Even so, it still hadn't stopped a feeling of unease pervading the air at Yorkshire Portions.

Though Mim had relished being able to get stuck into her to-do list without the usual interruptions, her concentration had been broken on several occasions by the uncomfortable feeling that something amiss was creeping up on her. Honey's presence didn't help, and much as she was thrilled by the attention from Caspar, the unease she felt about him hadn't gone away. Instead, it quietly thrummed away in the background, jumping out whenever Mim's mind skirted too close to it, each time sending a prickle of worry racing up her spine and making her stomach clench. It reminded her of her childhood, of sitting engrossed in lessons at school when a nasty little reminder of the unpleasant things going on at home would spring into life, snatching her enjoyment away. Mim would feel her stomach go into freefall as a feeling of nausea washed over her. She was always glad when classroom distractions eventually helped push her worries back into the shadows, but they would never completely disappear, returning with a vengeance on the long walk home as she wondered what she'd be greeted with when she got there. It was fair to say, she'd spent her childhood as a tightly furled little ball of anxiety; it was no wonder she was plagued by psoriasis.

Sensing Aidey's eyes on her, Mim looked up and smiled at him. The one he returned was a mere glimmer, offering a barely discernible lift to the corners of his mouth. She couldn't help but notice his eyes didn't have their usual happy glint, instead they were clouded by a shadow brought down by his furrowed brow, and dark semi-circles hung beneath. She popped a sweet into her mouth and glanced across at Anna-Lisa to see her friend engrossed in her work, gnawing on the inside of her cheek as she read. Honey gave a theatrical sigh from her desk; she was making hard work of her latest task, making no secret of her lack of enthusiasm. If she'd hoped to get the others' attention with all her huffing and puffing, she was to be disappointed; everyone continued with their work as if she wasn't there. The spoilt teenager act was already beginning to wear thin.

Anna-Lisa, Aidey and Mim shared the growing suspicion that Honey was working as some kind of spy for the Pallister-Biggs, which meant the desire to punctuate their work with a bit of occasional friendly banter had deserted them. They didn't want to give her the opportunity to report back that they sat chatting rather than getting on with their work. Instead, they'd spent the morning working in virtual silence; it was a case of heads down and let's crack on with it. Well, all except for Honey who was wearing a petulant expression that said she'd rather be anywhere than there. Mim had to stop herself from asking her how she was getting on, and if she'd finished designing the new social media headers – a job Mim had suggested to her as it was one of the most enjoyable tasks on the to-do list. The words were poised, ready to be delivered, but the look Honey shot her told her she'd be throwing herself into very choppy waters. Instead, she bit her tongue; she couldn't be bothered with the grief that would ensue. It was far easier to let Honey complete her half-hearted attempts at whatever she'd been tasked with, then check over them herself when the other girl wasn't around. It was better than confronting her, or worse, just handing the work straight over to Susan to approve; she'd only go ballistic with Mim for not instructing Honey properly.

The only time Honey had spoken since she came back into the room was to ask Mim if Caspar had given her a lift to work that morning, and to see if anyone knew what he'd been up to over the weekend, and then to announce that she'd bumped into him on the landing and he'd looked at her as though he was undressing her with his eyes. 'He's got the hots for me, it's just so obvious; a man doesn't look at you like that for no reason,' she'd said. Anna-Lisa had glanced across at Mim and rolled her eyes. And though Mim hadn't believed Honey's boast for a second, it hadn't stopped a bolt of intense jealousy from tearing through her.

The only other interruption had come when Tamsin brought hot drinks in for everyone. She had a sweet face and wore an air of optimistic enthusiasm. Such a shame that won't last long, thought Mim, taking pity on the girl straightaway. It would be knocked out of her within the week, and by the time she went home on Friday – if she lasted that long, of course – she'd be feeling absolutely crap and totally useless, and would spend the weekend sobbing into her duvet. Certainly, after what had happened to Sara and her predecessors, it didn't bode well.

Mim had only seen Caspar once since their earlier meeting. She'd nipped along the landing to go to the loo and bumped into him coming out of Clarissa's office, wearing his familiar self-assured smile and a glint in his eye. Mim had dismissed the flicker of surprise followed by the expression of being caught out that had crossed his face when he'd spotted her, telling herself it was just her imagination running riot.

'Hi,' she'd said, her husky voice laden with hints of their little secret. She'd gone to reach for his hand but he'd pulled it away.

'Hello, Mim.' His reply had been cool and there'd been no sneaking into his office for a furtive snog to pick up where they'd left off like she'd hoped they might. Instead, he'd turned away from her, swaggered his way down the creaking floorboards of the landing and disappeared into his office, closing the door firmly behind him. Within seconds she could hear his voice on the phone, loud and confident.

His reaction had wrong-footed her, had hurt even, being so very different from their earlier encounter. A ripple of anxiety had run through her as she'd tried to ignore the little voice that told her Caspar had been flirting with Clarissa, discussing more than work with her or, worse, that their relationship was something more than that of simply work colleagues. After all, Mim had seen that look in his eyes earlier that morning, and she knew exactly what it meant. Her stomach had squeezed as the unpalatable feeling of déjà vu crept up her spine. Did he think that it was okay to play mind games with her? Be cruelly dismissive with her, and keep her dangling until he was ready for her. Keep her waiting for any tiny nugget of affection or acknowledgement that they were an item he was minded to throw her way. Well, she'd been there before – more times than she cared to remember – and she was damn sure she wasn't going to go there again. She hoped with all her heart that Caspar wasn't going to prove to be no better than her previous boyfriends.

Her mind had been charging all over the place when a little voice of reason whispered in her ear. *Don't be ridiculous, you're both at work!* Of course, that was it, and they'd been right outside Clarissa's door; it would've been too risky for him to respond in an affectionate way, after all, Clarissa might have heard. She'd quickly batted her worries away and continued along that preferable line of thought. Outwardly, he was trying to behave in a professional manner, speaking to her in the same way he spoke to other staff, not wanting to draw any unwelcome attention to them. He was being considerate and conscious of her worries about Susan and her job security, that's all. She should be thankful that he was behaving in this way. And, in truth, she certainly didn't want to attract any more negative attention from Susan, nor Honey for that matter. He was just being totally professional.

The door to Clarissa's office had opened and the woman herself had stepped out looking business-like in her neat fitted black suit, showing off her trim figure. She'd pressed her hand to her chest.

'Ooh! Mim, you made me jump! Are you okay, you look worried? Is something the matter?'

'Oh, er, no, nothing's the matter I'm fine, thanks. Just nipping to the loo.'

'Well, don't let me stop you.' Clarissa had flashed her usual friendly smile. 'Oh, and by the way, I love the latest Instagram advert you've done; very eye-catching and I like the humour in there. I'll be interested to see what the interactions are like.'

'Thanks, I was really hoping you'd like it, and they're already up quite a bit on average.' Mim hadn't been able to help but smile at the praise. It was impossible for her to have a negative thought about Clarissa; she was so incredibly decent and likeable.

'Great! I'll see you later.' Clarissa had smiled again before heading off downstairs.

'Yeah, see you later.' Mim had remained rooted to the spot for a few moments. There'd been nothing at all in Clarissa's business-like appearance to suggest that there was anything going on between her and Caspar. *I really need to calm myself down; it's just my crappy relationship history that makes me so suspicious and paranoid. There's nothing going on between Caspar and Clarissa; it's all in my daft head. I seriously need to chill.*

As Mim had headed off to the office's grimy little bathroom, she'd tried her hardest to ignore the annoying voice that had suddenly piped up and was telling her that Clarissa and Caspar would make a beautiful couple and were far better suited than herself and the man in question. 'Oh, just bugger off!' she'd hissed at it.

'Right, now that's done, I'm going to have a break for lunch, anyone care to join me for a bite to eat at the Nutmeg Tree? Aidey, Mim? Surely you're going to have a lunch break this week, Mimbo?' Anna-Lisa popped her pen into the jar on her desk and straightened her paperwork.

'I'm nearly done here; I could do with some fresh air actually, so count me in,' said Aidey.

'Yep, same here. I've got quite a lot done but I just need to finish this last little bit. If you two want to go ahead and get a table, I shouldn't be too long.'

'Good plan,' said Anna-Lisa. 'If the waiter comes before you arrive, shall we order your usual chai tea latte?'

'That'd be great, thanks.'

'Well, I'm afraid I won't be able to join you, I'm meeting a friend,' said Honey. She didn't see Anna-Lisa mime wiping sweat from her brow behind her computer terminal, nor Aidey pressing his lips together as he tried not to laugh.

14

Mim burst through the door at the Nutmeg Tree, her favourite eatery in the city. She was instantly accosted by a wall of warmth and the mouth-watering aroma of sautéed onions and freshly baked bread. She took a deep breath and pressed a hand to her stomach which had started growling noisily in response. It gladdened her heart to see a roaring fire dancing in the wood-burner that nestled in the vast inglenook fireplace, especially since mist still curled around the city, making it chilly and damp.

The coffee bar – the term really didn't do the place justice – in its current incarnation had opened its doors just over a year ago and had already gained itself a loyal following of fans, its plates of food regularly featuring on the blogs and Instagram pages of foodie bloggers. Like Yorkshire Portions, it was housed in a double-fronted, mediaeval timber-framed building which afforded it masses of character. The owners had cleverly married its ancient oak panelling and wonky wattle and daub walls with industrial furnishings; there were tables made of reclaimed floorboards set on heavy steel legs, while seating featured aesthetically worn leather sofas, squishy chairs, metal seats and a row of leather-upholstered booths that ran along the walls at the back. Lighting was courtesy of clusters of exposed vintage lightbulbs suspended from the low, heavily-beamed ceilings by cord-covered cables and vintage candlesticks on the tables. There were shelves made of reclaimed oak on the walls, housing battered hardback copies of classics as well as old bottles and pewter tankards that had been found buried in the ground at the rear of the property, betraying its history as a coaching inn. During this refurbishment a piece of hand-painted Tudor graffiti in an age-worn shade of ochre stating the name "Willyam Merywether" and the date "1532" had been uncovered on one of the walls. It was now on display for diners to admire, protected by a sheet of glass and surrounded by a rustic wooden frame. The well-chosen playlist of laid-back music added a happy vibe to proceedings.

Running late as usual, Mim was thankful the coffee shop was conveniently situated on the same row as the Yorkshire Portions' office on Smiddersgate. She loved the atmosphere, which was always warm and welcoming, and exactly what she needed on a dull, grey Monday – well, any day, actually. Her eyes scoured the tables, skimming over the sea of heads and, though the café was heaving, she easily managed to spot her friends – thanks to Anna's baby-pink hair – sitting in one of the much-coveted booths. She made her way over to them, squeezing through the tables in a flurry of apologies to the other diners whose shoulders she clipped with her new oversized bucket bag.

'Hi, guys, sorry I'm late.' She reached her friends and, noting the small fabric bundle of their coats and bags occupying the space beside Anna, slid into the seat beside Aidey where she breathed out a noisy sigh of relief. 'Crikey me, I thought I was never gonna get here.'

'Hey, no worries, you're here now,' Aidey said with a smile that lit up his eyes, making him look impossibly handsome. Mim smiled back, something indiscernible swirling in her stomach.

'That was good timing, drinks should be here any minute. Anyway, what took you so long, I thought you were supposed to be following right behind? Nice coat, by the way, Mimbo.' Anna watched as Mim undid the buttons of her faux fur jacket.

'Thanks – for the drink and the compliment – you won't believe it, but I picked it up from the charity shop at the top end of Smiddersgate, so though it's new to me, it's actually second-hand. I couldn't believe my luck when I spotted it hanging on the rail for a tenner. And I got this fab bucket bag, too; that was just a fiver.'

'Wow, amazing bargains; you were obviously meant to go into the shop on that very day at that very time. The bag's cute, it'd be enormous on me, but it's perfect for you being lovely and tall.'

'I think you could actually fit inside the bag, Anna,' Aidey said, laughing.

'Hey, you!' Anna-Lisa flicked his arm with the back of her hand. 'Anyway – before I was so rudely interrupted – I was going to say I absolutely love the coat, it's gorgeous, looks really good quality, doesn't it, Aidey?'

'It's very nice, Mim,' he said humouring them good-naturedly. He regularly got dragged into their conversations about hair and makeup or clothes, and they would teasingly ask his opinion.

'Why, thank you, Aidey,' said Mim. 'Even though I got it for a steal, it's actually designer, look.' She flashed them the label. 'And it looks like it's never been worn, either.'

'If that's the case, you were lucky it hadn't been snapped up by those people who go to charity shops looking for designer stuff to buy then re-sell on the internet for a small fortune,' he said.

'Ooh, check out the man with his finger on the fashion pulse but is sitting looking all innocent over there in the corner.' Anna-Lisa giggled.

'See, despite what you think, I do listen to what you two talk about.'

'Good to know,' said Anna-Lisa.

'Actually, it might come to me selling stuff on the internet if I lose my job at Yorkshire Portions, or if I get so fed up I hand my notice in,' said Mim.

'And I might be joining you.' Aidey's smile dropped.

'Well, if you two leave I'm coming with you. I don't think I could stand being stuck in an office with Honey.'

'Do you think she's really that bad?' asked Mim. 'Or do you think we're judging her because of what happened to me? I mean, after all, it was Rick who cheated on me; it wasn't really her fault, if you think about it, just she seemed to get more of the blame heaped onto her while he got off with just looking like a player, which knowing him he'll have been quite chuffed about. That hardly seems fair, does it? You could almost say it's sexist.'

'Is she drunk?' Anna-Lisa looked at Aidey, horrified.

'I reckon she must be.'

'Mim, chick, she's every bit as bad as him; she pursued him knowing he had a girlfriend. That's a big no-no in the sisterhood as well you know. Then the little witch went and had the bloody brass neck to rub your nose in it. And I couldn't give two hoots if you think she got more of the blame than that knob-head you went out with; from what I can gather, her big gob had a lot to do with it.'

'In case you were wondering, Anna's very much on the fence about her.' Aidey chuckled, earning himself a scowl from Anna-Lisa.

'You know I'm right; tell her, Aidey.'

'Anna is right; you're too soft, Mim. Don't let Honey trample all over you again.'

'Hey, I'm only playing devil's advocate; I just wanted to make sure we weren't judging her unfairly or making her feel unwelcome at Yorkshire Portions because of it, that's all.' She leaned across and put her coat on top of the pile beside Anna.

Anna-Lisa shook her head in frustration. 'Mim, you're not talking sense. Think back to how upset you were when you found out about her and Rick. And think back to the day she arrived last week; how she was with you, and how she's done all she can to wind everyone up.' She turned to Aidey. 'I definitely think Mim's still drunk from Saturday night.'

'It's looking more and more that way,' he said.

'I wish.' Mim laughed. 'Trust me, I still think she's a cow for what she did, and I wouldn't trust her as far as I could throw her. I just had a sudden thought that she might try to accuse us of bullying her, or excluding her or something, especially after what she said to you this morning.'

'What, because I stood up to her?' asked Anna-Lisa.

'Actually, Mim might have a point; we've seen how Honey twists things,' said Aidey. 'I don't agree with Mim that we've misjudged her or anything like that, but I think we should be very wary of her. And don't forget what your sister said about her experience of working with her, Anna.'

'Agreed, we should definitely be wary of her,' said Anna.

'Yep, agreed,' said Mim. 'And now no more talk of that girl over our precious lunch break or I'll end up with indigestion.'

'Fair enough,' said Aidey.

'Ooh, perfect timing, here's the drinks,' said Mim.

'Hi, guys, how are you doing today?' asked the waiter. He set three earthenware mugs down on the table.

'Hiya, Ed, this looks good,' said Anna-Lisa.

'Now then, Ed, we're good, thanks, how're you?' asked Aidey.

'Chai tea latté, you've no idea how ready I am for you,' said Mim, making everyone laugh.

'I'm good thanks – busy as ever – your food won't be long. I'll catch you later.'

When Ed had gone Anna-Lisa turned to Mim. 'Anyway, you were going to tell us why you landed here late.'

'Uh, yeah. I'm afraid I'm going to have to bring up "you-know-who's" name again.'

'S'alright, we'll make allowances, just this once,' said Anna.

Mim smiled. 'I was late thanks to Honey, quizzing me about Caspar again; honestly, talk about being interrogated. Wanting to know what I knew about him, and how the Pallister-Biggs knew him. Asking again what we talked about in the car on the way to and from work. Why he's still doing it when the roadworks aren't so bad this week, if he ever mentioned her, if I thought he fancied her, had I noticed the way he looks right into her eyes when he's talking to us, as if there's only her in the room; I honestly thought I was never going to escape. I had to make a quick dash for it when she got a call from Simon to go to his office.'

'Ughh! Rather her than me. I've been keeping well out of his way since he came on to me.' Anna pulled a disgusted face.

'Oh, I think she'd be able to handle him, that one,' said Aidey. 'And I think he'll know it, too, especially if she's grown up around him, being his aunt's goddaughter and everything. He'll have had plenty of time to see her in action and get the measure of her.'

'True, and vice versa.' Mim swirled a spoon around her drink. 'Though something tells me she likes the attention from him.'

'Hmm, after what Aidey said about how she looked when she was leaving Simon's office this morning, I know exactly what you mean,' said Anna. 'And I hope you don't mind, Mim, but I let slip to Aidey about you and the Dark Count.'

'Oh.' Why had she done that? 'It's okay, I know you won't say anything, will you, Aidey?'

'Of course I won't, it's none of my business, but, as one of your oldest friends, I will say I think you should watch him – and that's not just because of what happened with my job. There's something about him I'm not sure of, and I got the feeling he was trying to stitch me up the other day.'

Anna-Lisa snorted. 'That doesn't surprise me. And I hate to say it, Mim, but he seems to be sniffing around Clarissa quite a bit; and I don't think it's all work-related.'

'I agree,' said Aidey.

'Look, I know you both mean well, but I honestly think you've got him all wrong; he's just a bit different to us, that's all.' Mim chose to ignore the unpalatable fact that her friends shared her misgivings.

Just then, a waitress arrived with a large tray holding their food, a welcome change of subject.

'Mim, that look on your face is just like Herbert's when he's watching us eat.' Anna-Lisa giggled.

'Looking at what you two have ordered, I'm beginning to understand exactly how he feels.' She laughed. 'Everything looks delicious and I'm so hungry I swear I could eat a scabby horse between two mattresses.'

Aidey cut a slice from his portion of slow-roasted beef cheek and popped it onto Mim's plate. 'There you go, don't say I don't give you anything.'

'Thanks, Aidey, you're a babe.'

'So I'm told. Want some, Anna?'

Anna-Lisa shook her head. 'No, thanks, I doubt I'll be able to eat all of this salmon, it's bigger than me.'

Mim cut a slice of her herb roasted chicken breast and popped it onto Aidey's plate. 'See what a lovely friend I am, I wouldn't do that for just anyone, you know.'

'Thanks, Mim, you're a babe, too.'

'Anna?' Mim nodded to her plate.

'No thanks, chick.'

'That was the right answer.' Mim giggled taking a forkful of the beef cheek Aidey had given her.

The friends spent a few moments tucking into their food, enjoying the comfortable silence between them. Mim tapped her foot and nodded along to the R&B playlist as she chomped away, the flavours in the salad dancing on her tongue; sometimes spicy, sometimes earthy and sometimes sweet. She finished her mouthful, pondering for a moment before she stole a herbed roast potato from Aidey's plate.

'This is seriously good,' she said. The others nodded enthusiastically.

'Mmm. It'll save me having to cook something big for dinner tonight. Caleb can see to himself, if he can be bothered to pull himself away from his computer, that is,' said Anna-Lisa.

'Ah, do I detect a hint of annoyance there, Anna?' asked Aidey.

'It's not so much annoyance … well, maybe it is a bit, but you both know he's always been keen on his computer games, only now it's become something more like an addiction with him. He's on that bloody computer the whole time. I've even known him get up extra early on a morning to squeeze in a quick go at slaying dragons or whatever it is he does. Honestly, you'd think he was a fifteen-year-old with no responsibilities, not a grown man of twenty-seven the way he goes on.' Anna-Lisa sighed resignedly. 'He behaves like he's single, too, we never do anything together; we don't even nip out to the Mucky Duck for a quick pint anymore.'

'Oh, Anna, you look sad.' Mim reached across the table and gave her friend's hand a squeeze. It wasn't like Anna-Lisa to let a man get to her like this.

'Yeah, that's seriously out of order, Anna. You need to have a word with him,' said Aidey.

'Oh, I'm alright, just a bit brassed off with him, that's all; it feels like he's taking me for granted. Anyway, enough about that boring old fart, I'm not going to let him take the edge off us enjoying our food.'

Their conversation was interrupted by the loud rattle of coffee beans being ground in the machine, filling the air with their delicious aroma.

'How's your lovely mum, Aidey?' Mim felt a change of subject would be helpful.

'She's good thanks. In fact it's her fiftieth coming up soon, so Hamish and me are keen to get her a really nice gift. We thought a day of pampering over at Kirkbythwaite Hall Hotel followed by dinner and an overnight stay for her and Dad would go down well.'

'Ooh, that sounds lovely and thoughtful; she'll love that. And I can't believe Shona's going to be fifty, she could easily pass for a good ten years' younger,' said Mim.

'She so could.' Anna-Lisa nodded in agreement.

'I'll tell her you said that, it'll make her day,' Aidey said with a smile.

Mim had a soft spot for Aidey's mum whom she'd met on a few occasions when she'd popped into the Yorkshire Portions office. She was a bubbly, friendly woman with a trim figure thanks to her dedication to Pilates and running. She sported a short asymmetrical bob with a scattering of subtle, golden highlights. Mim loved how she wore skinny jeans and crisp white shirts with chunky brown brogues; she was fashionable but not in a way that didn't suit her age. It was fair to say she was the polar opposite of Mim's mother who favoured anything that was too short and too tight, and if it was too revealing, then even better. Her clothes most certainly didn't suit her age.

'So you don't think she'd rather have something to keep, you know, something, like an object, to remind her of her fiftieth?' Aidey asked.

'No way. She'll come away with heaps of wonderful memories of her time there and they last forever,' said Mim.

'Plus the fact it'll mean a lot to her that you and Hamish put thought into the gift, knowing how much she'd enjoy it. And, to be honest, I think it's a bit old fashioned to buy presents as keepsakes for milestone birthdays,' said Anna-Lisa. 'After all, who wants to clutter up their home with stuff that just reminds you you're getting older?'

'Oh, right. I didn't think of it like that,' said Aidey.

'And, what you could do, rather than just hand her an envelope with the voucher in, is pop over to Kirkbythwaite Hall Hotel and buy a box of the products they use in the spa there, then wrap them up with the envelope.' Mim felt pleased with herself that she'd come up with this idea.

'Good plan, Mimbo.' Anna-Lisa nodded.

'Oh, I like the sound of that; we were actually wondering how we could make it look like a nice gift, there's not a lot you can do with a humble envelope really. And they actually sell the stuff they use, do they?'

'I believe so, and it's supposed to be absolutely gorgeous, too,' said Mim.

'Wow, I'm really chuffed I ran it by you two, I'd never have thought of that. I'll mention it to Mish tonight.'

'Glad we could be of service.' Mim beamed.

'Anyway, with that sorted, I don't suppose either of you have any idea what's going on at work?' Aidey asked. 'Surely you can sense the atmosphere as much as I can, it seems to have intensified since last week. I've got a horrible feeling some more changes are going to be sprung on us and it isn't half making me feel uneasy. There was a lot of whispering going on between Susan and Simon this morning when I walked past her office; I got the impression they weren't very happy to see me at work so early; like they were wanting to discuss things without anyone else being there. It was very odd.'

'It's not just you, Aidey, me and Mim can sense it, too. I mean it's bad enough the way you two have been treated without worrying about other things happening.'

Mim nodded. 'And don't forget what happened with poor old Dennis who suddenly left or was sacked, or who knows what, so Simon could take over the accounts,' said Mim. 'And is that legal anyway, to push someone out of their job without any notice? It's like what they did with Aidey.'

'I don't suppose the Pallister-Biggs care whether anything's legal or not; they just seem to do what they like and bugger the consequences; they just bully their way to get what they want. And since when does Simon know anything about accounts?' asked Anna-Lisa.

'Since he took Dennis's job apparently. And I honestly don't know how he's going to manage that role as well as being the production manager, but I dare say we'll find out sooner or later. Having said that, Clarissa's always carried him anyway, so she'll be the one who has the problem of the extra workload,' said Aidey.

'Makes you wonder what other nasty surprises Susan and Kenneth have up their sleeves,' said Anna-Lisa wryly.

'Ughh! Don't, say that. There's so much going on my brain can't keep up.' Mim's shoulders sagged.

'Same here,' said Anna-Lisa.

'And have either of you noticed the car Simon's suddenly driving?' asked Aidey. 'It's seriously flash and will have cost a fortune. I've no idea how he'd be able to afford that. I mean, I know his aunt owns the magazine, but his wages aren't going to be that high, are they?'

'Is that the swanky motor that's parked beside Susan's battered old banger out the back of the office?' asked Anna. 'I thought it must've been some cheeky person parking there without permission. Did make me wonder why the old bag wasn't up in arms about it.'

'Yep, it's his.'

'It's the same with Caspar and his fancy wheels, I suppose,' said Anna-Lisa.

Ughh! Mim's heart sank to her boots.

'I wonder how he's managed to afford it?' she continued, looking enquiringly at Mim.

'He works for his parents at the weekends sometimes; they have a company apparently, and he helps them out. From what I can gather, they're quite well-off so maybe they pay him well.' Her cheeks started to burn and she felt herself squirm under the weight of two sets of eyes boring into her.

'Oh, right,' said Anna-Lisa.

Mim could sense the cogs of her friend's mind going into overdrive, while Aidey just remained quiet. She didn't know which was more unnerving.

'So, what do they do?' asked Anna-Lisa.

'I'm not really sure; he didn't say.' In truth, he'd been pretty evasive when Mim had asked him. He'd managed to confuse her such that she felt if she asked more, she'd have made herself sound stupid. And she didn't want to sound stupid to Caspar.

'Well, if he was going to tell you, I dare say he'd have done it before now. After all, he's had plenty of opportunity when you've been in the car together. He seems more than happy to share the details of everything else he does,' said Aidey.

Not quite *everything*, thought Mim. She couldn't shake the feeling there was a huge black, swirling hole full of Caspar's secrets.

'Hmm, the Dark Count; just remember what we said about being careful, Mim,' said Anna-Lisa. 'There's definitely something dodgy lurking behind those dark eyes.'

Mim wished Anna-Lisa would ease up on the criticism of Caspar; it was having the unwelcome effect of galvanising her own concerns about him, and she hadn't found the courage to face them yet. But she wasn't going to fall out with Anna over it; she knew she meant well. 'Hey, you two, I thought we weren't going to spoil this gorgeous food by talking about work. I think we should change the subject to what we're having for pudding. And, can I just say, there's a cheeky salted caramel muffin winking at me from the cake stand over there on the counter. One of those in a bowl with a huge dollop of butterscotch ice cream beside it, drizzled with toffee sauce. Mmm-mm. Oh, yes indeedy.' Mim rubbed her hand across her stomach.

'I'm surprised you've got room, especially since you've eaten half of Aidey's food,' said Anna-Lisa, laughing.

'Where salted caramel muffins are concerned, I've always got room.'

15

THE TENSE ATMOSPHERE at Yorkshire Portions stood in stark contrast to the warm and happy one they'd just left at the Nutmeg Tree. The three friends exchanged unhappy glances as they made their way up the stairs and along the landing.

'Where've you lot been? You've had way longer than an hour for your lunch break.' They'd just got through the door to their office when Honey pounced. 'And Auntie Susan's not very happy.'

Oh, what now? 'Why, what's happened? And I haven't had more than an hour for my lunch break, I didn't leave here until I'd finished speaking to you,' said Mim.

'Didn't realise you were keeping tabs on us.' Anna-Lisa shot Honey a black look as she shrugged off her coat. 'And anyway, the three of us regularly work through our lunch break or work late; if we sat down and added it all up I think you'd find we're owed weeks' worth of time in lieu.'

'It's your problem if you choose to work late without running it by the bosses,' said Honey.

'I'm sure they wouldn't begrudge us an extra ten minutes on our lunch today,' said Aidey. 'Anyway, what's Susan getting het up about?'

All eyes were on Honey who was clearly getting immense pleasure out of delivering her news. 'Her pen's gone missing; you know, the expensive one.'

'It's her pen now? She's always loosing stuff, it'll turn up,' said Mim.

'I don't know why she insists on buying expensive things if she just keeps losing them. We must've wasted hours of work time looking for things she's lost over the years,' said Anna-Lisa.

'Yeah, well she's seriously angry about this, apparently it's worth nearly two hundred quid. She said she hasn't used it at all this morning so thinks someone must've been in her desk or her bag and taken it deliberately.'

Anna-Lisa tutted. 'Yeah, like one of us would do that. She's probably left it at home. And that's a serious allegation, accusing someone of stealing; are you sure she actually said that?'

'Of course I'm sure, I don't just make things up you know. And she said she hadn't left it at home, she brought it to work this morning. She's had that new intern girl, what's-her-name?'

'Tamsin,' said Mim.

'Yeah, her, hunting all over for it.'

'And no doubt you helped her look,' said Anna-Lisa.

'Me? No, I was too busy.'

'There's a shock.' Anna-Lisa shot a knowing glance over at Mim and Aidey. 'I don't know about you two, but I'm not too concerned about this, it'll just be the same as all the other times Susan's lost stuff. We can have a quick scout about, but I'm not going to waste too much time over it, I've got too much to do.'

'Yep, same here,' said Aidey.

'Shame you were back late then, isn't it? And I don't think Auntie Susan would be very pleased if she heard about your couldn't-care-less attitude; if I were you, I'd be keeping my eyes seriously peeled for it.' She looked pointedly in Mim's direction. 'We don't want her to think we've got anything to do with it going missing, do we?'

'And what's that supposed to mean?' asked Anna-Lisa.

'Nothing, I was just saying. Auntie Susan said the pen means a lot to her, that's all, apparently it was a gift from Kenneth.'

'If it means so much to her, it makes you wonder why she doesn't take better care of it,' said Aidey wearily as he switched on his computer.

'My thoughts exactly,' said Anna-Lisa.

Mim hung up her coat and got settled back at her desk. The way Honey had looked at her just then, and the obvious pleasure in her eyes as she was reporting what had happened made Mim feel unsettled, but she couldn't quite put her finger on why. If she didn't know better, she'd say Honey had taken the pen; the girl's covetous nature was nothing new, maybe she didn't discriminate; men, jobs, pens. But then again, like Anna-Lisa said, theft was a serious allegation, and, much as she disliked Honey, Mim felt bad just thinking about it. No, she was sure the silly pen would turn up, just like it always did. At least, she hoped it would.

16

Caspar pulled up outside Pear Tree Cottage. He turned to Mim, the familiar glint in his eyes. He leaned in and kissed her, sending her heart leaping about in her chest. 'Listen, why don't we leave it a few minutes before you go and get the dog? You know how he doesn't like me, and I'd like to have a bit of time, just you and me, without the distraction of him barking and snarling. I'm sure your friend won't mind.'

'Oh, right.' Mim was distracted by the taste of him as she tried to marshal his words. How long was he intending to stay for? His request suggested not long. Had she read that right? She couldn't stop thinking about the delicious effect his lips on hers had created, which was currently working its way through her body; desire fuelling the anticipation of picking up where they'd left off in the crumpled sheets of her bed on Saturday morning. How she wanted that so badly. Is that what he intended? Would Carly feel Mim was taking advantage of her if she didn't go and collect Herbert straight away? As she processed her thoughts, all the while, snaking around them was a little niggle that he'd referred to Herbert as "the dog", despite being well aware of his name. She didn't like how he'd sounded dismissive, it rankled with her loyalty to Herbert. She pushed that peeve briskly away, choosing to ignore it, telling herself he didn't mean anything by it; it was just his way, and she was just being petty by letting it bother her. But she knew, deep down, if anyone else had done the same, she'd have put them straight – albeit very nicely. Herbert was so much more than just a dog, as anyone who knew him would testify. And, much as it went against her better judgement that she'd be taking advantage of Carly, she found herself agreeing to Caspar's request.

Once inside the house, he pushed her up against the wall in the hallway, his lips pressing urgently on hers. She dug her fingers into his hair as he pushed her skirt up and tore at her tights. He fumbled in his pocket for the small foil packet, his mouth never leaving hers. He picked her up and she wrapped her legs around him, their lovemaking over with in a flash. 'You drive me crazy, you know that, don't you? I couldn't wait a second longer for you,' he said. His warm breath on her neck sent a thrill deep to the pit of her stomach.

'That was amazing,' she said, her heart still pounding as she smoothed her skirt down. 'I'll just get my breath back, then I'll go and get Herbert while you make yourself at home by sticking the kettle on.'

He pushed his floppy black fringe back with his fingers. 'Ah, about that, you see, I can't stop this time, but I so desperately needed a fix of you, Mim. And from what I could see, you felt the same; hit the spot, didn't it?' He kissed her again, fixing her with his dark eyes. She looked into them, trying to read him, but it was useless, all she could see were deep pools of black; it was anyone's guess what was swirling behind them.

Disappointment landed with a thud on her shoulders, dampening her mood. 'Oh. You don't even have time for a quick coffee?' She hoped she didn't sound needy.

'Sorry, darling, I have to get to my parents' house. Urgent business I'm afraid.'

'Oh. Okay, of course.'

'I'll see you in the morning, usual time.' He kissed her once more before he left.

Mim closed the door, resting against it while her mind caught up with what had just happened. She couldn't help but feel that her latest romantic encounter with Caspar was a little bit "wham, bam, thank you, ma'am". Yes, her passion had matched his in urgency, and the experience had been hot and heady, but she'd hoped he'd at least stay for a coffee afterwards, not shoot off practically before he'd had time to pull his zipper up. *Ah, but he'd wanted me so badly, even though he was pushed for time and in a hurry to get to his parents. He shouldn't really have been here, or even given me a lift home, but he did, just so he could spend time with me.*

Mim's thoughts had the pacifying effect she hoped they would; the last thing she needed after such a crappy day was to feel she'd been used, or worse, simply used for sex. She shuddered at that thought.

'Right, I'd best go and get Herbert,' she said aloud. She ran her fingers through her hair in attempt to straighten it, and headed through the door.

As ever, Herbert hurtled towards her as soon as Carly opened the door, his tail wagging so hard his whole body wiggled. Mim couldn't help but smile. 'Hello, lad, I hope you've been good.' His tail wagging came to an abrupt halt as he reached her, his nose sniffing at her legs, the happiness in his body language slipping away. Mim went to straighten her tights which were feeling a little uncomfortable, not to mention that things felt unusually draughty down there. She noticed Carly's eyes drawn to her legs and followed her gaze to see huge, glaring holes looking back at her, accompanied by bold ladders running down the full length, all the way to her boots. 'Oh!'

'Been having fun?' Carly giggled, arching a knowing eyebrow at her.

'Oh, I, er, I'm not sure how that's happened.' She could feel her face flaming and hoped her friend wouldn't notice in the soft hues of the light by the door.

'I bet I could hazard a guess.'

Carly's amused smile made Mim giggle. 'Uhh! Sorry.'

'What on earth are you sorry for?'

'For not calling straight round for Herbert when you've been looking after him all day.'

Carly looked at her watch. 'You're not that much later than usual, and he's no trouble at all. Must've been a real quickie.' She gave a knowing smile.

Mim clamped her hands over her face and groaned, her blushes intensifying.

'Hey, there's nothing wrong with that; I can remember me and Owen having to grab a few whenever the opportunity presented itself. Needs must and all that.'

Mim laughed and pulled a face. 'It's just been a bit of a crappy day, and Caspar couldn't hang around for long.'

'You don't say.' Carly's eyes twinkled with amusement. 'And you do know you'll have made the curtain twitcher's day, don't you?'

'Oh, no, I hadn't thought of that.'

'Well, I wouldn't worry about it; you're a grown woman, allowed to do what you please as long as you're not hurting anyone – which you aren't. It's not like you're running naked down the street or anything.'

'I can promise you, I have no plans to run naked around the village – or anywhere else for that matter! And on that note, I'll get this boy home. Thanks again for having him, Carly, I really appreciate it.'

'No probs at all, chick.'

'That's good to hear.' Mim ruffled Herbert's ears. 'Right, come on, young man, let's get back for a snuggle in front of the fire. See you, Carly.'

'See you, hon.'

MIM WAS STIRRING a pan of baked beans on the hob, anxiety building inside her as her thoughts wandered on to her brief encounter with Caspar, and what Aidey and Anna-Lisa had said about him earlier. Was he really sniffing around Clarissa? The ringtone of her mobile phone drew her back into the present. She slid the pan off the heat and followed the sound, first checking her coat pockets before realising it was coming from her bag which was hanging on the hook beside it. She lifted it down and set it on the kitchen table but the ringing had stopped before she'd had chance to find it. Though her bag was new, it was already full of her usual junk as she'd simply transferred the contents of her backpack straight across to this one with the plan to sort through it all later. It was a habit she'd developed with each new bag, gathering clutter and detritus that just grew and grew. 'I really must go through this lot.' She pulled out empty sweet packets, one of which was now home to a dried out piece of chewing gum that she'd got tired of and had nowhere to get rid of so had just popped in the old paper bag with a view to putting it in the next available bin. Which, of course, never happened. 'Well, that can get chucked for starters.'

She opened the bag wide as she began rummaging around in the clutter. She pulled out a spare pair of knickers she hadn't seen for months. 'Why?' They were followed by her favourite lipstick she'd thought was lost forever; on close inspection it might as well have been since the lid had come off and all sorts of unpalatable gritty bits were stuck to it. 'I am such a minger,' she said. She found an ancient manicure set. 'Think I'll keep this, who knows when it could come in handy.' Her voice tailed off as her eyes alighted on the last thing she expected to see in there: a turquoise-blue pen. She lifted it out, her eyes taking in the details. 'Oh, shit!' Her heart started pounding hard against her chest as a feeling of worry prickled up her spine. It wasn't just any pen, it was Susan's pen.

Mim leaned against the table, her hand pressed to her mouth, as panic flooded her body. 'How the hell did that get there?' Thoughts were running riot around her mind, none of them making any sense. What was going on? She'd never used the pen. Ever. She never would! And she hadn't even set eyes on it today – until just now. The only time she'd touched it was when she'd found it in some random place a few weeks previously and taken it back to Susan. Mim knew for certain she hadn't put the pen in her bag. She was the first to admit she was a scatterbrain – messy, clumsy even – but she didn't take other people's belongings. Someone must have planted it there, and the more she thought about it, the more she began to realise there was only one person who would do something like that: Honey. She cast her mind back to the conversation they'd had in the office when Honey was telling them with such relish that the pen was missing. At the time, Mim had felt sure Honey was up to something devious, but it hadn't crossed her mind that it would be something as potentially dangerous as this. Honey's childish, playground behaviour had been cranked up several notches. Mim suddenly felt very scared.

Sensing her distress, Herbert trotted over to her, his claws clicking on the quarry tiles. He sat beside her and looked up with concerned brown eyes. 'Oh, Herbert, I have no idea what's going on, but I'm worried.' He responded with a whimper and a swish of his tail. Mim bent to smooth his ears, his velvety fur soft and reassuring beneath her fingertips.

She stood for a moment, trying to make sense of her thoughts, when her phone started to ring again, making her jump. She put the pen on the table and delved into her bag, finding her phone, relieved to see it was Anna-Lisa's number. 'Hi, Anna.'

'Hi, Mim, are you okay? You sound upset.'

'I am, upset that is.' Mim's voice wavered and she felt her eyes brimming with tears. 'I don't know what to think or why it's even happened.'

'Oh, chick, don't cry. Is it Caspar?'

'No, it's nothing to do with him but, Anna, you won't believe what's happened. I'm just so shocked and scared, and I really don't know what to do about it.'

'What do you mean? Do you need me to come over? I can be there in half an hour.'

'No, honestly, don't trouble yourself, I'll be fine, it's just I've, well … oh, jeez, it's Susan's pen … I've, er, found it.'

'Well, we always knew it would turn up, you know what the daft old bat's like. So, where was it?'

Mim swallowed as a fat tear rolled down her cheek. 'It was in my bag.'

A couple of beats fell before Anna-Lisa answered. 'Which bag?'

'The bag I had at work today.'

More silence.

'Your new black bucket bag?'

'Yes.'

'How the hell did it get in there?' Mim could hear the frown in her friend's voice.

'I have no idea.' Mim's heart was thudding so loud, she felt sure Anna-Lisa would be able to hear it. 'I swear on my life I didn't put it there, Anna. I hadn't seen it at all today until just before you rang. It was when I was looking for my phone that I found it. Got the shock of my life.'

'I'm not surprised.'

'I honestly don't know how it got there. Somebody else must've put it in there, or it might've fallen in if Susan had left it on my desk or something.'

'But don't you remember, Honey said Susan hadn't seen it all morning – not that that means anything, or Honey could've got it wrong. But, listen, don't worry, I believe you didn't put it in your bag, chick, but I'm getting pretty fed up of all the weird stuff that's going on at work; it's unsettling as well as being bloody annoying.'

'I agree, but how did it end up being in my bag of all places?'

'I don't know, unless…' Anna was silent for a moment, Mim

could almost hear the cogs whirring. 'It's Honey! The little witch! I'd put money on it being her, it has her nasty little hallmarks all over it. My sister said things like this started happening when she worked at White Sprite Media, and it looks like she's up to her sly bloody tricks again.'

Relief washed over Mim as her friend vocalised thoughts that matched her own. The last thing she needed was for Anna to start doubting her or thinking her capable of theft. 'I must admit, Honey's was the first name that sprang to mind, once I'd got over the shock of seeing it there. But why would she do something like that? Surely she'd know the implications for me? It makes me look like a thief; I could potentially lose my job over it.'

'Yeah, well, she's not going to get away with it, but we need to get that pen back to Susan first thing before Honey gets a chance to start stirring things up.'

'Well, that won't give us long; she makes trouble as soon as she sets foot through the door.'

'Listen, I'm going to come over to yours tonight. You can give me the pen and I'll go to work early in the morning and sneak it back in Susan's room before anyone gets there.'

'Are you sure you don't mind?' Mim sniffed and dashed her tears away with the tips of her fingers. 'I feel bad involving you, and won't Caleb be huffed if you leave him on his own and come here?'

'Course not; he can fend for himself, he's a big boy. And anyway, he's in his computer room on his bloody game as per usual; I'll probably be back home before he's even noticed I've gone. But please don't feel bad, you're my best mate and you're having a horrible time of it at the moment so I'm coming over. All I ask in return is you save me some of what you're having for tea; not that I'm too hungry after that awesome lunch we had at the Nutmeg Tree.'

'Beans on toast do?'

'Ever thought about entering cooking competitions with those culinary skills?'

Mim managed a small laugh. 'The thought had crossed my mind. Tell you what, how about I grate some cheese on top; take it up another level?'

'Sounds good.'

'Fab, I won't have mine till you're here, we can have some wine with it, Lord knows I could do with a drink.'

'Hey, don't let anyone ever tell you we don't know how to live; beans on toast washed down with supermarket wine.' Anna-Lisa gave a throaty laugh.

'I know, we're a couple of stylish birds, aren't we?'

'You'd better believe it. Right, hon, I'll see you in half an hour.'

'See you, Anna. And drive carefully, it's foggy out there.'

'Will do.'

Mim felt her mood lift a little; she was lucky to have such a loyal friend as Anna, Aidey too. She wondered what he'd make of things when he found out; she hoped he wouldn't doubt her, think, for even the tiniest of moments, that she'd taken the pen. Her mind segued to Honey. *Jeez, that girl has certainly made an impact in the short time she's been at Yorkshire Portions.*

She pulled out a chair and flopped down, absent-mindedly sorting through the contents of her bag as she got lost in her thoughts. From the moment she'd arrived Honey had seemed determined to get everyone's back up – well, except for the Pallister-Biggs and Caspar. And it was becoming increasingly obvious she'd got it in for Mim. But Mim couldn't understand why. Yes, there was a history of bad blood between the two of them, but it should be Mim who felt bitter towards Honey, not the other way around. After all, it was Honey who'd stolen Mim's boyfriend, and it was Mim's heart that had been left shattered, her pride battered and bruised. For a fleeting moment she wondered what had happened between Honey and Rick. The only time the girl had mentioned him was on her first morning at Yorkshire Portions but, judging by her behaviour, there was nothing to suggest that they were still an item. *Honey probably got what she wanted, and then, "boom!" it suddenly lost its appeal; it wasn't shiny and new anymore and, more importantly, it didn't belong to someone else.*

But that didn't explain why Honey was still hounding her; why she appeared to dislike her so intensely that it had manifested in her going to such lengths as trying to make Mim look like a thief. Mim hadn't put up a fight for Rick; she'd quietly accepted defeat without challenging either of them. She'd simply disappeared. Honey had won and Mim had melted away, humiliation and hurt haunting her for months afterwards. And if there were any tiny scraps left in the dust to fight over, she had no appetite for it. She'd moved on. But it was looking increasingly like Honey hadn't.

Mim heaved a sigh. If she was honest with herself she knew the answer to Honey's latest grievance with her: Caspar. If the three friends had learnt one thing since Honey's first day at the office, it was that she couldn't hide her jealous and vindictive streak. But what had started out as snide comments appeared to have taken a sinister turn, and that scared Mim.

17

THERE WAS a rap at the door followed by a voice shouting through the letter-box: 'Little Mim, let me come in!'

Mim smiled and jumped up from her seat, while Herbert barked and trotted off down the hall. 'Coming,' she called back, feeling suddenly brighter at hearing her friend's voice. She opened the door to see Anna-Lisa on the step looking tiny, snuggled up in her roomy overcoat and a thick scarf, mist swirling around her in the muffled light of the street lamps.

Mim did her best to muster up a smile as she felt the threat of fresh tears brewing. 'I'm so glad to see you.'

'And I'm chuffed to bits to see you again, even if it is just a couple of hours since I last saw you.' Anna-Lisa laughed.

Mim felt her tears abate as a giggle took their place. Good old Anna. 'Mmm. Never thought of that.'

'Anyway, come 'ere, chick.' Anna stood on her tip-toes and pulled Mim into a tight hug, enveloping her in the scent of the cold night air and a heady mix of hair products. 'It'll be alright, you know. I'll make sure of it. That little witch doesn't know what she's messing with.' She rubbed her hand in sympathetic swirls over Mim's back.

'That sounds like fighting talk to me.'

'You'd better bloody believe it. Now, come on, let's have a look at this flaming pen. Hello, there, Herbert.' She bent to ruffle the Labrador's ears.

'Are you sure Caleb doesn't mind you coming here?' asked Mim.

'Not a bit; he was ensconced in his precious games room when I got back home from work, couldn't tear his eyes away from his bloody computer screen when I went in and said hello. He just grunted at me and carried on as if I wasn't there. Honestly, chick, he probably hasn't even noticed I've gone.' Her voice tailed off as she cast a critical eye around the kitchen. She shrugged off her coat. 'I see you've managed to keep this place tidy, well, except for the pile of junk on the table.'

'Ah, that's just me having a sort out of my bag.'

'Your new one?'

'Yeah.'

'It needs a sort out already?'

'I got into the habit of just transferring whatever was in the one I'd been using to the one I wanted to use next, turns out it's not such a good idea. I've found all sorts of grotty stuff, including a train ticket to Newcastle from two years ago and a packet of mints that look like they belong in a museum.'

'Sounds about right, you little scruff.'

Anna-Lisa was like a welcome ray of light. She hadn't even got through the door before she'd already made Mim feel brighter.

Anna walked over to the table and picked up the pen, examining it closely. 'Well, it's definitely Susan's; I don't know anyone else who has a pen like this. And I think we're pretty certain how it got into your bag. And I think I know when the little witch did it.'

'You do?'

'Yeah, I reckon it was when you went along to Clarissa's office this afternoon. I noticed Honey watching you; she jumped up as soon as you'd left the room, made some excuse about needing to look for something on your desk. I remember thinking it was a bit strange, and I did wonder at the time why she'd waited till you'd gone out. She was rooting around for a while and could have very easily dropped the pen into your bag then, with it having an open top like it has.'

'The devious little madam.' Mim took a moment to mull Anna's theory over. 'But why do you think she did it, what motive do you think she has? It's not like I've done anything horrible to her, and she knows as well as I do that I cover for her at work; the standard of the stuff she actually completes is pretty shocking and there's no way I could show it to Susan. Honey knows I have to change most of it, that I'm doing her a favour, and she doesn't seem at all bothered by it. Surely she can see that trying to set me up and essentially get rid of me won't be doing her any favours in the long run.'

'I don't think she thinks that far ahead. And I reckon her motive is Caspar. She's jealous of him giving you a lift to and from work; she's always wittering on about it when you're not in the room, it drives Aidey and me bonkers. Plus the fact that he asked you to go to his office today and not her, it's obviously pushed her jealousy over the edge. I'm afraid I think you're going to have to watch her.'

'Don't say that, Anna, it makes me feel really nervous.'

'Don't be nervous; don't let her win.'

'I can't help it, like you said, she's devious, and she's trying to make me look like a thief; that's really serious.' Mim paused. 'Does Aidey know what's happened?'

'He does, I called him after I'd spoken to you – I didn't think you'd mind, and I didn't think you'd call him 'cos you sounded like you were too upset to.'

'I was, I am. What did he say? He didn't think I'd taken the pen, did he?'

'Don't be so daft, of course he didn't! He was furious that it had been planted in your bag but said to tell you not to let it get to you – he's sure Honey's behind it, too, but we've got your back, we just need to make sure the little witch knows it.'

The fact that Aidey didn't think she was a thief was a relief; it mattered more than she could express that he trusted her.

'Aidey and me will watch her like a pair of hawks. We've already decided there's always got to be at least one of us in the room at all times so she won't get the chance to do this again.'

'Thank you, Anna, I really appreciate your help.'

'Hey, you're my best buddy, what else would I do? And I know you'd do exactly the same if the shoe was on the other foot.'

'I would, but thank you all the same, it's like having a weight lifted off my shoulders that you and Aidey are so supportive. I don't know what I'd do without the pair of you.' She pulled Anna into a tight squeeze.

'Watch out! You're going to strangle the life out of me if you're not careful.' Anna laughed. 'Now, I seem to recall you promised you'd feed me. Wasn't there talk of some beans on toast with a cheeky little grating of cheese to add that extra touch of luxury?' She put her hands on Mim's shoulders and guided her towards the oven.

'Hey, don't mock it, beans on toast is as good as it gets here, ask

Herbs. And with some cheese grated on the top, well, that's pretty much my full culinary repertoire you're getting tonight.'

'Now don't go selling yourself short; you've been known to do a mean fish finger butty, and I swear no one can slather tomato ketchup or dollop mayonnaise as expertly as you.'

'Ah, so true.' Mim couldn't help but giggle. 'I'll put the beans on while you get the wine from the fridge.'

'Sounds like a plan, but if it's okay with you, I'll skip the wine since I'm driving and the fog was like a thick pea soup on the way over here; it's chance to be even worse on the way back so I'll need my wits about me.'

'You could always stay here for the night, the spare bed's made up – remember, you put fresh bedding on it the other day when we had the blitz on the place.'

Anna-Lisa smiled. 'Thanks for the offer, but I haven't brought my toothbrush or a change of clothes with me and I don't think anything you've got will fit; last time I tried a pair of your jeans on they went up to my armpits and hung over the ends of my feet. Not a good look. And, anyway, I want to get to work bright and early so I can get that pen back in the dragon's room.'

'Oh, right, of course, thanks, Anna.' Mim's chest tightened at the reminder of the pen.

'You don't have to keep thanking me.'

'Okay, sorry.'

Mim slid the pan of beans on the hob again then popped four chunky slices of bread in the toaster while Anna set the table, all under the watchful gaze of Herbert who was curled up in his bed.

'I quite fancy a mug of tea with my beans on toast, if that's okay, Mim.'

'Yeah, course, help yourself, you know where everything is. Come to think of it, I'll join you; I don't fancy drinking wine on my own like a saddo. And it's not exactly the best accompaniment to beans on toast.' The thought of washing her meal down with a large mug of builder's tea suddenly felt very appealing.

Mim hadn't realised just how hungry she was until she sat down at the table – stress always seemed to increase her appetite, much to her chagrin. Her stomach growled in appreciation as she popped a forkful into her mouth, savouring the flavour of melted cheese as it mingled with the tangy tomato sauce of the beans. Sometimes the simple things were the best. She felt herself relax a little as the knot of anxiety in her stomach slowly began to unfurl. 'Mmm. This is so good,' she said with a sigh.

'Mmm, it is. Cheers to comfort food.' Anna-Lisa picked up her drink and Mim followed suit as they clinked their mugs together. 'Cheers, chuck.'

'Cheers, Anna. I've got a tin of rice pudding if you fancy some for afters.'

'Is it that really creamy one?'

'Mmm-hmm.' Mim nodded.

'Ooh, that's my favourite; I'm definitely up for some of that.'

MIM SPOONED the rice pudding into two bowls and set them down on the table before dolloping a spoonful of strawberry jam in the middle of hers. She passed the jar to Anna-Lisa.

'Thanks, chick. So did you ever find out what happened with Honey and Rick?' she asked.

'Nope, no idea. And I don't want to know. I've moved on and I've wasted too much energy thinking about him; it just used to make me feel rubbish about myself and set me back.'

Anna-Lisa gave her a sympathetic look. 'Don't blame you; he's not worth making you feel like that. And he was punching way above his weight anyway. All your boyfriends that I've seen have been; present one included.'

'What do you mean?'

'You sell yourself short. Big time. Always have done.'

Mim thought for a moment, casting her mind back over her dating history. She hadn't had many boyfriends, but even she could see they all shared similarities, not just in looks but in attitude as well; they all displayed the same swaggering disregard for her feelings. And each and every relationship had ended in the same painful way, with her being taken for a mug and cheated on. Still, she thought, it didn't mean that they'd been, as Anna put it, "punching above their weight", it was just that she had a habit of choosing men who weren't exactly suited to her.

'But that's hardly the case with Caspar; it's more like the other way round,' Mim said. 'Even you have to admit, someone like him is way out of my league. I honestly don't know what he sees in me.' Her thoughts swept to Anna and Aidey's warning about him sniffing around Clarissa, then to seeing Caspar leaving Clarissa's office, his air of coolness towards her. It was glaringly obvious that a woman as stunningly beautiful and as classy as Clarissa was so much better suited to him than raggle-taggle Mim. No wonder he wanted to keep their relationship under wraps; he knew what the reaction would be if folk found out as well as she did. They'd laugh in disbelief, and say that it was Mim who was punching above her weight. Of that she was certain.

Anna gave Mim a stern look. 'It so isn't the other way round. He's the one who's punching, not you. And you need to keep that in mind, my girl.'

'What do you mean?'

Anna shrugged. 'Just that feeling he gives me I keep telling you about; call it women's intuition. But promise me you'll not be totally blinded by him; if you ever get a little niggle – no matter how tiny – you must listen to it. Don't let that heart of yours rule your head like it usually does. Promise me, Mim.' She was looking at her so intently, Mim found it slightly unsettling.

'Okay, I promise.'

'Good, I'll hold you to that. Now, on a more palatable subject, is there any more of that rice pudding left?'

'There is.'

'Then what are you waiting for?'

18

BY THE TIME Anna-Lisa had left for home, Mim was feeling much brighter. Between the two of them, they'd managed to put her latest worries into perspective.

It was getting late, and Mim took Herbert for a quick walk around the village, the pair of them returning soaked through thanks to the mist that had started to fall as a heavy mizzle. 'Ughh, Herbs, you smell like soggy cabbage again.' She found his towel and went to dry him, which wasn't easy when he saw it as a game. He tugged at the towel and wriggled around on the floor, his legs kicking out all over the place. 'Herbert, sit!' She tried injecting a firm tone into her voice, but he ignored her; he was clearly having way too much fun. Eventually, Mim managed to get the towel off him and he jumped to his feet, happiness shining in his eyes. It triggered a surge of affection through her. 'You do realise you're the naughtiest boy in North Yorkshire, don't you?' She laughed as he grabbed the towel between his teeth, tripping over it as he did a lap of the kitchen. 'Come here, you little rascal.' She chased after him and snatched the towel back, giving him one last vigorous rub down before he shot off again, indulging in a final roll around on the mat by the door.

'I'm exhausted after all that mischief!' In truth, it felt good to have her headspace occupied by Herbert and his escapades, instead of the worries that had begun to fill it up recently. Not for the first time was she glad he was in her life, especially at this time of night, when her thoughts had a habit of wandering off to the dark corners of her mind.

Herbert finished his fun, made his way over to his bed and flopped down in it. He glanced across at her and yawned.

'Yep, you're right, Herbs, it's that time of night. I think I'll make one of those special sleep-inducing cups of tea and go and have a soak in the bath, see if the combination works and I actually get a good night's sleep for once.' Mim had picked up some teabags from the village shop that were full of fragrant herbs whose powers, the blurb on the box claimed, would help lull you to a "soothing and restful sleep". She'd liked the sound of that and had popped them into her basket. Tonight would be the first time she'd tried them, and her expectations were high.

MIM SLIPPED into the bubbles of the bath, propping her feet up by the taps at the other end. She released a sigh as she savoured the warmth of the water lapping over her body, her anxiety slowly ebbing away. It felt delicious. Over the last week her body had developed some unwelcome aches and pains, mostly across her shoulders and in her neck. She was sure stress was responsible, creating tension in her muscles; she'd experienced the same thing when she'd broken up with Rick. It never ceased to surprise her how stress manifested itself in her body – not least the patch of psoriasis on her stomach which had increased in size, and had been joined by a new outbreak on the inside of her elbows. She ran her finger over the raised scaly patch; she'd keep an eye on it, make sure it didn't get out of hand. Much as she was reluctant to order a repeat prescription of the usual smelly cream from the doctor, she had to concede, it did the trick, and pretty quickly at that.

Closing her eyes, she lay back and drew in a slow, deep lungful of the soothing fragrance that lingered in the bathroom; it was courtesy of some expensive-looking bubble bath of Josie's that Mim wouldn't normally dare touch, but after the day she'd had she figured her sister wouldn't mind, just this once.

After what had happened with the pen, Mim wasn't expecting her body and mind to submit to relaxation so easily but, like Anna-Lisa had explained, if you put things into perspective, they were nowhere near as bad as they seemed. As far as Honey's behaviour was concerned, they were merely dealing with childish games, no more, no less. And they were nothing that couldn't be sorted.

As Mim continued her slow, rhythmic deep breathing, she felt a wave of relaxation spread from her shoulders, all the way down her body. She allowed herself to succumb to it, the sensation of sleep slowly wrapping itself around her. Oh, bliss! It was only when the sound of her own snort pulled her back to consciousness that she reluctantly heaved herself up and climbed out of the bath. She was hopeful this was a sign she'd sleep well tonight.

But as soon as Mim climbed into bed and rested her head on the pillow the feelings of unease returned, slowly creeping out from the shadows and stealing into her mind, their strength growing with every passing minute. In no time, her heart rate had accelerated and her pulse was thrumming in her ears.

'Ughh! Not this again.' She rubbed her eyes with the balls of her hands. She'd been sleeping better since Caspar had started showing her attention, images of him dominating her bedtime thoughts, scenarios of their future together playing out until she drifted off to sleep, not giving her usual worries the time of day. Yes, she'd had a good stretch by her standards, and had felt better for it, but after today's happenings, it would appear that her insomnia had returned with a vengeance. Once again, the tight feeling in her chest was making itself known. She turned onto her side, dragged the duvet up close to her chin and closed her eyes. Her body felt exhausted, surely her mind would feel that way soon.

Another hour dragged by with sleep still eluding her. Wearily, Mim heaved herself up, slid her feet into her slippers and, grabbing her dressing gown, she padded downstairs.

As she grated nutmeg over the surface of her drink, Mim was pleasantly surprised to find the comforting, spicy aroma triggered a memory of Grandma Joyce, of the times they'd sat together in the neat kitchen of Primrose Cottage when Mim hadn't been able to sleep, their whispered conversations punctuated by the soporific ticking of the clock on the wall.

A wave of happiness enveloped her as distant images swept through her mind, offering precious glimpses of happy times spent at her grandparents' house; the handmade quilt that had covered her bed, its pretty hexagons of little ditsy flowers in shades of pink, green and primrose yellow all painstakingly sewn together by the neat, uniform stitches of her great-grandmother. The memory made Mim smile. She remembered it being a little worn in places, slightly faded in others, but that hadn't detracted from its beauty; she'd loved it and the comfort it had brought as she snuggled beneath it.

More images floated into her mind's eye, sylph-like gossamer wisps, tantalising snatches of the pale pink wallpaper, decorated with cheerful sprigs of flowers that covered the walls of the room, the small Georgian windows trimmed with matching curtains. There was a fleeting glimpse of fingers of sunshine poking through the gaps on bright, spring mornings, their warmth caressing her face. Whenever Mim thought of the time she'd spent with her grandparents at their homely little cottage, it was always to the backdrop of a gloriously sunny day.

Mim popped the nutmeg back in its jar, smiling as she recalled the frothy mugs of warmed milk Grandma Joyce used to make for her and how they'd sit by the old range in the spotless kitchen, crocheted blankets wrapped around their shoulders, while Grandma Joyce told her stories of when she'd been a young girl in that very village, and of how she'd always known she was going to marry Grandad. 'I didn't let on to him, mind; I made him chase me. And he did just that, bless him; never gave up even when I made it hard work for him.' Fond tales that had soothed Mim, filling her with a sense of contentment, and coaxed her desire for sleep out of its hiding place.

Mim and Josie had been regular residents at her grandparents' two-up-two-down home when they were children, sleeping in what had been their mother's childhood bedroom. Jeanette had developed a nasty habit of upping and leaving the girls, unceremoniously dumping them with their grandparents while she pursued her latest love interest, without a backwards glance nor a hint of remorse. Mim remembered it as a confusing and unhappy time, and one that had become such a regular occurrence that Grandad had insisted they put an extra bed in the room. He'd even made a sign for the door with their names painted on it in pink swirly writing. This small gesture had a big impact on Mim. Somehow, labelling it as theirs had an inexorably galvanising effect on her; she could think of it as her home. Where she belonged.

Cradling the mug in her hands, Mim walked over to the kitchen table and sat down. She didn't like to think of how things would have turned out without the care and guidance of her grandparents. She sighed; how she wished they were here now, with their wise words and uncomplicated view of the world. Their loss a couple of years ago had hit her hard. Grandma Joyce was the first to go, the cruel spectre of dementia taking hold and ending her days at the age of seventy-two. Mim's grandfather had been beside himself with grief, there'd been no consoling him. But what could you say to a man who'd had his soulmate and wife of over fifty years snatched away? After the funeral he'd floundered, looking pitifully lost and helpless, all traces of the capable man he'd previously been obliterated by sadness. It had been distressing to see, and his expression still haunted Mim.

Adding to her heartbreak, he followed his beloved wife just three months later. It had been a bitter blow for his granddaughters, but where Josie had Russ to offer support and keep her grounded, Mim had no one, and had sunk her grief by throwing herself into bad relationship after bad relationship. Without realising, she was following the same sorry path as her mother, the one saving grace being there were no children involved to get hurt.

Herbert padded over to where Mim was sitting and with a noisy "harrumph" he flopped down at her feet. She looked down at him, envious of his contented life and his lack of worries.

19

Mim lay under the warmth of her duvet for a few minutes after the alarm had gone off, her mind a melting pot of worries – the first one being Honey and the dreaded pen. Anxiety bloomed in her chest. She tried to quash it, reminding herself that Anna-Lisa would secretly deliver the offending item back to its owner before anyone else got to work. Mim hoped it would go to plan; the worry that her friend risked getting caught with their boss's treasured pen gnawed at her and she knew she wouldn't be able to settle properly until it was back in Susan's room, and Anna was safe in hers. Mim was thankful she had a friend like Anna-Lisa; she didn't know what she'd do without her. Aidey, too.

She pulled the duvet up close around her chin; it was too dark and too cold outside to get up, and it was too snuggly and warm in her bed, plus she felt overwhelmingly tired. The prospect of facing the day and all it entailed just wasn't appealing, so Mim gave in to temptation and closed her eyes for a moment. But she knew she was too comfortable, and that was risky, so she forced her heavy eyes open until the danger of falling back to sleep became too great and she reluctantly heaved herself out of bed. Why did she find it so easy to fall asleep first thing in the morning, but nigh on impossible when she went to bed at night? It felt desperately unfair. She couldn't wait for the weekend and the lack of need for a hideous, piercing alarm; the only alarm she needed then was Herbert, and he wasn't keen on early mornings either.

Her thoughts turned to Caspar and how much she was looking forward to seeing him again. She savoured every minute of the time they shared, just the two of them, in the intimate environment of his car. The anticipation of the feel of his lips pressing against hers was building and sent a delicious thrill through her, making her wiggle her toes.

But later, as she watched for him from the living room window, it didn't stop her from harbouring a little niggle about having a lift to and from work with him, much as she relished it. After Honey's remarks during the grilling she'd given her the previous day, she'd felt a sense of guilt bloom. That girl was too pushy for her own good but, much as Mim hated to admit it, she did have a point; the bulk of the roadworks had gone, with just a handful of stragglers causing minimal disruption on the periphery of the city; they shouldn't really make her late for work now. Caspar had already confessed to her that he was going out of his way by picking her up and dropping her off. Maybe she should mention that she could go back to getting the bus; see what he had to say about it.

Having said that, it was a cold, miserable morning and the cottages of Skeltwick were shrouded in a heavy mist which was falling as a cold, soaking mizzle. Mim hated this type of weather, especially since it had a nasty habit of making her already unruly hair go frizzy; she'd got drenched when she'd dropped Herbert off at Carly's earlier and that was no distance. The thought of travelling to work in Caspar's fancy car had made her secretly pleased she didn't have to trek to the bus stop at the other end of the village where there was no shelter. Instead, she had the luxury of waiting for Caspar in the comfort of her home.

She glanced at the time on her phone; it confirmed her suspicions: he was late, which she'd already learnt wasn't at all like him – apart from when he'd had hot coffee splashed down the front of his crisp, clean shirt on his way to a new job, of course. If she'd known he was going to be this late, she'd have tried to do something with her frazzled frizz-bomb of hair. Was he still coming for her? They hadn't discussed it, but the fact that he'd picked her up yesterday suggested he was. Was he playing a game with her? She didn't think so, but she wished he'd text to say he was on his way and for her not to worry, but then again, he didn't have her number, and she didn't have his. The anxiety of waiting and not knowing was adding to the horrible nerves she'd woken up with.

~

FOR THE LAST ten minutes Mim had been nibbling on a hang nail until it stung, looking out of the window and craning her neck every time she heard the sound of car tyres swooshing along the wet road. The feeling of nausea she'd had when she first got up, rendering her unable to face any breakfast, had started churning around her stomach again. The time waiting for Caspar had given her time to dwell; after the pen incident, she was dreading what today had in store. It didn't help that he was now over ten minutes late.

Relief swept through her when he finally showed up, swinging his car in front of the cottage and pulling up with a whiplash halt. 'Thank goodness.' Wearing the smile his presence always seemed to trigger, she hurried out of the house, ducking out of the rain and into his car as quickly as she could. Her heart thrummed with excitement as soon as the now familiar scent of his expensive cologne and even more expensive new car filled her lungs. Her eyes locked with his, sending a bolt of lust right through her. *Woah! Talk about sensory overload! Calm your jets, Mim, you're on your way to work – and running late at that!*

'Sorry I'm late; I had some urgent business to attend to.' The kiss he pressed to her lips was lazy and loaded with meaning; he followed it up with a heart-melting smile. 'I'll still get you to work on time, don't worry, darling.'

'It's okay. I just appreciate that you come out of your way for me.' Reeling from the effect of his lips on hers, Mim resisted the urge to suggest they both call in sick and spend the day in bed. It would only arouse suspicion which wasn't what she needed when she was only just hanging onto her job by the skin of her teeth.

Caspar reached across and squeezed her knee, running his hand up her leg. 'Ah, but you're worth it, especially with your lovely long legs that drive me crazy.'

She shivered with delight, her smile getting wider as he drove off down the road and out of the village. *Am I dreaming? I must be. Either that or the lack of sleep has made me delusional and I'm just imagining all of this.* She surreptitiously pinched the underside of her leg between her forefinger and thumb to make sure, making herself jump in the process. 'Ouch!' *Nope, that was very real; I'm definitely not dreaming.*

'You okay?'

Mim nodded, rubbing where a bruise would no doubt develop.

'Yes, thanks. Though I was wondering, now that most of the road-works have finished and the buses shouldn't be running late anymore – well, hopefully, at least – would it be easier for you if I got the bus? It would save you having to trail over here twice a day when you don't need to.'

'Mim, darling, it's really not a bit of trouble to me, and as I've said, it's a good way of spending a little extra time with you, just the two of us without the prying eyes of work, but if that's what you'd prefer…'

'Oh, not at all … that's not what I meant … I mean, I love spending time with you, too, but I don't want you to think I'm being a nuisance or that I'm taking advantage of you. Or what if it makes people gossip? I know you're keen to keep quiet about us, and I totally get that, but, well, I just thought I'd better mention it.' *Ughh! Why do I always make a clumsy mess of these things?*

'Gossip's one thing, proof's another. And as far as work's concerned, they think I have a good reason to head this way – they think I'm doing something to help with my parents' company, which I have been doing sometimes, this morning for example – at least that's what I've told them, and they've no reason to think otherwise.'

'Oh, right, when you put it like that, I suppose it does make sense.'

'Then let's just leave things as they are, eh?' His disarming smile made her heart squeeze with happiness.

'Okay.'

Caspar pressed his foot hard on the accelerator as they made their way onto the A64. The low cloud had lifted but the rain had suddenly become much heavier, firing down from sky like well-aimed arrows before bouncing back up off the road. Visibility was poor and the thudding sound the rain was making on the roof of the car was almost deafening. 'This isn't much fun.' Caspar flicked the windscreen wipers, increasing their speed.

Mim tried to ignore her rising concern that he was driving a little too fast for the conditions. Her heart was in her mouth as he bombed through huge puddles, the car aquaplaning a couple of times. She tried to take her mind off her fear by gazing out of the window, watching the countryside and catching glimpses of the trees bending in the wind, but they were whizzing by in such a blur that it did little to help. She figured striking up a conversation would work better. 'Come to think of it, Aidey's given me a lift home loads of times which is right out of his way, and no one's ever gossiped about that; everyone just sees us as mates.'

'Hmm, not quite everyone.' He glanced across at her.

She wished he'd keep his eyes on the road. 'What do you mean?'

'I mean he… Woah! What the? … Jesus! Bloody maniac!' Without warning, the car swung violently into the side of the road, bouncing over the kerb as Caspar swerved to avoid colliding with a lorry that was relentlessly ploughing towards them, filthy spray flying up from its huge tyres and spattering the car's windscreen. The sound of beeping horns and screeching tyres filled the air around them.

Mim screamed, gripping onto her seat for dear life, her heart hammering hard against her chest as the car came to a halt in the open gateway to a field. She felt the burn where her seatbelt had dug into her shoulder. Her breath was coming out in shallow gasps. 'Oh, my God, that was absolutely terrifying! What happened?'

Caspar's usual composure had deserted him and he looked ashen as he rubbed his fingers across his brow. 'That was seriously close. That bloody lorry driver was on my side of the road, swerving round a car that had broken down by the looks of it. Stupid idiot should've waited until he had a clear stretch of road in front of him, instead of using his size to bully me out of the way. If I didn't have such sharp reflexes, we wouldn't … well, it doesn't bear thinking about. Idiots like him shouldn't be on the road. This car could've been ruined; it's worth a fortune. If it's got a scratch on it, I won't be responsible for my actions.' He turned to her. 'Are you okay?'

Traffic continued to whoosh by, the drivers concentrating on the road ahead, oblivious to the fact that they could've been caught up in a serious road traffic accident. Mim started shivering though it was anything but cold in the car. 'Yeah, I'm fine, thanks; a bit shocked, but okay.' In truth she was doing all she could to quell the urge to throw up, thinking of anything to take her mind off the feeling, and the fact that Caspar seemed more concerned about his fancy car than anything else. 'Are you okay?'

'I'm bloody furious, but I'm fine. Just glad my reactions are so sharp.'

'Me too. Will your dashcam have recorded the lorry's number plate do you think? Couldn't you report him to the police for dangerous driving?'

'It should've recorded the whole thing. But I don't think we'll need to trouble the police, it was a McHubbard & Smithy van, they're based on the outskirts of York and my parents use them regularly. They're a small firm so it shouldn't be difficult to track down the driver; that lunatic needs to be taught a lesson.' His expression had changed, his eyes looked cold and dark, almost sinister, it sent a prickle of fear over Mim's skin. She got the feeling that Caspar wasn't someone she'd like to get on the wrong side of.

20

By the time they arrived at the Yorkshire Portions office, Mim felt much calmer and, despite the fact she was dreading seeing Susan, she was glad to be there and out of the car. Yes, the lorry driver had been in the wrong, but if Caspar hadn't taken his eyes off the road and had been driving at a more sensible speed, they wouldn't have had to swerve so dramatically to get out of harm's way. It was a notoriously busy road, and today she couldn't shake the feeling they were lucky they'd come away with their lives. And she knew Caspar was aware of that, too.

'Just in time, Jemima, only three minutes to spare before Auntie Susan would be hauling you over the coals for your lateness. Again.' Honey moved her gaze away from the clock on the wall to Mim in a theatrical gesture, the familiar annoying smirk on her face that was just itching to be removed.

Mim slipped her coat off, shaking the rain from it before hanging it up; she'd got a soaking on the dash to work from where Caspar had parked his car. 'Well, I'm here now.'

'You all right, Mim? You look a bit pale,' said Anna-Lisa.

Mim gave a watery smile and nodded; she wasn't in the mood to elaborate in front of Honey nor tempt her arrogant opinions.

'You sure? Anna's right, you don't look very well. Can I get you anything; cup of tea?' asked Aidey.

'Ah, check out Florence Nightingale; always coming to your rescue, Jemima, and you just keep him dangling there by a little thread.' Honey mimed dangling something between her forefinger and thumb.

'Just drop it, Honey,' said Aidey.

Honey ignored him. 'Anyone would think you had something worrying you, Jemima. Care to share it?'

Mim's stomach lurched; she knew Honey was referring to the pen. Before she could answer, Anna-Lisa came to the rescue.

'Oh, just back off, will you, Honey? Mim's clearly not feeling well. And have you never heard of the expression, if you haven't got anything nice to say then just keep your big, fat mouth shut?'

'Er, not sure that's how the saying goes.' Honey folded her arms across her chest in a defensive gesture.

'Well, I reckon it does a better job of getting my point across.' Anna-Lisa glared at her.

Mim looked across at her loyal friend; she often wondered how such fierceness could come out of such a tiny, sweet-looking individual. Anna-Lisa was totally fearless when she got going; she took no prisoners.

'There's no need to take that tone with me,' said Honey.

Aidey sighed and shook his head. 'That's enough, Honey.'

Mim tried to make discreet eye contact with Anna-Lisa, hoping to get a hint of the current state of play with the pen, but she was giving nothing away; there was no way she'd risk giving the tiniest of hints to Honey that they'd rumbled her and were already one step ahead.

'Well, she's not my superior, she can't tell me what to do. And she should realise, if I decide I want rid of her, all I have to do is just click my fingers and she'd be gone, just like that.' She clicked her fingers to demonstrate. 'I have a lot of sway with my godmother; you'd all be well-advised to remember that.'

'I don't think there's any need for that, do you, Honey?' They all turned as Clarissa stepped into the office. She was armed with a cardboard cup carrier filled with a variety of hot drinks and a carrier bag containing what looked like breakfast pastries. 'I thought, as it was such a grotty day out there, we could all do with some yummy takeaway breakfast things from the Nutmeg Tree.' She set the drinks down on the desk next to Aidey and picked out a cup, reading the name penned onto it. 'Right, there's your coffee, Aidey – splash of milk, no sugar, Mim, chai tea latte for you, Anna-Lisa, tea – teabag left in. Honey, hot chocolate for you. Actually, Honey, can you just pop to the kitchen and grab some plates for the croissants and muffins, please?'

'Me?' Honey looked at her in disbelief.

'Yes, you.' Though Clarissa was smiling there was a firmness in her voice that indicated she'd brook no argument. Honey stood up and flicked her glossy dip-dyed hair, glaring at the others as she left the room.

Clarissa gently pushed the door to. 'I overheard what Honey was saying before I came in and want to tell you not to pay too much heed to it; she really doesn't have the power to get anyone sacked. I don't know why she says such things, other than she doesn't really understand the impact of her words, and she's a little immature for her age.'

'Hmph. You're telling me. I reckon she must be about twenty-two or twenty-three,' said Anna-Lisa. 'Way too old to be acting like that.'

'I think she's twenty-two,' said Clarissa.

'So, she's not much younger than Anna and Mim but she acts like a sassy fifteen-year-old with a serious chip on her shoulder; she's got a hell of a lot of growing up to do,' said Aidey.

Mim listened in silence. Her head was thumping and she felt indescribably tired. There was always so much to worry about at the moment. Her eyes found their way to the window, watching as the rain pounded against it, running in rivulets down the wonky Georgian glass, some trickling in through the tiny crack in the corner of one of the panes. She was half-aware of the muted conversation going on around her as her mind insisted on going over the earlier terrifying near-miss in the car. There was no doubting they'd been incredibly lucky not to have been involved in a potentially catastrophic accident. A shudder ran down her spine and she turned to Clarissa, her kind voice a welcome distraction.

'Yes, I think that's got a lot to do with her parents spoiling her as a child to compensate for them not spending much time with her while they concentrated on growing their business, plus the fact that her father has always treated her like a little princess who could do no wrong. I gather she ruffled a few feathers when she briefly worked for them which is why she's had to look for work elsewhere; her parents didn't want to risk losing staff they valued who'd worked for them for years. And I don't actually think she realises how her behaviour comes across, which you have to admit is unfortunate for her; she has a lot to learn. You lot will just have to make sure the wonderful way you are rubs off onto her.' Clarissa looked around at the three friends, smiling.

'Talk about mission impossible,' Anna-Lisa muttered, making them all laugh. 'And now you come to mention it, I can recall my sister saying something about how Honey had worked for her parents but that things hadn't worked out and that's why she'd joined White Sprite Media. I think Honey claimed the women were all jealous of her at her parents' company, or something like that. Anyway, she'd only been at White Sprite a matter of weeks before she had to leave.'

Mim flashed her friend a warning look in the hope that it would remind her that she was talking about a close friend of the Pallister-Biggs family. Anna-Lisa was fearless when it came to expressing her opinion, but with things being so volatile at Yorkshire Portions she didn't want Anna to say anything she might regret if it was reported back to the bosses. But maybe she was being unfair to Clarissa…

'Really?' said Clarissa. 'I actually feel a bit sorry for her; I've got a sneaking suspicion she's a bit insecure, so – and I know this won't be easy – if you could just be patient with her, maybe…'

Anna-Lisa snorted just as Honey huffed her way back into the office, plonking the plates noisily on the desk. 'There,' she said, and flounced over to her chair.

'Thank you, Honey. Right, get stuck in, folks. Enjoy.' With a smile, Clarissa turned to leave. 'Oh, and, by the way, I don't know if you're aware, but Mum found her pen. It had rolled under her desk and was hidden under a scrap of paper on the floor. Panic averted.'

'What?' Honey's shock was palpable. 'How did it get there? I thought everyone had checked everywhere.'

'She must've knocked it off her desk, it's easily done,' said Anna-Lisa, flicking a quick glance at Mim. 'And if it was under some paper, maybe Susan didn't think to look there.'

'I always knew it would turn up, it always does,' said Aidey. 'I was just a bit surprised at the drama it caused.'

'Same here,' said Anna-Lisa.

'Well, that's a relief.' Mim tried to sound casual as Honey's eyes bored into her.

'It is, we can all do without the hassle. I do wish she'd leave her precious stuff at home, as for that ring of hers … honestly, I'm going to have to suggest it to her again, though I doubt she'll listen.' Clarissa shook her head good-naturedly.

'What I don't get is that surely Auntie Susan will have looked everywhere in her office for the pen yesterday, including under her desk. Don't you think it's odd that she didn't spot it then? I certainly do.' Honey still hadn't taken her eyes off Mim, whose heart was hurling itself against the inside of her ribcage.

'I don't think it's odd at all, it's very Mum.'

'Really?' said Honey.

'Yes, really. Actually, Honey, if you could just pop down to my office for a word before you get started. It won't take long.'

'Me?'

'Yes.'

'Now?'

'Yes.'

'Before I have a croissant or anything?'

'Yes, as I said, it won't take long.'

'But what if they eat everything and there's nothing left for me?'

Anna-Lisa rolled her eyes. 'Jeez, give me strength. Why can't you follow a simple instruction without arguing about it?'

'We'll make sure we save something for you,' said Aidey. 'Looks like there's more than enough for everyone, anyway.'

'Now, please, Honey. I've got quite a busy day ahead of me, so I'd like to get on.'

They watched as Honey reached into the bag Clarissa had brought in, grabbed a pain au chocolat and a double chocolate muffin and set them on a plate by her desk. 'They're mine, okay?' She stomped past Clarissa and headed down the landing to her office.

'Good luck,' said Aidey to Clarissa.

'Yeah, make sure you're wearing your body armour,' said Anna-Lisa.

Clarissa gave a quick flick of her eyebrows and followed Honey.

Anna-Lisa turned to Mim, concern etched across her elfin features. 'Mim, chick, what's up? You look dreadful. I thought you'd be pleased that Susan's pen has "turned up".'

'Yeah, you don't look yourself at all,' said Aidey. 'Should you really be at work?'

Mim sat back in her chair and took a deep breath, rubbing her sore shoulder where the seatbelt had dug in. 'Yeah, I'll be fine. Thank you so much for doing that, Anna, I really appreciate it, and I'm more relieved than I can put into words but I'm feeling absolutely knackered. I think the stress of yesterday's caught up with me and I had the worst night's sleep last night; I don't think I managed two full hours together. And Honey's naturally suspicious about the pen being found; it's all adding up.'

'Yeah, well, that's behind us now, but it's a shame you had to lose sleep over it,' said Anna. 'I thought that had been getting better.'

'It had been, until the pen situation. But that's not the only reason I'm feeling rough; on the way here this morning, we nearly had a head-on crash with a lorry. It's really shaken me.' Her voice wavered.

'What?' Aidey sat up straight, his eyes full of concern.

'Honestly, we were a millisecond away from being taken out by it; we wouldn't have stood a chance.' She shuddered. 'I know I might sound dramatic and all that, but it was really scary and I honestly thought that was it … there was no way we would've come out of that alive.'

'Jesus, Mim. Was Caspar driving like a lunatic or something?' Aidey looked furious.

Mim swallowed; it wasn't like him to get angry and she didn't want to be the cause of any more bad feeling between the two men. She shook her head; it wouldn't help to mention that he'd been driving too fast and hadn't been looking at the road. 'No, the driving conditions were terrible, what with all the rain and the flooding, but the lorry driver overtook another car when he shouldn't have done and ended up on our side of the road. Caspar had to swerve off into the side. I'm just thankful he acted so quickly.'

'Oh, my, God, Mim, that sounds terrifying. No wonder you look so pale,' said Anna-Lisa.

Mim was aware of Aidey's eyes on her, and she could sense the weight of his concern. 'Yeah, ordinarily I'd be raring to wolf these croissants and muffins down, but I still feel a bit queasy to be honest. But I'm sure I'll be fine soon, when everything's had chance to settle down – including my stomach.'

'Well, don't bust a gut for Susan today; you're no better thought of for it. Let Honey do a bit for a change; that one could do with having her mind occupied, it might even keep it off making trouble for once.' Anna-Lisa reached for her tea and took a sip, her eyes peering over the top at Mim who had suddenly burst out laughing 'What? What's so funny.'

'Oh, Anna! Aidey, have you seen what's written on Anna's cup?'

'No, what?' He craned his neck to see the name "Anal Lisa" scribbled on the cardboard cup in black permanent marker, and promptly spluttered with laughter.

'What?' Anna turned her cup around. 'Bloody hell! Not again! I don't believe it! How difficult can it be to spell my name? And why the hell would they think anyone would ever call their kid "Anal Lisa"?'

'Hah! Anal Lisa. Suits you.' Honey had returned to the room and overheard the conversation.

'Shame Honey doesn't suit you,' said Anna-Lisa.

'What's that supposed to mean?' Honey asked.

'Think about it,' said Anna-Lisa.

By mid-afternoon Mim still hadn't seen anything of Caspar since they'd arrived at work that morning, and his usual phone calls were conspicuous by their absence. For the last couple of hours, she'd toyed with the idea of making an excuse to go to his office, but each time had talked herself out of it. But now the urge to see him, see if his mood had improved, had got the better of her. She scooped up her notebook and rushed out of the office, aware of three sets of eyes on her.

'Hi.' She peered around the door to see him gazing out of the window. He turned, greeting her with a wide smile.

'Mim! I was just thinking about you.'

'You were?' Her body flooded with relief.

'I was; come in, close the door.'

He met her half-way across the room, pulling her towards him and kissing her hard on the mouth. 'Mmm. What I'd give to get you on your own right now.'

The kiss was intense, but she was distracted by subtle hints of Clarissa; the faint whiff of her perfume, her silk scarf casually draped over Caspar's seat. A quick look in his eyes, so full of lust for her, dispelled her doubts; there was bound to be a simple explanation for it; Clarissa was his work colleague for goodness' sake.

A knock at the door made them quickly pull apart. 'I'm not interrupting anything, am I?' asked Susan, eyeing Mim suspiciously.

'Nothing at all.' Caspar smiled. 'Thanks, Mim, that was very helpful; I'll get back to you on it.'

'Happy to help.' Mim left his office, thankful that her boss hadn't arrived a minute earlier.

'TIME TO PICK up where we left off this afternoon.' Caspar gave Mim a wolfish smile as they arrived at Pear Tree Cottage.

'I like the sound of that.' Mim beamed back at him. 'I'll let you in, then I'll go and get Herbert.'

'I don't think I can wait a moment longer to get my hands on you; you've no idea what you do to me, delicious Mim Dewberry. Come on, let's go straight in; you can collect the dog later.'

'Oh, okay.' Mixed feelings began jostling for headspace; it gave her a thrill that he was so attracted to her, but at the same time, she felt a prickle of annoyance at the way he regarded Herbert. It triggered an unwelcome reminder of the animosity the two shared for one another, but for now she didn't want to dwell on the reasons behind it.

Caspar barely waited for the door to close before he was pushing her jacket off, his hands roaming over her body. In a flash, her doubts were banished as she lost herself in the moment.

'Lord, I needed that.' Caspar pushed his floppy dark fringe out of his eyes. 'And, much as I would love to stay and have a coffee with you, I'm afraid I'm going to have to dash off.'

'Oh.' Disappointment landed like a wet blanket.

'Now, don't be like that; I thought you'd be as pleased to snatch a little romantic encounter as I am. I shouldn't really have stopped off here; my parents are waiting for me.' He dropped a kiss on the tip of Mim's nose.

There wasn't much romance involved! 'Oh, I am, it's just, well, it would just be nice to spend a bit more time with you, that's all.'

'I know, darling, I feel the same. Don't worry, we'll be able to soon.'

Once Caspar had left, Mim beat herself up for sounding needy; choosing to ignore the little voice telling her that things with him just didn't add up.

21

'JEMIMA, I want to run a feature on the best roast dinners in the area, and I've heard the pub where you live is getting a pretty good reputation for them. It's for our "Three of the Best" section, which is proving enormously popular, so I want three lots of Sunday dinners to feature in each of the three price ranges; the one near you should be perfect for one of the cheaper options.'

The cold and damp of Tuesday evening had segued into an equally dreary Wednesday morning, the weather reflecting the mood of the building. Susan burst into the office full of bluster and with little regard to the fact that Anna-Lisa was speaking to someone on the phone. Mim's heart leapt with surprise, her concentration scampering away. Anna-Lisa put her finger in her free ear, turning away from Susan in an attempt to carry on with her call.

'Got that, Jemima? Three bargain basement, three mid-range and three up-market roast dinners.' Susan counted them off on her fingers. 'I want you to speak to the landlord of whatever the place is called near you, and reserve a table for two, for one night next week. Tell them they'll need to serve up a three course meal and all the trimmings – with the main being a roast, of course – and there needs to be a bottle of wine thrown in as well. And don't forget to make it clear they'll be expected to waive payment in exchange for a review in Yorkshire Portions. Hopefully they'll have the sense to realise what an honour it is and what a huge favour we're doing them. Aidey, you can take Honey for the meal there.'

Mim looked across at her friend as she processed Susan's barrage of words; she vaguely registered that his face had dropped, while she negotiated the thinly-veiled insult to the White Swan which was anything but "bargain basement". *Bloody cheek of the woman!*

'Oh, I, er, wouldn't it make more sense if Mim goes rather than Honey? After all, it would save Honey the trek over to Skeltwick.' There was no mistaking the pleading look in his eyes.

'Don't be ridiculous, you know as well as I do, Jemima won't be able to give the place an unbiased review.'

'But will that matter if it's meant for the "Three of the Best" feature? Aren't you after glowing reviews?' Anna-Lisa had ended her call and joined the conversation.

'Not necessarily; if one of us has a meal somewhere and it's diabolical, or falls short of the expected standard, then we can always use it in the separate, longer dining reviews, where we have the luxury of being able to go into much more detail. Whether they be good or bad, they're useful for lending an air of credibility to our reviews, and puts a stop to people being able to say we're paid for them.' Susan looked around theatrically. 'And where is Honey? I thought she'd be working on that Christmas feature I had to give her, since she said Jemima only gives her boring stuff to do. She knows I need it by early afternoon.'

Before Mim had chance to respond to the slight, Anna-Lisa caught her eye as she spoke. 'She said she was going to see Simon; she's been gone a while actually. And, from what I've seen, Honey picks and choses what she wants to do; when she's actually at her desk to do anything, that is.'

Oh, bugger! Mim held her breath as her heart rate gathered speed; much as she admired the fact that Anna had the balls to walk where angels feared to tread, she wished she didn't have them today. She gritted her teeth, hoping her friend's comments wouldn't backfire.

'What do you mean by that?' Susan pressed her mouth into a hard line and glared at Anna-Lisa.

Mim looked on, conscious of her anxiety levels escalating.

'All I mean is that Mim works really hard, and Honey's away from her desk a fair bit, that's all. Just makes me wonder how she's able to get much work done. I'm sure I'd get next to nothing done if I was out of the room as much as she is.'

Oh, jeez! Please stop, Anna! This can only lead to trouble.

Aidey flicked a concerned glance Mim's way; he was clearly thinking along the same lines.

Susan continued to glare at Anna-Lisa, the cogs of her mind almost audible as she processed Anna's words. Before she had chance to speak Honey bowled into the room, with what was left of her lipstick smeared across her face. Her smug expression disappeared as soon as she spotted her godmother.

'Auntie Susan, I was just—'

'Honey, where have you been? And what the devil's the matter with your face? You know I need the Christmas article by this afternoon. And why are you troubling Simon? You know how busy he is since he took over the accounts.'

The girl shot an accusatory look around the room before she rubbed at her mouth. Mim looked on in morbid fascination as Honey began simpering. 'I was just asking Simon's advice on the article; he's so knowledgeable and no one in here was being particularly helpful. I'm just keen to do my best for you.'

Ughh! There was that infuriating little-girl voice. Hard as it was, Mim resisted the urge to call her out for her blatant lies.

Anna-Lisa clearly had no such scruples, with her top lip curling into a snarl she said, 'I didn't hear you ask anyone for help, Honey. But if you show us what you've done, maybe we can give you some advice. Come on, let's see what you've come up with so far.'

Tension sapped the air from the room as all eyes rested on Honey. Mim held her breath as she awaited the girl's response to Anna so blatantly calling her bluff. Mim felt a little guilty at not speaking out and, much as she was grateful Anna had jumped in, saving her from the need to defend herself, she really didn't have a clue what to say without making Honey look worse. After the pen incident, Mim was keen to avoid any more of the girl's wrath. She was concerned that Anna's comments would antagonise her, and no one knew how that would manifest itself.

Honey glowered at Anna-Lisa, which lent an odd edge to the little-girl voice she used in her reply. 'For your information "Anal Lisa", the ideas for the article are in my head, but because I'm new here, I just wanted to make sure I was on the right track, that's all. I didn't want to risk wasting time on something that might not be right or not what Auntie Susan wanted. And I didn't bother to ask any of you because you give the impression you don't really like to help me for some reason.'

Susan stood in silence, her eyes darting back and forth between Anna-Lisa and Honey as she weighed up the situation. It was obvious to everyone that Honey was shirking her work, and it was equally obvious that their boss's loyalty to her goddaughter would quash the dressing-down she'd give anyone else in similar circumstances.

'Hmph. Yes, well, we need to crack on. And, Honey, I was just explaining that you need to accompany Aidey for a meal at the pub in Skeltwick; it's for our "Three of the Best" feature. And, since it's Jemima's local, she's going to deal with the booking of the table and tell the landlords what we expect.'

Mim felt her heart sink at the reminder; she hated having to explain to restaurant and teashop owners that she wanted to book a table but wouldn't actually be paying for the meal. She'd had to do it several times, and it never got any easier. The explanation that it would be in exchange for a review was invariably met with a wary response, concern hovering in the tone of the owners' voices. And she couldn't blame them; there had been times when Simon or Kenneth had used such free meals to slate an unsuspecting restaurant or teashop in a separate food feature of the magazine. Having to deal with it at her local and explain Susan's demands to landlady Julie was filling Mim with utter dread. Just as she was wrestling with her thoughts, Susan's booming voice spliced through them.

'And there's that place over at Lytell Stangdale, The Sunne Inne, I believe it's called. From what I can gather, the local landed gentry over there – the Hammondelys – seem to favour it; that should do for the mid-range category.' She waved a dismissive hand at Mim. 'You can call them and reserve a table for Kenneth and I for one night next week – not Thursday or Saturday, though, we're busy then. You never know, Lord and Lady Hammondely might be there; I'd quite like to meet them, see if they'd be interested in us doing an exclusive feature on the family seat at Danskelfe Castle; they haven't opened the doors to anyone yet, and I quite fancy a nosy around that old place. I think we'd be the perfect publication to do them justice.'

'Oh, erm, right okay.' Mim's heart was sinking even further as she added the job to the top of her to-do list.

'And I want Kirkbythwaite Hall Hotel as our expensive option. Caspar and Clarissa can go to that; it's more their type of place.'

Mim felt the words hit her like a slap in the face. Caspar and Clarissa. Dining together at one of North Yorkshire's most sumptuous hotels. Anxiety jostled with a generous dash of jealousy as she recalled the look on Caspar's face as he was leaving Clarissa's office the previous day.

Ignorant of Mim's turmoil, Susan steamed on. 'The remaining reviews for the feature can just be cobbled together from whatever info you can glean from their respective websites and social media pages, as well as public reviews as usual – goes without saying, only use the good ones. And be sure to make them sound authentic, add your own words; I don't want to see the tiniest of hints that the reviews are anything but genuine.'

Mim looked at her boss, the words rushing over her and very little sinking in.

'Have you got that, Jemima?' Susan clicked her fingers. 'Jemima! Will you stop daydreaming, girl, this is important.'

'Oh, yes, sorry. My mind was racing ahead.' She smiled, hoping Susan wouldn't suspect it was a fib.

'Hmm. Good. Right, I'll leave you all to it. And don't forget I need that feature after lunch, Honey.'

Mim watched Susan flounce out of the room, too distracted to notice the dark looks Honey was sending her way. Instead, her mind was frantically going over various heart-wrenching scenarios of Caspar and Clarissa and their evening together. From the photos in glossy magazines Mim had seen of Kirkbythwaite Hall Hotel's restaurant it was intimate and romantic. Ughh! She tortured herself, picturing Caspar, achingly handsome in a well-cut designer suit, his dark floppy hair and film-star good looks lending him an air of effortless sophistication. Clarissa would be sleek and elegant, the neat curves of her figure shown to their best advantage in an expensive body-con dress, with her long, glossy hair tumbling over her tiny shoulders. Her naturally beautiful face would be emphasised by skilfully applied make-up, complete with sultry, smoky eyes. *Being everything I'm not.* Mim felt her mood sink even further. How could she ever hope to compete with someone like Clarissa? The situation was somehow made worse because Mim genuinely liked her.

A more worrying thought crept in: how would they end the evening? Surely they wouldn't stay the night? No, of course they wouldn't, that place was so popular it would more than likely already be fully-booked; in fact, they'd probably struggle to get just a table booking for next week. *Fingers crossed!* That thought offered Mim a tiny glimmer of hope. But what if they did get a table, would

Caspar take Clarissa back to his place – wherever that was? Mim wondered if she'd ever get to see it herself; it was beginning to feel odd that he'd never mentioned spending time together outside of work other than the brief moments they snatched at her cottage. She doubted if he'd spent half an hour there in total this week, which was something considering how they'd spent that tiny amount of time. The whole situation was beginning to make her feel more than a little unsettled. It would seem her idea of Caspar just being a bit of "no-strings fun" hadn't quite gone to plan.

Her mind was busy wrangling with this latest cluster of worries when Anna-Lisa's voice brought her back to the conversation in the room.

'Mim! Mimbo!'

She looked up to see Anna and Aidey smiling at her. 'Aidey's nipping out to the Nutmeg Tree and wondered if you fancied anything bringing back for your lunch? I'm going to head out later, but he's bringing me back a hot chocolate and a tuna sandwich since I'm starving.'

Honey snorted. 'Wonder if you'll get "Anal Lisa" on your cup this time?'

Anna rolled her eyes and reached for her bag to get her purse.

'I like the sound of a hot chocolate but I'm not sure I could manage it with a tuna sandwich.' The thought of that combination made Mim feel slightly nauseous. 'I think I'll just have a toasted teacake; I'm not feeling too hungry. Actually, I think I might go with you, Aidey, I could do with a breath of fresh air.' In truth it wasn't just Anna's food order that made her feel queasy; the thought of Caspar and Clarissa hadn't helped either.

'That's weird, I could've sworn I had a twenty pound note in here.' Anna's brow was furrowed as she checked through her purse.

'Are you sure you haven't spent it and forgotten?' asked Aidey. 'I've done that loads of times.'

'Uhh! You know what I'm like, I'm always doing it,' said Mim.

'I don't think so. I was sure I saw one in the wallet part when I checked just before I left the house this morning; I wanted to see if I needed to pop to a hole in the wall before work, save me having to waste time standing in a queue in my lunch break.' She rubbed her forehead with her fingertips.

It was very much like Mim to forget what she'd got in her purse, but it wasn't at all like Anna-Lisa, who prided herself on being extremely organised. Mim regularly teased her friend for being OCD about everything, but today she could see Anna was rattled. 'Don't worry about it, chick, I can sub you; you've done the same for me loads of times.'

'Yep, it's not a problem, Anna. Your twenty pound note will probably turn up at home; I wouldn't give it another thought,' said Aidey, pulling on his jacket. 'Right, Mimbo, shall we head out now before the weather gets too bad? Looks like there's a gap in the rain.'

'Sure, it's a good place to stop on this, I can pick it up easily when we get back.'

'Ahh, how sweet,' said Honey. But the others ignored her, and her comment was left to fall on stony ground.

As Mim and Aidey were making their way to the Nutmeg Tree, wrapped up well against the wind and rain that had started up again as soon as they stepped outside, a voice calling her name interrupted their conversation. Mim turned around to see a familiar figure hurrying down the street towards them, dodging the scurrying shoppers and their dangerously wielded umbrellas. It was Rick; a not particularly welcome blast from the past.

'Oh, bugger.' Though Mim's mind was telling her to keep walking, her feet didn't appear to be listening and she remained rooted to the ground while her heart thudded in her chest. She could really do without this today.

'What's wrong?' asked Aidey. 'Oh,' he said when he saw who was heading towards them.

'Mim, I thought it was you.' The owner of the voice gave a warm smile that crinkled the corners of his chocolate brown eyes.

'Hello, Rick. Yep, it's me.' She gave an awkward laugh.

'How are you doing? You look great.' He seemed genuinely pleased to see her.

'I'm fine, thanks. You?' The last thing she needed was to be making small-talk with the man who'd cheated on her, not least the one who'd cheated on her with Honey.

'I'm okay, thanks.' He looked at her for a moment, as if working out whether or not to say something. 'Look, I don't suppose you've got a minute?'

Mim groaned inwardly; much as she would love to tell him to get as far away from her as possible and to leave her alone, her soft-hearted side took over – as it usually did. 'Erm, okay.' She turned to

Aidey. 'You might as well go ahead and get out of this rain, I'll catch you up; I'll only be a couple of minutes.'

'Are you sure you'll be okay?'

'I'll be fine, I promise I won't be long.' She hoped Rick would get the message that she wasn't going to devote much time to him. Having a conversation in this weather meant it wouldn't take long or they'd get absolutely drenched.

'I've been meaning to get in touch with you, but after what happened, I thought I'd be the last person you'd want to hear from.'

Mim was relieved to see that Rick at least had the decency to look guilty, and there was no evidence of his usual cocky swagger. 'To be honest, I think it's fair to say I wouldn't exactly have been over the moon to hear from you.' The cold was creeping into her bones and mingled with the anxiety that had started to swirl in her gut, making her shiver.

'No, I don't blame you, but I owe you a hell of an apology, Mim. I honestly don't know what I was thinking of; you were the best thing that ever happened to me – everybody said that, and it's true – but I had to go and mess things up, and get taken in by some meaningless girl's flattery; she was so bloody pushy, practically offering it on a plate. Me and my bloody pathetic male ego; I don't know where my head was at the time. I'm really sorry, Mim. If I could turn the clock back I would never have even looked at her. What we had was so good, you and me, I realised that pretty much straight away; I was such a bloody idiot.' He paused for a moment, gnawing at his bottom lip. 'Look, I'll kick myself if I don't ask this, but I don't suppose there's a chance … for us, I mean?' He went to reach for Mim's hand but she quickly stuffed it into the safety of her coat pocket.

'I'm sorry, Rick, there isn't, it's too late.' If he'd asked her this a few weeks ago, she knew her answer would have been very different; her heart would have leapt at the chance. But not today. Her life was complicated enough. He needed to know they were very definitely over; that there was no going back. She took a fortifying breath. 'I've moved on since we broke up; I'm a different person now.'

'Oh, right, okay. Shame.' A few beats passed as he searched her face. Mim couldn't work out if he was trying to read her thoughts or if he was waiting to see if she'd change her mind. 'So, are you seeing anyone at the moment?'

'Mmm-hmm.' She nodded. 'Yep.'

'Is it serious?'

'It's early days, but it has potential.' *That's wishful thinking and you know it.*

'It's Aidey, isn't it? I always thought you two would get—'

'It's not Aidey, it's no one you know.' The look in his eyes set her heart pounding, making her wish she hadn't stopped to speak to him. Rick was tugging at feelings she'd had for him not so long ago, rifling around her mind in the detritus of their relationship. Looking at him today, with those mesmerising dark eyes, it was easy see why she'd fallen for him. But equally, a part of her felt numb to his charms; the attraction she'd once felt had faded and morphed into something very different. It took her by surprise when she recognised this feeling as something akin to pity. She felt sorry for him? She doubted he'd be very happy to hear that. But the more she looked at him the more she became aware of the unmistakable shadow of sadness in his eyes, and the air of loneliness about him. It almost made her want to reach out to him. Almost … but not quite. Like she said, she'd moved on, and she wasn't going to be a mug for him anymore.

'Listen, if it doesn't work out with this new bloke…' Rick pushed his fingers through his dark, floppy fringe that was now dripping wet with rain. 'What I'm trying to say is that I'd do anything for the chance to give things another go with you, Mim. I've been desperate to put things right. I feel really stupid saying this, but I didn't realise until it was too late that I've, erm, well, you mean a lot to me; a hell of a lot. When it sank in what had happened, what I'd done, I was gutted.'

You're not the only one. And why did you have to go and say that now of all times?

Mim was lost for an answer, being tough and hard didn't come naturally to her. She swallowed her discomfort. 'I'm really sorry, Rick. Much as I think you're a lovely guy, I couldn't run the risk of it happening again. You really hurt me, doing what you did with Honey. I know I probably gave the impression of being a soft touch before, but I've changed now; I've had to. I never want to go through that again, and I'm afraid I don't feel that way about you anymore.'

The rain was falling more heavily now, icy splashes slicing at her cheeks, making them sting. 'I can't just forget about what you did; you really hurt me, made a fool of me. And, to make matters worse, that girl you cheated on me with now works in my office, at the next desk to mine.' *A constant reminder.*

'What? You're joking?' He looked stunned. 'How the hell has she got a job there?'

'Her godmother owns the magazine. Very convenient, eh?'

Rick shook his head. 'Watch yourself with her, won't you, Mim? She's trouble. Seriously. I wasn't with her for long; I couldn't stand all the mind games and manipulation; she messes with your head big time. Singles people out and makes their life hell. Got quite a reputation for it from what I can gather, as well as a nasty jealous streak.'

'Tell me about it.' It felt a little surreal, Rick doling out advice about someone he'd dumped her for. Evidently, the grass isn't always greener. 'Anyway, this rain's getting really heavy, you're getting soaked and I told Aidey I wouldn't be long. I'd better go.'

'Oh, okay.' Disappointment clouded his eyes. He leant across and kissed her cheek, lingering just a little too long. 'It's been good to see you again. Look after yourself, Mim. You've got my number so you know how to reach me if ever you fancy meeting up.'

'Bye, Rick.' His familiar cologne set her nostrils tingling, stirring dormant memories. A warning in her gut kicked in, a timely reminder of Anna-Lisa's words. Sensing he was about to say something more, Mim turned and hurried off towards the Nutmeg Tree, depriving him of the chance. *Don't look back, just keep on walking. Don't look back.* She continued, head down, collar up, dodging puddles and shoppers huddled against the rain. She was conscious of the weight of his eyes on her until she disappeared amongst the sea of umbrellas. As far as she was concerned, there was nothing left to say. And she was relieved to find his kiss hadn't rekindled the deep feelings she'd once had for him. Yes, it had evoked a tiny flicker of something but it felt like little more than a superficial attraction.

For the first time, she'd made a decision based on what *she* wanted to do instead of what some man wanted her to do. It was surprisingly empowering and it felt bloody good! She couldn't wait to tell Anna; her friend would be so proud of her.

But a little part of Mim couldn't help but feel she'd been unkind for leaving Rick standing there while rivulets of rain poured down his handsome face, his gorgeous eyes looking unbelievably sad. She quickly pushed a pang of guilt away and strode on; Anna wouldn't be quite so chuffed if she knew about that.

Mim was relieved to be in the warmth of the coffee shop, the easy playlist and chatter of customers mingling with the delicious aroma of food that sought out her appetite and assuaged her guilt as she squeezed her way to Aidey. His kind face was etched with concern. 'You okay? You're drenched. I bet you're frozen; here, you stand next to the heater, get yourself warmed through.'

She did as she was bid. 'Thanks, Aidey, you're a star.'

'So, you're alright?'

'Never better,' she said, linking her arm through his and giving it a squeeze. 'Well, I dare say my hair could be; it'll be a frizzy mess when it dries but hey-ho, I'm used to it now. Anyway, I honestly thought I'd be really upset if I ever saw Rick again, but it turned out to be the opposite. I didn't really feel anything for him, other than pity. And I didn't feel upset or heartbroken like I thought I would.'

His face broke into a wide smile. 'Well, that's great news, Mimbo.' He wrapped his arm around her shoulders and pulled her close. 'I must admit, I was a bit concerned about leaving you, but didn't want to look like I was sticking my nose in.'

'It wouldn't have looked like that, but I needed to face him on my own; prove to myself I was well and truly over him – which I did, and I am. Would you believe he asked me if we could start again?'

'No way. And what did you say?'

'I told him there was no chance.'

'Wow. You actually said that?'

'I did, well, words to that effect.'

Aidey smiled, unmistakable happiness in his eyes. 'Good for you, Mimbo.'

'I know it was the right thing, but it didn't stop me from feeling like a mean old moo.'

'After what he put you through? That's the last thing you are; you're way too soft for your own good.'

'Not today! Today, I've been a hard ass! Boudicca eat your heart out!'

22

'So what do you think the thing with Anna's money is about?' Aidey asked as they were leaving the Nutmeg Tree, arms laden with cup carriers and paper carrier bags bursting with sandwiches and traybakes.

'I don't know, it felt a bit weird, didn't it?' Mim negotiated the slippery cobbles that lined the road along Smiddersgate. The rain had stopped but it was still bitterly cold and underfoot could be dicey.

Aidey nodded. 'It did and it's not at all like Anna, she's the most organised person I've ever met; right down to the smallest details of her life.'

'Yeah, she is – total opposite of me. It's her way of dealing with life since she spent so much of her childhood in care. She explained it once, said being organised gave her the feeling that she had control of at least some aspect of her life.'

'Poor Anna.'

'For Christ's sake, don't let her hear you feeling sorry for her; she'll have your nuts for earrings faster than you can say "castration"!'

Aidey threw his head back and laughed. 'Noted!'

'Still, she did seem genuinely thrown by the money not being in her purse.'

'Yeah, she did.'

Mim's appetite had returned and she took a sip of her hot chocolate, noisily sucking a marshmallow through the hole in the lid of her cup.

'Enjoying that?' Aidey asked, grinning at her.

'Mmm. It's seriously yummy, especially when the marshmallows go all warm and gooey. I couldn't resist a quick sip when the chocolatey smell wafted under my nose.'

'So me and half of Smiddersgate gathered.'

'Cheeky.' Mim nudged him with her arm.

Aidey laughed. 'Here we are, walking along the road, dodging traffic and folk rushing around, it's absolutely chucking it down, there's rain dripping off your nose, yet you still have to stop for a quick hot chocolate fix.'

'Can't see what's wrong with that myself, and you should know better than to come between a girl and her hot chocolate. And my nose is huge, that's why so much rain drips off it.'

'Don't be daft, there's nothing wrong with your nose, it's perfect; you need to stop putting yourself down all the time, Mim.' He flashed her a quick smile that made her heart squeeze; typical Aidey, always wanting to make you feel better about yourself.

'Anyway, this thing with Anna and her dosh, you don't think Caleb might've just taken it and forgotten to mention it to her, do you? You know, if he was in a hurry,' he asked.

'It's a possibility, though I can't see him going in her purse without asking her first, can you?'

'Not really. And who would do that sort of thing anyway?'

'I'm not sure,' said Mim.

'Well, as far as I'm aware, Caleb's never done it before. And, thinking about it, it's unlikely he had the chance since Anna was so sure she'd checked her purse just before she left for work; he leaves before her.'

Aidey was right. That thought sent Mim in a different direction. 'You don't think it's got anything to do with Honey, do you?'

'It had crossed my mind, but since the pen we've been careful not to leave her on her own in the room whenever possible; we both know that's why Anna didn't come out with us just now.'

'True. You don't think we're jumping to conclusions, do you, because of what happened with the pen? I mean, when has Honey had the chance to take money from Anna's purse?' As the words left her mouth Rick's warning flashed up in her mind, "Watch her, Mim … she messes with your head…" Maybe there was some substance to their suspicions. 'Oh, bugger, Susan called me to go down to her office, said I had to go straight away, she wanted to talk to me about the Facebook and Instagram adverts for the Christmas edition. You and Anna were with Clarissa; I wasn't gone long – I don't know why Susan couldn't have told me what she wanted over the phone, but you know what she's like. Anyway, I was only gone a couple of minutes, so if Honey did take it, she had to be flippin' quick.'

'Did she look suspicious when you went back in the room? Was she in her seat?'

'She was fiddling with her chair, muttering about it being the wrong height or something. I didn't pay much attention, but come to think of it, she did look a bit flustered, I just thought it was another one of her attention-seeking things.'

'Hmm. I dare say if she'd been in Anna's bag she wouldn't have had time to sit down and look like she was working; sounds like she was putting on a little performance so she didn't look suspicious.'

The worried tone to Aidey's voice sent anxiety scurrying up Mim's spine. 'I'd better check my bag, make sure she hasn't stuffed it in there like she did with the pen.'

Once they reached the entrance to Yorkshire Portions, Aidey held her bag open as she searched through it, a task made much easier since she'd got rid of the clutter. He lowered his voice. 'Listen, I think it's probably best if we don't say anything about our suspicions to anyone just yet; we don't know it's Honey for definite, and we don't want to go making false accusations. I think we should keep it to ourselves till we know what we're going to do about it. Obviously, we need to talk to Anna, but we can do that after work. Are you getting a lift with Caspar?'

Mim nodded. 'Yep, he's heading my way anyway.' Why did she feel the need to add that bit? 'And, there's no sign of the money in my bag, thank goodness.' Her shoulders slumped as relief washed over her.

'Well, that's something at least. Anyway, I'll tell Anna what we think when we're walking to the carpark after work tonight; I'd rather not mention it in the office, you never know who's listening there. But we definitely need to say something to her before she goes home and accuses Caleb of taking it.'

Mim nodded. 'You're right, things aren't exactly rosy between the two of them, and that definitely wouldn't help, but let's hope she hasn't already texted him about it.'

'I've got a feeling she won't have done.'

'What on earth are you two doing, dithering about on the doorstep looking like you're plotting something?' Kenneth appeared behind them, making Mim jump. 'Anyone would think you weren't aware there's work to be done and we've got a deadline looming.'

'Blimey, Kenneth, you gave me a shock!' Mim pressed her hand against her chest.

'We're on our lunch break,' said Aidey. 'And we're back early.'

'Lunch break? What's a lunch break? It's years since I took one of those; wouldn't recognise one if it slapped me in the face.' He pushed past them, turned around and shook his umbrella out, sending cold droplets of rain splashing up Mim's legs.

'Arghh!' She jumped back.

'Well, what do you expect if you stand in the way?'

Rather than tell him that any decent person wouldn't have the bad manners to do such a thing, or that she'd like to stick his umbrella where the sun didn't shine, Mim kept her thoughts to herself and watched him disappear up the stairs to his office. 'Pompous arse,' she muttered.

Aidey shook his head in disbelief. 'I don't know why that family think they're so superior and that it's okay to treat us like worthless peasants.'

'It's because he's our superior boss and he can do what he wants, we're just simple Yorkshire folk which means we do what he says,' said Mim. 'That's how he sees it in his little world.'

'And I if I have anything to do with it, I won't be part of that pathetic little world for much longer.'

'You're not the only one.' The thought of not working with Aidey made her feel suddenly rather sad, but she knew neither of them could stick it out at Yorkshire Portions for much longer if things continued the way they were.

23

Mim and Aidey found Anna-Lisa alone in their office, concentrating hard as she proof read an article Tamsin had been tasked with. She looked up and smiled as they walked in. 'Now there's a sight for sore eyes, I'm absolutely starving.' Her eyes settled on Mim, taking in her soggy appearance. 'You look like a drowned rat, Mimbo; have you been diving into puddles again?'

Aidey chuckled. 'For a change, no, she hasn't but sipping hot chocolate in the pouring rain and a close-encounter with Kenneth and his umbrella hasn't helped.'

'I won't ask.' Anna pulled an amused face.

Mim shrugged off her coat and hung it up. 'You won't believe it when I tell you why I'm practically soaked through to my knickers.'

'I can't even begin to imagine,' said Anna-Lisa.

'I got drenched because I was standing in the rain talking to Rick when the heavens decided to open.'

Anna-Lisa took a moment, as if waiting for the words to sink in. '*Rick*?'

'Yep.'

'As in slimy, cheating rat Rick?' Anna-Lisa's eyebrows had shot up to her hairline.

'Poetically put, Anna,' said Aidey.

'I do my best.'

'Yep, the very one,' said Mim.

'And?'

'And, you won't believe this either – where's Honey, by the way?'

'Last I heard, she'd gone out for lunch, she's meeting a friend apparently, though how she's got any beggars belief. Anyway, enough about her, what happened with Rick-the-slimy-cheating-rat?'

'Well…' Mim sat at her desk and opened her sandwich as she shared the conversation she'd had with him, her friends listening intently, expressing their outrage in a mixture of eye rolls, head shakes and exclamations of disbelief. Mim still found it hard to believe she hadn't crumbled, especially when he'd kissed her cheek. But at the back of her mind she knew that if Caspar hadn't been on the scene, the story would have had a very different outcome.

Anna-Lisa chewed vigorously on her mouthful of sandwich, swallowing so she could speak. 'He's got a bloody nerve after what he did to you. But I'm so proud of you, chick, I know how much you liked him, and he'll have been expecting you to go running straight back into his arms as soon as he clicked his grubby little fingers; it'll do that massive ego of his good to have a bit of a bruising. I reckon he'll have been expecting you to have been pining for him since you split up. Turns out it's the other way round. You can't beat a bit of poetic justice, can you? Looks like the Dark Count has his uses after all; I doubt you'd have been so keen to turn Rick down if he wasn't entertaining you.'

There was no fooling Anna. 'I'd like to think I'd still feel the same, but I take your point; him knowing I was seeing someone else made it easier in that I think it made him reluctant to push things.' Rick's assumption that she was seeing Aidey jumped into her mind again. Mim looked across at him and he smiled at her over his paper coffee cup. It set a little flutter away in her stomach as warmth rose in her cheeks. She smiled back, hoping he wouldn't notice her blushes. *Time to change the subject, I think!* 'Actually, before Honey gets back, I don't suppose your twenty quid turned up?'

'Nope.'

'You haven't asked Caleb about it yet, have you?' Aidey spoke quietly.

Anna-Lisa shook her head. 'I haven't. I've got a funny feeling about it and a certain person if you see what I mean? But I don't want to discuss it now, just in case, well, you know, little ears and all that.'

Aidey nodded. 'I thought we could talk about it on the way to the carpark; I'm not sure what you should do about it though.'

The sound of footsteps making their way along the landing ended their conversation. Anna made a zipping gesture with her fingers across her mouth and the others nodded.

Clarissa stepped into their room on a cloud of floral perfume. 'Hi, folks, I don't suppose any of you have seen my notebook have you? The one I always keep on my desk for scribbling ideas down, the fabric-covered one with the peacock feather print. Only, I'm sure it was on my desk this morning but I can't seem to find it now. I think I might've had it in my hand when I left my room earlier on and then I must've put it down somewhere and forgot to pick it up again.' She laughed, her grey-blue eyes lighting up her pretty face. 'Ughh! I'm beginning to sound like my mother, aren't I?'

Mim's heart started to gallop. *No, not something else! Not Clarissa!*

'I haven't seen it anywhere, I'm afraid, but I'll keep my eyes peeled. I'm sure it'll turn up,' said Aidey.

'Have you tried re-tracing your steps?' asked Anna-Lisa.

'Pretty much; I just need to double-check in Caspar's office, but he's having a meeting with Kenneth, so I haven't had a chance.'

Mim's heart sank, her mind wandering to the reason Clarissa had been in Caspar's office earlier that day. She pictured them together, smiling and laughing and looking like the beautiful couple they'd make. Her mind moved on to Susan's suggestion of their meal together at Kirkbythwaite Hall Hotel; it couldn't help but be anything other than romantic. She chewed on the inside of her cheek as her new-found self-confidence slowly started to disintegrate. She caught Anna-Lisa looking at her and batted her worries away; she was letting herself get carried away again.

'Maybe we have another ghost?' said Anna-Lisa.

'That thought had crossed my mind,' Clarissa said, laughing. 'Anyway, I'm sure it'll turn up, but I'd be grateful if you could keep a look out for it; it's full of ideas for features I've scribbled down so it's pretty valuable to me.'

'Will do.' Mim mustered up a smile as Clarissa left.

'Are you two thinking what I'm thinking?' asked Aidey when the coast was clear.

'Yup,' said Anna-Lisa.

Mim gave a weary sigh. 'But why on earth would Honey take a notebook?'

'Because it's worth a lot to Clarissa; you just heard her say it's packed full of ideas and is valuable to her. But we all kind of know that anyway and I dare say you-know-who does too.' Aidey took a sip of his coffee.

'Ughh! This is all getting exhausting. I can't keep up,' said Mim. 'I'm just going to stay glued to my seat until Honey's left the office for the day. There's no way I'm going to give her a chance to sneak anything else into my bag. In fact, when I get home, I'm going to swap it for my backpack, then it won't be so easy to quickly slip things in.'

'Yep, I think we need to be extra vigilant now, just in case,' said Anna-Lisa.

24

Mim was relieved when five o'clock finally arrived. It had been a long, drawn-out afternoon with Susan being in a foul mood for reasons she hadn't bothered to share. It appeared to have rubbed off onto Kenneth and Simon, so everyone had kept their head down and kept quiet, even, surprisingly, Honey who seemed to have heeded her godmother's words and got stuck into her work. There'd been a great deal of heavy sighing as was usually the case when Honey was given something to do but, for a change, Mim didn't ask if she could help nor volunteer any suggestions. Instead, she let Honey get on with it, hoping it would allow Susan to see the standard of work she was capable of. It had been sent back several times, and each time Mim could sense Honey glaring at her as if it was her fault, and, hard as it was, Mim resisted the temptation to make eye contact with her; she had a suspicion Honey's black looks had the power to turn people to stone. By quarter to five Susan declared she was almost satisfied with it.

Throughout the course of the afternoon, the quiet of the room had given Mim's mind free rein to drift as she worked through her to-do list. She replayed her conversation with Rick many times over, triggering a mixture of emotions ranging from relief to sadness. Caspar had featured highly, particularly the mixed signals he was sending her. When they were together, he made her feel like the most attractive woman in the world, but when they were apart, there was something about the way he was with her she couldn't quite put her finger on, and she became riddled with insecurity. Though, she couldn't lay all of the blame for that solely at his feet, she'd become pretty accomplished at making herself feel that way; her litany of dating disasters had ensured she'd had years' of practice. But his actions definitely didn't help, especially his reluctance for others to know that they were dating – if that's what you could call it – despite the reasons he gave.

By mid-afternoon, temptation had got the better of her, and she'd found an excuse to pop along to his office where he'd greeted her enthusiastically, pulling her onto his lap. 'Mmm. I can't get enough of you,' he'd said, kissing her passionately and running his hands up inside her top despite her protestations that someone could walk in at any moment. 'Don't you think it adds to the thrill?' he'd asked. But thrilled wasn't the word Mim would have used, when all she could think about was the scent of Clarissa's perfume that lingered on his shirt.

She'd heard Clarissa go into his office earlier that afternoon, remaining there for a good forty-five minutes, their laughter filtering along the landing; they clearly weren't discussing work. It had plunged Mim into turmoil; his actions were seriously messing with her head. She wondered if he'd stay long enough for a coffee after dropping her off after work, but something in her gut had told her he wouldn't.

From what Mim could gather, Clarissa's notebook still hadn't turned up. Honey hadn't mentioned it, which had surprised Mim since she'd taken great delight at wittering on when Susan's pen was missing. The three friends hadn't discussed it any further in case Honey was responsible; they didn't want to give her the satisfaction of knowing it had made them feel uncomfortable. It still didn't stop a prickle of fear from running up Mim's spine at the thought of what the girl was capable of.

'Right, that's me done.' Mim crossed the latest task off her to-do list with a swipe of her pen. She pushed her worries aside; Friday was almost upon them and that thought gladdened her heart for several reasons; the first one that sprang to mind was that Friday was followed by two blissful days away from Honey and her spiteful, barbed comments – and her mind games, if the missing items were anything to do with her. The second because it was inching closer to the night of Carly's get-together. Mim couldn't wait to see her friends from the village; they could always be relied upon to make her laugh and see the lighter side of life, helping her to momentarily forget her troubles. She was desperately in need of that. And the third was the chance to catch up on the hours of lost sleep she'd had this week. *Nearly there, Mim. Hang on in there.*

She looked up to see Anna-Lisa watching her, smiling as if she could read her thoughts. Mim smiled back before glancing across at Aidey who was wearing his familiar expression of concentration, his mind deeply engrossed in his work. A pulse of something indefinable shot through to her core, catching her off guard. As if tuned into her thoughts, he looked up at her, flashing a quick smile, his eyes warm and friendly. It made her heart squeeze. He was such a lovely bloke; it always puzzled her that he didn't have a girlfriend, or at least one who lasted longer than just a few weeks.

THE DRIVE HOME with Caspar was filled with the usual banter about work; his mood brighter than Mim anticipated after the vibe in the office. She was thankful of it. 'I enjoyed our moment together this afternoon,' she said.

'Mmm. Me, too.' He reached across and ran his hand up her leg, making her shiver with anticipation. 'It was a tasty little appetiser. I'm looking forward to getting back to your place so we can pick up where we left off.'

'I like the sound of that.' Something held her back from asking how long he'd be staying for, she didn't want to sound needy –which was something she'd been accused of in previous relationships, the memory of which made her cringe – and she had a feeling she wouldn't like the answer.

The car purred along the road out of York with understated confidence. Their conversation was dotted with a liberal sprinkling of laughter as they relived the times they'd grabbed together over the last few days; illicit moments, stolen under the noses of everyone at Yorkshire Portions, just avoiding getting caught. All the while, Mim fought a silent battle with images of Clarissa that persistently tried to sneak into her mind; she didn't want to let her paranoia smother the happiness of the moment.

'Imagine what Susan would say,' said Caspar.

'Oh, don't, she'd kick me out straight away; you'd be okay though, she thinks the sun shines out of your backside.'

'Are you trying to say it doesn't?'

'I hate to disappoint you, but I'm afraid it doesn't. Well, not quite.'

'Yes, well, sod the risk, it still isn't going to stop me from taking every opportunity to get my hands on you whenever the chance arises.'

'Yes, but we need to be careful, look how close we came to Honey and Susan walking in on us.' She knew Honey suspected something, and Mim was well aware that if she had concrete proof, Honey wouldn't waste a second before running to Susan.

'Yes, I suppose that would've taken some explaining,' he said with a chuckle. He took the reins of their conversation, chatting away, taking his usual dig at Aidey which annoyed Mim. It set little alarm bells ringing which she tried to ignore, telling herself it was just fragile male ego at play and Caspar didn't really mean anything by it. But, deep down, she wasn't so sure and she wished he could keep his thoughts on Aidey to himself, especially since such comments caused an air of awkwardness between them.

As they drove on, Mim toyed with the idea of touching on Anna-Lisa's missing money, but something made her hold back; she was unsure how he'd react. Instead, she decided to test the water with the notebook.

'Do you know if Clarissa managed to find her book?' She turned so she could catch his expression, wondering if it would betray any signs of his feelings for Clarissa.

He paused for a moment before replying, his face frustratingly impassive. 'You mean the blue one with peacock feathers she scribbles all her ideas in?'

'Yes, she came into our room this afternoon, asking if we'd seen it.'

'No, I don't think she has, but I haven't seen her for a few hours so I suppose it might have turned up by now.'

'I hope so.' Mim gazed out of the window, watching the dark clouds creep across the sky forming a thick barrier to the stars, building up her courage to speak further about Clarissa whilst not wanting to sound like she was fishing. 'I really like Clarissa, she's so friendly and really quite thoughtful.'

'Yes, she is.' His expression remained inscrutable.

'And she's so beautiful.'

He paused for a moment. 'I suppose she is. And it's pretty obvious she's the talent behind the magazine.'

Mim couldn't argue with that. 'Yes, I used to read it when it was just an online version before her mum got involved.' She paused and said with a laugh, 'She's nothing like her, is she?'

Caspar followed with a laugh of his own. 'She's nothing like her at all. Simon's more like Susan, as is Kenneth. And despite input from the three of them, the magazine would be nothing without Clarissa, or people like you, Mim.' He turned and flashed her a smile that triggered a bloom of happiness inside her, chasing her doubts about him away.

'I agree with what you say about Clarissa, but you're just being kind about me.'

'I do wish you wouldn't do that.'

'What?'

'Sell yourself short, Mim Dewberry. You never accept a compliment; you do it all the time. You're not only incredibly sexy, you're intelligent and brilliant at your job, too. Yorkshire Portions wouldn't be the same without your input; Susan and Kenneth are well aware of it, and how skilfully you manage all the different hats you have to wear for them. That's why they treat you the way they do, they don't like how you're more creative than them; it scares them. They know you're vital to the success of the magazine and that intimidates them, so by bullying you – for want of a better word – it keeps you doubting yourself, and keeps you in your "place" – in their minds, at least.'

'Oh.' Was there any truth in that?

'Think about it, Mim, you're the epitome of the down-to-earth "Yorkshire lass next door", which is the very demographic they're wanting to target. Why else do you think they get you to write so many features? Your dry, northern sense of humour shines through; it's adorable and approachable. I knew I had to get better acquainted with you before I'd even met you; your writing style draws people in, makes them want to be your friend.'

Mim was lost for words. He'd wanted to get to know her *before* he'd even started at Yorkshire Portions? *Did* the Susan and Kenneth really think that about her? Is that what Caspar really thought of her writing, or was he just paying her lip-service to spare her feelings? Having said that, she had to admit, as much as she enjoyed marketing, she loved getting stuck into a bit of writing, letting her creative side loose on the page. And, come to think of it, Anna had regularly complimented Mim on her features as she'd been proofing them. But, in typical Mim style, Mim thought Anna was just being kind because they were best friends.

'You're pulling my leg.'

'I most certainly am not.'

'Really? You honestly think all that, you're not just teasing me?'

'Why would I tease you? I mean every word of it, Mim, from the bullying right through to how talented you are. Though, I'd appreciate it if you wouldn't share what I've just told you with anyone else, I don't think it would go down too well with the bosses.'

Mim winced at the thought. 'I wouldn't dream of it, my lips are well and truly sealed.'

Basking in the glow of his words, feeling inexorably happy, Mim couldn't believe she'd allowed herself to doubt Caspar. Somehow, whenever her worries and insecurities were beginning to rear up, he seemed to have the ability to dispel them and, in the process, make her feel as if she was the luckiest girl in the world. It was almost as if he knew when it was necessary, when to deliver just the right words.

As they travelled along, she pushed her worries about Honey and her job to the back of her mind, allowing happiness to take over. She leaned back in the warmth of the leather seat and smiled, thinking how lucky she was to have someone like Caspar in her life.

25

As they pulled up outside of Pear Tree Cottage, Mim was hopeful that tonight would be different to the other nights this week when Caspar had dropped her off. If their earlier conversation was anything to go by, she felt sure it would be. Still, she resisted the urge to say something to him since she didn't want to come across as complaining or pushy, but she couldn't help but hope for more than a hastily grabbed encounter in the hallway, with Caspar disappearing before she went along to collect Herbert from Carly's. And, much as she enjoyed the passion and urgency, Mim couldn't shake the thought that it was starting to almost feel a little sordid; cheap even. Yes, the odd once or twice, when passion got the better of you or there was no other opportunity, then a "quickie" was fun. But not every time.

Was it unreasonable to want to spend more time with him, she wondered, or was she being clingy? With her history of getting it wrong so many times, she was keen to do things right with Caspar. What would other women expect? What would Clarissa expect? Mim had to admit, she was beginning to feel a little confused by the dynamics of their relationship. Before his complimentary words in the car, she'd tried to face facts, be honest with herself, wondering if they were actually going anywhere. But she didn't want to be honest. Being honest didn't give her the answers she wanted to hear, and she didn't want to let the tiniest doubt sneak in. And she certainly didn't want to think of herself as someone's "quick shag", or that she was being used just for sex; that would hurt. All she wanted was to spend a little more quality time with Caspar. Was that so bad? She was desperate to tell him that travelling along in the car together was all very well, as was their fast and furious sex, but it couldn't compare to having a relaxed conversation over a coffee or a glass of wine, or snuggling up together on the sofa and getting to know more about one another, or spending lazy nights in bed like they had last Friday. But Mim was afraid she wouldn't like his response, or that it would push him away, so she kept her thoughts to herself. It didn't help that this week, there'd always been a reason for him to shoot off and not even stay for a coffee. Did he really dislike Herbert so much he didn't want to be in the same building as him. Did Herbert really dislike Caspar so much? Hmm. She knew the answer to that. Or was Caspar really only after one thing? Mim quickly shoved that unpalatable question out of the way.

Caspar followed her down the path and into the cottage. The door had hardly had the chance to click shut before his lips were on hers, his hands roving hungrily over her body. And, much as she was desperate to pull away and suggest they take things to the comfort of the bedroom, she bit her tongue; she knew he wouldn't be interested in that, besides, at this very moment, she wanted him as badly as he appeared to want her.

'You're so hot.' He dropped a trail of kisses down towards her breasts, the pupils of his eyes so dilated his dark eyes looked almost black.

Mim felt her face flush with desire as Caspar worked his magic. She pushed away the voice telling her she was being used, and focused on what was happening in that moment; how he was making her feel. She shrugged off her coat as he pushed up her flimsy cotton skirt.

'You do realise that working with you is absolute torture, don't you?' he said when they'd finished.

Mim's heart sank. 'It is?' *This is it, he's going to dump me.* She hardly dared breathe as she anticipated his answer.

'Well, when I'm there, all I can think about is how you're working just a couple of rooms away from me in your naughty little tops displaying your rather fabulous cleavage, and your tiny little skirts with your divine legs that go on forever. It really is very distracting when I'm trying to get on with my work, and my mind wanders on to how much I'd like to get my hands on you.' He kissed her hard. 'Mmm. You're delicious.'

Mim's heart picked itself up off the floor and soared. 'Stop teasing me,' she said with a giggle. 'I know you don't think anything of the sort. And Susan would be after you if she thought you weren't concentrating on your work. Then she'd be after me if she thought I was the reason for it.'

'Let's not worry about her. But I do know that I'm going to have to do my best to get a fix of you at some point at work tomorrow; I don't think I'll be able to last till the evening again.' He looked at her and smiled, tucking his shirt back into his trousers.

'Ah, well, Anna will be bringing me home tomorrow night.' Why did Mim feel like she was doing something wrong?

'Oh? And why's that?' His eyes took on a cool expression which unnerved her slightly.

'Because she's staying over. It's the monthly get-together with our group of friends in the village; Anna always comes to them.'

'But she doesn't live in the village.'

If Mim didn't know better, she could have sworn he seemed a little huffy about it. 'I know, but with her coming over to see me as much as she does, she's got to know everyone here and fits in really well; they're her friends as much as mine now.' She could see he was mulling this over. 'What's the matter? Have I said something?' And there was her infamous boyfriend paranoia, creeping in.

As if suddenly remembering himself, Caspar's expression changed, the dark cloud lifting from his face. 'No, not at all, darling. It's just that I was looking forward to spending a romantic evening with you, and I'd planned on picking up a takeaway for us to share from my favourite Indian restaurant, as well as another bottle of fine wine from my parents' cellar. And then, you know…' He lifted a strand of her hair and started to twirl it around his finger. 'I was hoping we could have a little repeat of last Friday night.'

Oh. My. Days! Mim's mind was thrown into turmoil. She'd been so looking forward to tomorrow night with her friends and the fun time she knew she'd have with them, her worries temporarily chased away by their hilarious stories and the face-ache-inducing belly-laughs they always had. But the idea of spending the evening with Caspar and his hint at a repeat of the previous Friday had triggered a powerful desire to be with him. She found her resolve slipping away as her heart went into battle with her head. It was a feeling she'd had so many times before with previous boyfriends, and she didn't like the fight one little bit. And it was one in which her heart was always victorious.

'And I have an important question I'd like to ask you.' He ran his finger along her bottom lip before dropping a tantalising kiss on it.

Her mind was all over the place, the heat of his kiss sending lust swirling around inside her once more. *What could be so important that it would have to wait until tomorrow night for him to ask her? Surely it wasn't…? No! Don't be so bloody ridiculous girl; you've only known him a fortnight! Why on earth would he be about to ask you that? Get a grip!* 'I don't suppose you could ask me it now?'

'Not really; I'd prefer to ask it when we're both feeling a little more relaxed with the weekend ahead of us.'

What could that mean? Once again, myriad thoughts were racing around Mim's mind and she was making sense of none of them. She looked into the dark eyes that were looking down at her so intently, hoping to see a clue lurking in the deep, black pools. But that only served to turn her heart and legs to mush. Before she knew it, a little voice was telling her to scrap her plans with her friends. Surely they'd understand that she'd want to spend time with him when she had the chance; after all, they were always saying they wanted the best for her. Wouldn't spending time with Caspar be the best for her tomorrow night, especially when he had an important question for her? Her pulse surged as images of their heady love-making the previous Friday filled her mind. She was just about to speak when her mobile phone started ringing from her bag.

'Who the hell is that?' The impatience in Caspar's voice snapped her back to reality.

'I don't know; it doesn't matter, I'll call them back later.' It was probably Anna-Lisa or Aidey, but Mim had the feeling it would annoy Caspar if she mentioned either of their names, so she kept quiet. And, for some reason, she wasn't keen to speak to either of them while he was there to overhear the conversation. Her happy thoughts silently slipped away. They were immediately replaced by the voice of common sense. Mim hadn't heard much from that one over the years but right now it was telling her she should stick with her plans to meet her friends and not bow down to Caspar's wishes, regardless of his intriguing question. She was surprised to find it had a strangely bolstering effect upon her.

'As lovely as a repeat of last Friday night sounds, I really can't let my friends down by not going tomorrow night; it's been arranged for weeks and it'd be particularly unfair on Anna if I don't go. We're best mates, and best mates don't do that kind of thing to each other.' For the second time that day, her head had defeated her heart and Mim didn't know what to make of it. One part of her felt proud and strong, while the other part felt like screaming, "No! Don't say that! You don't mean it! You want to spend tomorrow with Caspar, have hot and furious sex with him, eat the delicious Indian takeaway with him, drink the sophisticated wine with him. And, more importantly, hear the question he wants to ask you!"

He stood looking at her, his eyes almost boring into hers; he clearly hadn't been expecting that for an answer. 'Are you sure?' He cupped her face in his hands and kissed her, knocking her thoughts right off balance, just as he obviously intended.

She pulled back. 'I am.' *Am I? Oh, those eyes, oh those lips...* 'I'm free on Saturday, though.'

He paused for a moment. 'I'm afraid that's no good for me, plans and all that.'

'Oh, okay. Working late for your parents?'

'Amongst other things. Anyway, I won't keep you any longer. See you in the morning.' His mood reverted to the cool one she was learning he adopted when he didn't get his own way. He strode off into the dark of the night leaving her standing on the doorstop watching after him.

'Bye, thanks for the lift.' Mim closed the door, her mind and heart in conflict. His sudden change in mood had left her feeling uncomfortable, as did his evasive answer when she'd asked him what he was doing on Saturday. And what on earth did he want to ask her? He'd made it sound so intriguing. Maybe he was planning a romantic break, just the two of them, somewhere where no one would recognise them. That would be lovely! That thought was quickly followed by another: he clearly wasn't happy about her seeing her friends, though he'd tried to hide it. Another thought was hot on the heels of that one: would he always want to keep them a secret? She hoped not, it was beginning to feel like there was another reason for keeping their relationship under wraps. Was he embarrassed by her? Did he already have a girlfriend? Neither thought made her feel particularly good about herself. 'Get a grip, woman!' she said out loud. 'Caspar's a busy man and is being a dutiful son by helping his parents out. And he's keeping quiet about your relationship to save you from a load of crap from the bosses. That's all! You should be glad of that. End of!'

She puffed out her cheeks and released a noisy sigh. Feeling this way was exhausting; she should be thankful someone like Caspar had even looked at her when he could have someone as gorgeous and sophisticated as Clarissa. She needed to stop over-analysing everything he said or did. She picked her coat up from the floor and shrugged it on; it was time to go and get Herbert from Carly's. The thought of seeing the pair of them sent a wave of happiness washing over her.

She was about to leave the house when she remembered the missed call that had niggled Caspar; she fished her phone out of her bag to see it had been from Anna-Lisa, no doubt she'd have asked Caleb about the missing money. The reminder sent a spike of anxiety through her. Mim was sure he hadn't taken it, and she hoped it hadn't caused any unnecessary tension between the pair. She'd call her back as soon as she'd collected Herbert.

'Hi Anna, sorry I didn't pick up before, I was just getting Herbert from Carly's.'

'Hey no worries, chick. I just wanted to let you know that Caleb didn't know anything about the money, not that I thought he did, but I just had to rule it out before we go accusing people.'

Mim's heart sank. 'And there's no point asking if you're sure you had it in your purse this morning because we all know how organised you are.'

'I'm absolutely positive. Like I said before, I can remember specifically checking and seeing a twenty pound note just before I left the house.'

'The question is, where's it gone?'

'I know where I'd point the finger, but it's difficult when we have no proof, a suspicion isn't enough. And I know twenty pounds isn't a huge sum of money, but the thought that someone's been in my bag and in my purse makes me feel really uneasy.'

'I can imagine, and it's not like we can blame it on the ghost, is it? Blaming it for moving things around is one thing, but it's hardly going to go rifling through people's bags.'

'Ughh! I'm getting seriously brassed off with that bloody place.

The atmosphere's getting worse, and what with Honey, I don't know how much longer I can stick it there.'

'Same here, and that's what Aidey said, too, not so much about Honey, more the way he's been treated.'

'Can't say I blame him.'

Sensing they were venturing onto a sensitive area, namely Caspar, Mim thought it best to change the subject. 'At least we've got tomorrow night to look forward to; it'll be good to have a laugh with the lasses and let our hair down.'

'I honestly can't wait. I'm practically counting down the hours. It'll be nice to have some company in the evening for a change. Surprise, surprise, Caleb's disappeared into his computer room to slay more dragons with his buddies. I might as well live on my own.'

'Oh, chick, I'm sorry to hear that, but I suppose it's all the more reason to enjoy tomorrow night then.'

'Too true. And, while I remember, we need to find a moment over the weekend to have a chat with Aidey about Honey's campaign of terror at Yorkshire Portions; work out what we should do about it,' said Anna-Lisa.

'Well, you're welcome to stay an extra night here, and we could see if Aidey would like to come over on Saturday afternoon, once we've shaken off our hangovers; he could stay over, too,' said Mim.

'Sounds like a plan, we can run it by him tomorrow.'

The friends finished their call and Mim turned to Herbert. 'Right, Herbs, it's time to flex my culinary skills again.' She opened a tin of tomato soup, tipped it into a pan and set it on the hob while the Labrador looked on intently, his ears twitching as she spoke to him. 'See how I did that? The skill involved in using a tin opener is seriously underestimated.' She fished a tub of cream out of the fridge. 'And a dollop of this will elevate that humble tin of soup to a whole new gastronomic level. Don't let anyone ever tell you I'm not a culinary genius.'

26

THAT NIGHT, when Mim had gone to bed, she closed her eyes and felt herself giving Caspar's words free rein to gallop through her mind, which they did with utter abandon. Her imagination chased wild ideas and scenarios, scattering them everywhere – she even allowed herself to indulge in the crazy thought of a marriage proposal. That had made her heart thump and she quickly shooed it away as being ridiculous, making herself blush that she'd even thought of it.

It didn't take long for her thoughts to venture onto Clarissa and where she fitted into Caspar's feelings. A comment Honey had thrown at her earlier in the day sprang to mind. 'Clarissa seems to be spending a lot of time in Caspar's room, I reckon they're having a fling.' At the time, Mim had brushed it off as just another of Honey's spiteful barbs. But now, in the depths of night, when she had time to analyse it, it added fuel to her suspicion that the pair were more than work colleagues.

She lay awake for hours. Only when the early glimmer of daybreak sneaked in through the gap in the curtains and the dawn chorus kicked in could she feel her eyelids getting heavy and the soothing warmth of slumber throw itself over her.

IT FELT like she'd been asleep for a matter of minutes when her alarm clock cruelly invaded her dreams at seven o'clock the following morning. Rain was hammering against the window and the wind was howling angrily around the house. With a groan, Mim reached for the clock and flicked it on to slumber mode. She was tired, it sounded horrible outside and her bed was so lovely and cosy; just five more precious minutes would make all the difference. And another five, and another five until: 'Oh, shit a brick!' The last time Mim had set the alarm for five more minutes' slumber, she'd accidentally turned it off, only to be woken with a start by Herbert barking from the kitchen. She checked the time, it was five to eight. 'Bugger! Bugger! Bugger!' She jumped up and pulled her dressing gown on before racing downstairs to let Herbert out for a quick toilet trip. She could wave goodbye to breakfast and a shower, she barely had enough time to get dressed and get Herbert to Carly's. Ughh! Mim hated mornings like these; in her experience they set you up badly for the whole day; that horrible feeling of having to race around to get ready, heart galloping, and adrenalin coursing through your veins. It was the last thing she needed for today; the day she'd been looking forward to all week.

Despite getting up late, Mim somehow managed to get herself ready in time for when Caspar arrived to take her to work. In an ideal world, she'd have washed her hair but with time being in short supply, she'd improvised and pinned it up in a makeshift, messy up-do.

'You're looking very sexy this morning. I like your hair like that, looks like you've been up all night doing naughty things, if you know what I mean. Reminds me of how it looked last Saturday morning.' Caspar leaned across and kissed her. 'Mmm-hmm. Don't suppose you've changed your mind about tonight, have you?'

Mim's heart somersaulted. She wished he didn't make her feel so torn like this. 'Erm, no, I can't, it's too late, and wouldn't be fair. I'm pleased you like my hair, though, it's actually a case of desperate measures.' She went on to explain about how she'd slept in and had no time to shower, never mind wash and dry her thick mane of hair.

'Well, can I just say, for the record, I prefer you dirty.' He flashed her a wicked grin, showing the snaggle tooth that Mim found so appealing.

'MIMBO, I think you're going to have to tidy some of the clutter off your desk, it's starting to migrate over to me.' Anna-Lisa nudged an empty sweet packet with her pen. 'Your scruff gene is getting a little carried away with itself again.'

Mim looked at her desk; she couldn't argue, there were remnants of her old to-do lists and a variety of pens scattered over it keeping company with a half-drunk cup of tea that had been there for a couple of days; it had developed an unappetising-looking film on its surface. 'Mmm, you have a point, sorry, Anna.' She picked up the jug of wilting gerberas that Aidey had bought her the previous week and threw the flowers in the bin, scrunching up her nose at the foul smelling, stagnant water. 'Ughh! That stinks like rotten eggs.'

'That's what happens when you don't chuck them away when they're dead. And it looks like all those bits of paper you have over there have been breeding,' said Anna-Lisa.

'Yeah, I think it's reached the point where my desk needs a tidy up. By the way, did you mention tomorrow night to Aidey?'

'I did, yep, he's keen. He's just having a word with Susan. The mighty one summoned him to her office in her usual pleasant manner.'

Mim rolled her eyes just as Honey walked in. 'What's the matter with your face, Jemima?'

Mim groaned inwardly; that girl aroused feelings in her nobody else ever did. She bit down on her annoyance. 'Nothing whatsoever.'

'I see Aidey's late. Looks like you lot have got no better with your time-keeping.'

Anna-Lisa glanced up at the clock. 'For your information, Honey, Aidey's been here a good forty-five minutes and is in with Susan at the moment. It's you who's late.'

Honey pouted, at ten past nine, she couldn't argue with that. 'Okay, keep your knickers on, Anal Lisa.' She took her coat off and hung it on the back of her chair. 'Don't suppose Clarissa's found her notebook?'

Mim stole a look at Anna-Lisa; from her expression they were clearly thinking the same thing: Honey knew something about it and the girl was trying to antagonise them.

Mim remained quiet, reluctant to get involved in a conversation with Honey.

'Not that I've heard, but I'm sure it'll turn up,' said Anna-Lisa.

'I'm sure it will. Probably in the most unexpected place.'

The tone of her words sent a prickle of fear up Mim's spine.

THE SHRILL RING of the phone on Mim's desk snapped her out of her concentration. She kept one eye on her work as she picked it up. 'Hello.'

'Oh, that sexy, husky voice of yours does unmentionable things to me.' It was Caspar; she tried to hide the smile a surge of happiness had triggered.

'Oh, hi.' She felt Anna-Lisa's eyes on her.

'Could you just pop down to my office for a moment?'

'Sure. I'll be there in two ticks.' She put the phone down and scooped up a notebook and pen.

'Who was that? I bet it was Caspar, judging by that daft grin on your face,' said Honey. 'Does he need me to go with you?'

'He didn't mention you, and I can pass on any information if it's necessary. It's pointless two of us being away from our desks.'

'Yeah, well, if I'd answered the phone it would've been me who he'd ask to go to his office.'

'But you didn't, Honey.' Mim was getting tired of dealing with Honey's spoilt teenager act.

'I'm sure I saw Clarissa leaving his room earlier; she was looking very happy with herself. Can't think what they'd been up to,' Honey said with a satisfied smirk.

Mim ignored her and hurried out of the room before she could say any more.

As soon as Mim stepped into Caspar's office, he pulled her into a passionate kiss that turned her knees to jelly.

'You've no idea what you do to me, Mim. I've never felt this way about anyone.' He pressed his lips against her neck, running his hands over her breasts.

His words sent her pulse racing, while Honey's words hovered in the periphery of her thoughts. Did he really mean that?

There was a sharp rap at the door and they pulled apart just in time as Clarissa entered the room. She glanced between the two of them. 'Hi, I just wanted to check that I hadn't left my notebook in here after our meeting yesterday.'

'Yes, I'd heard it was missing, but I haven't seen it in here. I'll have a proper look around after I've run my idea by Mim, just in case it's lurking somewhere.' He flashed her a charming smile.

'Thanks, Caspar, I honestly can't think where it's gone so I'm checking everywhere.'

'I'll let you know if it turns up in here.'

Clarissa smiled and left the room.

Had Honey been lying or was that just a convincing act to cover the real reason Clarissa had come to his office, Mim wondered. She pushed her doubts away. 'Phew! That was close.'

'Just a bit.'

'You don't think she suspected anything, do you?'

'I doubt it, she seems too hung up about that bloody book.'

His dismissive tone surprised Mim.

'Anyway, lovely Mim Dewberry, back to us.' He planted a lingering kiss on her lips that sent her stomach swirling. 'I just wanted to make sure I definitely can't tempt you to spend the evening with me and put your get-together with your friends on hold until the next time – I mean, it's not like you don't ever see them, is it?'

Not this again. After Caspar's kisses, Mim was thrown into turmoil. But it was too late in the day; Anna had brought her overnight bag and was expecting to stay at Mim's, the two of them spending the evening at Carly's. And, besides, Mim had been looking forward to it. 'Sorry, Caspar, I'm afraid it's only fair that I stick to my original plans; I don't want to let my friends down.'

A shadow crossed his face and his eyes took on a cold expression. Mim felt unnerved; he clearly didn't like to be turned down.

Before she knew it, his smile had returned and he delivered another delicious kiss to her mouth. 'That's what I like, a woman who knows her own mind, and is always keen to do the right thing.'

'My friends mean a lot to me, that's all.'

'I can see that, and it's actually probably a good time to ask you that question I mentioned yesterday. I don't think it's fair to keep you hanging on. No doubt you've been wondering about it.' Caspar gave one of his familiar disarming smiles; if only he knew just how much she'd been wondering about it.

'Oh?' Mim's heart rate cranked up several notches.

'Mmm. It's quite an important one.'

Oh, my days! She looked across at him. A muscle twitched in his cheek; he looked like he was trying to choose the right words. It was sending a mixture of emotions racing around her insides. 'Is everything alright?'

'Yes, everything's fine. It's just that I need a little favour from you.'

A favour? From me? Disappointment crushed any hope of it being anything she'd like. 'A favour? What kind of favour?'

'Well, it's complicated, but it's really to help my parents out. You see, they've been having a spot of bother with their bank – they're actually in the process of changing who they bank with but it's taking a little longer than expected – you know what banks can be like. Anyway, they have a client who's very keen to pay them for a car they've bought, well, it's two clients actually, and they're both very keen. But my parents being in limbo with their bank means they have no account for their clients to transfer the money into.'

'Oh, so how can I help with that?' This was nothing remotely like the question she was expecting.

'Well, I was wondering if it would be possible for their clients to pay the money into your bank account and then, when my parents are sorted out with theirs, you can transfer the money across. It's a very simple solution that wouldn't inconvenience you at all. They'd even let you take a cut for the inconvenience.'

'Oh. Right. But why can't they pay the money into your account?' Mim was hopeless with money and knew very little about banks other than that was the place her wages got paid into and she had a card to take money out of a hole in the wall. Was she being really stupid here and missing something obvious?

'Ah, good question. They can't transfer payment into my account because I'm having the same problem as my parents.'

'Oh, I see.' This felt a little odd. 'How much money would it be exactly?'

'It'd be roughly a hundred and twenty thousand – you can see why my parents are keen to get a solution straight away. We'd need your account details as soon as possible, otherwise the clients won't be able to have their cars. You can imagine how that would affect my parents' reputation. They've spent years building it up through sheer hard work, they're very well-respected.'

'They must be pretty fancy cars to be worth that much.'

'They are, my parents deal in high-spec motor vehicles, selling them to the rich and famous abroad.'

'Right, well, no one's ever asked me to do anything like this before. If you don't mind, I'd like to think about it over the weekend and let you know on Monday.' Alarm bells were ringing and Anna's words of warning earlier in the week crept into her mind. Something in her gut didn't feel right.

'Well, if you must. I was really hoping to have this sorted out for my parents before then. And it goes without saying, I'd prefer it if you kept this to yourself, my parents are very private about their business.'

'Oh, okay.' This felt wrong on so many levels. Was this what he wanted her to give up an evening with her friends for, ditch Anna-Lisa while he worked on her to do a favour for his parents? She felt suddenly hurt, and not a little stupid.

Mim was thankful when Susan rang, asking Caspar to pop to her office. 'Right, I'd better head down there. Let me know if you change your mind about tonight.'

'I really can't.'

'Shame I can't meet up with you on Saturday, I'd much rather spend it with you than what I'm actually doing.' He cupped her face in his hands and kissed her. 'And it's a shame we didn't get to take things further just now. Looks like the Pallister-Biggs are conspiring against us.'

Despite her misgivings, the smile he gave her still had the power to send butterflies fluttering in her stomach.

When Mim returned to her office there was no sign of Honey, and Aidey was sitting at his desk. 'Morning, Mimbo.'

'Hi, Aidey. Has Anna mentioned tomorrow to you?'

'She has, sounds good.'

'If you fancy coming over early afternoon, we could go to the pub for a roast dinner.'

'Sounds even better.'

'We can't guarantee we won't be a little hungover,' said Anna-Lisa.

Aidey laughed. 'That I can imagine once you lot get together. Is Pat Motson still up in arms?'

'Thankfully, I haven't seen much of the old witch, apart from her hovering behind the curtains, but according to Carly she witters on at her every time she sees her, telling her we're lowering the tone of the village.'

'Why would having a few drinks around at your friend's house lower the tone?' He looked puzzled.

'It might have something to do with the fact that they've been spreading a rumour that it's a kinky underwear party complete with a male stripper called Hosé Horny,' said Anna-Lisa.

Aidey clamped his hand to his brow. 'You lot are terrible, winding up a little old lady like that.'

'For one, she's not that old, and secondly, she's such a miserable old prude, it makes it hard to resist.' Mim flashed him a mischievous smile, thoughts of her recent conversation with Caspar slipping away. 'And, just for the record, we're not having a kinky underwear party—'

'Not that it would matter if we were,' said Anna-Lisa.

Aidey opened his eyes wide and shook his head. 'Course not.'

Mim continued, 'And there's no stripper coming. It's just our usual get-together, but the new vicar's wife's joining us for the first time.'

'Brave woman.' Aidey laughed, ducking as Mim threw a rubber at him.

'Hey, you, we're a friendly bunch,' she said.

'Yeah, we just know how to have a bit of fun,' added Anna-Lisa.

'My point exactly,' said Aidey. 'Oh, and while I remember, I'd keep a low profile with Susan, she's in a foul mood.'

'Just for a change,' said Anna-Lisa.

'It's looking very industrious in here.' Caspar popped his head round the door of Mim's office. He looked heart-meltingly handsome. She noted Aidey didn't look up.

'Yep, that's us, industrious,' said Anna-Lisa. 'We're trying to get everything done so we're free to enjoy the weekend.'

'Mmm. So I gather. Anyway, the reason I'm troubling you is to see if anyone's seen the paperweight I usually have on my desk? The round glass one? It's an Italian antique and, as well as being worth quite a bit, it has great sentimental value since it was a present from my parents. It was there on my desk first thing this morning, but it seems to be missing now.'

Mim's stomach clenched with anxiety. She looked over at Anna-Lisa whose expression mirrored her concerns. Her eyes travelled over to Honey who had fixed Mim with a determined stare. 'As far as I'm aware, Mim's been the only one in your office today. You haven't scooped it up, have you, Mim? Added it to the clutter on your desk?'

'I certainly have not!' Mim could feel her anger rising. Was this Honey and her mind games again? From the goading look on the girl's face, she was sure of it. She resisted the temptation to ask her if she had anything to do with it; she didn't want to alert Honey that they were on to her.

'Maybe it was the ghost again? He seems to be up to quite a bit recently, don't you think, Anna-Lisa?' Honey shared her antagonising look with Anna. Mim was relieved that her friend didn't bite.

'Maybe. We'll have a look around for it for you, Caspar, let you know if we find it.' Anna-Lisa gave him a tight smile and got back to her work.

'Er, okay, thanks.' Caspar seemed wrong-footed that Anna-Lisa still hadn't succumbed to his charms.

'Wonder where it could be?' Honey said when he'd left the room.

'No idea,' said Anna-Lisa. 'But if you don't mind, we've all got work that we'd like to get finished before we leave tonight.'

'Sorry.' Honey used the petulant tone that meant she wasn't sorry at all.

27

MIM'S HEART felt light as she travelled along the roads to Skeltwick in Anna-Lisa's little car. The pair were singing along to the radio at the top of their voices. 'Ughh! This one's boring.' Anna-Lisa pressed a button on the dashboard, changing the station. 'That's better.' She drove along, tapping her fingers against the steering wheel.

'Not that I want to spoil tonight with talking about work the whole time, but what do you think about Caspar's paperweight going missing?' asked Mim.

'Honey's responsible, without a doubt. Did you see the look on her face when he asked about it?'

'I did.'

'I don't suppose you noticed if it was on his desk when you were in his office this morning?'

'You know what I'm like, it wouldn't register if I did.' The temptation to bring up Caspar's question was on the tip of her tongue, but something held her back.

'And why would you feel you had to take notice of everything that was on his desk? You'd hardly expect anything to go missing from his room.'

'Well, we didn't expect Clarissa's notebook to go missing, but it has. What do you think's happened to them? And your money, for that matter. I'm just relieved she hasn't seen fit to put them in my bag again.' That thought sent a ripple of disquiet through her.

'Hmm. True.' She turned to Mim and grinned. 'Anyway, enough

about miserable, bloody Yorkshire Portions and the weird goings on there, tonight we're going to have fun.' Anna-Lisa turned up the radio and launched into her singing with gusto.

Mim opened the door of Pear Tree Cottage and headed down the hallway followed by Anna-Lisa. 'It doesn't seem the same without Herbert's enthusiastic greeting,' said Anna.

'I know, but Carly says he might as well stay at hers since we're going along later. He and Maisie are joining the fun, too.'

'That's what I like to hear. Am I alright to pop my stuff upstairs, before I go back to the car and get the tub of food I made to take along tonight?'

'Course you can, I can't wait to see what it is. It'll be far more adventurous than my corn chips with grated cheese and soured cream.' Mim loved Anna's cooking which was way ahead of hers in the ability and quality stakes.

'Hey, don't knock corn chips, everyone loves them.'

'I've even got some salsa.' Mim grinned, shaking the jar at her.

'Perfect.'

'Right, while you're doing that I'll stick the kettle on; I think it's a little early to start on alcohol just yet.' Mim made her way over to the sink and filled the kettle.

'Very wise, I think I need to line my stomach a bit before we touch any, to be honest. Have you got any biscuits or cake?'

'Of course.'

'True, daft question, I've never known you not to have a plentiful supply.'

'Right, I think we're ready to paint the town red, or at the very least Carly's.' Mim made the final adjustments to her hair. 'And I can't wait to get my teeth into those millionaire's chocolate brownies you've made, they look heavenly.'

'Thanks, I hope they're alright.'

'They'll be delicious.'

'Hardly great for the waistline, but what the hell, it's Friday.'

'I've heard calories don't count from a Friday right through to a

Sunday night. Not that you need to worry about calories, you're tiny. It's folk like me with a rather large elephant physique who need to take note.'

'Right, before we go any further, that's the last time I want to hear you put yourself down tonight. Okay?'

'Hey, I was only joking.'

'I wish I could believe that, but you always do it, and you shouldn't. So no more tonight, right?'

'Right you are, captain.' Mim grinned and saluted her friend, recalling how Caspar had said something similar the other day. *Caspar? Huh!* She pushed thoughts of him right out of her mind; he was way too confusing to think about on a Friday night when she was going to have fun with her friends.

Mim rang the doorbell, triggering a commotion behind the door. As soon as Carly opened it, Herbert shot out, in raptures at seeing Mim and Anna-Lisa.

'Wow, that's a greeting and a half,' Anna-Lisa said, laughing.

'Come on in out of the cold, lasses, you're the first ones here.'

'That's because we're keen to get started,' said Mim.

'Nothing new there with you two,' Carly said with a giggle.

The two friends stepped into the warmth of the hallway, dodging the dogs who shot by them, racing into the kitchen.

'Looks like we're not the only ones keen to get started,' said Anna-Lisa.

'Hi, ladies, just pretend I'm not here.' Owen popped his head round the door of the living room.

'Hi, Owen,' said Anna-Lisa.

'Hi, Owen, I hope we don't disturb you with all our noisy chatter,' said Mim.

'Don't worry about that, I've got a few films lined to keep me entertained. You lot just enjoy yourselves.'

'Don't worry, we will. Come on through,' said Carly.

Before long the kitchen was filled with the laughter and chatter of the group of friends.

'So what does your husband think of you joining us tonight, Gemma?' Carly asked the vicar's wife.

'Yeah, we can be a bit of a rowdy bunch when we get going – all very harmless I should add,' said Lou. 'I get disapproving reports coming back to me at the shop from Pat Motson and the likes, as if I have nothing to do with it. It's hilarious.'

'Ooh, she'll be turning herself inside out tonight, especially since she thinks we're having a racy party complete with a male stripper,' said Mim.

'She doesn't?' Gemma pressed her hand to her mouth, her eyes growing wide.

'Oh, but she does. And she knows all about you joining us, too,' said Debbie, who lived two doors away at Yew Tree Cottage.

'Hmm. Should be interesting explaining that to David,' said Gemma.

'Shame we don't have a stripper.' Michelle, who was new to the village herself, gave a throaty laugh.

'And you should've seen the curtain twitching at Cuckoo's Nest Cottage as I walked by. It was in overdrive,' said Amy. 'Pat Motson actually stopped me when I was on the way back from a run the other day and asked if there was any truth in the rumours that you were leading us all astray, Carly.'

'Hah! Really, she put it like that?' Carly asked, giggling.

'She did, and I told her, yes, you very much were, and we were all thoroughly enjoying it, which sent her scurrying back into her house with a face like a slapped backside.'

'Oh, fabulous.' Sharon from Rosemary Cottage joined in the giggling.

Anna-Lisa picked up a corn chip and popped it into her mouth. 'Fab nachos, by the way, Mim.'

'Thanks, it's down to the skill of how you grate the cheese. I think I've perfected my technique.'

'Actually, there's something I've been meaning to ask you, Mim,' said Sharon.

'Oh, what's that?'

'Who's that gorgeous hunk you get a lift to work with? He looks very tasty.' Sharon waggled her eyebrows mischievously.

Mim felt herself flush. 'Oh, erm, that's Caspar. Caspar De Verre, he's new at our office and travels in this way so he picks me up and drops me off.'

'Oh, I know of that family,' said Gemma. 'They have some sort of company that, from what I can gather, deal with, well, nobody knows what really. But I've heard their name mentioned in relation to property development. Actually, I do believe the family used to be called Cleghorn but they changed it to De Verre in the eighties. As I say, no one's really sure what kind of business it is they run, but they have a certain reputation, if you know what I mean. They seem to have their fingers in lots of pies, some of them supposedly unsavoury – but I didn't say that.'

'Hmph. Why doesn't that surprise me?' said Anna-Lisa.

'Yes, rumour has it they're not the sort of family to get on the wrong side of.' Gemma looked over at Mim. 'But they're only rumours; I'm sure Caspar's very nice.'

Mim mustered up a smile despite the clench in her stomach.

The evening passed quickly and soon Carly, Mim and Anna-Lisa were waving Gemma and the rest of the friends off at the doorstep. 'Thanks for coming, lasses,' said Carly. She raised her voice. 'And how many pairs of crotchless knickers did you say you wanted to order, Gemma?' She gave a theatrical wink followed by a cheeky grin.

Gemma managed to make herself heard amongst the giggles. 'Ooh, let's make it seven, one for every day of the week.'

'Woah, Rev Dave'll think it's his birthday and Christmas all rolled into one.' Amy roared with laughter. 'We'll all have to go to church and see how big his smile's got.'

'It's not his smile getting bigger I'd be worried about,' Sharon said, cackling.

'Get your mind out of the gutter, Sharon. That's smutty talk about our local man of the cloth,' said Lou.

'Come on you lot, let's get home. Thanks for inviting me, Carly. I'll play hostess for the next one if you like? You can all come and join me at the draughty vicarage,' said Gemma.

'Sounds great,' said Carly.

'Good to see we haven't scared you off.' Amy slotted her arm through Gemma's and they made their way along the path and into the night.

'Well, that's what I'd call a great night.' Carly pressed the door shut with a click. 'Can I tempt you ladies to any more wine?'

'Sounds like a plan. I'd do anything to stretch tonight out, make the weekend seem longer,' said Anna-Lisa. 'And it has been a brilliant night.'

Mim curled up on the floor next to Herbert who rested his big, square head in her lap, making little grunts of contentment as she smoothed his ears. 'Yep, it was a brilliant night, Carly, thanks for playing hostess.' It felt good to forget her worries for a few hours, though what Gemma had said about Caspar's family had unnerved her a little, but she'd done her best to push the thoughts away.

'Yeah, it was great, just what we needed after the week we've had at work,' said Anna-Lisa. 'And Gemma's great fun, isn't she?'

'She is, I'm glad we invited her. I bet she's like a breath of fresh air up at that vicarage,' said Carly. She turned the lights down, leaving just the glow from the under-cupboard lighting boosted by the fairy-lights that were woven around the branches of a large lemon tree that sat by the bi-fold doors. It lent a cosy air to the kitchen. 'And from what you were just saying, I'm guessing things haven't got any better at work then?'

'No,' Mim and Anna-Lisa chorused, taking it in turns to tell her about things going missing.

'Hmm. Sounds pretty dodgy to me. And you think that Honey girl's got something to do with it?'

'We're pretty certain,' said Anna-Lisa. 'And, for some reason, she seems to have got it in for Mim.'

'It sounds to me like a case of the green-eyed monster,' said Carly.

Mim rubbed her eyes, trying to get her contact lenses back into place. She found whenever she was tired or had had a bit too much to drink, they had a habit of floating about, making it difficult for her to focus. 'It's created a horrible atmosphere at work, and we honestly don't know what to expect next. If I think too much about it, I actually feel really scared about what she might do next.'

'I'm guessing your thing with Caspar hasn't gone down well with her,' said Carly.

Mim noted her use of the word "thing" rather than relationship; it said a lot. She nodded. 'I think so. I do know she likes him; she's asked if I think he fancies her, but her reaction to it's a bit extreme.'

'How old did you say she was? She sounds like a teenager.' Carly topped up their wine glasses.

'Tell me about it. She's a very immature twenty-two,' said Mim.

The three friends continued chatting away, picking at the leftover snacks and sipping wine. Owen ventured into the kitchen, padding across the floor in his chunky socks. 'Sorry to intrude, ladies, I'm just going to grab a plateful of left-overs for my supper, then I'll be out of your hair.'

'Hey, it's us who should be out of your hair, we're getting dangerously close to outstaying our welcome,' said Anna-Lisa.

'Rubbish! The night is young.' Carly filled a plate with snacks and handed it to her husband. 'There you go, lovie. Enjoy.'

'Mmm. This lot looks good. Right, I'll leave you in peace.'

Once Owen had gone, Anna-Lisa turned to Mim. 'While I remember, I keep meaning to ask how the Dark Count's driving has been after your near miss with that McHubbard & Smithy lorry? Please tell me he's calmed it right down.'

Before Mim had chance to answer Carly jumped up. 'Ooh, that reminds me, there's an article in this week's York Gazette about one of that firm's drivers. Apparently, he was found on some waste land. He'd been quite badly beaten up.'

Mim's blood ran cold as she remembered Caspar's reaction the day they came off the road. Gemma's words of earlier swirled around her mind. Surely neither he nor his family would have had anything to do with the lorry driver being hurt. Caspar certainly didn't give the impression he was the fighting kind. But what if he'd got someone else to do it for him? Would he do that, rather than getting his own hands dirty? After what she'd heard tonight, she had a horrible feeling he probably would.

'Are you okay, chick? The colour's drained from your face,' said Carly.

'It has, Mim. What's up? I can tell there's something the matter. Has it got anything to do with what Carly's just said? Do you know something about it? Does Caspar's family have something to do with it?'

Mim looked across at her friends, marshalling the thoughts that were tumbling around her mind. The feeling of unease about Caspar and his family was increasing by the second. She couldn't say with all honesty that she didn't think they had anything to do with it. And she couldn't shake the suspicion that there was clearly more to that dangerous look in his eyes than she'd bargained for. And, much as he'd told her not to tell anyone about the favour he'd asked of her, she decided to share it with her friends whose views she'd always valued. 'I'm okay, and I honestly don't know if Caspar had anything to do with the lorry driver, he hasn't said anything to me. But … there's something I'd appreciate your opinion on.'

'This sounds serious, Mim. You're worrying me,' said Anna-Lisa.

'The more I think about it, the more I think it is serious. He's asked me to do him a favour, a pretty big one actually, and I'm a bit uneasy about it.'

Mim shared the conversation she'd had with Caspar, adding how keen he'd been for her to cancel that night with her friends. They listened, their expressions growing more and more alarmed. 'So, what do you think it's all about? Do you think it sounds legit?'

'Flaming hell, Mim, no, I don't. I think it sounds seriously dodgy. He casually asks if some clients of his parents you've never heard of can pay a hundred and twenty grand into your bank account like it's nothing.' Anna-Lisa wore an expression of utter disbelief.

'And he said it was payment for cars that are being sold abroad? Makes you wonder what kind of cars they are to cost that much between them. Are they gold-plated or something?' Carly looked as concerned as Anna-Lisa. 'It's hardly your run-of-the-mill favour, is it?'

'I must admit, it made me feel a bit suspicious. I really wish he hadn't asked me,' said Mim. 'And I can't understand why he did; surely his parents must have plenty of their own friends who could do it for them.'

'Which makes it all the more worrying,' said Carly.

'You realise if you agree to it your bank might start asking questions? After all – no offence, Mim – it's hardly like you, or any of us, to get deposits as huge as that on a regular basis,' said Anna-Lisa.

'None taken. I've never had anything remotely like that in my bank.'

'How did you leave it with him?' asked Carly.

'I told him I'd let him know on Monday. He wasn't very happy about it, but with it being such an odd thing, I wanted to have a chance to think it over.'

'Hmph. I bet he expected you to say yes straightaway,' said Anna-Lisa.

'If I'm honest, I think that was probably why he was keen for me to cancel tonight with you guys, so he could come over and work on me.' Much as Mim hated bad-mouthing Caspar to her friends, she knew there was more than a grain of truth in her words. A wave of sadness washed over her, making her wonder if his flattering words were nothing more than a cold-hearted ploy to manipulate her so she'd do what he wanted.

'Jeez, Mim, imagine if you'd backed down about tonight and he'd plied you with drink and managed to get your bank details out of you,' said Anna-Lisa.

'Ughh! Don't.' Mim put her head in her hands, remembering how close she'd come to giving in to him.

'Looks like you've had a lucky escape tonight, chick, but I'm surprised he hasn't pushed to see you tomorrow,' said Carly.

'When I first told him I wasn't free on Friday, I suggested Saturday – it was before I'd arranged to do something with Anna and Aidey – but he said he was doing something with his parents so couldn't meet up; he seemed a bit weird about it.'

'I'll bet he did. I knew he was dodgy from the moment I set eyes on him,' said Anna-Lisa. 'I couldn't put my finger on it, but I just knew there was something shifty about him. That's why I told you to always trust your gut, Mim, which is exactly what you did today, and I'm so bloody pleased you listened to it, hon.'

'Me, too, but I'm dreading Monday, that's if he doesn't turn up on Sunday.'

'Wouldn't he text you first? You could always pretend to be out,' said Anna-Lisa.

'He doesn't have my mobile number, and I don't have his. I did offer him mine but he said he didn't need it since he saw me pretty much every day.'

'Really? Didn't that strike you as odd? Everyone has each other's mobile number these days; we've even got Susan and Kenneth's, not that I'd ever be tempted to text them.'

'I suppose it did a bit.'

'I'm worried about you in case the slime-ball decides to call round and work on you, so I think we should do all we can to make sure you're not left on your own this weekend. I'm happy to stay on Sunday night, too, if you'd like?' said Anna-Lisa.

'Really?' That thought was very appealing to Mim; there was no love lost between him and Anna-Lisa, and there was no way Caspar would hang around if she was there, but all the same, she didn't like to think of her coming between Anna and Caleb when their relationship was on such shaky ground.

'And it goes without saying that you only have to text, call or whatever and Owen or I would be along like a shot,' said Carly.

Mim looked at the two women. 'You two are the most amazing friends I could ever have, thank you.'

'You'd do the same for us,' said Anna-Lisa.

'True, and I know it's easier said than done, but just do your best not to think about it over the weekend. You're entitled to switch off; it's bad enough worrying about Honey without him adding to your problems. From what I can gather, he ain't worth it, chick,' said Carly.

28

'MORNING, sleepy-head. Did you sleep any better than usual last night?' Anna-Lisa was sipping coffee and gazing out of the window as Mim made her way into the kitchen, squinting.

'Not really, but at least I could have a lie-in today which has helped.' She yawned and gave her head a vigorous scratching. ''Ughh! This mop of mine's driving me mad, it's so dry and frazzled and is always full of knots and stuff.'

Herbert trotted over to her, his tail swishing happily. 'Hiya, Herbs.' Mim bent and rubbed his head.

'Stuff?' Anna-Lisa pulled a face of disgust.

'Mmm-hmm. I've found food crumbs in there before now, a clump of congealed scrambled egg, bits of fluff, bits of paper, you name it.'

'Why doesn't that surprise me?'

'I'm actually surprised I haven't found any wildlife nesting in there.'

'You're such a delight. Here, get your mouth around this, it'll give you the kick-start you need.' Anna-Lisa handed Mim a mug of coffee which she took gratefully.

'Mmm. Thanks.'

'And where are your glasses? You wouldn't need to squint if you wore them.'

'Haven't seen them for months. Don't worry, they'll turn up. I lost them before the delightful Honey started working with us so I know it's nothing to do with her.'

'Ughh! Don't mention that girl this morning. Anyway, how's your head?'

'I've known it worse after one of our get-togethers.'

'Yep, me too. We must've been taking it steady.'

'Or we ate enough to soak up all the alcohol.'

'Yep, that's probably more accurate.'

After a cold and soggy week, they'd been blessed with a bright sunny autumnal morning. It was almost as if Mother Nature was trying to cheer them up after the tough time they'd been having at work. Mim sat down at the table and closed her eyes, letting the sun's rays melt over her, warming right through to her bones. She sighed. 'This is bliss.'

Soon she was overheating and she slipped off her pyjama top, leaving her vest top underneath. 'Phew! I'm roasting.'

'Yeah, there's a lot of warmth in that sun behind glass. It's a nice change after the rai… Mim! Your arms.'

'What? Ah, I'd forgotten about that. Yeah, my psoriasis has been acting up a bit recently.' Mim felt herself flush, though she wasn't embarrassed about Anna-Lisa seeing her like this, more that she would know the cause and would attribute some of the blame to Caspar. And she'd be right.

'Oh, chick, they look really sore. Haven't you got any cream for it?'

'I've run out, and since it's such a long time since I had a repeat prescription, I have to make an appointment with one of the doctors before they'll give me any more, which I just haven't had time to do.'

'More like you're too scared to take time off work in case Honey does something when you're not there.'

'Pretty much, yeah.'

Anna-Lisa shook her head. 'It shouldn't be like this, Mim. I can't bear it at Yorkshire Portions but I honestly don't know how you can stand everything that's going on, what with Honey and Caspar, and the way Susan treats you. It's because you're a people-pleaser, but you're no better thought of for letting them make a mug of you, you know that, don't you?'

Mim hung her head, scratching the itchy patch on her arm. 'You're right, I know, but I don't know how to stop.'

'Then it's time we taught you. Actually, you've already taken a step in the right direction by turning Rick down and not giving Caspar the response he wanted straight away, so that's a good start.'

Mim felt suddenly brighter. 'You're right; it's about time I got seriously bad ass'.

'I think it is,' Anna-Lisa said, laughing.

ONCE THEY'D HAD breakfast and showered, the two friends enjoyed a leisurely walk across the fields with Herbert charging about, darting into hedgerows and chasing sticks. The crisp sunshine picked out the warm shades of autumn that decorated the landscape, emphasising their rich, jewel-like glow.

'I love the way Herbs is always so upbeat,' said Anna-Lisa.

'Me too, I'd be lost without him. I'm dreading Josie telling me they're coming back to live over here.'

'Has she given any hints that's likely to happen?'

'No, quite the opposite in fact. But if they did, it wouldn't be so bad having to move out of the cottage, but it would break my heart not to have Herbert anymore; he's totally stolen my heart.'

'If it's any consolation, I think he'd feel the same. You can tell just by the way he looks at you he absolutely adores you.'

'Really?' Anna-Lisa's words gave Mim a warm glow. 'Well, the feeling's mutual.'

Though Mim had felt herself relax she hadn't managed to chase away the growing worry about Caspar and his family, especially after what Gemma had said. It went head-to-head with her feelings for him, making her feel all the more confused. Honey might have a reputation for messing with people's mind, but it would seem Caspar was giving her a run for her money.

Herbert, as usual, was always there to lighten her mood exactly when needed. He trotted up to her and Anna-Lisa and dropped a half-decomposed tennis ball at their feet. He sat down in anticipation, swishing his tail through the remnants of a muddy puddle sending droplets flying.

'And what do you expect us to do with that manky object, Herbs?' asked Mim.

He glanced down at the ball and back up at her, his tail wagging increasing in speed.

'Much as I love him to bits, he's got another thing coming if he thinks I'm going to touch that thing, it could be crawling with all sorts,' said Anna-Lisa.

'I think in Herbert's mind that adds to the appeal.' Mim giggled and picked up a stick. 'How about this, Herbs, this looks much more fun.' With that she threw the stick as hard as she could and he raced off after it, the tennis ball all but forgotten.

'Well, that was easy.' Anna-Lisa watched him, laughing.

'Yep, the only other thing that could distract him like that is food.' Mim glanced at her watch. 'Speaking of which, it's probably time we headed back. Aidey'll be here soon and I need to call in at the butchers for a bone for Herbs, then I need to get some more sweets from the village shop. Oh, and I need some bread and milk, too.'

'I love how you add bread and milk as an afterthought.'

The friends looked at one another and giggled before Mim whistled for Herbert who came tearing back to them, the stick clamped between his teeth.

29

By one-thirty there was still no sign of Aidey and Mim had started to worry. 'Where do you think he is?' She glanced up at the kitchen clock. 'It's not like him to be late, or at least not to let us know.'

Anna-Lisa frowned. 'Hmm. You're right, but I'm sure he'll be okay. How about another coffee?'

'I'm sure you're right, and a coffee sounds good. I'll give it another fifteen minutes and I'll call his mobile again.'

Five minutes later, relief flooded through Mim when Aidey's familiar knock at the front door made her jump. Herbert leapt up from his bone in the utility room and charged down the hall, barking as he went.

'Aidey! Where've you been? We've been worried sick.' He'd barely stepped over the threshold before Mim had thrown her arms around his neck, while Herbert danced around him, his nose nudging at Aidey's legs.

'Give the lad chance to get over the doorstep, you two.' Anna-Lisa laughed and went to relieve him of some of the bags he was carrying. 'Here, I'll take these, you look like a packhorse.'

'Thanks, Anna. And, I'm really sorry, I didn't mean to worry you. I ended up having a slight detour and the traffic was really bad. I meant to call but I think I must've thrown my phone in my overnight bag when I was packing this morning. I thought if I just carried on driving, it'd be quicker than me stopping to try and find it.'

'You're here now, that's all that matters, and there's still time to go to the pub for a roast.' Mim released Aidey from her embrace, the familiar comforting smell of his woody cologne dancing around her nostrils. It triggered a feeling of warmth inside her.

'Well, that is good news.' Aidey followed the two friends down to the kitchen. He deposited a large paper carrier bag onto the table next to the two bags Anna-Lisa had put there before sliding his overnight bag off his shoulder and setting it on the floor. Herbert dived on it instantly, giving every inch a thorough sniffing. 'I'm afraid there's nothing exciting in there for you, fella, but I think we might find something in one of those bags Anna took.' He checked the carrier bags, reaching in and pulling out a huge chewy stick. Aidey looked across at Mim. 'Am I okay to give him this?'

She nodded. 'I think it would torture him if you didn't. He's already on with a bone from the butchers, but he loves those.'

Aidey bent to Herbert, offering the chewy bone which the Labrador took gently. 'That's a good lad, you go and enjoy that.' He patted Herbert's head, watching as he trotted off to his bed.

'Fancy a coffee before you get settled in? Anna and I have just made one.'

'Sounds good.'

While Mim filled the kettle, Aidey turned his attention to the paper carrier bag. 'So, I mentioned I had a detour and, to cut a long story short, Hamish was meant to book Mum's spa treat over at Kirkbythwaite Hall Hotel but he hadn't got round to it what with the house move and everything. Anyway, I said I'd do it but, as you ladies suggested, I wanted to get some of their products to wrap with the voucher, so I thought the best thing to do would be to head that way and get it sorted today. Mum's birthday's on a Saturday in January and I didn't know how far in advance they'd get booked up. Hamish and I thought it'd be nice for her to spend her actual birthday there.'

'That's really thoughtful of you, Aidey,' said Mim.

'Ooh, what was the place like?' asked Anna-Lisa.

'Absolutely amazing. I've never been anywhere like it. I'm so pleased we chose to get Mum a voucher from there. They showed me round the spa, which was out of this world and I know she'll absolutely love it. And the products, well they all smelt fantastic so it was hard to choose, but I managed in the end – not an easy task for a bloke, I have to say. And, of course, I couldn't come away from there without getting either of you two something, so, Anna, this is for you.' He handed her a bottle of lemon verbena bubble bath. 'And, Mimbo, this is for you.' He handed Mim a bottle of purple coloured bubble bath that was fragranced with lavender and patchouli. 'It's just a little something, but it's a way of saying thank you for coming up with the idea of getting Mum some products to go with the voucher; Mish and me would never have thought of that.'

'Thanks, Aidey, but you shouldn't have,' Anna-Lisa clicked open the lid and inhaled the fragrance. 'Mmm. This smells heavenly.'

'Oh, Aidey, you really didn't need to, but thank you, it smells absolutely gorgeous. I can't wait to use it.' Mim reached up and kissed his cheek, his day old stubble tickling her lips. She didn't spot the blushes that swamped his freckles.

'RIGHT, here we have two roast dinners.' Julie set the plates down in front of Mim and Anna-Lisa. 'Bethany's on her way with yours, Aidey. I'll just go and get you some more gravy and a bowl of horseradish.'

Mim's eyes widened. 'Thanks, Julie. Wow! This looks fantastic; look at the size of the Yorkshire puddings; they're enormous!'

'Here's your roast, Aidey.' Bethany, blushing profusely, set his plate of food down on his mat before scurrying off.

'Ahh, bless her, I think someone's got the hots for you, Aidey,' said Anna-Lisa.

'Me?'

'Yes, you. And don't sound so surprised, you're a babe, isn't he, Mim?'

'Yep, you're a total babe, Aidey, and it's time you recognised that fact.' Mim glanced across at him; there was no denying he was attractive, and the blue checked shirt he was wearing seemed to make his moss-green eyes take on a deeper hue. That, combined with his easy-going, pleasant personality, made it easy to see why young Bethany thought he was cute.

'Here you go.' Julie placed a jug of gravy and bowl of horseradish sauce on the mat in the middle of the table. 'Just shout up if you want any more.'

'Thanks, Julie,' said Mim.

Julie leaned in. 'I won't keep you, but thought you'd like to know

Pat Motson's practically having a melt-down over last night. Apparently she heard Carly ask Gemma about the crotchless knickers.'

Aidey's eyebrows shot up. 'I won't ask.'

'Gemma's the vicar's wife, she's a good laugh,' said Mim.

'Old dragon Motson told Cath Jones she's going to speak to Rev Ferrers about it and about the suitability of his wife being friends with us.'

Mim burst out laughing. 'Oh, my God, can you imagine how she's going to start that conversation?'

'I'll tell you what, it would be fun to be a fly on the wall,' said Julie. 'And can you imagine poor Rev Ferrers' face when she does?'

'The woman needs to get a life instead of sticking her nose into everybody else's business and stirring up trouble,' said Anna-Lisa.

'Well, let's hope when she finds out we've been winding her up, she'll stop and think,' said Mim.

'Here's hoping. Right, I'll leave you folk to your food.'

'I KNOW we were going to talk about Honey and the missing stuff at work, and what we thought we should do about it, but today's been so lovely, do we have to spoil it?' asked Mim. The three friends were sipping coffee in the garden at Pear Tree Cottage, watching Herbert chase leaves. In truth, her anxiety about it had been building by the day, and she didn't want to have to go over the details when she'd rather switch off with her friends. It was only putting off the inevitable, but that suited her just now.

'I agree, let's save it until tomorrow, Sunday's a much better day for it,' said Anna-Lisa.

'I'm happy with that. Anything to put off thinking about that place,' said Aidey.

'So why don't we find a decent series and do a bit of binge-watching? I've got a huge bag of popcorn, heaps of crisps and loads of sweets, we can have the perfect movie night.' Mim beamed at them. The thought of having an easy-going evening with her two best friends was suddenly very appealing.

'Sounds like a top plan to me, though I can't really think about any more food at the moment,' said Anna-Lisa.

'Yep, I like the sound of that, but – and it's not a deal-breaker or anything – do you mind if we steer clear of chick-flicks?'

Mim and Anna-Lisa looked at one another and giggled. 'Ooh, I'm not so sure we can make such promises, what you do you think, Anna?'

'Hmm. It's a tricky one, but seeing as though it's you, Aidey, we'll give chick-flicks a miss, just for tonight.'

THE HEAVY CURTAINS were drawn against the dark of the October night, and the light from the table lamps cast a warm, cosy glow over the living room. Herbert was curled up in front of the stove, snoring in gentle contentment – something Mim couldn't imagine him doing if Caspar was here. Anna-Lisa was sitting in the large armchair, her feet tucked underneath her, while Mim and Aidey had opted for the squishy sofa. Mim plumped a cushion behind her back and aimed the remote control at the television. 'Right, here goes.'

'Can I just say, it's easy to get spoilt for choice when you're trying to choose something to watch and before you know it, the evening's half gone and you haven't settled on anything, so why don't we make a mental note of any series we like the look of and set ourselves a time-limit?' said Anna-Lisa.

'That sounds sensible,' said Aidey.

'I agree,' said Mim. 'Ten minutes okay?'

The friends were pleased when it didn't take them long to find a suitable series they all liked the sound of, and they settled back and launched into the first episode.

After a two hour session of watching episodes back-to-back, they declared it a good time to take a break for a leg stretch or a nip to the loo. Aidey offered to take Herbert for a toilet break in the back garden and top drinks up on the way back.

'While I have a minute, I'm just going to upload this photo I took of my roast dinner onto my Instagram feed before I forget,' said Anna-Lisa.

'Ooh, let's see it,' said Mim.

Anna-Lisa dropped onto the sofa beside Mim and showed her the photos she'd taken. 'There, that's the one I'm going to use, shows the Yorkshire puds off to their best advantage.'

'Mmm. And you can just tell that beneath the crisp exterior of the roasties, they're going to be all fluffy and buttery.'

After Anna-Lisa had added an array of hashtags she went on to have a quick scroll through her feed with Mim watching over her shoulder. She was flicking through, pausing to like the occasional one that caught her eye, when a photograph of a smiling couple made her stop. 'Oh!'

Mim stared in disbelief. Surely that couldn't be right, her eyes must be deceiving her. But the closer she looked, the more she realised they weren't. 'That's Caspar and Clarissa.' Her voice came out in a whisper.

'I know.'

'Why do you think they're together like that?'

'I don't know.'

30

Mim's heart was pounding as her eyes scanned the image of the couple, Caspar's arm around Clarissa's tiny waist, her leaning into him, each holding a flute of sparkling champagne. They looked very comfortable being in such close proximity, their radiant smiles anything but the polite ones of work colleagues. Mim's eyes drifted to the caption, "Publishing's Golden Couple". 'What? What does that mean?' Panic tore through her. Why would anyone say that? They weren't a couple!

'Looks like they're at some kind of party. I could see if there are any other posts from the same event, it might help clarify things, if you want me to, that is?'

'What's up? You two look like you've had some bad news or something.' Aidey came back into the room with Herbert. Anna-Lisa held her phone up to him. 'Oh, right.'

'So, do you want me to check for any more, or do you just want to leave it?' asked Anna-Lisa.

Mim hesitated; what if more photos of Caspar and Clarissa together only served to confirm her fears? 'I don't know. When was this one posted?'

'Tonight; it looks like they're at a charity auction over at Kirkbythwaite Hall Hotel.'

'That explains why there was a massive marquee there. I thought it must've been for a wedding or something, but it was obviously for this.' Aidey made his way round the sofa and sat beside Mim, giving her shoulder a squeeze. 'It might not be what it seems, Mimbo.'

'That'll be why he couldn't come here tonight, though he told me he was doing something with his parents.'

Anna-Lisa's search turned up more and more photos of the couple in various happy poses, some with an older couple Mim assumed were Caspar's parents, and some with Susan and Kenneth. She looked at each one with morbid fascination, the horrible, familiar feeling of being played for a fool slowly creeping over her, extinguishing the carefree, happy feeling she'd had just ten minutes earlier.

'I think we've seen enough, Anna,' said Aidey.

'Sorry, Mim, maybe I shouldn't have gone searching.'

'It's not your fault.' Mim sat back, her mind all over the place. Why hadn't he told her the truth about where he'd be? And why were he and Clarissa being labelled a "golden couple"? She felt tears burning at the back of her eyes and before she knew it, they were tumbling down her cheeks.

'Oh, Mim, don't cry.' Aidey pulled her into his arms. 'Like I said, it might not be what it seems, the captions might just be referring to them as a couple in the professional sense.'

'Mim, I'm so sorry, I wish I hadn't picked my phone up, I was in two minds about it.' Ann rubbed her friend's arm.

Herbert whimpered and nuzzled closer to Mim.

'It's alright, lad,' said Aidey.

'It's really not your fault, Anna. And we all know those photos are exactly what they seem. I've just been a bloody idiot again. When am I ever going to learn?' Mim sat up and wiped her eyes, smearing mascara across her cheeks. 'And who was I kidding thinking someone like Caspar would seriously consider someone like me? He and Clarissa are so much better suited, that's why he wanted to keep things with me quiet, I'm just not in his league.'

'More like the other way round, Mim!' Anna-Lisa looked outraged. 'You're a decent person, he's a slimy rat.'

'I agree,' said Aidey.

'I can't believe I let myself fall into the usual trap. I wouldn't care, I had a feeling at the back of my mind that something wasn't right, but would I listen to it? No, I just go and end up making myself look an absolute laughing stock again.'

'I think you did listen to it, Mim, I think that's why you didn't agree to his favour straight away. And you're not a laughing stock.'

'Yeah, well, tell that to my heart, not to mention my pride.'

'What favour's this?' asked Aidey.

'Ah, well, apparently his parents have sold a couple of expensive cars to some customers abroad, but they're having problems with their bank – or they're switching it or something; it was all a bit confusing – so Caspar asked me if these clients could transfer the payment directly into my account then, at a later date, I'd transfer it to his parents' new account.'

'What?' Aidey frowned.

'Oh, it gets better; tell him how much, Mim,' said Anna-Lisa.

'It's over a hundred grand; he said I'd be able to take a cut of it as some kind of "thank you".'

'You've got to be kidding me! That's seriously dodgy, Mim. And am I right in believing you haven't agreed to it?'

Mim couldn't remember a time when she'd seen Aidey look more annoyed. She shook her head, a sob escaping her mouth. 'I told him I'd think about it over the weekend and let him know my answer on Monday.'

'Thank God for that. Promise me you'll say no.'

'I promise.'

'Good. And as for this business with the photographs, he's so not worth it, Mim, you're way better than him,' said Aidey.

'That's what I keep telling her.'

'No, I'm not, I'm a disaster. I look like a disaster and I am a disaster.' Mim dashed away the tears that had started falling again.

'Right, I think this calls for a hot chocolate and a long-overdue talking-to, Mim Dewberry.' Anna-Lisa pushed herself up. 'Come on, let's get a change of scenery and move to the kitchen for a bit.'

'But I don't want to spoil your night, we were supposed to be having a chilled time together, not spending the evening listening to me whinge about my pathetic life choices.'

'You're spoiling no one's night, and I agree with Anna, come on. I know how you love a hot chocolate, I heard as much yesterday after you sucked the life out of that poor marshmallow.' Aidey took her hand and pulled Mim up, his words eliciting a watery smile from her.

Anna-Lisa sloshed milk into a pan before adding the chocolate powder and set to whisking, all under the watchful gaze of Herbert.

'I'm afraid you can't have any of this, Herbs, chocolate isn't good for hounds.'

Mim glanced up. 'He likes boiled milk, I usually do extra for him when I'm having some. Would you mind putting some in a separate pan for him?'

'Course, no problem, can't have you missing out can we, Herbert?'

The Labrador's ear pricked up at the mention of his name.

Soon, the friends were sitting around the table. Anna-Lisa was the first to speak. 'Look, Mim, I have to say, after seeing those photos of Caspar and Clarissa tonight, it didn't come as a surprise. I've never made a secret of the fact that I don't trust him, and that added to the favour he's asked of you only goes to confirm my doubts about him.'

'I can understand that.' Mim nodded.

'But what I really want to say to you is that you're worth so much more. Much more than Caspar, and much more than the men you seem to be drawn to – Rick's a classic example. From what I've seen over the years, it's almost as if you're subconsciously pursuing relationships with men that are doomed to fail. Anyone looking at the situation from an objective viewpoint might be tempted to say your relationship history mirrors that of your mother's.'

'I'm inclined to agree with Anna; I can remember what Josie used to say about your mum and her boyfriends when we were at school,' said Aidey.

Mim sat staring into her mug, pondering her friends' words. She'd never thought about it like that before, but they were right, her relationship history was scarily similar to her mother's – the very last person she ever wanted to be compared to. What a fool she hadn't seen it before now. Her eyes brimmed with tears. 'You're right, I can see that now you've said it.'

'Oh, Mim, don't cry.' Aidey pulled his chair up beside her and wrapped his arm around her.

'Mim, chick, don't waste any more of your tears on those losers.' Anna-Lisa squeezed her friend's hand. 'You just need to put them behind you and move on. You've had a lucky escape with Caspar.'

Mim nodded.

'And you need to stop going into relationships as if you don't deserve any better,' Anna-Lisa added.

'But I don't deserve any better, I'm a disaster. Look at me

compared to our Josie. She's got her perfect life and what have I got? Everything I touch seems to turn to crap.'

'That's not true, she's just used your mum as an example of how not to live her life; I can remember her saying words to that effect when we were teenagers,' said Aidey.

He was right; Josie always used to say she was going to use their mum as an example of how not to be and, if she ever got married, she wanted her marriage to be just like their grandparents'. Looking at Russ, he was about as far removed from any of their mother's boyfriends as possible. Mim's, too, for that matter.

'I promise you, Mimbo, you just need to get Monday out of the way, deal with Caspar and his favour, then things will feel better.' Anna-Lisa flashed her a warm smile.

Mim sniffed and wiped her nose on her sleeve. 'The thing is, I'm nowhere near as gutted as I thought I'd be after seeing that photo of Caspar with Clarissa. I thought I'd be devastated if I ever found out he was the same as the rest, but weirdly I'm not. Yes, I'm hurt, but in a funny way, I feel almost relieved it's over; it didn't seem real somehow.'

Aidey gave her a squeeze. 'Well, that's got to be good news.'

'It is, that scumbag's so not worth you being upset, chick,' said Anna-Lisa.

Mim sighed. 'I know.'

They finished their hot chocolates and migrated back to the living room where they continued watching television until sleep beckoned, for Anna-Lisa and Aidey at least. Mim had only half-watched the series, her mind regularly sloping off onto the photo of Caspar and Clarissa. She pushed the image away when she felt fresh tears threaten; she didn't want to spoil her friends' night any more than she already had done. And, though she felt emotionally and physically drained, she was dreading her head hitting the pillow and having to face the usual agonisingly long hours of lying awake until the dawn chorus kicked in and, as if in some perverse way, sleep suddenly decided to lay claim to her.

31

Mim woke to the sound of a wood pigeon cooing from the branches of the pear tree in the garden. Judging by the level of light pushing its way into the room she reckoned it must be at least ten o'clock. Her nostrils twitched as she detected the aroma of bacon frying, making her stomach rumble appreciatively. She pushed her hair off her face and reached for her alarm clock; it was nearly ten thirty. Thank goodness for weekends and the opportunity to have a lie-in. The memory of last night kicked in. Caspar and Clarissa. Her heart sank. 'Here we go again.'

She'd lain awake for hours the previous night, her mind a toxic mix of Caspar, Clarissa, Yorkshire Portions, Honey, and all of the individual problems attached to them. Mim hadn't even tried to fight it as she usually did, hadn't attempted to clear her mind and let sleep find its way in; she'd known it would be futile. Instead, she'd just let her worries do their worst, which they had, bounding from one anxiety to the next.

'Actually, bollocks to "here we go again". I'm taking control of my life and I'm not going to let another man make me feel like crap again.' She pushed herself up and climbed out of bed. 'I knew he was trouble; I should've listened to my gut.'

Mim followed the delicious smell of bacon frying into the kitchen where she found Anna-Lisa standing over a pan full of fried breakfast goodies. 'That smells seriously good.'

'Morning, Mim, how did you sleep?' Anna-Lisa slid the pan off the heat and rushed over to Mim, pulling her into a hug.

'Ughh! I'd love to say I slept like a log, but that would be a big fat lie, but I did manage a few hours once the birds woke up, like I usually do.'

'Well, that's something at least. Coffee?'

'I'll make it. And since there's no drooling Labrador watching your every move at the oven I'm guessing Herbert's somewhere with Aidey.'

'Yep, they're out in the garden having a bit of male bonding time.' Anna-Lisa smiled and nodded towards the window.

Mim looked out to see Aidey, still in his pyjamas, having a game of fetch with Herbert. The Labrador was tearing backwards and forwards, his breath coming out in a cloud of steam. His happy expression made her laugh. 'Look at the state of him, he's having a whale of a time.'

'Who, Aidey or Herbs?'

'Herbert,' Mim said with a giggle.

'He loves Aidey to bits, doesn't he?' Anna-Lisa came to stand beside her.

'He does, it's because Aidey's always been lovely with him.'

'Aidey's lovely with everyone.'

As if aware of being watched Aidey turned and beamed a smile at the two women. It sent a flutter of something stirring inside Mim. Anna-Lisa made an eating gesture to him and he nodded, giving one last throw of the ball before venturing back inside.

'Hiya, Mim.' He entered the kitchen on a blast of fresh air, his cheeks ruddy. 'How're you this morning?'

'I'm good thanks, Aidey. How about you? Now then, Herbs, been having fun?' She bent to fuss Herbert who'd charged straight over to her.

'All the better for having some fresh air with the "fetch" king over there,' Aidey said with a chuckle. 'He's got so much energy.'

'Tell me about it. He'll think he's earned himself a sausage or two after that, won't you, Herbert?'

'That's because he has. I've set a couple aside for him to have when they've cooled down. Grub's nearly up by the way.' Anna-Lisa started ladling food onto the plates.

Over breakfast they agreed to avoid all conversation related to

Yorkshire Portions, so as not to spoil their enjoyment of their food. It proved easier said than done since the company, and all its associated problems, occupied such a huge chunk of their thoughts at the moment. Mim swallowed her mouthful of toast. 'So, Aidey, tell us all about Hamish's new pad.' She felt pleased at her choice of "safe" topic.

'Oh, yeah, did you say it was a farm?' asked Anna-Lisa.

'It's more of a small-holding really, but it's called Dane's Garth Farm and it's in Mistleby, the same village where our parents live. It's an amazing place, needs a fair bit doing to it – hence why he and Laura got it for such a good price – but it's got loads of potential. It's got a huge barn that's been converted into a couple of offices, so he's going to be running his planning consultancy business from one of them, and offering the spare one up for rent.'

Mim nodded. 'I can remember you telling us about that, it'll save him having to pay rent to someone else; that place he was using in the centre of York was getting expensive, wasn't it?'

'It was.' Aidey took a sip of his coffee.

'And he'll save a fortune in petrol, not to mention parking in the city,' said Anna-Lisa.

'Yeah, and there's ample parking for his clients, too, so they won't have to worry about that.'

'And is Laura still chuffed about it?' asked Mim.

'She's over the moon; the school in the village has a great reputation, there's loads of room for little Rory to run around safely and get loads of fresh air, and she can't wait to get stuck into the smaller barn which they're going to convert into a holiday let.'

'Sounds perfect for them,' said Anna-Lisa.

'It is.' Aidey nodded. Mim noted he looked thoughtful but didn't like to ask. She wondered if he was thinking that Hamish seemed to have it all, despite being a year younger than him.

Anna-Lisa appeared to pick up on Aidey's expression, too. 'So, how do you fancy a walk after breakfast?'

Herbert's ears pricked up and he looked across at them hopefully.

'I'm up for that. Though, I'll need to head off early in the afternoon, I've got some freelance work I want to finish today,' said Aidey.

'You won't find Herbs and me complaining about going for a walk on a gorgeous sunny day like today.' In truth, Mim was glad of the distraction; she knew as soon as her friends had gone, her mind would turn straight to Caspar and Honey.

'RIGHT, so we're in agreement, there's nothing we can really do or say to Honey about all the missing stuff, our only option is to remain vigilant and make sure she's not left on her own in the office.' Anna-Lisa slung her backpack over her shoulder and picked up her overnight bag; she'd offered to stay another night, but Mim had refused, feeling guilty about keeping her away from Caleb.

'Yep, and we mustn't lose sight of the gravity of what she's doing: if she really is trying to set us up to look like thieves then that's serious.'

Aidey's words sent a shiver down Mim's spine.

'Yeah, much as we hate working at Yorkshire Portions, we don't want to leave it because we've been set up by an evil little cow like her,' said Anna.

'Too right.' Aidey turned to Mim. 'Are you going to be okay getting a lift from Caspar in the morning?'

Mim felt anxiety swirl around her stomach. She was absolutely dreading seeing Caspar. 'I should be okay, we won't be in the car for long, and I've no intention of mentioning the photos of him and Clarissa.'

'Yes, but he's bound to ask if you've given the favour any more thought. Will you be okay telling him on your own?' asked Anna-Lisa.

'I'll be fine, stop worrying.' She didn't want to tell her friends, after seeing a glimpse of his anger, she was more than a little anxious about how he'd take the news. They worried about her enough, she didn't want to add to it.

'Okay, well, as long as you're sure,' said Anna-Lisa.

'And you only have to let me know if you've changed your mind, I can easily come and get you.'

'Thanks, Aidey, that's really kind, but I think I'd prefer to get it out of the way, rather than having it hanging over me at work.'

Mim watched her friends drive off down the village, Herbert sitting beside her at the garden gate. The house would feel very empty without them.

32

Mim's heart was thudding as she looked out of the living room window waiting for Caspar to arrive. The sunshine that had graced Skeltwick over the weekend had disappeared and been replaced with a low-slung sky, heavy with thick, black clouds that threatened to burst at any moment. How very apt for a Monday, she thought.

Before long, his sleek car pulled up outside the cottage. Mim did her best to quell her nerves as she slid into the warm leather seat and clicked her seatbelt into the socket.

'Morning, Mim. Good weekend?' Caspar leant across and kissed her as if nothing was out of the ordinary. It took her by surprise, and if he noticed her response lacked the usual passion, he didn't let on.

'Er, morning, yes, thanks. How about you?' Maybe the photos weren't what they seemed after all, she thought. Maybe they were just of two work colleagues, looking happy together for the sake of the camera, all completely innocent. But deep down, Mim knew that wasn't true.

'Not bad, thanks.'

Mim waited for him to elaborate, but he clearly had no intention. She steadied her breathing and gazed out of the window, watching the car eat up the country lanes as he made small-talk.

Eventually, he flexed his fingers against the steering wheel, his body language suggesting he was building towards asking the thing she dreaded most. 'And did you give any further thought to that little favour I asked of you? The one that would really help get my parents out of a sticky situation.'

His words made her heart clench; he hadn't waited long before broaching the subject. His choice of manipulative words sent a flicker of annoyance through her, his blatant intention of heaping guilt onto her shoulders transparent. Though she thought she'd prepared herself for this, it didn't stop her from feeling anxious; her heart was beating so hard she could feel it thrumming in her ears. She took a deep breath and steeled herself. 'Actually, I have given it some thought, and I'm sorry but I don't think I can help out.' Her face was burning, but she felt utterly relieved once she'd set her words free.

Caspar increased his grip on the steering wheel, his knuckles blanching white. 'I see. So when you say you don't *think* you can help out, do you actually mean you *won't* help out?'

'Yes, I'm afraid so. I mean, you hardly know me, and your parents don't know me at all, and with it being such a huge sum of money, well, my bank are going to think it's very odd. What would I say if they started asking questions? Would they believe it if I told them the truth? It just doesn't feel right, that's all, makes me feel uncomfortable.' Mim was aware she was gabbling. She stole a look at Caspar to see his face set stern, a muscle twitching in his cheek. The atmosphere in the car had been a little awkward to start with, but now it was downright uncomfortable.

'Right. This doesn't sound like you talking, and I get the feeling, despite me specifically asking you not to, you've spoken to those friends of yours, Anna-Lisa and Aidey, who've advised you against helping out. And, can I just add, it doesn't surprise me one little bit of Aidan, his advice will not have come from a selfless place, Mim. He's jealous of me, and has been from the moment I started at Yorkshire Portions; he knows my work is light years ahead of his and he can't bear it. There's no way he'd want you to help me and my family out.'

His reference to Aidey made her blood boil, but now wasn't the time to defend him. 'I didn't mention it—'

'I'm disappointed in you, I expected more loyalty from my girlfriend.'

Girlfriend? Is he for real? 'And I had no idea you considered me to be your girlfriend. I thought we were just a fling. Why else would we have to keep us secret?'

'I thought I'd explained that to you clearly enough, it's because it wouldn't go down well with Susan and Kenneth, and I didn't want to cause any trouble for you with them, we both know what they can be like. And I think they have plans for me and Clarissa, not that that's ever going to happen.'

'Oh, really?' Mim fished around her backpack for her phone, hurriedly scrolling through it until she found what she was looking for.

'Really; she's not my type.'

'And there's me thinking you were "publishing's golden couple". Seems I've got it all wrong.' She thrust her phone under his nose, giving him an eyeful of the image that had spoilt her Saturday night.

He looked shocked for a moment, before pushing her hand out of the way. 'I can explain.'

'There's really no need.' Where was this fearless version of herself coming from?

'The photos were staged; it was all Susan and Kenneth's idea, to attract attention to the magazine. I can assure you, I'm not in a relationship with Clarissa; much as she'd like me to be.'

'Well, that's not my problem anymore. What we had was nothing serious, it's run its course.'

'You know you don't mean that.'

'I actually do.'

'Let me make it up to you tonight when I drop you off, we can spend the evening together, get things back on track, and maybe have another think about that favour; I can explain how it's totally risk-free for you.'

'Caspar, there's absolutely no chance. And I won't be needing a lift from you anymore.'

A muscle twitched in his cheek. 'You really are a silly little girl, aren't you? You've no idea what you've turned down. But I won't ask you again, you've had your chance.'

'I don't feel silly, not anymore, at least. And I think I've got a very good idea of what I've turned down, and I know I've absolutely made the right decision.'

Caspar was livid. He pressed his lips together and pushed his foot hard down on the accelerator. The car increased speed effortlessly, the scenery soon nothing more than a blur. Mim was terrified, her heart beating faster as adrenalin surged around her body. Memories of their near-miss the week before flashed through her mind. She resisted the urge to scream at him to slow down, there was no way she'd let him see he had this power over her. She closed her eyes, telling herself they'd be parked up and out of the car soon. Now there was another reason for her to look for another job; the sooner she got away from him, the better.

ONCE THE CAR had come to a halt in York, Mim climbed out and, without a backwards glance, ran off in the direction of the Yorkshire Portions office. Though her legs felt like jelly after that ridiculous journey, she pushed herself on, stopping only when the building was within sight.

'You okay, Mim?' Aidey looked up from his work, taking in her wild, bedraggled appearance.

Still gasping for breath, she nodded. 'I am now. Honey?'

'Not here yet.' The concerned look in Anna-Lisa's eyes matched Aidey's. 'What's up? Have you told him?'

Mim nodded and spoke quietly. 'Yes, I wasn't expecting to first thing, but he kind of forced the situation.' The sound of the front door closing with a loud bang and someone thundering upstairs made the three of them jump. Mim pressed her hand against her chest. 'Jeez! That'll be him, he was furious, drove like a bloody maniac on the way here. Don't let on you know anything.' She pressed her fingers to her lips until Caspar's footsteps could be heard heading towards his office, the door closing firmly behind him.

Mim blew out a sigh of relief.

'Am I right in guessing it didn't go down well?' asked Anna-Lisa.

'Not well at all.' Mim spoke in a whisper. 'He's actually quite scary when he doesn't get what he wants.' Her heart was still thudding, her voice a little shaky.

Aidey's expression was like thunder. 'What kind of man sets out to scare a woman? He's nothing more than a thug in expensive clothes. Promise me you won't get in that car with him again, Mim.'

'Trust me, there's no way I want to experience that again, it was terrifying.'

'He's a hideous bully. I'm so glad you can see him for what he is,' said Anna-Lisa.

Before they could say anything further, Honey came into the room. 'What have I missed?'

DESPITE THE TENSION in the air, the friends got their heads down and got stuck into their work. Mim had prepared herself a new to-do list and had managed to get through a couple of things on it by lunchtime, her mind occasionally drifting to Caspar before moving on to the items that had gone missing the previous week. There'd been a shouty email from Susan, asking if she'd booked a table at the White Swan for later in the week for the planned feature. Though Mim had told her boss she had, she hadn't actually got round to it; the prospect of having to tell Julie that she'd be expected to provide her wonderful food for free was just too humiliating and insulting, and Mim hadn't had the courage to mention it.

Her thoughts turned to Clarissa's notebook and Caspar's paperweight, wondering if they'd turned up. Surely if they had, someone would have said something. At least nothing else seemed to have gone missing. In any event, they'd been careful not to leave Honey on her own recently, which seemed to be a source of frustration to her.

'So aren't you three going out for lunch together today?' Honey asked.

'Not today, we've each got different plans.' Anna-Lisa didn't bother to look up at her.

'I'm going to nip out for a short time before the heavens open,' said Mim, looking out of the window at the grey sky that hung above the city. The wind was picking up, making her glad she'd brought her warm coat.

'And I'm going to get this finished before I head out,' said Aidey.

Their responses didn't seem to suit Honey, and she flounced out of the office on the pretext of having some idea to run by Susan. The three friends looked at one another and rolled their eyes. Mim did her best to quash the feeling of unease Honey's question had triggered.

Before long Honey returned, a jubilant glint in her eye. 'Auntie Susan's not very happy; she says her ring's gone missing again and what with everything else that's happened, she's getting very suspicious. Says she last remembers taking it off in the bathroom, where she's convinced she left it by the sink at around ten this morning.'

Mim groaned inwardly. 'Is she sure? I mean, she's lost it before but it's turned up.'

Honey glared at her. 'I don't think Auntie Susan would be very pleased to hear you say that. She sounded pretty certain about things to me, but if you doubt her, why don't you go and have a word with her, tell her yourself?'

'Don't be so childish, Honey. You know as well as the rest of us Susan's always losing stuff, that ring included. I'm sure it'll turn up like it did last time.'

'Okay, keep your hair on, Anal Lisa.'

'Honey, that's enough.' Aidey shot her a stern look which seemed to do the trick.

'Right, I'm going to take my lunch break now. Can I get anyone anything?' asked Mim.

With no one taking her up on her offer, she pulled her coat on, slung her backpack over her shoulder and headed out, glad to be away from the intensity of the office and into the fresh air, cold though it was. Her first stop was the florists where she picked up a bunch of brightly coloured pink gerberas; her favourite flowers always made her feel cheerful and she had a feeling she was going to need all the help she could get with that this week. Next was the sweet shop where she bought a double-sized bag of penny sweets. Mim nibbled on them as she walked towards the Nutmeg Tree where she stood in the queue for takeaway sandwiches. This morning in the car with Caspar seemed like a different day. Had she really stood up to him? Confronted him about Clarissa? A wave of nerves rippled in her stomach. What they'd had was very definitely over now, there was no doubt about that. But it still surprised her that she didn't feel as wrecked as she'd thought she would, that her feelings for him had been superficial. Was her heart getting hardened to love? Only time would tell.

33

'So, Honey hasn't had chance to be on her own in our office over lunch?' asked Anna-Lisa. It had been an hour since Mim had returned from her lunch break. Anna-Lisa had been out when she'd first got back which was when Aidey quickly took his turn to pop out. None of them had been away from their desks for long.

'The only time the room was empty was when you were both out and I nipped along to grab my printing. I was only gone a few minutes but Honey was out herself; I would've waited for one of you to get back otherwise,' said Aidey.

'Fair enough,' said Anna-Lisa. 'She can't get up to no good when she's not here.'

'Who are you talking about?' Honey bowled into the room.

'Oh, no one important.' Anna-Lisa arched her eyebrows at Mim.

Honey glared at Anna-Lisa before she delivered her news. 'Auntie Susan's on the war path and she wants to speak to you all individually in her office, straightaway.'

'Why, what's the matter?' asked Mim.

'Well, as you know, her ring's gone missing.' Honey was clearly enjoying delivering this news. 'She's convinced it's been stolen since Caspar's paperweight's vanished and there's money missing from the petty-cash tin, too.'

Mim's heart started galloping, panic making her breathing shallow. *Honey's been up to something.*

'Oh, here we go again,' said Anna-Lisa.

'That can't be right,' said Aidey. 'Nobody here would steal anything; she'll have just misplaced her ring like before. And none of us have ever seen the petty-cash tin.'

'True. All I've ever known about it is that it used to be kept by Dennis in accounts when he was here. I wouldn't have a clue where it's kept now. And as far as Susan's ring's concerned, she's always taking it off when she washes her hands. I've lost count of the number of times I've found it by the sink in the loo or the kitchen,' Mim said, trying to hide the concern in her voice.

'And you've given it back?' asked Honey.

'Of course, I have! And I haven't seen it today, if that's what you mean.'

'What do you think, Honey?' Anna-Lisa looked daggers at the girl. 'Before you go any further, don't even think about accusing anyone here, okay? We've all worked here a long time, and as you know full well, it's not the first time Susan's lost that bloody ring – though why she doesn't leave it at home somewhere safe is beyond me if it's worth so much – and it's always been found exactly where Susan left it.'

'Don't talk to me like that, I wasn't accusing anyone.'

'That's not what it sounded like to me.' Anna-Lisa glared at her.

Aidey splayed his hands. 'Look, I think we should all calm down. Like Anna said, it's not the first time this has happened and I'm sure it'll turn up. Did Susan say who she wanted to see first?'

'Mim.' Honey was struggling to keep herself from smirking.

'Well, I really don't know what she's expecting me to say since I haven't got a clue where any of the missing stuff is.'

'That's all you can say, chick,' said Anna-Lisa.

Mim's heart was pounding as she made her way along to Susan's office. Though she hadn't done anything wrong, an inexplicable feeling of guilt had started churning in her gut, no doubt triggered by Honey's accusatory words.

As she approached the door she could hear her boss's voice barking at some poor soul. Mim knocked before walking in. Susan was at her desk, glowering at Tamsin. Mim's heart went out to the young intern whose face was crimson, her eyes swimming with tears. There was no such thing as getting broken in gently at this place. It was a baptism of fire; sink or swim. 'And don't let me catch you making the same mistake again, girl. Got it?'

Tamsin nodded vigorously. 'Yes, Mrs Pallister-Biggs. I'm really sorry. I promise I won't do it again.'

'Right, get back to work. Start from scratch and send it to me as soon as you've finished. And don't take all afternoon about it. Go on, go.' Susan waved her hand, her ring conspicuous by its absence.

Tamsin barely had chance to scurry through the door before Susan turned her beady eyes onto Mim. 'Right, Jemima, I'm sure Honey has already informed you of my reason for wanting to see you all.'

Mim nodded. 'Yes, but I—'

'I haven't finished. You'll get your chance to speak in a minute.'

'Sorry.'

'My ring has gone missing. I last remember seeing it on my finger this morning at around ten-thirty or so. If I've taken it off to wash my hands, there are only two places it could be: the kitchen or the bathroom. It's in neither place. Since there are several items which appear to have gone missing recently – as of this lunchtime fifty pounds from petty cash can be added to that list – I'm afraid it leaves me with no choice but to think that it's been misappropriated.' She put heavy emphasis on the last word.

Mim's heart picked up its pace. Why was Susan talking to her like this? 'Misap—'

'Stolen! I don't need to tell you that the ring is not only worth a small fortune but it is of great sentimental value to me, having been passed down to me from my much beloved grandmother.' She paused for effect, pinning Mim with a piercing glare. 'I'm going to give it until the morning and if it hasn't turned up then I'll have no alternative but to involve the police. Do I make myself clear?'

Mim could feel her anger rising. Susan had no right to speak to her in this way! 'Loud and clear. From your tone, it sounds to me like you're accusing me of stealing your ring, which is something I have not—'

'Don't take it so personally, girl. Let me tell you that I have spoken to everyone else in this tone; there's only Anna-Lisa and Aidey left and I'll be saying the very same things to them in exactly the same way. However, I felt it was important that I speak to each of you separately.'

And we all know why, don't we? You live by the motto "divide and rule". A bully like you wouldn't have the first clue about staff morale.

'I'm simply asking that if you know of the whereabouts of my ring you let me know, or at least make sure it's on my desk by the morning.'

You toxic old bag! How dare you accuse people in this way? Mim was struggling to bite her tongue; it wouldn't take much for her to lose her temper and let her boss know what she really thought of her. She did her best to steady herself before she spoke. 'I'd just like to stress, Susan, that I have absolutely no idea where your ring is and I can't even remember the last time I saw it or noticed it on your finger. And the same applies to the other items that appear to have gone missing; I've had nothing to do with it and I have no idea where they are.'

'That's all I needed to hear.'

'Good. Is that it?'

'Yes, send Anna-Lisa in next.'

It took every ounce of Mim's strength not to slam Susan's door shut as she left her office, her anger propelling her down the hall and into the room she shared with her friends. And Honey. If Honey hadn't been there she would have felt able to properly vent her feelings, instead, she dropped heavily onto her chair and mimed doing a silent scream.

'That bad?' asked Anna-Lisa.

'Worse.' Mim felt tears welling in her eyes. She looked across at Honey whose eyes were glinting with pleasure. Mim was sure she was behind all of this; it made her blood run cold.

'Are you okay, Mim?' asked Aidey.

'Oops. You don't look very happy. Did you get a bollocking?' Honey asked, smiling.

'Not exactly.' It was hard to put into words what had just happened. Susan hadn't accused her directly, hadn't given her, as Honey put it, a "bollocking" but nevertheless, Mim had been left feeling like both of those things had happened.

'What, you're not "exactly" okay or you didn't "exactly" get a bollocking?' Honey was looking at her like she was an idiot.

'Both. And I'm afraid she's asked to see you next, Anna.'

'Bring it on.' Anna-Lisa pushed out her chair and left the room.

She returned five minutes later looking furious, her normally pale skin burning crimson. 'That bloody woman's got a nerve the way she talks to people. It's a wonder she's got anyone left to work for her.' She started moving things around her desk angrily. 'I'm afraid you're up next, Aidey. Don't take any of her crap.'

'Great. Just what we need on a Monday afternoon.' With a sigh he headed out of the room.

A CLOUD of gloom sat over the Yorkshire Portions office for the rest of the day. It didn't help that the heavens had opened and rain was now lashing against the windows, making them rattle in their frames. Wind howled eerily down the old disused chimney making Mim shiver. She hadn't seen anything of Caspar since this morning; from what she could gather, he hadn't ventured out of his office which she was glad about. Mim didn't like being on bad terms with people and, as a rule, did her best to avoid anyone she'd had words with until she'd had the chance to put things right – something that wasn't going to happen with Caspar.

From the snatched conversations the three friends had managed whenever Honey had nipped out of the office during the course of the afternoon, Mim gathered that Susan had spoken to Anna-Lisa and Aidey in much the same way she'd spoken to her. All three had been left feeling unsettled and searingly angry. Mim couldn't shake the feeling that Honey was responsible. If things continued, pretty soon there'd only be Honey and Caspar left as Yorkshire Portions employees.

Mim felt tense, her body on high alert. She'd been trying to concentrate on her work but it was proving difficult since her mind kept mulling over the items that had gone missing since Friday. She knew Honey was responsible, and the fear that any of the things would somehow find their way into her bag, just like Susan's pen, sat heavy on her shoulders. If that happened, there was a real risk Mim could lose her job, the police might even be involved with the potential for her to be prosecuted and end up with a criminal record. *Oh, shit!* The thought made her feel sick. It didn't help that every time she looked up, Honey appeared to be watching her. Mim had to keep reminding herself that the girl hadn't been on her own in their office at all that day, so nothing was going to find its way into her backpack.

She was searching through some stock images when Honey asked to borrow her stapler. 'I thought you had your own,' Mim said, puzzled.

'Yes, but I can't find it. Using yours will save me time. I can look for mine when I'm not so busy.'

You, busy? Since it wasn't in its usual place on her desk Mim automatically went to her drawer. She pulled it open and had a quick rummage, keeping one eye on her computer screen, but couldn't find it amongst the usual detritus of pens, random pieces of paper and such like. 'I really must sort this out; I don't need half the stuff in here.' As she glanced down her heart stopped and a gasp left her lips. She stared at the contents of her drawer and pressed her hand to her mouth, the feeling of nausea swirling violently in her stomach as she looked across at Anna-Lisa and Aidey.

'What's up?' asked Anna. 'You look like you're about to throw up. You haven't found another exploded yoghurt in there, have you?'

Mim shook her head, her mind scrambling for something to say, desperately wishing Honey wasn't there.

'Or worse, a mouldy cheese sandwich like last time?' asked Aidey.

'I think that box of eggs she'd forgotten about until they started to stink the place out was the worst.' Anna-Lisa scrunched up her nose at the memory. 'They were really rank and leaking foul-smelling stuff. I'm surprised we can't still smell it.'

'What's the matter, Jemima? You look like you've had a shock,' said Honey, a mocking tone in her voice.

Panic rose inside Mim, snatching away her ability to form a single word. Looking back at her accusingly from her drawer was Clarissa's notebook, on top of which was Caspar's paperweight and Susan's ring, a mixture of ten and twenty pound notes strewn amongst them. She swallowed, trying to compose herself. 'I'm fine. I just put my finger in a sticky sweet, that's all.'

'Are you sure? It was a bit of an over-the-top reaction for something as measly as that.' The taunting look in Honey's eyes was almost more than Mim could bear, but she was relieved to see from her friends' expressions they'd clicked that something wasn't right.

'Yes, but it's probably been there for the best part of a year, it could be growing all sorts of God-knows-what,' said Aidey.

'I think you're right. Anyway, I don't know where my stapler's gone, but it's not in there.' Mim pushed the drawer shut, her heart hurling itself against her chest.

'Here, have a squirt of that. It should help remove most of the stickiness from the sweet.' Anna-Lisa threw a small bottle of hand sanitiser over to Mim. 'And you can use my stapler for now, Honey, there you go.'

'Thanks,' said Mim.

'You two are total opposites when it comes to being tidy,' said Aidey. He sent Mim a sympathetic smile.

'Yes, but it's not going to help Mim find her stapler if I use yours, is it?' Honey clearly wasn't going to back down. 'Are you sure you can't find it? Here, let me have a look in your drawer.' Honey stood up and started to make her way over to Mim's desk.

Mim put her hand on her drawer, fear raging around her body. 'No, it's not there, I don't know where it is. In fact, I can't remember the last time I saw it. You'll have to use Anna's.'

Honey glowered at her. 'Fine. I was only trying to help, but the way you're acting is very odd, like you've got something to hide.'

'The only thing Mim ever wants to hide is the mess she makes, her drawers are notorious,' said Aidey.

'Careful how you talk about Mim's drawers, Aidey,' said Anna-Lisa. 'People might think you're referring to her knickers.'

'Oh, I wouldn't do that.' Two dots of colour appeared on his cheeks.

Mim gave her friends a weak smile, appreciating that they were trying to act as if nothing was going on. Panic was scrambling her mind; she had no idea how she was going to get out of this one.

Soon Honey left the office saying she was going to check the ink levels in the printer. Once she'd gone, Aidey pushed the door shut. 'What the hell's happened?'

Mim felt tears fill her eyes. 'The missing things, Susan's ring, the book, the paperweight, the money, they're all in my drawer.'

'What?' Aidey looked at her in disbelief.

'No! When did she get the chance to do that?' Anna-Lisa ran her fingers through her hair.

'Oh, damn! She must've still been in the office when I went down to get my printing. She told me she was going to meet a friend. I wasn't gone long. I'm so sorry, Mim.'

'It's not your fault, Aidey. But what am I going to do? It'll look like I've stolen them.' Fear increased its grip on her chest.

'Quickly, get them out of your drawer and stick them in the cupboard over there before she gets back,' said Anna-Lisa. She jumped out of her seat and hurried over to the cupboard just as Honey returned with Susan.

'Jemima, I want you to open your drawer,' Susan barked, her hands on her hips.

'Please, Susan, I honestly—'

'Just do as I say.' Susan and Honey were looming behind her as she pulled open the drawer.

She closed her eyes, not daring to look. 'I didn't put them there.'

'Well, how else did they get there? Are you saying someone else put them in there without your knowledge?'

'Well, I didn't do it,' said Honey in her little girl voice.

Mim nodded, a tear spilling down her cheek. 'Yes, honestly, Susan, I have no idea—'

'This leaves me with no alternative but to call the police.' Susan marched out of the room, thundering her way along the landing.

'Can't you at least hear what Mim has to say?' Aidey called after her.

'She's had her chance.' Susan didn't bother to turn round.

'That is so unfair, Susan.' Anna turned to Honey, jabbing a finger at her. 'And you're a spiteful little cow. We know you're behind it all.'

'How dare you accuse me?' Honey narrowed her eyes at Anna-Lisa. 'It serves Jemima right that something doesn't go her way for a change. She gets everything she wants, it just falls into her lap while the rest of us have to work for it, and don't get the recognition we deserve.'

'You're deluded and toxic.' Anna-Lisa gave her a look of utter contempt.

Mim was sobbing now. 'This isn't right. I've done nothing to you, Honey, I don't deserve your spite and I'm not going to stay here and get the blame for something I haven't done. I'm not a thief; I've never stolen anything in my life.' She snatched up her bag, grabbed her coat and ran out of the office. As she raced down the stairs she could hear Clarissa's voice asking what was going on, mingling with Aidey and Anna-Lisa's voices calling for her to wait up.

Once outside, she ran, not caring that the rain was torrential or the wind lashing and cruel. She raced through the streets, tears pouring down her cheeks, dirty puddles splashing up her legs, the need to get as far away from Yorkshire Portions as possible pushing her on.

She continued running until she was well away from the busy streets of shops. She didn't know where she was going and cared even less. Her mind was a mess, unable to process what had happened. How was her life ever going to get right after this?

34

Darkness had descended over the city. The rain was falling in broad horizontal swathes, the odd flash of lightning streaking across the sky. Mim was soaked to the skin and shivering but she didn't care, she'd had enough. Her mind was still in turmoil, turning over everything that had happened over the last few weeks. She couldn't see how she was going to get out of this mess; Honey seemed dead set on persecuting her for reasons Mim couldn't fathom. But her persistence had paid off, Honey had won and Mim had lost her job and looked like a thief to her employers; it would be impossible to get another job without a reference from them.

She'd been walking around for hours, eventually collapsing on a bench by the river when her legs had felt too weak to go any further. She'd lost track of how long she'd been there when a figure dropped down beside her, wrapping their arms around her. 'Mim! Oh, jeez, Mim, thank God I've found you. We've been worried sick, you haven't been answering your phone.'

Relief at hearing Aidey's voice and feeling his arms around her, squeezing her tight, made her burst into tears once more. She leaned into him. 'I'm sorry, Aidey. I, I just had to get away. I can't believe what's happened. I'm not a thief.'

'Hey, you've got nothing to apologise for, and we all know you're not a thief.' He smoothed her hair. 'You're absolutely drenched. Travis and Sarah are having a night in at my place, but why don't I take you to my parents' house? My car's just over there. You can have a nice soak in the bath and I can tell you what happened after you left the office.'

His suggestion sounded indescribably appealing. 'But what about the police? Won't they be looking for me?'

'Don't worry about them, they're not looking for anyone. Come on, I'll tell you all about it on the way.' He hooked his arm under Mim's and helped her to her feet.

'I need to tell Carly I'll be late for Herbert.'

'That's already dealt with. Anna's been in touch with her, Herbert's having a sleep-over at her house. She sends her love, as does Herbs.'

The thought of Herbert brought a half-smile to her lips. 'Thank you, Aidey.'

'No worries. We'll just get you in the car, then I'll text Anna, tell her I've found you. She'll be so relieved.'

'I'm sorry I've worried you; I just had to get out of the office. I was wandering around and lost track of time.'

'It's gone seven o'clock. You've been wandering a long time.' Aidey pulled her drenched coat off her and wrapped a blanket around her shoulders. Once they were in the car, he put the heating on full and set off out of the city.

Mim couldn't remember ever feeling so cold, it felt as though it had permeated right through to her bones. Her teeth chattered as she listened.

'Clarissa came into the room, asking what all the yelling was about. As you can imagine, Honey started making her mouth go straight away until Anna and me shouted her down.'

'I bet that went down well.'

'Like a lead balloon.'

'Did she stay quiet?' Her hands lay in her lap, pain throbbing through them as they slowly thawed out.

'She did when Clarissa told her to shut up. Anyway, between us, Anna and me told her what had been happening, and that it had all begun after Honey had started working here. Clarissa's face was a picture as she listened.'

'I can imagine.'

'Anna played a blinder when she told them about what had happened when her sister had worked with Honey and how trouble seems to follow her around – Honey got a bit vocal then.'

'Well, there's no way she'd take any of that lying down, not with a strong personality like hers.'

'True. So, after Clarissa had heard everything, she went back to her room and made a few enquiries amongst her contacts. Turns out Honey's got quite a track record for this sort of thing, but no one would risk giving her a bad reference as everyone knows her parents and had offered her work as a favour to them. But they were all pretty keen to see the back of her.'

Mim felt relief wash over her; people might finally see what Honey was really capable of. 'So what happened after that?'

'Apparently, Clarissa had a word with Susan who called Honey down to her office – she'd still been in our office up to then – Kenneth was there, too, and by all accounts they gave her a right dressing down and told her to leave. Turns out Honey's been jealous of you; she said it wasn't fair how everyone likes you, everyone goes on about how good you are at your job, everyone says how pretty you are and how you get all the men you want without even trying.'

'What?'

'Apparently, she said no one seems to notice her.'

Mim snorted. 'Oh, I think we do!'

'Yep, that's what Anna and me thought. And, get this, she owned up to planting the pen in your bag and the stuff in your drawer, claiming it was a "joke" and that she just wanted to give you a bit of a shock.'

'Well, it was some sick joke; and it gave me more than a bloody shock.'

'I know.' Aidey reached across and squeezed her hand. 'She also said your mum had been having a fling with her dad sometime last year, and she wanted you to feel some of her pain.'

Mim shook her head. 'Nothing could surprise me as far as my mother's concerned, but it's hardly fair that I get punished for it. I've already felt plenty of pain over the years thanks to her actions.'

'I understand, but everything Honey does is a bit extreme. After that, Clarissa came to see us and said that her mum was really sorry she'd made a mistake and that she wouldn't be calling the police. Once we'd heard that, Anna and I told her we were going to look for you and we left the office.'

'So, Susan accepted that I didn't know anything about the missing stuff?'

Aidey nodded. 'Yep. Might make her stop and think, and get both sides of a story before she starts shooting her mouth off. But she's a bully, and that's not how she works. Though it looks like your job's still there, if you want it.'

Mim was relieved that her name had been cleared, but the thought of going back to work at that office held no appeal. 'I'm not going back. I can't face it. I haven't been happy there for a while. I've got a bit of freelance stuff that can keep me ticking over until I get another job. I should be okay, it's not like I've got rent to worry about and I don't have a wild lifestyle.'

Aidey was quiet for a moment, the lights of the cars heading towards them lighting up his face every now and then. 'Well, you don't have to make your decision now. You just need to concentrate on getting warm and dry.'

Before long the car headlights picked out the sign for Mistleby and the pair were pulling up outside Aidey's parents' home. Lights glowed from the downstairs windows of the large Georgian house, lending it a cosy air. The door opened, sending a shaft of light onto the path, and an elderly black Labrador with a broad, grey muzzle waddled out. Aidey's mum Shona appeared behind him, her pretty face etched with concern.

'Hello, Norman.' Aidey smoothed the old Labrador's head which was met with a steady wag of his tail.

'Oh, Aidey, thank goodness you found her. Mim, lovie, come on in out of the rain. We'll run you a lovely, warm bath, you can have a hot chocolate while it's filling.' She ran over to Mim and wrapped her arms around her. Mim could have cried; the last time she'd been shown maternal kindness like this was when her grandparents were still alive. She hadn't realised until that moment how much she'd missed it.

Mim followed Shona to the cosy, low-beamed kitchen at the back of the house. 'You sit yourself here where it's warm.' Shona motioned to a comfy-looking chair next to the Aga. She reached into a cupboard and pulled out a pan. 'Are you on for a hot chocolate, too, Aidey?'

'Think I'll just have a coffee, thanks, Mum.'

They were sipping their drinks when Mim suddenly became conscious of Aidey and his mum looking at her hair. She reached her hand up to it self-consciously. 'I cut it,' she said. 'I had to.'

'Oh.' Shona's eyes widened while Aidey looked puzzled.

'I got gum in it, a massive blob of it. I was sitting on a bench and leaned back into it. It must've been fresh since it was still soft and stuck in my hair. It wouldn't come out, so I cut it out with the nail scissors I had in my bag.'

'Nail scissors?' said Aidey.

Mim nodded.

'Oh, lovie, you needn't have done that, we could've got it out here, you just need to use something greasy to get rid of the stickiness, then it would slide out.'

Mim shrugged. At the time it had happened, she couldn't have cared less. It had been another thing to add to her problems, and she just wanted the disgusting stuff out of her hair. 'My hair's a frazzled mess anyway, it needed a good cut.'

THE DEEP, fragrant bath had gone some way to assuaging Mim's exhausted state. She'd dried herself on a huge, fluffy towel and pulled on the pair of Aidey's pyjamas his mum had set out for her. Shona had kindly said that Mim being so much taller than her meant that nothing she had would fit, but Aidey's legs being longer, the pyjamas she kept for if he stayed over last minute would do the trick. Mim knew that anything Shona had wouldn't touch her, her bum was easily twice the size of the older woman's. Not that she minded; she quite liked wearing something of Aidey's, especially since his cologne still lingered on the freshly laundered fabric.

When Mim padded downstairs she could hear a familiar voice coming from the kitchen. She pushed open the door to see Anna-Lisa sitting at the table, her hair glowing like a soft, pink halo.

'Mim!' Her friend jumped up, ran over to her and threw her arms around her. 'It's so good to see you. Are you okay?'

It felt good to see Anna, too, and Mim felt herself smiling. 'Hi, Anna, sorry to put you all to so much trouble, but, yes, I'm fine. Better now I've had a soak in the bath – thanks, Shona, it was lovely, just what I needed.'

'You're welcome, lovie. Fancy a glass of wine?'

'Mmm. Sounds lovely, thanks.'

Aidey got up from his seat and went to fetch her a glass, filling it with Pinot Grigio and handing it to her. 'You've got more colour in your cheeks now, I'm pleased to say; you were practically blue when I first found you.'

Mim giggled. 'I was pretty cold at the time.'

'Come and park yourself down here.' He pulled out the chair next to him at the table.

'So, we've been discussing quite a few things while you were in the bath, Mimbo,' said Anna-Lisa.

'Oh? What kind of things?' Mim took a sip of her wine, its cold blast a welcome change to the warmth of the bathroom.

'Well, first off – if it's okay with you – I'm going to ring Stefan the hairdresser in the morning, and get you an appointment with him. Aidey told me what had happened with the chewing-gum and I have to say, nail scissors aren't the best things for cutting hair. I can understand why you'd want the revolting stuff gone, though. And you've been saying you fancied getting it cut for ages, so now's your chance. And you'll be in good hands with Stefan, he's awesome.'

Mim smiled, she loved Anna's friendly bossiness. This was a worry taken out of her hands, and she was grateful for it. 'Thanks, Anna.'

'And I don't suppose you've given work any further thought since our chat in the car?' asked Aidey.

'Only that I'm never setting foot in that place again. I like Clarissa, and I'll miss her, but I never want to see anyone else from there as long as I live. Susan accused me of being a thief before even listening to a word I had to say; she's a horrible bully. And I'm not working my notice; she can get lost.'

'I don't blame you. I'm going to pop in tomorrow so I can gather up all our stuff, tell them that I'll work my notice but take what holiday's left to me, which by my reckoning is nine or ten days.'

Mim looked at her friend in disbelief. 'But what will you do for a job?'

'Over to you, Aidey.'

'Well, you know Mish has got that spare office space he's wanting to rent out?'

'Yes.'

'I've asked him if he'd be interested in renting it to us.'

'Us?'

He smiled. 'I'm not going back to Yorkshire Portions, they can bugger off. The way they've treated you is the final straw and has given me the push I needed. I've been toying with the idea of setting up on my own and, funnily enough, so has Anna, and after what you said in the car about your freelance work, well, it got me thinking ...

why don't we set up a digital marketing firm together?' His eyes were shining, Mim could see how keen he was on this idea. 'There's plenty of work kicking about.'

'And we've all been doing increasing amounts of freelance stuff, so we've been steadily building up our individual reputations.' Anna-Lisa's eyes were sparkling.

'And we've already got our first customer; Mish wants a rebrand for his company followed by a new advertising campaign.'

'Ooh, this is all very exciting,' said Shona. She set a large, delicious smelling casserole dish in the middle of the table, then went to get three plates.

Mim felt a smile tug at her mouth; though she still felt punch-drunk after the events of the day, it was good to feel enthusiasm bloom for this new proposal. The day that had started so badly had now become one filled with promise, and it was all down to her amazing friends. 'It is, and I love the idea of us working together. I'm definitely up for it.' Her stomach rumbled at the mouth-watering aroma from the food; she hadn't realised she was hungry until now.

'Great!' Aidey's beaming smile matched hers.

'Yay!' Anna-Lisa held up her glass. 'Cheers to that. We just need to think of a name now.'

'Since Yorvik's the original Viking name for York, how about Yorvik Digital?' asked Aidey.

'Perfect,' said Anna.

'I love it! Cheers to Yorvik Digital.' Mim held her glass up.

'Cheers,' they chorused.

'THANKS, SHONA, THAT WAS ABSOLUTELY DELICIOUS.' Mim had devoured every morsel of chicken casserole from her plate.

'Mmm, it was so good, thank you,' said Anna.

'You're very welcome, I'm glad you enjoyed it.'

Yep, I definitely miss your fabulous cooking, Mum.'

Shona walked by and squeezed Aidey's shoulder, smiling. 'Glad you liked it, son.'

Anna-Lisa stayed for a little while longer before declaring it was time she headed off. 'I'll text you tomorrow with an appointment time for your hair.' She rubbed Mim's arm. 'Try to get a good night's sleep if you can. You've got no more worries to keep you awake now.'

'True.' Mim's body hadn't caught up with that memo, it still retained some indefinable tension that had been there as far back as she could remember, reluctant to let go, just in case…

'See you, Anna, thanks for coming over,' said Aidey. 'Speak tomorrow, and good luck at Yorkshire Portions. Shout up if you need a hand.'

Mim and Aidey had remained in the kitchen, sipping wine with Shona after Anna-Lisa had left. The soothing bath followed by the delicious meal had made Mim feel sleepy, but she didn't want to seem rude by saying she wanted to go to bed; Shona was so lovely, and the last thing she wanted was to offend her.

'So, you remember Aidey from school do you, Mim?'

'Yes, he was in Josie's year, in her circle of friends at secondary school.' Mim giggled, the wine making her feel bold. 'I actually had a bit of a crush on him.'

'You did?' Aidey looked shocked.

Mim nodded, feeling herself blush.

'Ah, he's always been a good-looking boy.' Shona smiled fondly.

'Takes after his handsome devil of a dad.' Aidey's dad Col walked by, ruffling his son's hair.

Aidey rolled his eyes good-naturedly.

Before long Shona laid a photo album out on the table. 'And that was taken on the day Aidey wet his pants in the school dinner queue. Apparently he didn't want to lose his place in case there was no dinner left, so he hung on until it was too late. I had to go up with fresh underpants and trousers for him. Socks, too, he'd saturated those. And it took ages for his little shoes to dry out, didn't it, Col?'

'Aye, it did.'

Aidey clapped his hand to his brow. 'Please stop now, Mum. Mortified here!'

Mim fought hard to stop her giggles. 'Well, if it's any consolation, Aidey, you'd never tell all that had happened from the photo.'

'Yep, that really helps.'

35

MIM SLEPT SOUNDLY, only waking when Shona brought a cup of tea to the bedroom. 'Morning, lovie, did you sleep well?'

'Like a log, thanks, Shona. This bed is so comfy.'

'I'm pleased to hear it. Enjoy your tea and just get up when you're ready. Aidey says to tell you Anna-Lisa's been in touch saying she's got you a hair appointment for two-thirty this afternoon.'

'Oh, okay.'

Once Shona had left the room, Mim lay staring up at the ceiling, catching up with the thoughts that had started trickling into her mind. The events of yesterday seemed weeks ago, and almost as if none of it had happened to her. Yet so much had happened, and she didn't know what to think about first. From the sound of the bird-song in the garden, it had stopped raining but she could hear the wind still rocking the trees, though it seemed to have lost some of its power from the night before. She lay there until the urge to see Aidey pushed her out of bed.

She found him in the kitchen, sitting at the table working on his laptop, still in his pyjamas, his dark blond hair sticking up at the front making him look sexily dishevelled. 'Morning.' He beamed when he saw her. 'Coffee?'

'Mmm, please.' She pulled out the chair opposite him and sat down, the urge to feel his arms around her taking her by surprise. 'You look busy.'

'Ah, yep, just working out a few things, logistics, for our new venture.'

'Oh, yes, how exciting.' Mim's heart leapt with happiness.

'We can talk some more when Anna gets here, but first I've got a suggestion for you.'

'Oh?'

'I wondered if you fancied a break before we got stuck into work straightaway? After all you've been through, I thought you might be feeling a little punch-drunk with everything, and might need time to recharge your batteries.'

Mim thought for a moment, absorbing his words. 'A break does sound good, but I've got Herbert to think about.'

'Herbs wouldn't be a problem, he can come, too.' He handed her a steaming mug of coffee.

'So what kind of break do you mean?'

'My parents have a holiday house at a place called Skappanish on the Isle of Connask just off the west coast of Scotland, they had it built earlier in the year. It's in a stunning spot, looking out to sea. It's free for the next week or so, and I wondered if you fancied spending some time up there, getting away from it all?'

'Just you, me and Herbs?'

'If you're okay with that. I promise I'm not going to turn into a raging axe-murderer once we're up there.'

Mim giggled. She couldn't imagine Aidey being anything other than the gentle soul he was. 'It sounds blissful. When can we go?'

'Is tomorrow too soon?'

'Tomorrow's perfect. I'll pack after I get back from the hairdressers this afternoon.'

'Great!' Aidey flashed her a huge smile.

'RIGHT, we're a bit early, so why don't we pop into that teashop over there and have a cup of tea and a sticky cake?' Anna-Lisa had just finished manoeuvring her little car into a tight parking place in the market square at Middleton-le-Moors.

'You know me, I'm never one to turn down the opportunity for some cake,' said Mim. 'And your parking's amazing by the way.'

'Thanks, I love this little car, you can turn it on a sixpence.'

Mim pushed the door of the teashop open, setting the brass bell jangling. She scanned the room to see just a couple of tables free, though the one by the window had a reserved sign on it.

The two friends were perusing the menu when the bell rang noisily again. Mim looked up to see three women walking in, one with a headful of glossy, purple waves. 'Oh, look at that woman's hair, it's amazing.'

Anna-Lisa followed her gaze. 'I've seen her in Stefan's before, she's a regular; in fact, I've seen all three of them before.' She smiled as the women walked by, the one with a dark pixie crop smiled back, a flicker of recognition in her eyes.

Mim watched them sit down. 'Fancying a change of colour are you?' asked Anna-Lisa.

'I'd love to, but I don't think I'm that brave.'

MIM COULDN'T BELIEVE her eyes when she walked into The Salon. The playlist was thudding away in the background, while stylists were busy performing magic at their stations. She would never have guessed that such a funky, contemporary place like this existed in somewhere as "well-to-do" and with an older population like Middleton-le-Moors.

Before she knew it, she was gowned up and sitting in front of a mirror. In this light, her hair looked brassy and as dry as straw, emphasising where she'd hacked at it the night before. She was dreading Stefan's verdict.

'Right, doll. What's been happening here, then?' Stefan rocked up behind her, sporting a friendly smile and a sleek short back-and-sides, complete with floppy fringe.

'Well, I'm not sure where to start, but it's probably best to say that I got some chewing-gum stuck in my hair last night and ended up cutting it out with nail scissors.' She giggled at Stefan's expression of disbelief.

'Okay.' He picked up a few strands gingerly, inspecting them more closely. 'And the colour, are we liking that?'

'Well, I don't mind being blonde, but maybe not as brassy as it is now.'

'Well, I'm glad you said that, babes. But what I will say is that it's pretty dry and could do with a good five or six further inches off to take it up to just below your jaw line. If I give it a really good conditioning treatment, add a base colour then weave a mix of warm highlights through it, that should look amazing. What do you think?'

'Sounds great.'

'Fab. I'll get Amber to take you over to the sinks to give your mane a good wash, then we'll get to work.' Stefan looked excited at the prospect.

SO ARE YOU PLEASED WITH IT?' asked Anna-Lisa as they were hurrying over to her car before the rain started.

'I love it, it doesn't feel like my hair, it's so soft.'

'It looks gorgeous, those warm highlights really suit you.'

'Thanks, Anna, and thanks for booking it for me, I know Stefan squeezed me in as a favour to you.'

'No worries, chick. Right, now off to Skeltwick to see that gorgeous boy Herbert.'

'Ooh, I can't wait! Carly says he's been a really good boy again. Wait till he finds out he's going on holiday and he'll have to pack his tennis ball.'

36

Dusk was approaching as Mim and Aidey reached the holiday house. They'd had a steady drive up, breaking the journey halfway and enjoying a picnic on the banks of a loch. The crossing on the ferry had been surprisingly smooth, the wind having thankfully died down. The pair had stood on the deck with Herbert, watching seals bob in and out of the water as seabirds cried overhead, the tang of salty water in the air. Once they'd reached the Isle of Connask, it had been a thirty minute drive to Skappanish. Mim sat back, gazing out of the window at the quaint white crofts that dotted the lush landscape.

The house was a contemporary build, oak-clad with a corrugated iron roof and huge windows facing out to sea. It almost appeared to huddle into the undulations of the land at the rear, while the views to the front were broad and uninterrupted.

'Wow, this is amazing.' Mim stepped inside, taking in the clean lines of the interior. Herbert shot in, keen to start exploring, his tail wagging, his nose to the floor. If it wasn't for Shona's soft purple and green tartan furnishings, the space could have been almost clinical, but instead there was a tasteful homeliness to it. The walls were adorned with black and white photographs of local scenery and paintings by local artists. In the living room was a huge window framing the view of the beach and the sea beyond, while a sleek, black wood-burner sat at an adjacent wall. The large, squishy seating was turned to face the stunning view.

'It's been Mum and Dad's dream to have their own home here. I think they quite like the idea of retiring up here actually.'

'I can totally get that.' Mim watched a couple of sea otters scrambling over the rocks on the beach. She couldn't wait to get out and explore.

'It's a bit late to go for a walk now, it'll be dark soon, so I don't know what you fancy doing? We can pop out to the pub for a bite to eat, or I can rustle up something here and we can do the pub tomorrow. It's up to you, I've brought plenty of supplies.'

Aidey was right, it would be getting dark soon. 'Why don't we save the pub for tomorrow and just get settled in here tonight? I can help out in the kitchen, but you know how limited my culinary skills are, so I can't guarantee I'll be much use.'

Aidey chuckled. 'That's fine, I enjoy cooking, I find it therapeutic. You can be in charge of wine pouring, how does that sound?'

'Perfect. I'm very good at that.'

They spent the evening laughing and chatting, while Herbert lay stretched out on the oak floorboards, embracing the underfloor heating, snoring softly. Aidey had dimmed the lights so they could enjoy the last of the view, the golden glow of the sunset glittering over the ripples of the sea that was slowly inching closer. Soon, the light had faded and all they could see were tiny dots of light from houses on the other side of the water on the mainland, and the crofts that peppered the arc of the natural harbour that swept around the bay. Mim sighed and walked over to the window, peering out into the inky darkness, feeling utterly relaxed. 'This is a wonderful place,' she said. 'So tranquil.'

Aidey smiled, his eyes shining with happiness. 'It is.'

She made her way back over to the sofa and flopped down beside him, curling her feet underneath her. It didn't cross her mind that some people would find it odd that she was here with Aidey and they weren't an item. He was one of her best friends, and she felt as comfortable with him as she did with Anna-Lisa. 'Thanks for bringing me here.'

'Hey, you're welcome. I think the break will do us both good.'

'Yeah, it feels good to get a bit of distance from what's been happening.'

'And you look so much better already, your eyes have lost that exhausted look, and it goes without saying your hair looks great like that.'

'Thanks, Aidey, I wish I'd had it done like this years ago.' She beamed at him.

The pair passed a companionable evening, watching mindless television and sipping wine until Mim started to doze over. She followed Aidey's advice and headed up to bed where she slept right through until she was woken by the screeching call of a seabird the following morning.

~

Mim headed downstairs to find Aidey sipping coffee on the decking, looking out to sea, Herbert sitting beside him. 'Morning.' She joined them outside, the air cool on her skin.

'Morning. Sleep well?' He turned to her and smiled.

'Right through. I was only woken by those birds over there with the red beaks who are making all the noise– what kind are they?'

'They're oystercatchers.'

'Well, they make one hell of a flippin' racket.'

After breakfast the pair went for a walk along the beach which they had to themselves. Herbert raced down to the sea that had retreated since yesterday evening. He charged through the foam and lunged at the waves, his delight making Mim and Aidey laugh. Aidey threw stones that skimmed across the water and Herbert charged after them. The air was deliciously crisp and fresh, the sky overhead a vivid blue with fluffy white clouds scudding by on the light breeze. Mim took a lungful of sea air; it felt invigorating, a balm for the soul. Her eyes found their way to Aidey, who was smiling as he watched Herbert tear about the beach. She felt something stir inside, a feeling of warmth, of deep affection. Aidey felt good to be around, as though being together like this was meant to be. He caught her watching him, his smile widening. She felt colour rise in her cheeks and smiled back.

As they walked on, she linked her arm through his and they continued in companionable silence. At one point he looked as though he wanted to say something, but thought better of it. And, much as she was keen to find out what it was, she didn't like to push him.

That evening, they walked the half mile to the Skappanish Inn. They had a cosy table for two by the fire and dined on freshly caught scallops followed by plump monkfish and fresh vegetables, washed down with a crisp bottle of house white. Mim finished her meal with a bowl of homemade rice-pudding and a dollop of raspberry jam. 'That was heavenly.' She patted her stomach; she couldn't remember the last time she'd eaten such delicious food. Herbert had excelled himself and been a well-behaved boy, curling up on the floor beside them.

'Yep, the food's always good here, and the seafood's freshly caught by local fishermen.'

Mim went to bed content again that night. The anxiety and stresses of recent weeks receding into the shadows with every passing day. She was starting to feel her old self gradually re-emerge, as her self-confidence returned.

The following day, they went for a drive across the middle of the island, an area known for its stunning views and resident golden eagles. The huge, snow-capped mountains looked surreal, almost as if they'd been super-imposed in the background. Mim had never been anywhere like it. The roads were precipitous at times, but the reward was a view so breath-taking no amount of photographs could ever do it justice. Aidey parked the car up so they could get out and see the full length of the valley from the vantage point.

'How do you know about such an amazing place?' she asked.

'I used to come here every summer as a child; my parents rented the same holiday cottage and my dad used to drive us around the island, soaking up the views.'

'I can see why.' The air was imbued with a sense of tranquillity. Mim took a deep breath and let it wash over her.

That evening, the pair retraced their steps to the pub, tempted once more by its scrumptious food. Mim sat back in her seat, swirling the wine around her glass. 'I haven't felt so content for a long time. It's as if being here has washed all my worries away, and reminded me what it is to feel properly happy again.'

A smile spread over Aidey's face. 'Yeah, it kind of gets you like that, this place.'

'It's as if all of the horrible build up, Honey, Caspar, everything to do with Yorkshire Portions, hasn't actually happened, like I've never actually had anything to do with them.'

'I'm pleased you haven't let it affect you, you needed to be free of the whole lot, needed to move away from them.'

'I did, I just didn't realise it would be so simple at the time. I couldn't imagine ever being free of the stress, I'd convinced myself it would follow me everywhere.'

'I'm glad it hasn't.'

'Me, too.' Mim met his gaze. He looked so handsome, his eyes soft and kind. Butterflies fluttered around her stomach and she felt the colour rise in her cheeks again – something that had started to happen with increasing regularity when she was around Aidey.

'Mim, I—' Aidey's words were cut off by the sound of her mobile phone ringing.

'Who could that be this late?'

'You'd better get it, signal must've made a rare appearance.'

'It's Anna's number. I hope everything's okay.' She shot Aidey a worried look as she pressed her phone to her ear. 'Hi, Anna, how's things?' Mim's expression changed as she listened. 'What? No!'

'What's the matter? Is she alright?' asked Aidey.

Mim turned to him. 'She's been trying to get hold of us all day. She says the police turned up at Yorkshire Portions this morning, took the bosses off for questioning. Caspar conveniently disappeared as soon as he got a whiff of trouble, but it looks like his family are being investigated for money laundering, and the Pallister-Biggs and Kenneth are implicated.'

'What?'

Mim turned her attention back to her phone. 'Are you okay, Anna? Did the police speak to you?' Mim strained to hear her friend, putting a finger in her free ear. 'I can't hear you very well – I'd put you on speaker phone but we're in a pub.' Before long, the line went dead. 'Blast; she's gone!'

'Did you manage to hear much more?' asked Aidey.

'A bit.' Mim nodded, her stomach clenching. 'Apparently, the police took a statement from her at the office – we're going to have to give one when we get back.'

'Flipping heck, this is serious stuff. You realise you've had a lucky escape, don't you? That'll be why Caspar wanted you to have that money deposited into your account.'

She clamped her hand to her mouth. 'Oh, my God, the slimeball! So, if I'd agreed to it, the police would be investigating me, too?' Mim's heart was pounding.

'I would've thought so.'

'Thank goodness I followed my gut, and asked yours and Anna's advice; without it, he might've had the power to talk me round.' She paused for a moment. 'I bet that's why he was interested in me and kept paying me compliments; it was all just so he could manipulate me to do what he wanted. What a creep.' The realisation didn't hurt as much as she thought it would.

'And I'll bet that's why Simon took over the accounts; then no one else could see the ridiculous amounts getting paid in.'

'No doubt. And more than likely why they gave Caspar a job there.'

'Bloody hell, it's all starting to fit together.'

'I'm so glad we left when we did. I hope Anna'll be okay till we get back– I'll try and get in touch with her again.' Mim frowned. 'And what about Clarissa? I can't see her being involved in anything dodgy.'

'I'm sure Anna will be fine for a few more days; she's a tough cookie. But Clarissa? I can't imagine her being involved in anything illegal either, though who knows?'

'When I think of how Susan reacted when she saw those things in my drawer, like she was all holier-than-thou, it just makes me so angry. She made me feel like the worst type of criminal when I hadn't done anything wrong, and all the while she was sitting there, busily laundering money for the De Verres.'

'The woman's got a nerve. But it looks like karma's taken a massive bite out of her backside and she's going to have to live with the consequences.'

'And, it might sound unkind, but I think she deserves everything she's got coming to her, as do Caspar and his family.'

'It doesn't sound unkind, they could've wrecked a lot of people's lives with their dodgy dealing, yours included. But don't let it spoil your break; we can deal with it when we get back, a few days aren't going to make a difference.'

'True.' There was no way Mim was going to let anything to do with Yorkshire Portions make her cut short her time here with Aidey.

37

AFTER A BREAKFAST of porridge and toast, the news of the previous evening seemed like a distant memory and had a strangely liberating effect on Mim; as far as she was concerned, all ties to Yorkshire Portions and Caspar had been severed; they'd already taken up too much of her headspace and they weren't getting any more. She was moving on with her life and, once she'd spoken to the police, she wasn't going to give either of them a backward glance.

With Herbert in tow, Aidey and Mim jumped into the car and drove to a beach at the bottom of the island that Aidey had been keen to show her. 'It's great for beachcombing,' he said. 'And Herbert will love having a good run around.'

The beach was everything Aidey had promised, teeming with seabirds, dotted with rockpools that were full of a whole variety of marine life, and amongst the tiny pebbles Mim found a plentiful supply of sea glass and smoothed pieces of blue and white china. She gathered her finds and put them in her pockets; she wasn't quite sure what she was going to do with them, but they were too pretty to leave behind.

She stood with her back to the sea, the wind nipping at her cheeks, as she cast her eyes along the shoreline. She pushed her hair off her face. 'I never want to leave this beautiful island, it's so perfect and I feel so happy here.'

Aidey smiled. 'It is, I love it here. And Herbert would seem to agree.'

The Labrador came bounding towards them, his tongue lolling out of the side of his mouth, his coat drenched and covered in sand where he'd been rolling after swimming in the sea. He stopped in front of them and shook, showering them in salty droplets of water.

'Ughh! Herbert! Stop that!' Mim scrunched up her face.

'Thanks for that, Herbs.'

Herbert looked at them, a happy expression on his face. Aidey and Mim looked at one another and roared with laughter.

THE FRESH AIR was doing a good job of bringing colour back to Mim's cheeks, making her feel invigorated and carefree. She watched Aidey, frying two succulent pieces of hake in a pan, bathing them in bubbling herby butter. She set a basket of crusty bread on the table and filled their wine glasses. 'That smells seriously good. Who knew you were such an accomplished chef, Aidan Lister?'

'I don't know about that, it's simple stuff I'm doing.' He removed the pan from the heat and served the portions onto the two plates, adding chunky slices of lemon to each one.

'I think we both know that if I tackled anything like that, it would bear no resemblance to what you've just put on those plates. I'll stick with cooking beans on toast.' She giggled and took the bowls of vegetables and potatoes while Aidey carried the plates to the table.

'Beans on toast is good,' Aidey said with a smile.

'Hmm. You're just being kind. Anyway, cheers.' Mim lifted her glass aloft.

'Cheers.' His eyes twinkled as he looked at her, making her heart squeeze with happiness.

After they'd eaten, the pair decided to get a breath of fresh air on the decking. A pale moon was suspended in a clear, star-strewn sky, its light pouring over the sea like molten silver. Waves were gently lapping against the rocks below. 'It's so beautiful, whatever the time of day,' said Mim.

'It is. I'm pleased you love the island as much as I do.' Aidey turned to her and their eyes locked.

Mim felt her heart somersault. She reached for his hand, weaving her fingers through his, her other hand reaching up to cup his face. 'Aidey,' she whispered, and before she knew what she was doing, she felt her lips pressing gently against his. He paused for a moment before putting his hand behind her head, pulling her closer and kissing her hard.

The intensity of the feelings unleashed by the kiss took Mim by surprise; she could barely stop her knees from giving way beneath her. She'd been aware of her feelings growing for Aidey, aware that the crush she'd had on him as a teenager had never gone away, but now it had grown up and morphed into something she realised was love. It had been hiding in the wings, waiting for the right time to show itself. Being around him felt so right, they slotted together so perfectly, it was as if they were meant to be together. The realisation filled her with a happiness she hadn't thought possible. And, from the look in his eyes, Aidey clearly felt the same.

'Mim,' he whispered when they eventually pulled apart. 'I hardly dared hope you'd feel the same way.'

'It's kind of crept up on me.'

He bent to kiss her again, cupping her face in his hands. Feeling her passion rising, Mim took his hand and led him inside and up to the bedroom.

'Are you sure about this, Mim?' Aidey asked, his eyes dark with lust.

'I've never been more sure about anything.'

THEY LAY ENTWINED TOGETHER in the crumpled sheets of Aidey's bed. With her head resting on his broad chest, Mim could hear his heart beating in time with hers.

'I couldn't ever imagine feeling as happy as this.' He brushed his fingers over her shoulder.

'Same here.' She pushed herself up to look at him. 'And to think you've been there all along. I was stupid not to realise.' Love for him rose in her chest with an intensity she'd never felt before.

'Yep, I've been waiting for you to realise, hoping one day you would.' He rolled her over and kissed her hard. 'I love you, Mim Dewberry.'

'I love you, too, Aidey Lister.' She smiled, pushing her hands into his hair, joy dancing in her eyes.

'I can't tell you how good it is to hear you say that. Now, where were we...

THE END.

AFTERWORD

Thank you for reading Tell That To My Heart, I hope you enjoyed it. If you did, I'd be really grateful if you could pop over to Amazon and a leave a review – if you click on the link below it will take you right there:

Tell That To My Heart - Amazon UK

Tell That To My Heart - Amazon US

It doesn't have to be long – just a few words would do – but for us new authors it makes a huge difference. Thank you so much.

If you'd like to find out more about what I get up to in my little corner of the North Yorkshire Moors, or if you'd like to get in touch – I'd love to hear from you! – you can find me in the following places:

Amazon author page: Eliza J Scott - UK or Eliza J Scott - US

Website: Eliza J Scott

Twitter: @ElizaJScott1

Facebook: @elizajscottauthor

Goodreads: Goodreads.com

Instagram: @elizajscott

Bookbub: @elizajscott

ALSO BY ELIZA J SCOTT

The Letter – Kitty's Story (Book 1 in the Life on the Moors Series)

You can get it here:

UK: www.amazon.co.uk

US: www.amazon.com

The Talisman – Molly's Story (Book 2 in the Life on the Moors Series)

You can get it here:

UK: www.amazon.co.uk

US: www.amazon.com

The Secret – Violet's Story

www.amazon.co.uk

www.amazon.com

A Christmas Kiss (Book 4 in the Life on the Moors Series)

You can get it right here:

UK: www.amazon.co.uk

US: www.amazon.com

Coming soon:

The Man Who Stole My Heart (Book 2 in the Heartshaped Series)

THANK YOU!

I have to admit starting a new series felt rather strange at first. I'd got to know the characters in the Life on the Moors series so well that I thought it was going to be difficult to leave them behind and focus on a new batch of folk. However, once I started to write about Mim, Anna-Lisa and Aidey, and got to know their individual characters a bit better, the words just flowed; by the end, they all felt like old friends. And, on the subject of friends, just like the books in the Life on the Moors series, friendship and loyalty has been at the very core of this story too.

While Tell That To My Heart was set predominantly in the very real city of York, Smiddersgate – the street on which the Yorkshire Portions magazine is situated – is fictitious. Anyone who is familiar with York will be aware that the streets in the city centre are known as 'gates', which is a throw-back to its Viking heritage. The 'Smidders' part also comes from this rich time in history and is a corruption of the word 'smith', which I've used as a reference to the many blacksmiths whose work would have thrived at that time when the city was a bustling melting-pot of trade.

So, I've reached the point where I get to thank all of the people who have helped make this book possible. I'm going to start with my family for keeping me topped up with copious quantities of Yorkshire tea and ginger biscuits while I'm writing.

A huge thank you to Alison Williams for her wonderful editing skills and kind words of support. I really enjoy working with Alison and continue to learn a huge amount from her.

A great big thank you to Berni Stevens for yet another gorgeous cover! I wanted a different style for the Heartshaped series and am so thrilled with this one for Tell That To My Heart.

Special thanks go to Rachel Gilbey of Rachel's Random Resources whose blog tours are fantastic and her organisational skills second to none! Despite being very poorly this year, she battled on and still managed to keep the blog tours going. You're truly awesome, Rachel!

Thanks also to my lawyer friend for advising me on the complexities of money-laundering, how it's investigated and then proceeds to trial. I owe you a pint!

I'd like to say an enormous thank you to all of the wonderful book bloggers who have taken part in the blog tour for Tell That To My Heart and for featuring it on their fabulous blogs. Their kindness and generosity of spirit is very humbling.

Finally, I'd like to give a shout out to all of the fantastic folk I've got to know in the book community; what a kind and supportive bunch you are!

THANK YOU!

ABOUT THE AUTHOR

Eliza has wanted to be a writer as far back as she can remember. She lives in the North Yorkshire Moors with her husband, two daughters and two black Labradors. When she's not writing, she can usually be found with her nose in a book/glued to her Kindle, or working in her garden, battling against the weeds that seem to grow in abundance there. Eliza enjoys bracing walks in the countryside, rounded off by a visit to a teashop where she can indulge in another two of her favourite things: tea and cake.

Printed in Great Britain
by Amazon